SH
PRO
BY
JENNA RYAN

AND

HIS CASE,
HER BABY
BY
CARLA CASSIDY

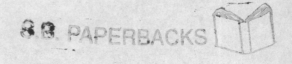

MILLS
BOON

SHADOW PROTECTOR

BY

NINA RYAN

AND

HIS CASE, HER BABY

BY

CARLA CASSIDY

SHADOW
PROTECTOR

BY
JENNA RYAN

First published in Great Britain 2011
by Mills & Boon, an imprint of Harlequin (UK) Limited,
Eton House, 18-24 Paradise Road, Richmond, Surrey TW9 1SR

© Jacqueline Goff 2010

ISBN: 978 0 263 88549 1

46-0911

Harlequin (UK) policy is to use papers that are natural, renewable and
recyclable products and made from wood grown in sustainable forests. The
logging and manufacturing processes conform to the legal environmental
regulations of the country of origin.

Printed and bound in Spain
by Blackprint CPI, Barcelona

Jenna Ryan started making up stories before she could read or write. Growing up, romance alone always had a strong appeal, but romantic suspense was the perfect fit. She tried out a number of different careers, including modelling, interior design and travel, but writing has always been her one true love. That and her long-time partner, Rod.

Inspired from book to book by her sister Kathy, she lives in a rural setting fifteen minutes from the city of Victoria, British Columbia. It's taken a lot of years, but she's finally slowed the frantic pace and adopted a West Coast mindset. Stay active, stay healthy, keep it simple. Enjoy the ride, enjoy the read. All of that works for her, but what she continues to enjoy most is writing stories she loves. She also loves reader feedback. E-mail her at jacquigoff@shaw.ca or visit Jenna Ryan on Facebook.

To Samoa and Serendipity.
Part of the new Lucky Seven.

Prologue

The dream unfolded piece by resistant piece in Serafina Hudson's sleeping mind.

She heard disembodied voices overlapping inside a viscous black fog. They murmured words like "death" and "danger" and "serial killer."

The mood altered. The voices grew louder. Fear slithered in, making the blackness cold.

Where was she? Sera wondered. Why couldn't she see?

"We look inside too much, Sera. That's our problem and our burden. It isn't all about the mind..."

Andrea's voice joined the mix. But that was impossible...

Because corpses couldn't speak!

Reality swept in, churning, swirling, spinning the black into blood red. Like the pool of blood her friend and colleague had been lying in on their office floor.

Sera remembered a slow, painful rise from dark to light. There'd been people everywhere, most of them wearing uniforms, all of them unfamiliar to her. Except for Len, the security guard. And Andrea.

Click into clinical mode. She was a doctor. She'd seen blood before.

Just not pooled around a body.

She swore three times. The hands vanished. Lights

flashed red and blue. She'd be fine, a stranger promised. As for Andrea...

The voices stopped abruptly. The lights blurred. Her mind stuttered then seemed to wink out.

"Try to remember, Dr. Hudson..."

The mental prod repeated with an eerie echo. A man's face, hazy at first, solidified. He had creased, careworn features. He looked sixty and tough, yet she sensed an underlying kindness.

She also knew a cop when she saw one.

"I'm sorry your colleague's dead, Doctor. I wish I could change that, but I can't. Neither can you."

Had she thought the man was kind?

"You need to concentrate," he pressed. "We found a white bandanna at the murder scene. It's the signature of a serial killer. A phantom. You saw the person who did this—we're sure of it. You called Security. You screamed. The guard was down the hall, less than ten seconds away. He thought you were both dead when he found you..."

His voice trailed off. This really was a nightmare, Sera decided. Maybe if she did as the cop suggested and concentrated, she could erase some of the more gruesome aspects.

Determined, she willed the man away, shut out the blurred lights and, because she knew it was important, concentrated on the throbbing pain at the base of her skull.

For a heartbeat, the world went dark.

When it relit, she was being ushered through a door. And, damn, there he was again. The careworn cop.

"You'll be safe here, Doctor. Leo and I have been partners for twenty years. We haven't lost a witness yet."

She was a witness? Her mind snapped to attention. Had she seen Andrea's killer? Please, God, no, had she watched her die?

The walls and fixtures distorted. Two men spoke in the distance.

"Captain thinks there's a leak at headquarters, Leo. I agree with him."

"You're a pair of old ladies."

"She saw him. I know she did. If we can buy her enough time, she'll remember, and we'll have that bastard Blindfold Killer cold…"

The image of a white bandanna floated in. It fell over Andrea's lifeless, staring eyes.

Sera's mind gave a single convulsive shudder that had her surging upright in bed.

"Sera!"

The cop's voice cracked the night shadows like a whip. He caught her by the shoulders, held her steady and stared into her eyes. "Are you awake?"

Was she?

Sera's heart settled as the image of Andrea's rigid features faded.

"Yes." She breathed in, then out. "I had a nightmare."

"You only had the beginnings of one, Doc. Worst part's still to come."

Instinct had her bracing. "There's worse than my nightmare?"

"There's a leak in the department. I've suspected it for a while. I'm sure of it now. My partner's been killed. This place isn't safe."

Questions raced through Sera's head, too many to ask. She wanted this to be part of her dream, but she knew it wasn't.

Two people were dead, and if the man who'd murdered them had his way, she'd be joining them. She'd been there the night he'd murdered Andrea. She'd seen his face.

All she had to do now was remember it.

Chapter One

"You're the psychiatrist, Doc. You tell me what's going on in this guy's pathetic excuse for a brain."

Sig Rayburn pushed on his forehead as if to compress his thoughts. Pain, worry, even a hint of fear had clouded his eyes during the two-day drive from San Francisco. The long, hot drive that currently had them blasting along Wyoming's I25 in his rusty brown Ford.

Sera searched for another vent. "Murderers usually have agendas, but that's not a given. I worked with a man once who liked watching people die. He said it gave him a buzz."

"Sexual?"

"Probably, although victim gender didn't matter. Neither did age or appearance." She paused, sat back, sighed. "Sig, where are we going?"

He pushed harder. "Tenth time you've asked me that since we left the motel this morning. I'm still not gonna tell you."

"Which says to me you don't know yourself, you think your car's bugged or you're weirdly superstitious. You're too good a cop to drive a bugged car, and you strike me as a man who always has a destination in mind, so I'll go with superstition and point out that wearing the same ratty

T-shirt for three days straight at the safe house still didn't help the Giants win their series against the Dodgers."

"Got 'em close, though. Final game, eleventh inning. One little error in the outfield and poof, streak done."

The clouds rolled through his eyes again. Reaching over, Sera squeezed his arm. "I'm really sorry about your partner's death."

"Not your fault, Doc. You didn't fire the bullet that took out the back half of his skull. Didn't slit your friend's throat either." He slanted her a speculative look. "You know who did, though. That's why we're doing this. You need time, distance and a safe place to unlock what's hidden inside that pretty head of yours. No offense," he added gruffly. "I know you have impressive credentials."

"None taken, and they're not as impressive as Andrea's were." Setting aside a twinge of guilt, Sera fanned her face with a Wyoming road map. "I'm pretty sure it won't jinx anything if you tell me our destination."

Sig waved at a buzzing fly. "You're wrong, Doc. Leo carried a lucky rock from Sedona the whole time we worked together. Kept it in his pocket with his loose change. When we found him in that alley, the change was there, but the rock wasn't. Don't talk to me about jinxes."

"Yes, but…"

"My nephew gave him that rock. Gave me one, too. Only time I left it behind, I took a bullet in my right calf."

"Where's your rock now?"

He jerked his head. "Backseat. Jacket pocket." When she didn't respond, he cocked a brow. "You think I'm nuts, don't you?"

"I don't analyze every idiosyncrasy, Sig."

"Uh-huh." But the challenge lingered. "You gonna tell me you don't have a quirk or two?"

"Oh, I have lots." She smiled. "But, no, I'm not going to tell you about them."

A rusty laugh preceded a gruff, "One thing's sure, Doc. Leo's gone, and he shouldn't be. No one better in the country at spotting or shaking a tail than him. Except..." With a glance at the distant Big Horn Mountains, he lapsed into silence.

Sera left him to his thoughts. His partner and friend was dead. Who better to understand how he felt than her? Even though...

She and Andrea hadn't been friends so much as friendly rivals. They'd known each other since they were five years old, but it was circumstance that had truly defined their relationship. Coincidence had also played its wily hand. From where they'd started—not a pretty picture—to where they'd ended up—as psychiatrists who'd obtained their degrees within months of each other—the outcome read like a small universal anomaly to Sera.

She closed her eyes and let the memories in. The murderer had left Andrea face up and staring at the shadowed ceiling. Through a swarm of police and medical workers, she'd looked like a broken doll—her skin chalk white, her features frozen in a mask of astonished horror.

Pain stabbed, swift and sure, and made her open her eyes.

"You're doing it again, aren't you?" Sig demanded. "Trying to smash down that wall in your brain."

She regarded the impressive peaks of the Big Horns. "It's like I'm in an all-black room and there's a strobe light flashing at random intervals. I get split-second glimpses of things I don't understand, then it's back to black, and I want to scream, because no matter how hard I try, I can't make sense of them."

"Could be you're trying too hard."

She slid him a vaguely humorous look. "Your name's Rayburn, right, not Freud?"

"What, you've never said that to a patient?"

"Not any more."

Sig went back to pushing on his forehead while Sera contemplated the landscape. The scenery was magnificent, as was the clear, blue sky. July in Wyoming was all about pine forests, spectacular mountain ranges and wide-open vistas that possessed a beauty all their own.

She felt a tease on the edge of her brain and tipped her head from side to side in an effort to center it. One image, that's all she needed to extract. Unfortunately, research suggested that forcing a resistant memory tended to be as effective as striking a nail with a feather.

She watched a pair of hawks glide in a wide arc beneath a cloudless stretch of sky.

"What's that look for?" Sig asked.

"I have a look?"

"Like you'd rather be riding a cable car."

A smile tugged on her lips. "My face isn't that readable, Detective."

"Hell it isn't. You're sleek, sophisticated and polished. You probably wear high heels to the grocery store. I don't mean to sound patronizing, but I have to warn you, where we're headed, the only place you'll see five stars is in the night sky."

Sera's smile widened. "Putting on your bad cop hat, huh?"

"Doc, you haven't seen anything like bad yet. When we get—aw, hell, what's this?"

"It sounds like a siren."

"Was I speeding?"

"Unless the limit's upward of ninety, yes."

"Crap." He slowed and pulled over.

The officer who approached the car did so with long, easy strides. He rested a forearm on the roof while Sig stretched back to snag the jacket behind him.

"Is there a problem, Officer?"

"Not unless you make one. Got your license with you?"

"Got better than that." Sig fished in the pocket, handed Sera what she assumed was his lucky rock and produced his badge with a flourish.

"San Francisco, huh?"

She caught a trace of humor in the other cop's drawl. His surprisingly sexy drawl, she thought. As for his features, she couldn't see them under the brim of his hat.

She knew he glanced at her before pushing off. "Out of the car, please, Detective Rayburn."

"Have I done something wrong?"

"Depends how fast you get out of the car."

"Don't move," Sig told her. He had to shove twice on the door to open it. "You're starting to piss me off here, Officer. I'm a detective with the San Francisco Police Department, homicide division. Who are you to be ordering me around like a common criminal?"

Sera saw the flash of a surprisingly attractive smile. "I clocked you at ninety-six miles an hour as you flew past Moss Creek."

Sig's balled right fist drew an even wider smile. A second later, her companion went from a short punch on the other cop's shoulder to a backslapping hug.

It figured. Sera breathed out but couldn't bring herself to be annoyed. It was such a predictable male game.

"I'm damn glad to see you, Logan." Sig drew back, grinned. "How'd you know? License plate give me away?"

The taller man glanced from side to side. "This isn't

a car, Sig—it's dented metal on wheels. One of a kind." Without looking or pausing, he asked, "Does she know?"

Sig shook his head.

That did it. Shouldering her door open, Sera slid out. "Excuse me, gentlemen, but 'she' has a name. It's Sera, and the reason she doesn't know is because the man with the San Francisco badge refuses to tell her anything."

"It's for your own..."

"Protection. Got that one yesterday, Sig. But six diners, five gas stations and one truly crappy motel later, I think I've earned the right to know not only where we're going, but also why a police officer in another state is better informed than I am." She sent them a placid smile over the roof of the car. "If it's not too much trouble."

Apart from his badge and the lights on his Explorer, nothing about the man in front of her said law enforcement officer. He wore jeans and a short-sleeved black T-shirt. His boots were dusty, his hat was decidedly more cowboy than cop and if he was carrying a gun, Sera couldn't see it.

Sig matched her smile as he turned to his friend. "Handful," he said.

"See that," the man replied. He nodded forward. "Nadine'll be serving dinner about now. Her place is on the edge of town. You can follow me." Although his eyes were shielded, Sera felt his gaze across the top of the car. "Nadine runs her grandfather's diner, Dr. Hudson. You can ask your questions while we eat." Nudging his hat forward so the brim hid the entire upper portion of his face, he added, "Assuming once they're answered, you still want to eat."

She wouldn't react, Sera promised herself. That would be counterproductive. Instead, she let Sig concentrate on the road that wound away from the interstate through a majestic expanse of pines, boulders the size of city buildings and a steady stream of out-of-state trucks.

Five miles in, the truck traffic thinned, the boulders softened and houses began to appear. Farmhouses at first, followed by larger, turn-of-the-century homes that ambled back from tree-lined streets.

A rustic sign with a hand-carved mountain peak rising above a lake welcomed them to Blue Ridge, Home of the Happy Mountaineer. Population five thousand, six hundred and twenty-seven.

Sig glanced in the rearview mirror. "Do you see my smokes back there?"

"No, and I'm not digging through a pile of old food wrappers and napkins to find them. You're a rolling health hazard, Detective Rayburn. Cigar stubs, cigarette butts and God knows how many million bacteria, all alive and thriving inside your vehicle. You inhale coffee like air, pour enough grease into your arteries to kill an elephant and probably haven't gotten eight hours of smoke-free sleep since you joined the force."

He chuckled. "You're a shrink, Sera. What does a head doctor know about high cholesterol, lung disease and sleep deprivation?"

She lifted the dark hair from her neck. "Among other things, my uncle does a weekend medical clinic in Haight-Ashbury. I help out when he needs it, which is often because he tends to be overrun and doesn't like to turn anyone away. How do you know him, Sig?" she asked after a brief pause. "The cop with the…" She started to say sexy mouth but changed it to "…black hat?"

He peered into the setting sun. "Oh, Logan and me go way back." A finger tapped the windshield. "Is he pulling off the road? All I can see is dust."

"Gravel parking lot." She let her hair fall. "My skin hates you."

"Your skin's gorgeous, as, I trust, are your manners. Five stars…"

"Yes, I know. Only in the night sky. As long as the food's recognizable, I'm good."

And more than ready to stop, she realized, stretching her back as she slid from the car seat.

Every article of clothing she wore, from the pale-green linen halter to the white capris stuck to some part of her body. And it was going to be an adventure navigating the unpaved, pothole-filled parking lot in strappy three-inch heels.

A collection of trucks and SUVs sat at odd angles outside the weather-beaten one-story building whose sign read Frank's Diner.

She stopped stretching to do a humorous double take down the side. "Are those horses?"

"The bay's Billy the Kid. The black is Jesse James."

She suppressed an urge to jump when the cop in jeans wrapped his fingers around her arm.

"Nadine's grandfather swears one of his ancestors was related to Jesse."

"So he named a horse after him."

She caught the quirk of his lips in profile. "No one you know's ever been named for a dead relative?"

"Not a notorious one, Officer…"

"Leave it at Logan."

"Evening, Chief. Rain's coming." The man shambling past, sprinkling tobacco in a rolling paper, barely spared them a glance. "It's my night for poker if you feel like letting us win back some of our hard-earned cash. Wouldn't blame you a mite, though, if not. She's a real pretty lady."

Sera would have grinned if she hadn't caught the edge of a rut and almost snapped her ankle in two.

"Horses, poker and holes big enough to swallow small children. I'm charmed..." She cast the man who'd caught her a sideways look. "Chief."

"It's a label. Means nothing."

"Uh-huh. It only signifies that you're in charge of a town containing five thousand, six hundred and twenty-seven souls. Which would make sense at this point in Sig's life. But everything about you screams big city cop to me."

His lips quirked again. "You might want to check your inner voice, Doc. Cities and me don't get along these days."

Meaning they had once? Interesting, she reflected, as they reached the diner's porch. But it wasn't as interesting as the fact that he knew her name and undoubtedly her story.

Several feet behind them, Sig sucked smoke into his lungs at an alarming rate. Because her arm was tingling, Sera eased free and strove for an unimpeded look at the man called Logan.

He was tall and rangy, with sleek muscles, long legs and dark hair that curled well below the back of his hat. He needed a cut and a shave. And she needed distance because not only was her skin tingling, but also her pulse was doing an erratic tap dance.

Food would help, she decided, plucking at the front of her top. "Is Nadine a good cook?"

"Best down home in Blue Ridge."

"He means if you're expecting art on a plate, you won't get it here." Sig studied the black clouds massing over the distant Big Horns. "Those coming this way?"

"Joe says they are. He's usually right."

"Then we should get down to business."

Sera arched guileless brows. "We're doing business? I thought we stopped here for answers and a hearty meal."

"I'm stopping, Doc. Got something different in mind for you."

Where was a control button when you needed one?

"Sig…"

"You're not stopping, Sera. You're staying."

Prepared for that response, she met his hard stare and simply asked, "Why?"

"Because I trust Logan. He's the best, and as bad as I wanted that bastard Blindfold Killer before, I want him doubly bad now. He's murdered sixteen people over the years. That includes his most recent victims, your friend and my partner. You saw his face, Doc. I know it, and so do you. Unfortunately—and this is where my faith in Logan comes in—one hell of a vicious killer knows it, too."

Chapter Two

"Your captain told me about the Blindfold Killer, Sig," Sera said. "No one's sure why he ties a white bandanna over his victims' eyes. He's killed eleven people over a seven-year period, all in the Bay area. The San Francisco Police arrested a suspect four years ago, but they were forced to release him on a technicality."

"Illegal search of his living quarters," Logan said. "The officer in charge assumed a warrant was en route. He was mistaken."

"Said officer has since been demoted and put in charge of a desk," Sig added gruffly. Then he brightened. "Ah, here we go. Food."

Their dinner arrived courtesy of a buxom fifty-something blonde. It might not be gourmet, but it looked delicious. Almost as delicious as the man seated across from her.

Although she'd braced herself for sexy, Sera hadn't anticipated the punch of desire that had rocked her when he'd removed his hat.

And then, out of nowhere, a tweak of familiarity. But the sensory whisper came and went too quickly for her to capture it.

Sidestepping, she set her mind back on the man himself. To call his features arresting would be a serious understatement. And she couldn't imagine any woman not being wowed by the smoke-gray eyes that caught and held hers far too often for comfort.

One look at Logan's face, however, and she'd known he wouldn't be an easy read. Whatever haunted those mesmerizing features, he'd buried it deep and very, very well.

Sig dug into his steak. "What else do you know about our killer, Doc?"

Refocusing quickly, Sera sampled one of the wedge fries. "Two and a half years went by after the suspect's release. Nothing more happened. Then he vanished, and it started all over again. The killer has committed five new murders, including Leo, in the past eighteen months. His MO is consistent, but his motive remains a mystery."

When Andrea's lifeless face appeared in her head, Sera reached for her wine.

"There've been two witnesses to his crimes. Number one vanished five years ago, before the police could bring him in. That makes me the best hope you've got of identifying this guy. Unfortunately, because I hit my head while I was struggling with him, I can't tell you if his description matches the original suspect's or not."

Logan swirled his beer and sent a lazy look into the mug. "You don't remember the guy's face, but you do remember struggling with him."

Surprise halted the wine at her lips. The image reformed instantly. "He blindsided me," she recalled. "I fell against the edge of my desk."

"Anything else?" Sig asked.

She thought for a moment but couldn't pull any details from the blackness. "Sorry, the rest is still a shadow."

Around them, the diner, really a roadside bar and grill, began to buzz as groups of dusty workers in steel-toed boots filed in.

Sig tapped an unlit cigarette on the table. "New construction in town?"

With his eyes on Sera's face, Logan took a drink of beer. "West end. Developer from Cheyenne's building a—resort."

The amusement that climbed into Sera's throat felt good. "Translation—he's building a resort-style fishing and hunting lodge."

Sig tucked a pack of matches into his jacket pocket and scraped his chair back. "I can't think in the throes of a nicotine fit." He gave Sera's arm an awkward pat. "Keep poking at that memory, Doc. This killer's slick and slippery and far as we can tell random in his selection of victims. Logan." Cigarettes in hand, he made his way through the crowd toward the door.

"He didn't finish his dinner," Sera remarked.

Logan speared one of her fries. "Sig seldom finishes any meal that doesn't start with the prefix Mac."

"How old is he?"

"Fifty-six."

"He acts older."

"Drawn-out investigations do that to cops."

Leaning in on her forearms, she absorbed his unfathomable stare. "I'm sure I've seen…" she began, but the fleeting sense of familiarity vanished again. "Is that why you left?" she asked instead.

"Nope."

Door firmly closed. She picked up her wine. "How long have you been in Blue Ridge?"

"Two years, three months, give or take."

"And you became chief of police when?"

"Same answer."

Pulling teeth would be easier, she reflected, but nowhere near as challenging.

"How long have you known Sig?"

"Longer than most."

"You're not giving me much in the way of answers, Logan."

His gray eyes glittered. "Should tell you something about the questions."

Undeterred, she ran a finger around the base of her glass. "You don't like small talk or, apparently, polite conversation. No problem. I don't need to know your history, and you certainly don't need to know mine." She made a visual circle of the increasingly noisy diner. "This whole take-the-witness-with-the-faulty-memory to Wyoming deal was Sig's idea. It had nothing to do with me. I have relatives in Phoenix, Skagway, Tulsa and yes, Bugs, even Albuquerque. I have a cousin who's a law enforcement officer and an ex-military aunt who flies supplies from Washington state to central Alaska. I could have gone to any number of people for help, but I went with Sig and wound up here. Why? No idea, but hey, you put your life in someone else's hands, who knows what'll happen."

"Are you done?" Logan asked.

"My uncle Jeffrey says I'm never done, but as a shrink, I'm supposed to be a good listener, so the floor's yours."

He held her gaze. "What you're supposed to be—what you should be, Sera—is scared."

She summoned a faint smile, glanced away. "Believe me when I tell you, if I wasn't, I wouldn't be anywhere near you, your outlaw horses or your town." A shiver danced along her spine. "Nothing personal, Logan, but I get along very well with cities. Violent death, however, rattles me. I watched my partner's ashes being entombed last week. I watched her father break down and her mother lose a hard-fought battle to a bottle of cognac. I saw Sig lose a friend he's worked with for twenty of his thirty years on the force.

I did all that with the knowledge that lurking somewhere in my head is a killer's identity. If I can retrieve it, no one else will have to suffer at his hands. So, yes, I'm scared, but not as much as I am determined to watch the person who's responsible—and whose face I swear I'm going to remember—fry."

Unexpected humor glinted in Logan's eyes. "You must have some outlaw blood yourself, Doc. I've never met a shrink who wanted to see anyone fry."

Her first reaction was to defend the remark. Her second was to cover a smile with a bite of chicken. "I won't tell you what my uncle says about my mouth. I will tell you I'm sorry I dumped all that on you when we've known each other for less than sixty minutes."

He moved a shoulder. "Dumping's what people do on cops, town, city or state. It rolls off unnoticed after a while... Nadine?" He spoke to the blonde who was balancing six main courses. "You mind wrapping these dinners up for us?"

Sera's brows elevated. "Are we leaving?"

"Unless you want to get hit on by every guy here, yeah."

For the first time since Sig had gone outside, she looked around the room. Not every male eye was turned in their direction, but more than half were.

She let the amusement blossom. "Because I assume they're not staring at you, I'll go out on a limb and speculate that you don't get many female strangers in this town."

Logan picked up his hat. "Oh, we get plenty of strange females, just not many you'd call witchy."

The blonde returned with their bagged dinners. "You want the steak wrapped, too, Logan?"

He finished his beer. "No point. Give your dogs a treat, and put the dinner on my tab."

The woman flipped a dishtowel over her shoulder. "Your friend beat you to the punch there. He paid the bill on his way out."

Something unpleasant snaked through Sera's stomach. Although she recognized it for the blend of dread and certainty it was, she settled for a mild, "He's gone, isn't he?"

Logan assessed her as he returned the hat to his head. "He told you he wasn't staying, Sera."

"And I'm just supposed to go with that? With this?" She fixed her gaze in the general vicinity of his eyes. "With you? No questions asked or really answered, and no choice in the matter?" Her control slipped a notch and she leaned forward. "Logan, Sig broke a mirror at the safe house and freaked over it for days. We were driving east within an hour of his partner's death. 'Gotta leave fast,' he said. Yet, he went ten minutes out of his way because he wouldn't go past the path lab where his partner's body had been taken. Said he'd rather walk under a dozen ladders. He also didn't tell anyone in the department where we were going, and I know his captain personally. He's a forty-year man with commendations as long as my arm."

"What's your point, Doctor?"

Did she have one? Right then, Sera's thoughts were too scattered to collect, let alone organize.

It had to be exhaustion combined with a touch of hysteria that made her want to laugh. "You know what?" She pushed back. "I haven't got a clue what I'm saying or why I'm even talking. I need air, space and no more Willie Nelson for at least twelve hours."

She also needed to be away from the man across the table. The ridiculously sexy cop who disliked cities and personal questions and quite possibly his old friend Sig at this moment.

Standing, Logan drew her to her feet. "You look over-whelmed."

"You think?'

"If it helps, Sig left your bags behind my truck."

"Sorry, Chief, not feeling any better here."

The shadowed look he cast her brought a sigh coupled with a strong desire to bolt.

"Okay, fine. Message received. Sig's trying to keep me safe, as a person and as a potential witness. What I'm still trying to process is why he brought me to you. He talked about a potential leak within the department, but please don't tell me he suspects his own captain."

"Twenty years in homicide, ten in vice, what can I say, he's jaded."

"You sure you don't mean paranoid?"

Pressing a hand to her hip, Logan eased her behind him as he forged a path to the door. "Sig's a cautious man, Sera. He wants to keep you alive, and this was the best place he could think of to make that happen."

A man with no bottom teeth winked and offered her his drink.

Logan's unruffled, "Doctor, Billy," had the leer fading to a scowl and the man scuttling backward so fast he almost knocked the plates from Nadine's loaded arm.

Sera tapped his back. "Care to explain that reaction?"

"Billy's father turned ninety-eight last June. Doc Prich-ard said he needed a vitamin shot. The old man died that night."

"Uh—well, hmm." Unsure how to respond, Sera tried not to grin. "Ninety-eight, huh? Billy doesn't really believe it was the vitamin shot—" She let an oblique hand motion finish the question. "Does he?"

"Yeah, he does, and he's not alone. Most of the people you'll meet around here are perfectly normal, but for every fifty, there's a Billy or a Jessie-Lynn. Rumor has it aliens grabbed Jess twelve years ago after the Founder's Day parade." Logan opened the door—and closed it in the face of a large, hairy man whose hand had been mere inches from Sera's breast.

Removing his hat, he placed it on her head and smiled just enough to momentarily steal her breath. "I hate to be the bearer of bad news, Dr. Hudson, but you're not in Kansas any more. And while you might think the Emerald City is a little off the map—be warned, it has nothing on Blue Ridge, Wyoming."

HE SHOULDN'T HAVE said that, Logan thought as he started his Explorer. But, dammit, he didn't want the burden of a targeted witness's safety riding on his shoulders. Add in the fact that she was a jaw-dropping female of—what had Sig told him—twenty-nine, with credentials that shouldn't be possible for someone her age and a body just made for trouble, and yeah, you could say he was pissed off. Mostly at himself for reacting the way he was, but partly at Sig for putting him in this position.

He knew she didn't remember him. Why would she? They'd never met face to face. Their one and only patch of common ground involved the age-old cop versus shrink battle. Was the suspect the police had arrested for a brutal crime fit to stand trial or not? On their particular patch, a trio of shrinks, whose number had included Sera, said no.

Now, the way Logan saw it, he could let old resentments fester or, for Sig's sake, put the past in its place and deal with the current situation.

One glance at her face in profile, and he knew where he'd be going with that.

Although she had to know his thoughts weren't running

along pleasant lines, she opted to keep their conversation relevant and, for the most part, impersonal.

"The suspect was under surveillance when he disappeared, wasn't he?" she asked.

Logan shoved the Explorer in gear and his emotions in line. "His name's Hugh Paxton, and yes, he was. He dropped out of sight a few months after I came to Blue Ridge."

She regarded him from under the brim of his hat. "Did you hear about that from Sig, or did your alien abductee return from the mother ship a gifted clairvoyant?"

Humor stirred. "Jessie-Lynn has her moments, but the answer's no on both counts. Remote as this town is, we have a local newspaper, and believe it or not, Internet access."

Pushing the hat back, she lowered her sunglasses. "I'm not a snob, Logan, whatever you might think—and God knows it probably isn't flattering. I'm just a little—no make that a lot—out of my element here. I don't usually see horses grazing outside San Francisco diners, and unless we wander into the wrong area of the city, big, hairy men seldom make a habit of grabbing women's breasts."

"So, no conquest for Charlie, then. He'll be bummed."

She laughed, and the sound of it sparked a sensation Logan didn't need to feel in his groin. Keeping his eyes on the road, he returned to topic. "Paxton walked because the arresting officer screwed up, but he was the Blindfold Killer. Every cop on the coast knew it."

Sera regarded the dying orange glow in the western sky. "He'd have known the police were watching him, ergo, for a while at least, his desire for freedom must have outweighed his need to kill. Either that or he'd achieved his initial goal of eleven people dead. It's possible his more recent victims are unconnected to the first group."

"No one ever established a connection between the first

eleven victims." Logan chose to ignore the out-of-town driver who whizzed past in a mud-spattered four by four. "Any thoughts on that, Doc?"

"Without getting inside his head, no." But as he'd expected, after a moment she ventured to ask, "Were the victims primarily female or male?"

"Eight female, three male."

"Ages?"

"The youngest was twenty, the oldest forty-seven."

"And Paxton's age at the time of his arrest was?"

A smile touched the corners of Logan's mouth. "That's the sticking point. No one knows. He has no official record of birth and the kind of appearance every cop hates."

"Changeable?"

"Big time."

"Which explains why Sig showed me multiple versions of ten different men, more than a hundred shots in total. I figured there were disguises involved—but, big surprise—Sig refused to explain. He said the less he told me, the less chance that my memories, when they did return, would be colored. All he really needed to say was that the suspect took his cue from Lon Chaney."

Logan sent her a brief smile. "It's not a bad comparison. Twenty pounds more or less, from dreadlocks to buzz cuts, stubble to mustache to beard, tooth caps on or off, contact lenses in or out—Paxton knows how to alter his appearance. It's one of the reasons he was so difficult to nail in the first place. The other was the obvious lack of credible witnesses."

"I assume that's how he slipped under the radar. In disguise."

When the radio squawked, Logan reached down. "Probably, but I was gone by then, and Sig was so disgusted that they'd lost him, he wouldn't talk about it."

Her eyes slid to his, but she said nothing, and he pressed the Receive button. "Problem, Fred?"

"The Bulley boys are at it again, Chief."

"Home or town?"

"Home now, but they came through town on a big old tear. Near as I can tell, they're riled up over the workers who are camped out—quite legally, I might add—on their farm. Did some pushing and shoving on Main, went into Tommy Gray Wolf's bar, had a shouting match, punched someone, then took off for home when Tommy threatened to call it in. Which he did anyway ten minutes before Edgar Bulley did the same. Old Edgar says there's no point sending deputies. The boys'll just threaten to gore them and carry on 'til you show up."

Logan glanced over. "I'll be there in five. Tell Edgar to fire a couple rounds of buckshot into the barn wall. Might take the edge off."

"Always a first time," Fred returned cheerfully. "Good luck, Logan."

As the sun dipped below the mountaintops, he switched on the lights and siren. "How are you at following orders, Doc?"

She dropped his hat on the seat between them. "The mood I'm in, spectacularly bad. Did I hear the word 'gore'?"

"It's the Bulley's word for 'stab.' Used to be a kid's game involving plastic horns. Now it's a drunken threat when they're feeling ornery."

"Sounds like your Bulley boys have serious anger management issues."

"You could say," he agreed. "Their grandfather grazes a stingy herd of cattle, but the number's been dwindling over the years, so the boys, six of them, have been forced to find other ways to augment their income."

"Ways you *smoke* or *drink?*"

"Drink mostly. We've dismantled three stills since late March. Last one was five days ago. Supply's probably running low, so Bulley logic would dictate that they down the last of it and take their anger out on someone else."

"Like deputies and campers."

"They've also been known to fire warning shots at trespassers." Logan slowed as the lights of a ramshackle farmhouse came into view. "Challenge is to see how close they can come without actually hitting the person. Fortunately," he flicked off the siren, "they're not in love with firearms. Knives tend to be their weapon of choice."

Braking behind a stand of pines, he reached for his rifle, stuck the hat back on his head and caught her chin between his thumb and fingers. "Whatever happens, Sera, keep the doors locked and the engine running. Anyone who isn't me shows up, don't check for blood, just turn the truck around and head back to Frank's Diner. You got that?"

"Every word," she said. "Uh, tell me, are two of the Bulley boys tall, wiry and left-handed?"

A brow went up when her eyes touched on a point over his shoulder. "Coming from behind?"

"Faster than speeding bullets."

Anticipation glimmered. Releasing her chin, he reached for the door handle. "This is gonna be fun."

Chapter Three

"Logan?" As amused as she was amazed, Sera worked her way over the console to the driver's seat. She stared into the rapidly expanding darkness. "Forget Jesse James. Houdini must be one of your ancestors."

No matter which direction she looked, she couldn't see him. He was gone, and so were the two men. Obviously they'd vanished into the trees, but talk about witchy people—this place had it all over San Francisco—and that was saying a lot.

She was searching for the lock control when a face popped up at the driver's side window. A split second later the door flew open and a pair of grimy hands, one of them wielding a knife, shot inside.

Startled, Sera jumped back. She gave the passenger door a shove and the man's wrist a kick.

Spying Logan's gun, she grabbed it and tumbled from the truck.

It was hardly surprising that her heels unbalanced her and she landed on the ground. But she didn't spend three nights a week at the gym for nothing. She was on her feet before the man could wriggle through the interior.

His lips peeled back when he got his first good look. "Hoo-ee, you are a pretty thing, aren't you, baby doll?"

On her feet now, Sera raised the gun. "Don't make me shoot," she told him. "I don't want to hurt you."

He hopped out, snickering when her hand trembled. "You sure you got the right end pointed at me?"

"Do you want to find out?"

He didn't stop completely, but she saw him hesitate. He was drooling, she noticed. And limping slightly.

She kept her arm extended, and flicked her gaze down then back to his face. "How old were you when you broke your right leg?"

Shock halted him in a way the gun hadn't. "How'd you know about that? You Jessie-Lynn's cousin from Casper?"

"No, I'm…"

"A witch then." His already small eyes narrowed. "Gramps says there's a bunch of them living up Buffalo way."

"He means Wiccans."

"Don't matter what he means. How'd you know about my leg?"

"It wasn't set right so the bone didn't heal properly. I'm guessing you were young and still growing. Maybe ten or eleven?"

"Twelve." His lip curled. "You a doctor?"

"Yes."

He made a sound of disgust and spit to the side.

Sera kept her tone and expression calm. "I see."

"You're a jackass like Prichard."

"Only on weekends in Haight-Ashbury. Don't make me shoot," she said again when he lurched forward.

The snarl became a sneer. "Doctors don't go round shooting people, now do they, baby doll? Anyway, I think you're lying. Saw me limping, took a lucky guess."

Still fifteen feet away, Sera could smell the alcohol on

his breath. He whipped out a taunting arm, then laughed and feinted forward.

Double handing the gun, Sera put pressure on the trigger. "You really don't want me to do this."

"Want it more than you do, I figure. Come on, baby, show Benny what you got."

When he moved again, she fired. Missed him by several feet, but the shock of it had him hopping backward.

"You ain't no doctor, lady..." Then he stopped. "You ain't no kind of shot either." His eyes gleamed as he recovered lost ground. "Grab her, Danny."

She heard a twig crack. Waiting a beat, she plowed her elbow into the stomach of the man behind her, then spun away to fire a second shot. The bullet thwacked off a tree. From her knees—when had she lost her footing—she squeezed again.

The Bulley with the bruised stomach bared his teeth.

Sera knew she couldn't win this. Both men were advancing, both were drunk and she had a feeling it was the heel of her shoe snapping off that had landed her on the ground.

"Looks like we got a she-cat on our hands, Benny," the bigger Bulley growled. "How 'bout I..."

The rest of his sentence emerged in a whoosh of air as he hit the tree behind him with enough force to send him slithering down the trunk.

Swinging around, Logan used the butt end of his rifle on the other man's jaw. Benny pivoted in a slow half circle before dropping like felled timber.

"Might want to take your time getting up," Logan suggested. His eyes were on Sera as he spoke. Holding out a hand, he drew her to her feet. "You hurt?"

"No more than if I'd been working out with Hulk Hogan in his prime." She waved the tip of his gun between the two prone men. "Do you do this sort of thing often then?"

"Often enough." Raising his voice, he said, "Lloyd and Jake are cooling off in the barn. They were smart enough to ditch their knives when they spotted me."

"Didn't mean no harm, Logan." Benny's words were muffled by the dirt beneath his face.

"You threatened the lady with a weapon. It's called intent. On your feet, both of you, and into my truck."

"Come on, Lo…" But one look and Benny dropped his face back into the dirt. "Yeah, sure, whatever you say."

Danny worked himself into a squat. "I'm supposed to be stocking shelves at the grocery store tonight, Logan. Miguel won't be happy with you."

Ignoring him, Logan indicated the gun in Sera's hand. "I hope you pointed that a good long way off target."

"I did. Here." She handed it over.

"Her bullet came closer to my crotch than my knife did to any part of her," Benny called out. "Maybe I wanna press charges myself. Against you for bringing her here and her for almost shooting my balls off."

"Right." Sera extended her hand. "Give it back."

Logan grinned. "He's just pissed because he's going to be spending a couple nights in jail."

She wiggled her fingers. "Give it. I promise, I won't shoot them."

Clearly intrigued, he relinquished the weapon.

"Hey, wait a minute," Benny spluttered.

"Don't move," Sera said and, taking aim, sent one of the pebbles on the ground between his spread feet zinging into the bushes behind him.

AN AMUSED LOGAN said little on the drive into town. That was fine with Sera. After changing her shoes, she climbed into his truck and let Etta James drown out the Bulley boys' gripes.

Apparently, the police chief planned for her to stay in his home. It made sense, but it hardly set her mind at ease. The more time she spent with him, the stronger the feeling that she should know him.

They hadn't met—she'd have remembered that in a minute. Seen his name then? Possibly. She could see it well enough on the lighted dash.

Michael Richard Logan. And, ding, there went another bell. Had her memory been more compromised than she realized?

Unable to answer that, she returned to the moment.

The Bulleys' grumbles grew louder the closer they got to Blue Ridge. Inside the station, Logan handed them over to his deputy, Toby, a young man with bright red hair. "Separate cells," he said and tossed the young man the keys.

The deputy looked like he'd rather drink arsenic. "Uh, Logan, er, Chief, I'm not sure—I mean, they're my cousins. I can't just, you know, put them behind bars."

Logan searched through a drawer. "Don't sweat it, Toby. You're only the messenger."

"But don't messengers get shot sometimes?"

"Hang around here long enough, you'll get shot one way or another," Danny Bulley snarled. "Do what you gotta, Toby. Just know you won't be getting no freebies for a good long while." At Logan's raised brow, he added, "Dinners."

All in all, Sera spent less than fifteen minutes at the station. Ten more, and they were pulling up outside a very old, very large house that Logan informed her had come with the job.

Sera sensed his stare as he removed her bags from the back of his truck. With her skin prickling, she swung to confront him.

"What?" she demanded and received the kind of slow

smile she really didn't need to see right then. "Is it the gun?"

"Yeah, but it can wait until we're inside."

As he spoke, a drop of rain from clouds she'd failed to notice plopped onto her head.

"You've got about five seconds to decide...or not," he amended when the night sky simply opened up.

If this had been San Francisco and she'd been going to work, Sera would have run. But here, in the middle of no-where, with the lights of town a distant blur and her clothes already streaked with dirt, she simply lifted her face to the warm rain.

"I have to tell you, Logan, this qualifies as one of the strangest days of my life, and I've had some really bizarre days."

He set his hat back on her head and picked up the heavy bags. "Courtesy of your patients?"

"Not even close."

Hoisting her carryall, laptop and purse, she preceded him up a short walk to a porch that appeared to wrap around the entire farmhouse. She counted three floors, plus an L-shaped jut and an attic.

Lamps burned in three of the first floor windows. A dog barked deep inside.

"Her name's Ella Fitzgerald. She's a two-year-old golden retriever who thinks she's a lap dog. Can you handle that?"

She smiled. "I love dogs."

"Good, now how are you with..."

The door opened before he could finish and a small, thin woman with a frizzy gray bun whisked them inside.

She looked cranky, made rough tutting noises and, with a single sharp look, held them on the hallway mat.

"Moon Flower." Logan caught the towels she tossed from the closet. "Also came with the job."

"Use it." The woman pointed downward. "I waxed the floors today."

"Yes, ma'am."

"Call me Flo. You'd be Dr. Hudson, then. Sit, Ella. Her room's ready, like you wanted, Logan—the one across from yours. If you have a moment, Doctor, my sister's foot's been troubling her. And before you ask, she drinks plenty of milk."

Sera had no idea what to say. "I'm uh, glad to hear it."

Logan hung their towels on the doorknob and removed the dripping hat from her head. "She's not that kind of doctor, Flo, and she's not here to work in any case."

"I see. Fine then. Babe can just hobble around until that knot head who calls himself an MD decides to practice human rather than simian medicine. Room's this way, Doctor."

"Sera's good."

"You know, Babe can hardly walk some days. Doesn't matter how much milk she drinks."

"Phone's ringing, Flo." Logan nodded into the living room. "I'll take Sera upstairs." When the woman bustled off, he said, "Don't ask. She was part of the original hippie movement. She lived in a bus for three years. The engine died after one. She met my dispatcher Fred thirty-seven years ago. They got high, got married and started their own business in Sacramento."

"Would that be a hemp shop?"

He indicated a set of stairs that jogged to the right half-way up. "Fencing mainly, and not the white picket kind."

"So thirty some years later, it's only natural they'd be working for the chief of police in a northern Wyoming town."

"Life meanders, Sera. Why don't you tell me your shoot-'em-up story?"

Wet and dirty, with a big dog nosing her hip and a too-sexy man on the stairs behind her, Sera opted for the abbreviated version.

"An adopted aunt whose father was a Texas Ranger thought every girl heading to college should know how to fire a handgun. I put her off for two months. Then I got mugged and decided she had a point. Now can I ask you something? Or—no, I'll rephrase. Will you answer a question for me?"

He walked behind her down a surprisingly homey corridor. "I might."

She aimed a humorous look over her shoulder. "You said for every Jessie-Lynn there were fifty normal people in Blue Ridge. My question is, when do I meet one of the fifty?"

THE DRIVE THAT had taken Sig Rayburn two days going took him less than thirteen hours on the return trip. Fueled on bad coffee and hoarse from two and a half packs of cigarettes, he called his captain as he crossed the bridge into the city.

Ten minutes and a great deal of cursing later, the clearly out-of-sorts captain told him to report to his office at 9:00 a.m. and disconnected sharply.

Sig felt the sting but didn't care. Sera would be safe in Blue Ridge. Logan would see to that. He'd done the only thing he could, the right thing, he was sure. All he could do now was wait and hope her memory would return.

Unlike Wyoming, it was misty and cool in San Francisco. Fog slunk around the piers and the lower half of the city. He had time to grab breakfast, thirty minutes of sleep and a hot shower. By eight-forty he was back in the alley where he'd parked his car. He gave the dented roof a pat and the door a kick to open it.

A man in a black hoodie plodded past, drinking from a bottle in a bag. Sig spared him an uninterested look, then sighed at the interior of his Ford. He'd be swimming in trash soon.

He heard the sound behind him as he started to slide in. The blow to the side of his head stunned him—almost as much as the sight of the man who'd delivered it.

"You," he managed to croak.

Grinning nastily, the man stuck a gun in his throat. "No bandanna for you, cop." He shoved the tip in deep. "I'm saving it for the shrink." His face floated closer. "You're gonna tell me where she is."

"Go to hell," Sig managed to gurgle. "She's safe, and she will remember."

"Oh, I'm sure of it. What she won't do is live to testify."

"I'm not telling you squat."

"Not verbally," the man agreed. His gun made a quiet popping sound as the bullet discharged into Sig's throat. "But there are other ways, my friend." He folded his latest victim's body into the car, located his wallet and eyed the trash on the seat and floor. "Plenty of other ways."

Chapter Four

Sera could have slept for twenty-four hours. The twelve she got ended with a rough shake from Flo.

"Chief has to go to Casper for a meeting. You need to get up."

She stuffed Sera's clothes into a laundry bag, then picked up and examined her broken shoes.

"I can wear heels like this, but not Babe. She can hardly..."

"Walk some days. Got that, Flo." Sera fought off the effects of her latest nightmare. She was sliding from the surprisingly comfortable bed when the stack of suitcases caught her eye. "You unpacked for me?"

"I don't like ironing. What kind of doctor are you if you don't do feet?"

"I can do feet." In her dove-gray drawstring pants and white tank, Sera bent to look out the partly shaded window. "Will it be hot again today?"

"It's July, isn't it?" Flo dangled the strappy shoes. "You want me to see about getting these fixed?"

"Thank you." Biting back a smile, Sera offered the expected trade. "Would you like me to look at your sister's foot?"

"She'd appreciate that. But you tell Logan it was your idea. He said I wasn't to pester you."

"I will."

Cinching the canvas bag, Flo started for the door. "Logan'll be by in forty minutes. I've got flapjacks and blueberry syrup in the kitchen. Coffee too." She paused on the threshold. "When?"

Rocking the tension from her neck, Sera headed for the bathroom. "If you're talking about Babe, I can examine her when I get back from Casper, where I'm apparently going whether I like it or not."

Flo gave a satisfied nod. "Do your whatevers fast, and I'll feed you. Otherwise you're at Logan's mercy, and potato chips make a fine meal to him."

"It's a miracle cops live to retire."

"That last word's not one we use much in these parts, Doctor."

Why wasn't she surprised? Sera mused.

Still wondering where the normal people lived, she went into the bathroom to shower away her latest dream image—that of the Blue Ridge police chief's enigmatic face.

"DON'T LET HER out of your sight, Fred." Logan handed Sera a white hat with a braided black band, trapped her jaw and stared straight at her. "No guns, no clever tricks, no tricky questions. Agreed?"

She pulled free and smiled. "You have a very low opinion of me, Chief."

"Must be the city cop coming out. I mean it, Sera."

"Yes, I know. Go on." She tried the hat for size and was pleased to discover it fit. "I won't ditch your dispatcher."

"Dispatcher slash senior deputy," the man called Fred corrected. He gave his boss two thumbs up. "Don't you worry, Logan. Me and the pretty doc'll get on just fine till your meeting's done."

Sera turned to examine the window of a small shoe store.

Why couldn't the chief be more like his deputy? Huge, bald and in his late fifties, with a bull neck, a big belly and a smile as wide as the Platte River.

"You wanna walk, talk or shop, Doc?"

Fred's question brought a teasing smile. "You're okay walking the streets of the county seat in the company of a marked woman?"

"No killer with half a brain's gonna shoot up a busy street at midday, Doctor—sorry, Serafina. That's a pretty name, by the way. Mean anything special?"

The sun glinted off the roof of a white delivery van. Sera popped her sunglasses on. "It means my mother had high hopes for my future. Didn't happen. I like Sera now."

He regarded her from under his own hat. "You and your ma at odds then?"

"Fifteen years worth and counting. There's no middle ground for us," she added before he could press. "We didn't see eye to eye on my future, so now we don't see each other at all."

"That's a shame, and I can say that because Flo and me have a girl, maybe six years up on you. We see her, but every time we do, it's either behind glass or on our doorstep in the middle of the night. She's an addict. Addiction's made her a thief. Thieving's sent her to jail four times. Guess we shouldn't throw stones considering our past, but we straightened out. I'm starting to think she never will. She owes money now, so I'm hoping against hope she won't show up at Logan's place. We live there, you know."

"With Logan? No, I didn't know. Or maybe I just didn't think. It's a big house."

"Came with…"

"The job, I heard." Hooking his arm, she asked, "Where does your daughter live, Fred?"

He snorted out a laugh. "Wherever the wind blows her.

Like her ma and me that way. But you got your own problems, Doc. You don't need ours heaped on top of them. Word is you've got someone after you, someone who likes to kill. Any thoughts on why a person would do that over and over again?"

"A few, but nothing that really works. Whoa…" Raising her sunglasses, she ogled a purse dangling near a shop entrance. "That is one über cool bag. Bet it costs a fortune." She slipped around him and inside to flip the price tag. "Oh, yeah, fortune. Fourteen-ninety-five."

"That doesn't sound…"

"Fourteen hundred, Fred."

When he gaped, she caught his shirt and drew him back out. "Breathe deeply. The feeling will subside."

"Fourteen—fifteen hundred dollars? For a purse?"

"Well, it's leather." She glanced past him. "Dolce and Gabbana."

"But that's…"

"I know." Aware of the sun's increasingly strong rays, she steered him toward an outdoor café. "Do you like iced latte?"

"What?"

She grinned, then tugged on his shirt. "Coffee, cold, yummy. We can sit. You can tell me how you wound up in Blue Ridge and what it's like to work for Logan."

Fred ran a hand over his face. "Logan, right… Well, it's good. Best straight job I've ever had. You probably know that Flo and me have done some shady things."

"We all have a past, Fred. The present matters more, don't you…think?" The last word emerged on a frown as a picture suddenly streaked through her head. Swinging away from the street, she pressed her fingers to her temples, trying to recapture it. "No, don't hide. Let me see you."

Fred came up behind her. "Are you okay? You want me to get Logan?"

Ignoring him for the moment, Sera struggled with the hazy image.

"Music," she said at last and, pivoting, searched for the source. "There was music playing in the background the night Andi died." She closed her eyes. "There's something behind it."

Fred sidestepped. "I'll get Logan."

"I need to hear it again." When he started off, she trapped his arm. "I'm good, Fred, really. I just need the music back. I saw something for a second. A hand, I think. And some kind of motion." She zeroed in on a muddy four by four truck. "That might be where it came from."

"You sure it was music, Doc, and not what you were saying?"

She started for the truck. "What were we talking about, do you remember?"

"Coffee, wasn't it? Or purses."

She cut across the street, skirted a group of people waiting to board a Greyhound bus and wound up back at the sheriff's office, where the truck was parked.

The cab of the vehicle was empty, but she made a slow circle around the hood.

Fred caught up and mopped his face with a red bandanna. "It's awfully hot, Doc. We could go inside, sit for a minute, see if we can find...Logan!" Relief colored his tone. "Am I happy to see you."

"I forgot a file. What are you doing?"

"Recreating," Sera said over her shoulder. She wanted to look at him, but that would destroy any chance she had of resurrecting the memory.

"Maybe we should..." Logan must have silenced Fred because he trailed off.

Sera continued to circle. "I saw a man's hand and part of an arm. He was wearing a watch with a chrome band. It was scratched and corroded in spots."

"Not a Rolex then," Logan said from the front of the truck.

"Tell him about the music," Fred suggested.

"I heard a song, or part of one, as this—I think this—truck drove past us." She bit her inner lip, drummed the box. "Might've been Bob Marley."

"'One Love'?"

"Maybe." But the title didn't trigger anything more. She made a flitting motion. "Sorry, it's gone. There was a watch, though, and it wasn't high end." She rubbed her wrist. "I saw a glove, too, but that's a given."

This time when Logan spoke, he did so from directly behind her. "What color was the glove?"

Her heart gave several hard thumps, which she controlled before turning. "Black. His fist was clenched, and it was striking something. A hard surface, possibly my desk."

"So this striking happened in your office."

Sera's head began to throb, but she pushed through it. "My office door was open. Andrea was in Reception when the security guard found her. I hit my head on my own desk, so I must have run in there." Leaning back against the side of the truck, she waved her hat in front of her face. "Sorry again, Logan, but that's all there is."

"It's more than you had before."

"Must be the mountain air."

She was doing it, she realized suddenly. Looking at him. Getting sidetracked. A baby step away from fantasizing about what it would be like to have that incredibly sexy mouth of his on hers.

Pushing off, she said, "Okay, that's it. Sun's frying my mind *and* my skin."

"Do you want to come inside?" he asked. "Meeting shouldn't take more than an hour." Then he pulled a ringing cell phone from his waistband. "Logan," he answered with a trace of impatience.

Easing away, Sera searched her shoulder bag for the sunscreen she'd bought during one of Sig's filling station stops.

Logan's quiet, "When?" brought her head up and Fred away from his inspection of the four by four's front tires.

"Where?"

"Oh, hell." Her fingers stilled as a feeling of dread crept in.

"I'll get back to you, Captain." Logan broke the connection.

"He's dead, isn't he?" She said it simply and without inflection. But it hurt. It cut deep and it bled.

Fred looked from one to the other. "Who's dead? Someone in Blue Ridge?"

"His name was Sig Rayburn," Sera revealed. "He brought me here. He was a good cop with good instincts, but instead of being shot in the leg, this time he's dead."

Logan's eyes were steady on hers. "It's not your fault, Sera."

"Not directly," she agreed. "But indirectly—well, you decide." Removing her hand from her shoulder bag, she opened it. "I have his lucky rock."

HE'D DIED IN an alley. Like his partner, there'd been no bandanna, but every cop worthy of his badge knew who'd pulled the trigger.

That made it personal, Logan thought. Now, not only was he going to keep Sera safe, but he was also going to get the bastard who'd killed Sig and make damn sure he never saw the light of day again.

With his mallet, he drove a fence post deep into the ground, then gave the baling wire he'd been stringing a yank and secured it to the top.

He'd come to Blue Ridge to get away from this kind of crap—the gang leaders cops could never manage to touch, the targeted shootings, the senseless murders, all the garbage and destruction city life had to offer.

He'd been born and raised in a small town. He was where he wanted to be, doing what he wanted to do. And he still couldn't escape the urban nightmare.

He took a swing at another post and felt the impact race along his arms to his shoulders. He wouldn't let Sig or Sera down. But damn the woman, she was getting to a part of him he'd half forgotten existed.

Yes, she was beautiful. So were plenty of other females in the world. Surface meant nothing—he'd learned that lesson early on. And hormones tended to get in the way of good judgment.

Another slam, another shoulder-numbing jolt. It was after 7:00 p.m. According to the medical examiner, Sig had died around 8:30 a.m. He'd taken a single bullet to the throat, preceded by a sharp blow to the left side of his skull.

Fixing the last length of wire, Logan swiped an arm across his forehead. He knew she was behind him before he turned. She smelled like jasmine and late summer roses. She was every man's gypsy fantasy.

Except for the sea-green eyes. Those were pure, storybook siren.

Without looking, he took a final pull from his Bud. "I'm not feeling chatty right now, Sera."

"I didn't think you would be." Coming around him, she dangled a half-done bottle of bourbon with an overturned shot glass on the top. "My uncle does trauma clinics on

Sunday nights. He says sometimes we need a little poison to kick-start a difficult emotional process."

Logan drew his work gloves off with his teeth. "Sounds more like something you'd say."

"I just did." She glanced away. "Logan, I'm really sorry about Sig. I teased him a little—actually, a lot—for being superstitious. Now he's gone, and I have his rock, and who knows, it's a big universe, maybe there was something to his belief."

"Uh-huh."

Although her lips turned up, her eyes remained on the trees. "Figured you'd say that. But whether I believe in Sedona rocks or not, Sig did, and that's the point. What I don't understand is why he left town without it."

Logan downed the bourbon in a single swallow. When his throat reopened, he poured another. "Did he give it to you?"

"Only to hold."

"If he didn't ask for it back, he wanted you to have it."

"I was afraid you'd say that."

The ghost of a grin appeared as the liquor worked its magic. "Seems we're a step ahead of each other tonight." He handed her the glass. "To Sig," he toasted and raised the bottle to his lips.

Her eyes glinted before she tossed the liquor back. It amazed him that she only gasped once. "Med school," she explained at his prolonged look. "Real ass of an anatomy professor. His students, Andi and I among them, plotted his dissection at a dozen off-campus bars." Moving closer, she used her index finger to tip his hat back. "I'll be honest with you, Logan. You scare the hell out of me, and that's a big admission for me to make because I of all people know how to deflect this kind of fear."

"Yeah?" Capping the bottle, he set it and the glass on

the post beside him. "So what say we do this now, and get it out of our systems."

It might have been surprise that flitted through her eyes, Whatever it was, the gleam behind it chased it out. She almost jerked when he caught her jaw in a light V. But then she relaxed and went with it—as he drew her closer and crushed his mouth to hers.

Chapter Five

Sera's mind blanked out. Her blood fired as need spiked. He tasted like bourbon-flavored sex.

Logan took his time, exploring her mouth with lazy thoroughness. It wasn't what she expected. Heat seared the edges of her control, but he didn't rush her, didn't take her on a wild ride to nowhere. Instead, he let the anticipation rise, made the hunger build. She might even have taken a hungry bite back.

Somewhat dizzy but decidedly intrigued, Sera gave his lower lip a tug, then reluctantly made herself end it.

His left hand dropped and his lashes lowered, but he didn't step away. "Not the best idea I've ever had," he murmured.

"Not the worst either." A smile sparked her eyes. "But maybe not the smartest, all things considered."

"It's one of my bigger failings." With his fingers still wrapped around her neck, he stared down at her. "Sometimes I forget to consider the consequences of my actions."

Was any part of her body not tingling? Sera touched her thumb to each fingertip. "On the upside, Logan, that was some action you undertook. On the down, you're dredging up feelings I'm not sure I want to deal with. You're also undermining my resolve."

"Which is?"

"Present nightmare excluded, to control my own destiny."

"So there'll be no using the Force on you." The faint smile lingered as he unhooked his ringing cell phone. "Yeah, Logan."

Sera experienced a moment of regret when he moved away, then reminded herself that distance was good. Another shot of bourbon wouldn't hurt either, but giving in would be weak, and she had no intention of becoming— well, a weak person.

"You sure your grandsons didn't take them?" Safely out of range, Logan threw his mallet in a Dodge truck that had seen better days and tossed Sera a set of keys. "Okay, I'll come by tomorrow. Meantime, check the barn and whatever other outbuildings are still standing."

When he bent to retrieve his work gloves, Sera tried not to notice how good he looked in his jeans and red T. "Is Grandpa Bulley missing some knives?" she asked.

A roll of baling wire joined the mallet. "Old Edgar locked up his sharpest knives years ago. He can't find his father's Winchester rifle. He's also minus a box of bullets and some food from his pantry—cooking spray, candy bars, chips, Twinkies."

"All the basics."

"To the non-medical types among us." He glanced down, arched a brow. "Did you walk all the way out here in those?"

"Oh, I can hike up any San Francisco hill in heels, but I'll be honest and admit that Fred drove me most of the way. I only had to make it in from the road." Her humor faded. "He's going to show up, isn't he, sooner or later?"

"Probably." Logan added his work gloves to the pile of

tools and supplies. "Sig wouldn't have talked, but that never stops a serial killer. They find a way."

"Well, I feel better."

"You're a shrink, Sera. You don't need lies."

"No, but I wouldn't mind…" She stopped as a thought suddenly struck. "Dixon Dane! You—I—whoa." She spread her fingers. "I knew I'd seen you before. Did you know when Sig called—no, scratch that, you'd have known, because, although I don't believe in lucky rocks, a cop's memory, especially a pissed-off cop's, is pretty much infallible."

Logan scooped a second set of keys from the back bumper. "Dane killed a stranger on a train. Hacked a guy's head off with an ax he'd been carrying in his backpack."

"And that says sane individual to you?"

"It says he murdered an innocent man."

"He didn't fake us out, Logan. The voices directing Dane's actions make your Jessie-Lynn's aliens read like a ship full of Morks."

"He'll be on the street in seven years."

"Not based on my recommendation, he won't." But her right palm beat a restless tattoo on the leg of her jeans. "You're right, though, he will. And even if he's deemed fit to rejoin society, it won't erase what he's done." She sent him an assessing look. "That's why you're in Blue Ridge, isn't it, and not where you were?"

He shrugged. "New York, Boston, L.A., there was no difference in the end. Names, faces, coworkers. The crimes repeated, and time served became a joke. You want to drive?" He indicated the key ring in her hand. "Those are for you to use in case I'm otherwise occupied."

"Thanks." She exchanged the keys for the rock in the pocket of her jeans. "I know Sig gave it to me, but you were close to him so I figured you might…" She broke off at his expression. "What's that? Am I getting a look?" Dipping down, she peered under his hat. "Are you annoyed with me for offering to give you Sig's rock?"

"No. I'm not annoyed, and there's no look." Logan slammed the rear door of the truck. "I appreciate the gesture, but he wanted you to have it, not me."

"Yes, but..."

Reaching out, he closed her fingers around the smooth red rock. "Keep it until we nail the Blindfold Killer. You can give it to me then."

Heat speared up her arm, but she didn't react. "He told me it came from Sedona. But you already knew that, didn't you?"

"Yeah, I knew." He opened the driver's side door. "Choice of seats is yours, Doc."

She considered, then slid behind the wheel. "He said his nephew gave it to him."

"Yes."

"Look, I know you don't like answering..."

"I said yes, Sera." Before he slammed the door, he set his mouth on hers in a kiss that sent a streak of desire straight to her lower limbs and most of her thoughts into a black hole.

Most but not all, she realized as his answer suddenly registered.

Sig Rayburn hadn't merely been Logan's friend. He'd been his uncle.

BABE WAS LIMPING around the kitchen when she returned to the house. With a cryptic smile, Logan disappeared into the barn, leaving Sera to face Flo and her older sister alone.

Two hours and a long physical examination later, Sera had the woman booked for an X-ray at the hospital in Casper.

Flo waited until Babe was seated in Fred's truck for the trip home before giving the tabletop an accusing jab.

"What were the words you used, and why did Doc Prichard say milk would make the problem go away?"

Sera went to the sink to wash her hands. "The term was plantar fasciitis. It refers to the long ligament on the bottom of the foot. As for the milk thing, no idea, unless it had to do with milk as a source of calcium."

Flo sniffed. "Man's a jackass."

"It's been mentioned. In any case, an X-ray will pinpoint Babe's problem, at which point it can be treated."

"By you."

"Well, I'm not really..."

"You're a doctor, aren't you? Have to be one before you can get into the head shrink stuff. I didn't fry all my brain cells when I was young."

"That's not exactly the point, Flo."

"You don't want to get involved."

Closer, Sera thought. "I'm not staying," she said, searching under the sink for a towel.

Flo whipped a fresh one out of the drawer. "S'pose I can't blame you for that. Our girl, Autumn, couldn't wait to get out... Should I go to Casper with Babe and Fred?"

"It's up to you. X-rays are a simple-enough procedure. Driving in hundred-degree heat, that's a killer."

Hanging the towel on a peg, Sera regarded the spoked wall clock. 10:15. Logic said she should be tired, but of course her mind kept drifting toward the barn.

"If you're going out, take the dog," Flo told her. "Chief's orders. You don't go anywhere alone." She snapped the light off, plunging the kitchen into the kind of darkness Sera seldom experienced in the city. "Stars'll help, but there's a flashlight in the mudroom if you need it."

Sera knew better than to take the woman's cranky tone

personally. Still, she'd have thought someone called Moon Flower would have been a bit less prickly.

At her side, the dog gave a low growl.

"I know how you feel," she murmured.

And opening the door, she walked into a human wall.

It wasn't Logan—she knew that right away. This person kicked and flailed so erratically that a fist clipped her cheek and sent her stumbling into the jamb.

Ella barked, then leaped. At least, Sera thought she did. The room was so dark, she only caught glimpses of movement.

She heard shoes scraping on the floor as the intruder scrambled to avoid Ella's teeth.

Was it a woman? Didn't matter, she decided and grabbed the coat that billowed out in the person's wake.

"Let go, bitch," a raspy female voice snarled.

Sick of being jerked around by strangers, Sera hauled her sideways until she collided with the wall.

Or was it something else?

A light flared. "Are you hurt?" Logan demanded above the curses coming from the woman he was currently holding by the shoulders.

"No, but I can't say I think much of your visitors."

Twisting her head, the woman swore, first at her, then at Logan.

"Inventive," Sera remarked. "And I'm going to guess high as well." Letting her fingers fall from her bruised cheek, she summoned an unruffled smile. "You must be Autumn."

FLO'S DAUGHTER, a pixyish woman with hand-shorn hair and a wad of chewing gum in her mouth, vented her anger for a full minute until her mother appeared, apologized stiffly and marched her upstairs.

That left Sera alone with Logan, Ella and a sky full of stars.

"You don't get backdrops like this in San Francisco," she remarked as they picked their way over the rocks and scrub toward the barn. "I can almost believe that's the whole Milky Way up there."

"Half of it anyway," Logan agreed. "Stars are different in the southern hemisphere."

She glanced over. "Have you been?"

"Twice. You?"

"Only to Brazil for a pag… To Rio, actually, when I was seven."

"You were eight, Sera, and you got the crown. Your friend Andrea was second runner-up."

The band that tightened around her midsection was instinctive. And unwarranted at this point in her life. She avoided a string of thorny weeds. "Do I want to know how you learned about that?"

"Probably not."

Okay, now the tightness was warranted. She snared his arm. "Tell me you didn't talk to my mother."

"Sig's personal calls are being forwarded to my cell phone. He must have given her his number."

"Great. So now I have to suck it up and simmer, or let temper win and punch you."

Grinning, he helped her down a set of natural stone steps. "I'm flexible."

"My mother isn't. Was she drunk?"

"Maybe."

"Did she call me an ungrateful, self-centered bitch?"

"No comment."

"Bet she said I left her penniless, too, huh? Bled her dry, then let my uncle Jeffrey con me into coming to live with him."

"You know the woman, I'll give you that."

She wouldn't go for his throat, Sera promised herself. She'd deal, then she'd lock it away because it didn't matter any more. It couldn't matter—it could only hurt.

Her gaze touched on Orion's belt. "I was one of those kids, you know? With one of those mothers."

"Stage mother."

"That's the one. The beauty queen wannabe—her dream, not mine. I didn't 'wannabe' anything except normal."

"What happened?"

"Nothing I could control at first. Then later, nothing I could really object to. The prize money worked for both of us for a while."

"And after a while?"

Her smile had a sharp edge. "I didn't win. Fourteen years old, and I came in second at a tri-state pageant."

"Were you upset?"

"Not as much as my mom was. Does the word 'tantrum' bring any visuals to mind? On the surface, I got through it, but I was having a huge freak-out inside. Then I saw Andrea. We'd met at a pageant when we were five. At this particular event, I found her backstage, acting out every horrible thing I was feeling. She came fifth that night, probably because of a black eye she couldn't cover up. I remember thinking, well, yuck. Then I had an epiphany. I hated that world. I wanted to go to school like everyone else."

"Seriously?"

A portion of her tension dissolved at his tone. "Not a fan of the classroom, huh? Lucky for me, my mother's brother is a very grounded eccentric. He swooped in when my mother flipped out, said we needed some time apart and took me to live with him in L.A. I walked from the glam life that summer. End of story. Let's move on."

Once again, all she could see was Logan's incredible mouth—a mouth that had been igniting all kinds of feelings in her less than three hours ago.

His fingers skimmed down her throat while his eyes scanned her face. "Sera…" he began.

Then swore and shoved her to the ground as gunfire exploded out of the darkness.

Chapter Six

"You didn't see anything?" Draped over the seat of the Explorer, Fred looked from Logan to Sera and back. "Or anyone?"

"No and no," Logan replied.

They were en route to town from the Bulley farm, where Sera had been forced to spend a very long ninety minutes listening to old Edgar complain about his gout, his bursitis and the arthritic pain he continued to suffer in the two fingers he'd lost to frostbite thirty years ago.

After that, she and Logan had driven halfway to Casper to pick up Babe and Fred, whose SUV had died on the side of the highway. By the time they arrived, Babe had developed a whole new batch of symptoms for her to diagnose.

At this rate, Sera figured they'd be lucky to reach town by sundown.

The sun was in fact sinking when Logan noticed an approaching motorcycle. "Get the radar gun, Fred. That bike's coming fast. You belted in?" he asked Sera.

She shot him an exasperated look. "I have the front half of your dog on my lap, Logan. You couldn't launch me through the windshield if you tried." She swiveled her head as the motorcycle flew past. "Okay, rocket on wheels."

"Hundred and ten miles an hour," Fred confirmed.

"Guess that means lights and siren." Before sitting back, he tapped Sera's shoulder. "Why do I see a bruise on your cheek, Doc?"

"Bad night vision."

"You sure you didn't have a tussle with Autumn? Flo thinks you did."

"No tussle," she lied and held on as Logan swerved to avoid a rabbit. Braking behind the motorcycle, he shoved Ella's butt off his leg and climbed out.

Ahead of them, a man with long brown hair and a droopy mustache dismounted.

Fred snorted out a laugh. "Here we go. Big smile for the small-town cop. 'Honest, Officer, I didn't mean to speed. Bike got away from me while I was taking in the beautiful scenery.' He's wasting his breath with that soggy spiel. Logan snacks on guys like him."

Sera watched cop and rider square off. Fred was right. The more Logan said, the more agitated the other man became. All they were seeing at this point were teeth. "He wants to take a swing," she noted. "Or, hmm, maybe not. Cop's got muscle and height and a stance that's telling him to give it his best shot."

As she watched, the man gestured in several different directions. His jerky movements suggested a blend of nerves and anger, thinly veiled. Logan, she decided, was very good at this.

Tipping her head to one side, she asked, "How did he wind up here, Fred?"

"Luck mostly. Fate if you believe. Our last chief was one of those pickers. You know the kind. Step outside a shop to check the color of a tie—you're a shoplifter. Pop a button while you're walking—that's littering. We had him for five years, until the mayor got sick of everyone complaining and started looking for better."

"And that was Logan."

"Yup. He was driving through town one day, heading for Montana. Nadine got to chatting with him, found out he was a cop and ran straight to the phone. Mayor and three of the town council members beat Logan's dinner to the table. Next thing we knew, he was taking a tour of the station. Now, let's go back to last night. I need you to give me the lowdown in detail because you don't seem panicky enough for a person who got shot at twelve times. Someone fired that many bullets at me I'd be shaking for days."

"Oh, I'm shaking, Fred. I'm just afraid to let it show." But she did let her mind slide back and a chill skate along her spine.

"Logan and I were heading toward the barn. The guy must have been hiding at the edge of the woods. If he'd waited another thirty seconds, he'd have had a better shot, but lucky for me, he fired prematurely."

"Gun or rifle?"

"Logan says gun. The bullets are being tested today."

"Lotta stars out and a big old half moon. You didn't see anything at all?"

"Only leaves, branches and some kind of animal that startled me as much as I startled it. Logan shouted at me to stay down, then he took off with Ella, but by the time they reached the road, the shooter was gone, mixed in with a dozen or more trucks coming from Frank's Diner."

"Did Logan talk to any of the drivers? Never mind, stupid question. 'Course he did. And no one saw a thing because the more they said, the better the chance they'd get charged with a DUI. People," he added in disgust.

Sera returned her gaze to Logan, who was sending the scruffy biker on his way. She couldn't help wondering if there'd been a specific reason why he'd chosen to leave the city. Cops like him seldom traded pace for peace.

She watched him walk toward them in his jeans, black hat and, for today at least, the requisite blue cop shirt. At the door, he unhooked his cell, talked for a few moments, then slid inside and tossed the phone on the dash.

When Ella whined, he motioned to Fred. "She needs a tree."

"Her and me both. Come on, girl."

Something in Logan's tone had a knot of resistance forming in Sera's stomach. "That was the police lab in Casper, wasn't it?"

"Ballistics report's in." His shielded eyes met her wary ones. "The bullets fired last night came from the same gun that killed Sig."

THE MEETING WITH the mayor at Town Hall took more than an hour because, big surprise, the man was delighted to discover a competent doctor in their midst. So delighted that he dropped his pants and showed Sera the spot on his butt where a large insect had bitten him.

Logan had no idea what she prescribed. Close-up inspections of male body parts wasn't in his job description. He escaped the office and let Nadine's mother, who was the mayor's secretary, flirt with him for a while.

It was after six before he reached the station. Back in the cells, the Bulleys sniped at anyone who'd listen, although they saved their nastiest barbs for the young deputy who had the misfortune to be their second cousin.

Logan's other deputies ignored both the Bulleys and their boss and vied for a look at Sera, who'd been waylaid outside the hardware store by a pregnant woman in curlers.

Perched on the dispatcher's desk, with a good view out the station window, Logan kept an eye on the sidewalk while he skimmed the file he'd been piecing together since yesterday.

Front and center was the ballistics report from last
night's—whatever the hell it had been. Not a particularly
adept murder attempt, that much was certain.

The killer had unloaded a dozen bullets from a nine-
millimeter automatic, missed on all twelve counts, then
backtracked at warp speed to his vehicle, where he'd successfully melted into the traffic on Boulder Road.

He hadn't laid down any rubber that Logan could see, and
no one he'd questioned had noticed anything unusual.

Not that that surprised him. Workers heading back to
camp from Frank's might notice a naked woman on the
road, but one truck more or less, not a chance.

Okay, so the killer knew how to blend in. And he was
a piss-poor shot when his gun wasn't pressed to a specific
body part. What did that prove?

Not much in the grand scheme. But it did suggest he'd
need to get close to kill again.

An unpleasant thought curled around the edges of Logan's mind. It had taken root early on, and he'd never quite
managed to blow it off.

Sig had talked about a leak at headquarters, but what if
that leak came with a twist? What if none of this was as it
seemed?

Yeah, and what if he was jumping at old cop shadows?

Glancing up, Logan saw the pregnant woman drawing
some kind of air picture for Sera.

"Chief?" Fred joined him with papers in each hand.
"I got that playlist you wanted from the radio station in
Casper. Bob Marley's there."

Setting his thoughts aside, Logan nodded. "Go for thirty
minutes on each side and download the songs to an iPod.
What else have you got?"

"Two full pages on our speeding biker. The name he
gave you is real, but he's used others over the years."

"Arrests?"

"Three in Idaho, one in Colorado, two in Utah. He broke into a bank machine in Colorado and gave the cops stolen ID when he got picked up. Likeness on the driver's license was good though, and some time over the course of life's journey, he's had his fingerprints burned off, so it took them a while to sort things out. He's been living the free life for more than a year now, but—and here's the kicker—both the Colorado and Utah cops figure most of his crimes are someone else's brainchild. No idea whose, and he denies it all the way, but there you go. What kind of line did he give you?"

Logan read on. "He said his bike had been acting up, and he thought if he gave it a good, hard run, the problem would solve itself."

"Think he'll pay the fine or hightail it?"

"He hired on yesterday out at the resort. Says he's a roofer. He's put in eight hours so far."

"Might be worth losing the pay in order to finger you."

"I don't see it, Fred." Logan took another look at Sera. "The guy had five bucks and a driver's license in his wallet, nothing but dirty laundry in his saddle bags and nerves stretched so tight I could've blown and watched them snap. He needs a fix. Either he knows someone here who can supply it, or he'll try his luck with our bank machines. Put Annabelle on night patrol with Biggs and Wendell, then call Johnny Abraham at the construction site and get him to send me a list of all the workers he's taken on since yesterday afternoon. Tell him I want that list updated every time he adds a new name. Same goes for anyone looking to hire here in town."

Fred cast a worried look at Sera. "You think whoever's after the doc will try to hide in a crowd of strangers?"

"It's possible. He's good with disguises. He might also camp out in the woods. Give Walter and Toby that detail. I want all the sites in the area investigated, and that includes the big one on Edgar Bulley's farm. Ditto the bed and breakfasts, the Lake's Inn and the Bear Hotel. I want details on anyone who matches the general description I gave you. Clear?"

Fred scratched an ear. "That's a tall order at this time of year, Logan. Tourists everywhere. Hunters, fishing folk, backpackers, bird watchers and, I think, a group of naturalists out near Sprout Lake. Not sure any of us will want to check them out."

Logan flipped to the next page in the file. "You never seen anyone naked before?"

A flush crept up Fred's thick neck. "Saw things that would make your hair turn during the Summer of Love, but it's a bit uncomfortable interrogating people who're letting it all hang. Hard to know where to put your eyes."

That wasn't Logan's problem at the moment. His eyes didn't want to leave Sera, no matter how many directives they received from his brain.

"Just ask the necessary questions, and look anywhere that works for you."

The big man didn't speak for a minute, but he didn't leave either. When he shifted his weight for the fifth time, Logan gave up trying to ignore him. "Something else, Deputy?"

He cleared his throat. "About the doc. I was wondering…"

"I'm not going to tell you who's after her. You only need to know that someone is."

A windy sigh emerged. "I suppose that's fair. But twelve bullets? That's an awful big number. Whoever he is, he must want her pretty badly."

"He does."

The edgy feeling crawled through Logan's belly again. Something there, his instincts warned. Then his gaze rose to the window, and he felt a spike of fear shoot into his throat.

Sera was gone...

HE'D OBSESSED ABOUT her since it happened, reliving the scene again and again. Beat himself up over it.

He wanted to beat her instead.

He saw himself in his mind, prowling the street outside the medical building, waiting, watching. The light on the fifth floor was on. She was working late.

Minutes turned to hours. Rain bounced off the roof of his car. Then, finally, the front door opened.

He recognized her red trench coat instantly.

Not yet, not yet, he cautioned himself. She was going to the all-night deli. She'd go back up. He'd get her then.

She emerged from the deli with a box and hugged the building walls so the rain wouldn't soak her. She used a key card on the door and went back inside.

He counted to ten, then used his own stolen key card and followed.

Child's play. Five flights of stairs, and he was there.

Do it quick. That was the best way.

He eased the office door open. She had her back to him. She was hanging her coat on a hook to dry.

He knew where the light switch was. He snapped it down. It wasn't completely dark, but who cared? Five strides brought him to her. He hooked an arm around her neck. Bye-bye, gorgeous.

One slash of his knife, and she was dead.

He let her drop. Done.

No wait. What was that sound?

An inner door opened.

"Andi, this patient's…" Green eyes locked on his.

He wanted to lunge, but shock turned his legs to lead.

It took forever to reach her. When he did, she kicked him in the nuts and ran.

A door slammed. He heard her on the phone. Pain screamed through his body, but he knew she couldn't get out, couldn't get past him. She was trapped.

He almost tripped over the dead body. He wanted to kick it aside. Wrong, it was all wrong.

He crashed through the door, breathing like a bull, shouting. Plan, what plan? Nothing left now but to fix it fast and get the hell out.

She'd called someone. His palms went clammy, but rage kept him going.

She was fast. He was faster—and still between her and the door.

He caught her. She fought. He went for his knife. She kicked him again. He shoved. She fell, hit her head, stopped moving.

"Dr. Hudson?"

He heard a voice on the other end of the phone.

Run, he ordered his lead-weighted legs. People would come. Use the fire escape. Get away and hide…

He called in sick the next day. Ear to the ground, though. He listened to the other "invisibles." They heard it all.

His mind leaped ahead.

Luck was with him. She couldn't identify her friend's killer. She didn't remember…

Alone for the moment, he looked up at the vast Wyoming sky, arms spread, face rapt.

Yes, Papa, there is a God!

Chapter Seven

"You're going to pull my arm out of the socket, Logan." Sera twisted on her wrist. "I'm not a criminal, and I'm not your dog. Stop playing caveman cop and let me go."

He did, but only, she suspected, because they'd reached the front door of the drugstore and couldn't go through it at the same time.

"Back to Town Hall," he said once they were outside.

"Not your dog," she reminded. Bending, she ruffled the retriever's ears. "No offense, Ella."

The dog barked and plopped down next to her on the sidewalk. The dark sidewalk, she noted in surprise.

She felt Logan staring, then realized that more than a few people around them were doing the same thing and sighed.

"The woman's eight and a half months pregnant. She asked me what products she could safely use in order to sit for more than ten minutes at a time." Her temper pricked at his continued stare. Disinclined to smooth the edges, she retraced her steps and went toe to toe with him. "You're a cop, Logan, you protect people. I'm a doctor. I help those same people with medical conditions. Try not being able to sit in a chair, and see how you feel after six weeks. Oh, but first strap on a pregnancy suit. You won't be asking for help, pal—you'll be begging for it."

"You weren't in the drugstore the first time I looked."

"Yes, I was. You just didn't see me because the night clerk, who lives upstairs, was afraid that George, who's been losing weight steadily over the past six months, has stomach cancer."

"George is the clerk's dog," Logan said.

"Thank you, I discovered that. Unfortunately, he neglected to mention it until I'd gone up. What he did mention is that your Dr. Prichard dabbles in veterinary medicine. If I were you, I'd stick with the overworked but legitimate town vet. George has two teeth that need to be pulled and his diet consists mainly of kibble. Prichard didn't even look in his mouth. He felt his ribs, then pronounced that the dog had two months to live. As a tactless parting shot, he told the owner that Nadine's border collie is expecting a litter of puppies in August."

Catching her chin, Logan looked directly into her eyes. "Cell phone, Sera. You have one. Next time you decide to hold an impromptu clinic, use it."

"Love to." She moved her lips into a smile. "As long as, next time, you remember to clip yours on and not leave it on your dash." She widened her eyes. "I left a message, Logan. Twice."

He was swearing softly when a man with a prominent Adam's apple strolled past. "Evenin', Chief." He winked at Sera. "You tell him what's what, Doc. Just don't ride him so hard he leaves town."

"Keep walking, Harry," Logan suggested. His eyes were fixed on hers. "Town Hall, Dr. Hudson. Please."

Because far too many people were staring at this point, Sera located the large, wood-fronted building across from the drugstore and, with an unpromising look at Logan, started toward it.

The century-old structure had a wide, worn stoop,

mullioned windows and a sign above the entrance that had apparently been nailed in place by someone too inebriated to see straight. The hinges on both doors screeched, the pine floors sagged in the middle, and the air smelled of stored apples and old books. She noticed that one of the side windows was broken. A green trash bag duct taped over the hole flapped open at the top, allowing both insects and the omnipresent wail of country music inside.

When the overhead lights blinked on, Sera spied a stack of wooden crates with the letters BRD painted on the sides directly ahead of her.

"Blue Ridge Days," Logan said without looking. "It's a mid-summer tradition. Means more money for local businesses and more work for me and my deputies." He snagged her arm before she could evade him. "You could have called the station."

She could also tell him off and leave the hall. But that would be foolish and ungrateful. He was only trying to keep her alive.

So she released a breath and gave the stack of chairs beside her a vexed nudge with her knee. "I'm not used to living like this, Logan, under scrutiny twenty-four hours a day. Do you really think the Blindfold Killer would follow me into a drugstore half a block from the police station?"

"He fired twelve shots at you in the police chief's backyard. Yeah, I think he'd follow you and take out anyone who got in his way."

"Oh, good. Now I don't just feel bad—I also feel guilty for endangering the lives of a thirty-something store clerk and a woman with child."

"Children. Prichard says she's having twins."

"Don't think so, Ace. She's not large enough. I felt her

belly. That's one big baby she's carrying. No room inside for two."

"You sure, Doc? Twins run in her husband's family."

"They run in my mother's, too, but as you see, I'm an only one."

"Trust me, Sera, one's more than enough."

A round of cheers and catcalls reached them through the broken window. She hoisted herself onto a crate. "Sounds like stripper night at the Main Street saloon."

"You could say." Logan prowled a little. "Sometimes Ginny gets tanked and starts up a game of strip poker in the back room."

"Of her saloon?"

"Garage. She fixes vehicles—cars, trucks, motorcycles, strollers, anything that rolls. Her last name's Bulley."

"Of course it is. And she gets tanked on...?"

"Whatever's left in the barrels my deputies and I don't find and her cousins haven't sucked dry." A gleam in his eyes lightened the mood. "Wanna join the game?"

"FYI, Chief, I went to college. I've done more than..."

It came out of nowhere, a razor-thin beam that sliced through the wall in her mind and allowed a brief but vivid image to sneak out.

She focused her eyes downward and let her heel hit the side of the crate. "Okay," she said softly, "that was weird." Her gaze slid to the flapping trash bag. "I saw him—his watch, I think, and his coat, some kind of lightweight khaki." The bag flapped again as a breeze stirred the air. "I remember mothballs—and some other smell buried under it." She tried to separate the components. It wasn't men's cologne. She tapped the crates beneath her. "What's inside these?"

"Decorations. Streamers, bunting, signs."

"Stored in mothballs," she assumed. "Which must have

been the trigger. It's gone back to blurry now. But I saw a khaki coat and the chrome watch again, so I know it's the same guy." She breathed out. "Damn, this is so frustrating." On more than one level, she reflected, hopping down.

When the hoots and catcalls reached them again, her lips curved into a slow smile. "Tell me, Chief, can anyone join Ginny Bulley's game?"

"Far as I know." His eyes dropped to her breasts, then rose with a glitter. "You're not wearing much in the way of clothing, Sera. Couple bad hands, you'll be down to your underwear."

"Lingerie," she corrected and, giving into temptation, ran a finger from his throat to his chest. "Black and lacy, the kind of feminine garments men are terrified to buy."

"You think?"

"Probably not as clearly as I should, but what if we do this." She took a suggestive step closer, flicked a finger between them. "A one-on-one contest, you and me, beyond the parameters of the usual game. I win, you buy me dinner. You also agree to cut me some slack when I'm in a relatively safe place. You win, I buy, and I'll accept your twenty-four-seven surveillance rules without a fuss."

The glitter became a gleam. Trapping her hand he brought it to his mouth and kissed her knuckles. "It's a deal, Doc. We'll leave Ella at the station. She's not as big a fan of black lingerie as I am."

She gave him a quick, teasing kiss. "You're counting chickens, pal. Never a wise move in my experience."

With a smile she knew she shouldn't trust, he swept a hand toward the door. "After you, Doc."

A feather-light shiver danced along her spine as another image suddenly appeared. Not of a man wearing khaki and chrome, but of the man behind her wearing nothing at all.

"YOU CHEATED."

Sera preceded Logan into Tommy Gray Wolf's bar. She wore his hat, his cop jacket and all of her own clothes.

Kenny Chesney poured from four speakers mounted high in the dusty rafters. It was the barman's ode to the present. Given a choice, Logan knew Tommy would play Johnny Cash from morning to night.

Setting his mouth next to her ear, he nodded forward. "Head for the back corner. The people there are leaving."

"How many bars does this town have?" she asked over the music.

"Nine or ten." He stopped a tourist from snatching the hat off Sera's head. "Depends on your definition and whether or not you include Frank's Diner."

"Or Ginny Bulley's back room." Halting, she pushed the hat from her face and sent him a wary stare. "Back to the cheating thing. I saw you do it. What I don't understand is why you stacked the cards so I'd win." Her gaze fell to the front of his jeans. "You like women's lingerie, right?"

"Do I need to answer that?"

She smiled and started walking. "No, and maybe I understand after all. Not necessary, though. I played poker in med school. I also have a patient who's a compulsive pretty-much-anything-you-can-name. He talks to me, but only if we play five-card stud during our sessions. Because gambling's the least of his problems, I took the deal. He's taught me how to cheat and spot a cheater. I'm helping him overcome his need to set fire to any structure bigger than a phone booth."

"You're joking."

"I never joke about patients, Logan. It might seem like a lighthearted approach to a serious problem, but it's working. In any case, he isn't the most dangerous arsonist I've taken on."

By the time they reached the table, Kenny had given way to George Strait. "Sounds like an interesting career, Doc." Logan pulled out a chair for her, scanning the crowded room for the third time in as many minutes. "Ever worked with a serial killer?"

"No, but I've collaborated on several murder cases—beyond our creepy common dominator, Logan." She touched his arm. "If he's here, he won't do anything. Suicide's not this guy's deal. Completing his specific agenda is."

"Sure of that, are you?"

"As sure as I can be with only slivers of information to go on."

"I wouldn't call that a reassuring assessment."

"That's because you're approaching this from the perspective of a cop who's thinking protection rather than motive." She leaned in to stage whisper, "He's not done. If suicide was his goal and Andrea had been his final victim, Sig and his partner would still be alive, I'd be home in bed and the Blindfold Killer would be in a body bag. My guess is he has more people to murder, or he wants to go on hiatus for a while. Either way, not done."

When Logan didn't respond, she nudged his arm with her shoulder. "Ground Control to Major Tom. You still with me, or is the BK's motive starting to interest you?"

He ran his gaze around the busy room. "Everything interests me, Sera, but motive's not relevant here—unless Paxton's suddenly decided that killing beautiful brunettes is the way to go."

The thought of her partner brought a twinge of regret. "Andi and I should have been better friends." She drew an absent crown on the table. "Her ancestry was Scottish. Mine's Irish. People used to call us the Celtic sisters. One of her patients who was into astrology insisted we had a Gemini connection. She said we shouldn't work together because of it. Something about spatial displacement and overlapping dimensions. Bottom line, we should dissolve our partnership before all hell broke loose in our astrological spheres."

"Was this patient psychic?"

"No idea. She was definitely bipolar, which was Andi's main concern." Sera watched a man and woman unapologetically making out on the dance floor. "There's no professional connection between Andi and Hugh Paxton, Logan. The San Francisco police went over her life in detail. It has to be a personal link, if not to the first eleven, then somehow to his last three victims. Assuming there are any links involved."

Logan sat back. "You want my feeling, cop to shrink?"

She'd like a great deal more, actually, but truth had its place and this wasn't it. "Love it," she said. "Are we talking random or calculated here?"

"Calculated. Likely convoluted. Definitely personal in terms of each victim."

"So, pretty much textbook then. Some wrong being made right in Paxton's eyes."

"The investigational stumbling block being that said wrongs often seem perfectly right to a serial killer."

"Whose values are dictated by his emotional barometer, which in turn frequently harkens back to some childhood dysfunction either unnoticed or induced by the mentors and or peers... Blah, blah."

Logan chuckled. "Tired, are you?"

"And hungry."

As if cued, the drinks and appetizers they'd ordered at the door appeared on the table courtesy of a harried server. She had a cigarette tucked behind one ear and a cloth wrapped around her left hand.

"It's nothing," she said at Sera's raised brows. "Fire in a

frying pan. Tommy doused it." She rapped Logan's shoulder. "Abe's at the bar, says you want to talk to him. I'm due for a break. I'll sit with the doc, keep your seat warm."

Almost as good a bodyguard as Fred, Logan reflected. "Back in ten," he told Sera and was glad to finally see an amused expression.

Johnny Abraham, called simply Abe, owned seven plaid shirts, one beer buckle belt and a nineteen-fifties truck that only ran because Ginny Bulley was the best mechanic in Wyoming. He'd been hiring steadily since early spring and subcontracting for the last three months.

When he spotted Logan, he gave the man beside him a shove. "Find another seat, Mel."

"I'm Travis."

"Well, you smell like Mel. Go on, get. Chief wants a word."

"Yeah? Well, I've got a beaut of a word for you, Chief." The beer-bellied worker tapped the side of his nose. "It's Bulley—as in watch out for the ones who aren't behind bars. Heard rumblings about the two oldest." At his boss's glare, Travis shrugged and left.

"Man's got the brains of a billy goat, but he's strong as an ox." A trio of chins wobbled beneath Abe's fully dentured smile. "What's on your mind, Logan? Besides that pretty doc you've been showing the sights to these past few days?"

Because he'd left his mug on the table, Logan went with a glass of beer and another scan of the room. "I want names, Abe."

"I know." He dug in the pocket of his shirt. "Only have three, and all of 'em came with references."

Logan took the folded paper. "You check any of those references out?"

"Yeah right, I got oodles of friggin' time to do that. I'm

only a month behind schedule, and old gloom and doom Joe's predicting two feet of snow by Halloween. Hell, Logan, I'd hire Edgar Bulley if he came looking." Raising his beer, Abe squinted at the door. "Speaking of... Unless I need my glasses more than Travis thinks I do, two of old Edgar's dumbass grandsons just lumbered in. Could be they're looking for you."

"Looking for trouble anyway." Although he didn't expect it would amount to anything—the killer, a known suspect, wouldn't be likely to hire on to work in plain sight—Logan pocketed the list and kept his eye on the glowering men.

Swiveling back to the bar, Abe bumped his elbow. "She staying?"

"No."

"Why not?"

Because complication, strong emotions and lust were things he didn't want or need in his life. Because she was a psychiatrist and he was a cop, and those two professions, as proved by the Dixon Dane case, didn't mix. And because he'd been doing just fine without her.

She wasn't his type, and no way in hell was he hers. The big city burnout that had landed him here hadn't done its phoenix-rising-from-the-ashes thing yet. He was no bargain for any woman at this point, let alone a dark-haired, green-eyed siren whose job was to fix screwed-up people. To get inside messed-up minds.

To get under his damn skin...

Between that last thing and the growing twist of doubt in his belly, Logan's mood began to deteriorate. Raising his beer, he slid his gaze to the corner table.

And saw the biker he'd ticketed that afternoon skulking across the floor toward Sera.

Chapter Eight

"You cook, you get burned." The server, whose name was Jenny-Lynn, shrugged. "It's no big thing."

"Bet it stings." Sera rewrapped her hand and tore the ends of the towel to tie it. "I can write you a prescription to manage the worst of the pain."

"I wouldn't say no." Jenny-Lynn gave her fingers a casual flex. "You got something going with our chief of police?"

Mostly in her head, Sera thought, but shuffled the fantasy aside and went with Logan's story. "Actually, I'm on vacation. Logan's uncle told me about Blue Ridge Days, and I was free, so I figured why not explore the Big Horn Mountains?"

"Uh-huh." The woman, a self-described hot mama with a no-nonsense attitude, fifty-plus years under her belt and cabernet-colored hair, picked up Logan's beer, studied the thin line of foam and took a deep swallow. "You heard about my sister yet?"

Sera tread carefully. "If her name's Jessie-Lynn, yes, I have."

"She's ten years younger than me and loony as a Warner Brothers' cartoon. She saw you for the first time today. Called me straight away, said that pretty-as-a-picture doc was gonna steal our police chief out from under us unless we did something big."

"Should I be worried?"

"Hard to say. Knowing Jess, she's talking alien intervention. Now me, I'm more inclined to talk practical, and I get a little oochey thinking about this town without Logan. He keeps things running smooth, and, hon, you gotta know, the ladies love him, local and tourist."

"Fancy that." Leaning in, Sera let her eyes dance. "Police chief and tourist attraction rolled into one. That's some weighty twofer."

"You teasing me?"

She laughed. "Yes, I am. Look, would you and Jessie-Lynn feel better if I admitted that I'm really here because I had a stalker after me in San Francisco and the detective in charge of the case thought it would be a good idea for me to leave the city?"

Jenny-Lynn stopped a match halfway to her cigarette, shook it out and scooted her chair closer. "Honey-lamb, I am all ears. Do you think this stalker followed you to our little mountain town?"

"Maybe." Because her wine sucked, Sera took a sip of Logan's beer, and immediately wanted to spit it out. "That tastes like sewer."

"Lines need cleaning. We'll get to it when the regulars start griping."

Sera pushed the mug to the center of the table. "That's just plain gross, Jenny-Lynn."

"You think?" The server braved another large swallow. "Tell me, Doc, d'you know what this stalker of yours looks like, or are we talking stranger?"

Sera selected a red nacho from the plate. "Stranger, I think. I might have caught a glimpse of him once, but nothing definite. He wears a watch with a chrome band on his left—no wait—on his right wrist." She halted mid crunch. "How did I know that?" Then frowned. "How did I miss it?"

Jenny-Lynn struck a fresh match. "You're losing me, hon."

Sera's mind skipped back. The police report said the Blindfold Killer had slashed Andi's throat from behind with a left to right motion. With his right hand. Most right-handed people wore watches on their left wrists. Andi's killer hadn't.

She tapped a contemplative finger on the table. "Maybe he's ambidextrous."

"Still lost. Are we talking about your stalker?"

Sera zoned back in. "What? Oh, no. I was thinking about a patient."

"I heard you helped Babe and the mayor. And Nadine's cousin who's having twins she and her husband can't afford."

"I suppose I did, but…"

"You don't call them patients?"

"I was only trying to…"

"Sure, more people than you might like know your business, but those same people are also there when and if you need them."

"Look, I like it here. It's just…"

"Dr. Prichard is a complete jackass. Unfortunately, he's all we've got. Doc Faldo and his wife Doc Faldo retired last year and left town. Now a resort's coming in. We don't need one doctor, we need at least four, and for my money, Prichard can hightail it to some other state. Do you know anybody who'd be willing to help you out at the clinic?"

Sera regarded her with patience. "I'm not staying, Jenny-Lynn, and even if I was, technically I'm not a family physician. I'm a psychiatrist."

Jenny-Lynn hooked an arm around the back of her chair. "You got Babe to like you," she began, then rolled her eyes when the owner shouted from the bar. "Guess recess is over." She crushed out her cigarette. "Think before you decide," she said and was gone before Sera could respond.

She was sliding Logan's mug absently toward her when a man's fingers spread across the top.

"Hey there, sugar. Name's Wayne, and I got a powerful thirst building. D'you mind?" With his flat brown eyes on her face, the biker Logan had pulled over that afternoon removed the mug from Sera's unresisting fingers and raised it to his mouth.

"You must have a cast-iron stomach," she remarked when he didn't flinch. "That beer's crap."

"Whole town's crap. Except for you. Sheriff's a complete…"

"Police chief," she interrupted. "Former homicide detective. If that matters to you."

"Why should it?" His chin jutted. "You think I can't handle a cop? Watch it, pal," he snarled. "That's my arm you're poking."

Across from Sera, a big man with Bulley features and hands the size of ham hocks gripped Wayne's shoulder and lifted him off his feet.

"Go away." He set his other hand on the knife in his belt. "I got business with the lady."

This couldn't be good. Sera stood—only to find herself staring into a second man's chest. Bulley number two, she presumed.

"You're not leaving us, are you, Doc?" Number Two's smile mirrored his brother's. "'Cause we wanna get some things straight. Beat it," he snapped at the biker, whose mustache had begun to tremble.

"Leave him alone." Sera jerked back when the second Bulley reached for her.

A tanned arm wrapped around Number Two's throat, squeezing just hard enough to draw a chocking cough.

"Call her reaction a no and back off, Lloyd. You, too, Victor."

The Bulley named Victor tossed the biker aside as if he were made of cardboard. "We got a bone to pick with you, Logan."

"Figured you might."

"Her, too."

Sera sidestepped the finger he attempted to thrust in her face and glanced at his belt. "Uh, Logan…"

"I see it." Logan's flexed forearm turned the cough to a hiss. "For your brother's sake, you want to leave that knife where it is."

"Two of us and only one of you," the trapped Bulley growled. "Odds ain't exactly in your favor."

"No? Huh." Logan's elbow clipped Lloyd's jaw so swiftly that Sera missed the move.

The dazed man mowed the biker down, then staggered into a skinny man about to take a drink of beer. The beer flew, the biker landed on his butt and three pairs of hands made a grab for the fallen Bulley's shirt.

"Well, hell," Logan said on a breath.

It was the last really clear thing Sera heard. The flying beer seemed to galvanize half the males in the room and more than a few of the females.

A man in plaid with three chins and a frantic look on his face barreled into the fray. "Leave it be, Derek," he shouted.

"Put your glasses on, old man. I'm Travis."

"Behind the bar, Sera." Logan shoved her toward the pass-through where Jenny-Lynn was waving an arm.

"Come on, hon," she called. "Tommy's gonna hit the lights. That'll put a damper on things."

"Don't count on it." Sera did a double take as the biker yanked a switchblade from his boot. A second later, someone stumbled into her shoulder. "Toby?" She helped Logan's junior deputy regain his balance. "Did your cousin just punch you?"

He swiped gamely at a bloodied lip. "They're a little riled tonight is all."

A little riled and a lot drunk, Sera reflected. Either their whiskey barrels were bigger than Logan realized or the Bulleys had another still up and running on their farm.

Jenny-Lynn continued to motion her forward. Music blared overhead. It was like a scene out of a B movie, except the blood here was real and there was no way to separate the good guys from the bad.

She'd almost reached the pass-through when the room went dark.

"Gotcha, Doc," Jenny-Lynn said.

She caught hold of Sera's jacket—a split second before Sera caught the smell of mothballs.

She started to swing around. "Jenny, where's Lo…?"

It was all she got out, and the last thing she remembered.

Something came down hard on her head. Like thick fog rolling in, deep shadows gave way to solid black, where noise, thought and music simply disappeared.

"LOGAN?" HIS YOUNG deputy sounded unsure.

Logan blocked a full-face punch and swung the drunk in front of him into an arm lock. "Toby, get to the bar and tell Jenny-Lynn to turn on the damn lights."

He had to toss the drunk he was holding aside so he could yank his junior deputy out of the way of Victor Bulley's fist. When the big man snarled and raised an arm, Logan went with the obvious and kicked him in the groin.

"Go," he ordered Toby.

"I won't make it," Toby protested, but at a push from Logan, he endeavored to forge a path in the general direction of the bar.

Someone large and heavy slammed into his back. Logan spun, prepared—then blew out a breath when he realized it was Fred.

"What's going on?" the big man demanded. "I came in the door and almost got tackled by Lloyd Bulley."

Logan used his fist on a man who was lining Fred up from behind.

"How did you see him?" Fred demanded, peering at the floor.

"I worked a lot of night shifts in L.A." Logan shook out his bruised knuckles. "Follow Toby to the bar. I want the lights on—now."

A flashlight beamed wildly in front of him. "Logan!" Breathless and pointing, Jenny-Lynn clutched his wrist. "Someone took Sera."

"What?" Her statement cost him a hard shot to the ribs.

Ignoring the pain that screamed through his body, he gripped Jenny-Lynn's arms and propelled her backward. "What happened? What did you see?"

"The room was dark, so not much. I had my hand on her sleeve, then I didn't." She gripped him back. "I don't know how I know it, but I felt someone hit her. Air moving maybe. And I heard her say something about mothballs."

"Could you tell which direction they went?"

"No, but I'd guess one of the side doors. Back's too hard to get to through the kitchen, and you can forget the front."

"I'll go left," Fred volunteered and began plowing through the field of bodies.

Logan took her flashlight, used his forearm on someone's throat and deposited Jenny-Lynn at the pass-through. "Get those lights on and make sure both Bulleys are still here."

"I can hear Lloyd squawking, so he's here for sure." She dug stubby fingernails into his arm. "Find her, Logan, before…" A swallow ended the statement. Turning, she shouted the owner's name.

Logan followed the long bar to the second door. Could be a Bulley had grabbed Sera out of spite, but that was probably wishful thinking.

"Logan, I wanna…whoa, no, take it back."

Logan pointed the gun he'd drawn from his waistband at the ceiling and fixed his eyes on Victor Bulley's shadowed face. "Where's your brother?" he demanded.

A sneer appeared. "None of your f…"

An uppercut sent him sprawling over a table that cracked under his weight.

Logan had no idea what the killer's plan might be when operating on unfamiliar ground. The Bulleys would do anything short of murder if the price was right, and Sera's abductor could undoubtedly playact with the best of them. He might have paid a Bulley to take her.

He reached the exit and pushed through to the relative silence of the alley. A row of trucks lined one side, metal trashcans the other.

Toby rushed through the door behind him. "Fred just told me…"

"Go right," Logan ordered. "Check every vehicle."

He took the longer line on the left. He'd barely reached the first truck when an engine roared to life.

"Got you, bastard," Logan growled as light flooded the alley. Taking aim, he went for the tires.

The truck slammed into reverse. He shot twice. The man in the truck retaliated, letting five rounds go. Ramming the side of Abe's Hummer, he fired again, then jumped out and bolted into the night.

Logan heard Toby go down behind him and swore.

"I'm okay," Toby called weakly. "He winged my arm."

The truck's tires squealed. Logan smelled burning rubber. The box was wedged against Abe's heavy vehicle. Stones flew in all directions. Cutting through the twin beams, Logan raised an arm against the rock spray and yanked the driver's side door open.

He saw her in the back of the extended cab, facedown on the seat. Unmoving.

"Sera!" Kicking a stone off the gas pedal, he shoved the truck out of gear and reached for her.

Was she breathing? He pressed his fingers to the pulse point in her neck. Fast but steady. And there was no trace of red on the cracked seat.

Logan let his forehead drop onto her hair. She was alive.

And he was in deep, deep trouble.

Chapter Nine

"I don't have a concussion." Arms folded, Sera regarded the line one of his deputies had drawn on the station floor. "You don't seriously expect me to do this."

Logan sat back at his desk, hat forward, booted feet propped on top. "Walk the line, and the key to the clinic's yours. Otherwise it'll be up to Doc Prichard to deal with the fallout from last night's fisticuffs."

"It was a barroom brawl, and I happen to know you were in there brawling with the best of them. You also saved my life, so thank you. Again." At his placid stare, she sighed. "Still have to navigate the line, huh?"

"Do it, and I can go out to the practice range, blow the guy away a few dozen times."

The killer had left a white bandanna, Sera recalled with a chill. He'd stuffed it under the seat of his truck, or rather a truck stolen from Edgar Bulley's barn.

There'd been no non-Bulley paraphernalia inside, and she didn't anticipate any better luck in terms of fingerprints. Besides, what would it prove if they did find one of Hugh Paxton's prints? Identifying him wasn't the key. Unmasking him was.

Resigned, Sera walked to the top of the line. "I'm only doing this once, Logan, so sit up and take notice."

He didn't, but she saw his lazy smile and knew he was watching. Closely.

Five seconds later, she pivoted ninety degrees in three-inch heels, then strolled toward him, palm out. "Mission accomplished, Chief. Where's the clinic?"

It took two minutes to get there from the station and less than half that time for Sera to understand what everyone had been telling her from the start about Rufus Prichard.

Chimpanzees could have done a better job of organizing and maintaining the town's limited medical equipment. The BP monitor had a torn cuff, the stethoscope was dirty and the scale fell apart when she touched it.

"You have paramedics, right?" She flicked through the filing cabinet and wasn't impressed.

"Four of them," Logan confirmed. "They take emergencies straight to Casper."

Sera looked around, considered. "Jenny-Lynn's right. You'll need more doctors when the resort's done. What about nurses?"

"Only one. She's sixty-six and married to Jenny-Lynn's uncle. She worked with Prichard for two days after she retired from her hospital job in Casper. On Tuesday afternoon, she marched across the street to inform me that she was putting an old Norse curse on him. So far it hasn't kicked in."

With Ella nosing her arm, Sera inspected the medicine cupboard. Uncapped bottles sat alongside open boxes of tongue depressors, cotton wadding and gauze. "Why hasn't someone run him out of town?"

"He's all we've got, Doc."

"That's not an answer."

"You're desperate, you either drive to Casper or you take your chances with Prichard."

She thought of the pregnant woman she'd spoken to

and leaned against the cupboard to close it. "What about midwives?"

"She knows what she's doing."

"Caregivers?"

Crouching, Logan searched out a dusty coffee pot. "You do know where you are, right? You need care, you call a relative, a friend or a neighbor."

She grinned. "Everyone knows everyone, is that it?"

"Pretty much."

"So the Blindfold Killer probably won't risk staying in town."

"Probably not."

"Which leaves campsites, roadside motels...and you've already got that covered, haven't you?"

Logan regarded her from his crouch. "Come here, Sera."

It was his tone more than his expression that had an anticipatory shiver whispering across her skin. No fan stirred the air in the clinic. There was only the heat and her pulse points doing a sudden series of war dances throughout her body.

Stay away, her brain urged. But of course she ignored it and went with the challenge of holding her own against Logan.

"This better turn into a romantic moment because if you show me a dead animal, you'll find you're due for a very nasty vaccination."

"Probably be smarter to take the shot." But his lips curved, and he wrapped his fingers around her neck and held her eyes with his. "This is a really bad idea, Sera."

"I know."

"I can't watch your back if my head's as screwed up as I let it get last night."

"You did? It was?" Delight filtered in. "When? Why? How?"

"Strip poker, strip poker, vivid imagination."

She wanted to laugh, but the urge to kiss him won out, and with a soft "This is so wrong," she took his face in her hands, yanked his mouth onto hers and dived in.

Sensation rocked her from head to toe, wave after stunning wave. A need she hadn't known existed surged and swirled inside her.

It was like plunging head first over a cliff and not knowing if there was water below or a dry roadbed. Not that it mattered. Right then it was all about the fall, about the fiery rush of wind over her limbs and the dark, dangerous taste of him.

Drawing her closer, Logan changed the angle of the kiss, taking it from hot to molten. He used his tongue, his hands and somehow, without moving, his body. There was no gentle exploration this time—there was only greed and hunger and desire, skating on the slippery slope of control.

When his hand slid to her breast, a gasp leaped into her throat. He swallowed it. Sera fisted his hair and nipped his bottom lip. She needed to taste and feel all of him.

She also needed to breathe, and for a heart-thudding moment, she couldn't. Or wasn't. She eased back just far enough to get air and steady her spinning head.

"I feel like I'm on a carousel from hell—only in a good way." Very slowly, the room and her racing heart began to settle. Maybe. Her eyes rose to the ceiling. "Do I hear drums?"

The ghost of a smile crossed Logan's lips. "It's the door, Sera. Someone wants in."

"Ah." Her mouth curved, and she gave his bottom lip a last regretful bite. "For a second I was thinking subarachnoid hemorrhage. Blow to the skull followed by the trauma of a killer kiss." Her smile blossomed when he narrowed his eyes. "One of us should probably answer the door before..."

"Doc Sera, you in there?" A man's voice came from the other side. "It's Travis from last night. Bunch of us out here need looking at."

"Where's a good sub-hem when you need one? Logan, I only wanted to see the clinic. I'm not a family doctor."

"Yes, you are." He gave her a grin and a kiss and brought her back to her feet. "For today anyway." Eyes gleaming, he returned the hat to his head and scratched Ella's ears. "I'll talk to Beth about giving you a hand."

"The Norse nurse?"

"Doc Sera?" the man called again.

"I'll be right there, Travis." She arched meaningful brows. "You realize I need a license to practice medicine in Wyoming."

"I know what you need. I also know you're licensed to practice medicine in seventeen states, one of them being Wyoming. You're running out of arguments, Sera—unless you just don't want to help."

She kept her smile serene as she headed for the door. "It's no wonder you did so well in last night's brawl. Below the belt appears to be your specialty. Talk to Nurse Beth, think of somewhere nice to take me for dinner—your treat as per our poker game bet—and have fun at target practice."

"Sounds like goodbye to me."

"You think?" Then she opened the door to an overflowing waiting room and stopped thinking about anything.

Logan left with a twitch of his lips and, Sera imagined, a satisfied dusting of hands. Trap sprung. His charge was safe, and he was free to pursue other chiefly matters.

Beth arrived within thirty minutes. She wore a beaded

headband with a Native American drawing on the front, a feather and leather belt and a ruffled pink blouse.

"I don't like milk," she said and waited as a child might for Sera to respond.

Which she did with a twinkle while inspecting the bullet graze on Toby's right arm. "I don't like green vegetables. Way more problematic."

The young deputy drooped. "I don't like red meat. Try living here and saying that. You think I could go on patrol today, Doc? I mean, moving around's better than sitting behind a desk, right?"

"Depends. How many of your Bulley cousins are in jail now? Four?"

"Five. Logan caught Jake trying to sneak in the back door and jimmy the cell doors."

"People who have turnips for brains do that sort of thing," Beth remarked. "I'll dress that arm if you want to move on, Doctor. Toby's sweet on my granddaughter. He knows I'll only hurt him if he gets her pregnant."

What could she say to that? Sera wondered. With a final inspection, she stepped back. "All yours. I have a possible fractured femur in the next room."

"Any of the local boys get fresh, you tell them I'm here and I brought my enema bag with me."

Sera started out but paused on the threshold. "Toby, do you know if Logan talked to Dr. Prichard about any of this?"

"Prichard's gone fishing, but Logan'll handle him when he gets—ouch—back."

"Sorry." But the sweet-faced Beth didn't look it as she picked up a roll of gauze. "I'm sure that rumor I heard about you and Lily in the movie theater wasn't entirely true."

Grinning, Sera moved on.

One hour flowed into the next. Jenny-Lynn brought her a

sandwich and coffee and Ella a bowl of kibble at lunchtime. Then Babe, fresh off the round of flexibility exercises Sera had prescribed, hobbled in wearing a new pair of orthopedic shoes for which she wanted official approval. Ten minutes later, the mayor came by to tell her the gel she'd recommended worked just fine on insect bites.

It was after six o'clock when the last patient appeared. He had his left wrist cradled in his right, and he was pushing his tongue carefully against an incisor.

He watched her in uncertain silence until she walked past him. Then his face cleared. "I know you," he exclaimed. He gave her a sheepish grin. "Recognize your perfume anyway. But I guess it couldn't have been you I saw leaving the bar last night."

Beth poked her head inside. "I'm back with the supplies, Doc. I know we're closing, but I'll just see to the man who's been shuffling his feet on the sidewalk since I left. He's got a lump the size of a duck egg on his skull." She regarded Sera's patient. "Are you Babe's late husband's cousin Doug?"

The man looked baffled. "Uh, no, ma'am. I'm Roy—Parsons," he added, but he was talking to air as Beth disappeared into the waiting room.

"You get used to it." Sera examined his injured hand. "Is this from a fall or a punch?"

The man's neck went red. "Big guy took a swing at me. I took one back. Felt like I hit a stone wall."

"Sounds like you hit a Bulley." She regarded his swollen knuckles. "Can you move your fingers?"

"Hurts some, but yeah."

With her head bent, she glanced at his face. "You said you saw me leaving the bar last night. Did you see the person with me?"

The red deepened. "Man's about all I can say."

"Can you describe him?"

He shrugged. "Taller than me, maybe six two or so. Thin. Might've had some hair on his face. Mostly I noticed you."

She smiled. "Pretty sure I wasn't walking."

"He had you slung over his shoulder, you know, like firemen do."

"You saw that in the dark?"

He shrugged. "I do a lot of night work up at the construction site, so I'm used to dark. Soon as the lights went out, I closed my eyes and got them adjusted. Opened them and saw you."

"Did you notice anything about the man other than his height?"

Roy Parsons started to shake his head but frowned and wrinkled his nose. "Might've been him who smelled funny. I got a nose for smells. Now, your perfume, that's pretty, but I'm not so fond of mothballs. My old dad, he used to pack everything short of food in them." He wiggled his fingers for her. "I hope you weren't hurt bad, Doc. Some in there were getting mighty loose with their fists."

Beth's head reappeared around the door. "Sorry to interrupt, Dr. Sera, but Fred's here. He's got some kind of musical gizmo for you."

"Five minutes, Beth." Crossing to the medicine cupboard, Sera located a fresh tube of ointment.

She stopped the cap mid-twist as a sudden memory spiked. "Mildew," she murmured.

Her mind flew back. She'd been on the phone. He'd burst in and snatched it away. He'd pushed her. Maybe he'd struck her. She'd gone down. But before things went dark, she'd caught the combined smell of mothballs and mildew. On his coat, she thought now, possibly on that lightweight khaki sleeve as his arm had snaked around her.

The watch was clear enough, worn high on his tanned right wrist. And, yes, it was his sleeve that had smelled of mildew. Like damp, dirty laundry, she reflected now.

"Excuse me, Doc, are you all right?"

Sera blinked and the memory shattered. "Yes—thank you." But her eyes strayed to the door. Logan had said the biker's saddlebags were filled with dirty laundry. He was tall, wiry, probably stronger than he looked. And he'd been at Tommy's bar last night.

The man called Roy slid from the table. "I can come back tomorrow if you're tired."

"What? No, I'm fine." She motioned him back up. "I just got sidetracked for a moment. Can you do me a favor when we're finished here?"

"Don't have to be on site till eight. You got something needs fixing, I'm pretty good with my hands—well, hand."

Behind her, the door leading to the alley slammed open, and a tall man with murderous brown eyes strode in.

His lips peeled away from his teeth when he spied her. Reaching into the back of his pants, he produced a knife, flipped the blade up and whipped it to the underside of her chin.

"Thought you'd be alone by now, Doc, but I'm not figuring on this taking long." He shoved the tip in just deep enough to prick her skin. "No sirree," he snarled. "Not long at all."

Chapter Ten

Sera's heart skipped several beats. She heard Ella bark sharply in the waiting room. The man's small eyes bored into hers. The point of his knife scraped forward under her skin. She spied a movement in her peripheral vision but didn't shift her gaze.

"You're trouble, lady, in big, red letters. All my brothers are behind bars because of you."

"Which would make you the last free Bulley," she replied calmly. "If you want to keep it that way, I'd lose the knife fast."

"Why?" He sneered. "You gonna stick me with one of your needles, send me to my grave like Doc Prichard did to old Billy's dad?"

Then suspicion crept in. His eyes turned to slits and his mouth snapped shut. Swearing, he started to spin.

Logan blindsided him, catching him by the neck and arm. He might have been the biggest Bulley yet, but he yelped like a girl when his face plowed into the examining table.

"You know I busted a bone in that shoulder last spring, Logan."

"Best cure for a broken bone is a good long rest." With his forearm pressed to the Bulley's neck, Logan regarded Sera. "Did he hurt you?"

Before she could shake her head, Fred and Ella charged through the main door. "You put that knife away, Lester Bulley, or I'll—ah…" Fred spied Logan, and his doubled-up fists relaxed. "Well, that's better."

With the danger passed and Ella growling softly beside her, Sera raised amused brows. "Is this the last of the Bulleys then?"

Logan hauled his captive upright. "There's a couple dozen cousins, aunts and uncles around, but no one who'll want to avenge their so-called honor."

She looked past Fred into the waiting area. Beth was ushering a bandy-legged worker out the door, but otherwise the room was empty.

"I hope he remembers to change the bandage," she remarked.

"If you mean the guy who hightailed it out of here when this one," Fred gave Lester Bulley's ankle a none-too-gentle kick, "broke in, he looked to be wrapped up just fine. Told me there was an apeish Paul Bunyan holding the pretty doc at knifepoint, and if I didn't want her carried off like last night, I should get inside quick."

"Last night." Logan cuffed the seething Bulley and motioned to Fred. "Are we talking potential witness here, Doc?"

"Maybe. The patient's name is Roy Parsons. He saw a tall, thin man carry me out of the bar."

"I'll have Annabelle bring him in. Maybe we can come up with a composite for your assailant's current persona."

"Or maybe, like Clark Kent, he'll duck into a phone booth, whip off his glasses and woo-hoo, unrecognizable."

Logan grinned. "I think our guy probably has a better disguise going than Superman, but any description'll help."

Fred strong-armed the uncooperative prisoner toward

the waiting room. "I know you're talking about whoever's after Doc Sera, Logan, but just so you know, I heard some rumbles this afternoon about that biker you ticketed. Don't know where he got it or how, but word is he was out near the Bulley farm today, shooting beer cans off fence posts with a big old semi-automatic gun."

THE RUMOR COULD BE checked. Right then, Logan wanted to talk to Sera's patient. He locked Lester Bulley in with his grumbling brothers, sent Sera and Ella home with Fred and Annabelle out to search for the witness. He recalled her five minutes later when Roy Parsons presented himself at the desk.

"Figured you'd want to see me," he explained, flushing. "Not sure I can help, but I'd be happy to try."

Logan poured him a mug of coffee and phoned Jenny-Lynn at the bar.

"Jen does our composites." He set a hip on one of the desks. "Describe the man you saw, and she'll do a sketch."

It took more than ninety minutes, but when Jenny turned the sketchpad around for the last time, Parson's eyes lit up. "That's him. That's the guy, or mighty close."

Logan thanked him and nodded at Jenny, who gave Roy a tap on the thigh. "Come with me, hon. I'll get you fixed up with dinner and a couple free drinks."

"Dinner anyway. I'm working tonight." The man nodded as he stood. "I hope you find the fellow who hurt the doc. Not right he should go around hitting women."

"Hitting on, yes, hitting, no." Jenny-Lynn left with a wink for Logan and a follow-me swish of her hips for Parsons.

Logan glanced at the clock, made two quick phone calls and turned the station over to his night deputies.

He wanted to head home. Wanted it far more than he should. Dinner out sounded damn good, and he owed Sera a nice one. But he'd been doing battle with his hormones all day, and he suspected it wouldn't take more than a crook of her finger to send his tightly leashed control into a horny tailspin. Better to bolster himself with an extra hour of separation by keeping his mind tuned in to cold, hard fact.

One of those facts involved a phrase no law enforcement officer wanted to hear—copycat killer...

Parsons's description of the current suspect worked in terms of Hugh Paxton's physique, but something about the murderer's MO felt off to him. On the other hand, this was someone chasing down a witness, not looking to fulfill a sick wish.

As he braked at the construction site, Logan spied a scruffy-looking worker on the edge of the gravel lot. The guy was tall, rangy and wearing a three-day growth of beard. Not a ringer for the man in the sketch, but given Paxton's chameleon-like qualities and allowing for witness error, worth a chat.

"You new here?" he asked as the man approached.

Pale eyes flicked to the badge on Logan's waistband. "Thinking 'bout hiring on," he drawled. "Got tools, got a strong back. Figured I'd have a look-see before I talked to the man."

"Where're you from?"

"Speck of a town near Louisville. Don't have a record if that's your real question."

Logan glanced away and kept his tone pleasant. "Record's for Abe to determine. I'm just welcoming a stranger to town."

The man snorted. "Right. You got a smoke?"

"Nope. You got a name?"

"Cody." When Logan merely stared, the man hitched

a shoulder. "Jenkins. Hitchhiked here. Got a ride a couple days ago with a guy who was looking to sign on for a few months. Said he was looking to steer clear of his old lady awhile longer."

"So did he sign on?"

"Now how the hell would I know that? Told me his name was Truman if that matters."

"What did he look like?"

"Well, gee, officer, I didn't take notice of his pretty face—seeing as he didn't have tits and his truck smelled like chicken manure. Look, can I go? No law in this state about checking out a prospective employer, is there?"

Logan's lips twitched. "Abe's a good guy. As employers go, a person could do worse."

The man continued walking but with several mistrustful backward glances.

Tucking away what he'd learned, Logan climbed the metal steps to the trailer that served as Abe's project office.

Although it was after 8:00 p.m., the big man was still at his desk. The air smelled of stale cigarettes, coffee and sweat. A slab of raw meat covered his left eye, his shirt was open to the waist and papers were strewn from desk to doorway.

Logan chuckled at his dramatic sprawl. "Bad day?"

"Lost my best welder to a busted finger. Lost my stupid-ass bricklayer to a falling beam. First thing's your fault, second's my assistant's. Got myself a shiner and a gouged shin—also your fault. What is it you want, and do you know anyone who can handle a torch welder?"

"I'll ask around."

Abe squinted at the file Logan held as he spun a chair back to front and straddled it. "If that's paper, don't even think about putting it on my desk." He shifted the meat, cleared his throat. "Is it something I should see?"

Logan tossed a photo onto the pile. "This is from the station's surveillance camera. Have you got a worker named Roy Parsons on your payroll, and is that him?"

Abe blew out a disgruntled breath and worked his way to a semi-upright position. "Yes, I've got a Roy Parsons and yes, that's him. As electricians go, he's decent. Been with me for more'n two months," he added, anticipating Logan's question. "What's that other thing you're holding?"

"Possible serial killer."

Abe's thick fingers recoiled. "Well, hell, I haven't got any of those on my payroll. Pretty sure not, anyway."

"This one might smell like mothballs."

"Unpleasant."

"And mildew."

"Well, now you're talking gross—though I wouldn't turn down a good welder for a little stink." Turning the meat over, he blew out a breath. "You want me to keep my eyes and nose open and my mouth shut, am I right?"

"Thought crossed my mind."

"I'm surprised there'd be room for thought with the pin-up you got sleeping under your roof." His expression grew sly. "Though maybe not so much sleeping as cold showering, huh?"

"That's real helpful, Abe. Thanks."

"You're a man, aren't you, still breathing?" He drummed the desktop. "What kind of serial killer we talking about here?"

"There's a kind?"

"There's killing, clean and fast, there's raping, mean and nasty and there's butchering, sick and vicious. What does this one do?"

"Clean and fast so far, but MO's change and the victim

count's into double digits. You see him, you hear anything, you call me and only me."

Abe pointed to an ancient machine. "Run me off a copy. I'll keep it in my safe. Dammit, though, Logan, a serial killer, here in Blue Ridge?"

"I'm going to nail this guy, Abe."

"Yeah, but to do that won't he have to try and kill again? And if you don't catch him in the act…" His splayed fingers finished the grisly sentence.

In the corner, the copier made a grinding noise, but it did the job and spit out a replica of Jenny-Lynn's drawing. "The guy's here." Logan handed him the sketch. "And he's out for blood. It's my job to make sure he doesn't get it."

Abe squinted at the composite, then gave his head a dubious shake. "Makes me glad I'm only looking for a welder."

"Now, I NEED to head straight back out." Fred braked his truck at the back of the house. "Flo'll do dinner when you're ready, and I told you what Logan said."

"Yes, he wants a rain check for the poker game wager his sleight of hand dealing allowed me to win."

"Wouldn't be a gentleman if he'd let you lose even one piece of clothing in a game of strip poker."

Sera smiled and hopped out. "Good night, Fred. Thanks for the iPod. And tell your boss I'm tired, so he can come home any time."

"He's not avoiding you, Doc."

"No, he's just keeping his distance very, very well."

Which was as good for her as it was for him, Sera reminded herself. From the porch, she watched Fred drive into the gathering dusk, then, stretching her cramped shoulder muscles, turned and went inside.

Flo was nowhere to be seen, but raised voices drifting

down the third floor stairwell told Sera she was arguing with her daughter.

A warm bath scented with jasmine bubbles soaked away the day's tension. It didn't banish Logan from her mind, but she doubted anything short of a knockout punch would do that.

Relaxed in the claw-foot tub, she wished for a glass of wine and, if not Logan, then at least an inspired vision. Sleeves and watches were breakthroughs, but until they came with a face, Andi's and Sig's murderer was going to remain free.

Unless he killed again. But even given her limited knowledge of the case, Sera didn't see that happening. He wanted her, and everything she'd seen and heard so far indicated a single-minded man with a very specific purpose.

Resting her head on the curved edge, she let her mind float. Not surprisingly, it went straight to Logan. Strong, silent type, small-town born, drawn to the city and now returned to his rural roots. What had brought him back? Major injury? Doubtful. Sick of the system? Maybe. Lost a partner? Possibly.

He'd lost his uncle in any case. His uncle and his friend. What else might he lose before this was over?

"Okay, not going there," she told herself and, shaking off the haze, plugged into the iPod Fred had loaned her. Bob Marley's "One Love" was on the playlist, but her only memory now had to do with Logan and how hot he'd looked in his cop clothes.

She listened on as she traded water and bubbles for a pair of faded jeans and a black tank.

Ella was snoring on the bedroom floor. When Sera clapped her hands, the dog's head sprang up, and she gave two excited barks.

"Wanna run?" She grinned when Ella's tail began to

wag. "Thought so. Come on, then. You deserve some free-dom after being cooped up in a waiting room all day."

The retriever raced into the darkness the moment Sera opened the screen door downstairs.

She smelled spaghetti sauce and wondered if she was supposed to eat or wait for Flo. She was dipping a spoon in the spicy sauce when the housekeeper marched into the kitchen, thin-lipped and obviously displeased.

Because there was no point pretending, Sera asked, "How's Autumn?"

Flo set a large pot of water on the stove. "She left thirty minutes ago—took off in my old clunker while my back was turned. Must've hot-wired it. I hate to think where she picked that up. Girl needs an intervention, you ask me."

"Would she be receptive to it?"

"Does she need to be?"

"Makes it easier but, no, she doesn't. I've only been involved in a few. One went well then fell apart, second was a disaster from the start, and the third started badly but turned."

Flo dropped a double handful of noodles into the pot. "Define the word 'disaster.'"

"The man died two months after he was removed from his residence."

"Drugs or alcohol?"

"Old age mostly. Dementia, coupled with a troubled life. Was Autumn a troubled child?"

"She was thirteen when she slept with her first Bulley. Fourteen when she used her first needle." There was a long pause while Flo tracked and swatted a fly. "Speaking of intervention and dementia, Edgar Bulley's sister hasn't been right for some time. Sits in her attic room at the farmhouse, rocks and knits and sings old Patsy Cline songs. Once when I went up to visit her, I started to take her needles away so she could eat, and she stabbed my leg. A few seconds later, she went back to knitting and singing like nothing had happened."

"And Dr. Prichard said…?"

"She needed a vitamin shot."

Sera would have laughed if the woman's condition hadn't sounded so serious. "Edgar Bulley would be the relative to approach. If he agrees, the process could be initiated."

"A complicated process?"

"Can be. It depends on the individual involved and how dangerous the afflicted person is. Resistance and borderline competency can make things—well, sticky."

A deep rumble sounded in the distance.

"Storm coming," Flo predicted. Her mouth compressed to a line. "My clunker doesn't run in the rain. Do the girl good to spend a night stranded on the side of the road. She knows not to bring her drugs here, but she does it anyway. How many times can we expect Logan to look the other way?" She plated the noodles with a vengeance and ladled chunky marinara sauce on top. "Eat," she ordered in a no-nonsense tone. "You've had a long day, and you're too thin. Your mother should've pushed you harder."

"Oh, she pushed plenty hard, Flo."

"You don't like her?"

"Not particularly. By the Freudian yardstick, I love her because she's my mother, but like her? Not by any measure." Sera's eyes rose as the lights flickered. "That's not promising."

"There's a generator."

The housekeeper surprised her by bringing her own full plate to the table. Then she realized why and acceptance came out in a sigh. "Logan told you to watch me, didn't he?"

"Suggested it." Flo passed a plate of warm breadsticks.

"I had no argument. He's a fine man, our chief. Got some history of his own."

"Do you know why he left L.A.?"

"Not the specifics, but he had that look cops get when their defenses are running down. Pain starts to sneak in. Sometimes other feelings break loose."

Sera stopped twirling as thunder rattled the walls of the old house. "That's close. Has there been anyone special since he came to Blue Ridge?"

"Nope."

She smiled a little at the housekeeper's tone. "I'm not trying to pry, Flo."

"Yes you are. Wouldn't be a woman if not. Logan came here looking for something. Came looking to put something else behind him. I figure he's about halfway done with both things. Could be the right woman'll speed matters along, but being right means being open. Life's full of peaks and valleys. You've gotta roll to get through them in one piece. Me, I rock better than I roll, but Fred taught me how to combine the two. Seems like now it's your turn to do the same. Your choice anyway."

How had this shifted from Logan to her? Scraping her chair back, Sera went to the stove for more sauce. "I've made a lot of choices already in my life. Being in Blue Ridge wasn't one of them."

"Got a stalker after you, I hear."

"You hear very well."

"Logan'll catch him."

"Promise?"

She was dipping the ladle into the pot when the overhead lights snapped off. No flicker of warning, just off.

Sera tried to ignore the finger of fear that slid along her spine. "Please tell me the generator's not in the cellar."

"Nope." Flo's voice came from across the room. "In the barn."

"Well, I feel better."

"A little dark won't hurt me."

"Us," Sera corrected.

"If you want. Flashlight's in the mudroom."

"It would be." The blackness was so complete, she had to feel her way along the kitchen wall.

"Emergency gear's on the right, second shelf."

"Like I can see the shelves to count them," Sera muttered. But she located the door and remembered to step down.

She groped through a variety of jars and bottles before she reached the metal-cased light. "Found it," she called in.

"Got another one here," Flo returned. Then she made a sound of disgust. "Oh, now who left the door open? Fred are you home? I swear, if your shoes are muddy..."

Sera was testing her beam when the housekeeper broke off. Fear tickled her throat. "Flo?"

There was no answer.

She tried again, louder and with tension beginning to thrum. "Flo, are you all right?"

A bolt of lightning shot through the sky beyond the barn. On its heels, thunder rocked the foundation of the farmhouse.

Unless it had been Fred at the door and he'd swept his wife into a passionate embrace—unlikely from what Sera had seen—something was wrong.

Acting quickly, she scanned the shelves. On the highest one she found a box of bullets and an old .32 caliber gun.

There was a phone on a stand behind the door. Controlling her fear, she punched Logan's cell number. Then she wedged the handset between her shoulder and ear and shoved bullets into the empty chamber.

"Yeah, this is Logan."

"Where are you?" she demanded without preface.

"A mile south of the Bulley farm. What's wrong?"

"I'm not sure. The power went out. Flo and I split up to look for flashlights. She said something about someone coming in—through the side door, I think—then suddenly, she stopped talking."

"Is Ella there?"

Braced for his reaction, Sera shoved the last bullet in place. "I let her out for a run. I don't know where she is." She heard Logan's low curse and almost smiled.

"Where are you now?"

"Mudroom. I've got a gun. I'm going to look for Flo."

"Sera, don't…"

"There's no don't, Logan. For all I know, she fell and hit her head."

"You've met her, right? Stay where you are. Don't go looking for Flo or the generator."

More lightning forked through the sky. Sera glanced up. Then slowly down as something caught her eye.

Her heart, already hammering, sank into her stomach. "Oh, hell," she breathed.

"What?"

"I'm looking at the barn, Logan, in the alcove above the door. There's a light on."

Chapter Eleven

The power hadn't failed. Someone had cut the line to the house. Or worse, switched off the breakers from the inside.

Panic would have blocked all thought if Sera hadn't mastered the art of breathing through it as a child. Block nerves and focus on what was good.

Her eyes were adjusting. And she knew how to shoot. All she had to do was keep her back to a wall so whoever had cut the power couldn't ambush her.

Fear slowly gave way to determination. This madman would not take another innocent life. If Flo was alive, she was going to stay that way. They'd get out of here together or not at all.

With her gun pointed at the floor, Sera stepped up into the house. The thunder outside sounded like cannonfire. The darkness in the kitchen was thick and menacing, the air still and eerily silent.

She worked her way across the large room toward the pantry. "Flo?" she whispered.

Nothing stirred. Flo didn't answer.

Hugging the wall, Sera shone her light into the pantry. No Flo. But she spied clumps of dirt, the kind that came in on the soles of shoes, so someone had been here. Undoubtedly still was.

She breathed in and turned the beam back to the kitchen.

The swinging door presented a huge mental barrier. Releasing her breath, she gripped the gun and pushed through to the hallway. "Flo?"

A barely audible scrape halted her. On its heels, she caught a low creak, not directly ahead but somewhere on the ground floor.

Angry drops of rain spit fretfully against the windows. The thunder and lightning were almost simultaneous now. In the flashes, she saw Andi's lifeless face, then Sig's and finally, the hazy outline of a man. Real or imagined? In her mind, she saw his gloved hands reaching for her…

"Doc Sera?"

The image dissolved as a smaller pair of hands clutched her arm. A head toppled against her shoulder, and the body beneath it sagged.

"Flo!" Sera caught the woman before her knees buckled. "What happened? Did someone hit you?"

"From behind." The housekeeper's fingers dug in deep. "Room went black. When I came to, I was alone, but I don't think he's gone."

"So we'll go instead. Where's the closest door?"

"Front, but I heard a creak that way."

Sera kept her on her feet. "Second closest?"

"Back through the kitchen—unless we go into the cellar. Not sure I can make it down the stairs."

Making it down was a moot point as far as Sera was concerned. No way was she trapping herself in a dark, dank basement with a serial killer behind her.

"Let's go with the kitchen." Wrapping an arm around Flo's waist, she hoisted and gently pushed. "Logan's on his…" This time it wasn't a creak so much as a footstep that reached them. "…way. Did that come from the living room?"

"Might have. My ears are ringing."

Sera bumped against the banister. Up wasn't smart, but what choice did they have?

"Dr. Hudson?" A man's voice whispered her name. "Are you hiding in the dark, hoping I'll go away? Do you know me? Remember me? Remember any of it?"

Sera could barely hear him above the rain and thunder, but he felt close, as if he was breathing down her neck.

"I don't know where he is," she told Flo. "We have to go up."

The housekeeper nodded.

They went backward a step at a time. In the spread of darkness below, the killer chuckled.

"I have a bandanna ready for you, Dr. Sera. Hospital white. Sterile. Fools rush in, but some fools see nothing. They just close their eyes and jump."

"What's he saying?" Flo grunted.

"Shhh." Sera glanced upward. They'd climbed ten stairs. Four to go. Unless he rushed. Her heart gave a hard slam, but she kept moving. Two stairs left. And there it was, the upper landing.

"I'll find you, Doctor," he warned and chuckled again. "I'll simply turn the lights back on, and there you'll be. Beautiful as life and twice as deadly. The Hippocratic hypocrite."

Sera started along the hall. Where to? Flo was in no condition to shimmy down a trellis. She was trying to decide what to do when watery headlights swept across the wall beside her.

"Thank God." She breathed out. "Logan's here."

The housekeeper's head lolled sideways. "Going under,"

she mumbled. "Get to Logan's room. Best place. Big window. Should be able to climb down."

Sera didn't argue. Did she hear measured footsteps on the stairs? Maybe the killer hadn't spotted the headlights.

The door opened silently. The window faced the front of the house. If she could get to it, she could call down to Logan.

Depositing Flo in a chair, she ran. She was halfway across the floor when something surged up to her right. She felt a wet draft a split second before a body crashed into her side and sent her flying onto the bed.

Dodging a balled fist, she brought her knee up and used the gun she still carried to slam his ear. When he yelped, she kneed him again and rolled off the bed.

She landed on all fours on the plank floor. Righting herself quickly, she planted her forearms on the mattress and aimed at the doubled over silhouette darting for the door.

She went for his leg, heard the bullet embed itself in wood and fired again. A sharp zing told her the shot had ricocheted.

The door opened. Feet pounded. Then they stopped and thudded back again. The silhouette darted past the bed and vanished through the open window.

Sera let her head fall onto her outstretched arms. "Flo?"

"Still here." She sounded weak but aware. "Logan must be downstairs. Guess you showed that scumbag a thing or two."

Sera forced her head partway up. "Scared him anyway." While her heart searched for a semi-steady beat, she rested her chin on her arm and let the obvious question creep in.

The killer had been on the first floor when she and Flo

had started up the stairs. So how, she wondered, had he gotten into Logan's bedroom ahead of them?

"FLO'S FINE. SHE'S asleep," Logan said to Fred in the kitchen.

The lights were back on and Sera and Flo were safe. No thanks to him, Logan reflected with a thrust of self-directed anger. The Blindfold Killer had escaped again. Barely, but he'd done it, roared off in a cloud of rain and dust and sporting, he hoped, a crippled groin.

"How'd he do it?" Fred wanted to know. "Sera said he was threatening them down here, then suddenly, he was up in your room."

Logan braced his hands on the counter. "I checked the trellis. There's a lot of damage, and the window was only open a crack when I left this morning. Sera swears it was wide open when the guy jumped through it."

"So he used the trellis to get upstairs ahead of them?"

"It's one possibility."

Fred rubbed a guilty palm over his head and paced circles around the table. "I should've gotten Annabelle to look into that break and enter down the road. Only take a minute, I thought. But then my engine overheated, and Ginny Bulley doesn't answer her phone after hours. What if they'd been killed, Logan? Whose fault would that have been?"

"Not yours." Pushing off, Logan went to the fridge, pulled out a beer and tossed it to his distraught deputy. "Sera fired, the guy took off and I'm the one who should be kicking himself because this is the second time I've missed him."

"You weren't supposed to be here. I was. Fault's mine."

Logan debated, then thought to hell with it and pulled

another beer. "We could do this dance all night, Fred, but the fact is, I'm the chief of police in Blue Ridge. Sera's safety is my responsibility. End of story."

"End of fairy tale, more like." Arms folded, Sera leaned against the frame. She held the swinging door open with her shoulder and regarded them through mildly exasperated green eyes. "My life and safety are my own responsibility, gentlemen—and especially Logan. While I appreciate the effort everyone's making—again, especially Logan—I'm not a five-year-old child who requires constant supervision. People with goals, good and or evil, generally find a way to fulfill them. If one of you had been here tonight, he might not have done what he did, but you know he'd have done something at some point and maybe then, instead of failing, he'd have succeeded, and this conversation would look good by comparison."

Logan let a faint smile escape as he handed her his beer. "Sounds like the twisted logic of a tired shrink to me."

"Tired's better than dead." Fred glanced upward. "Can I see Flo?"

"She's sleeping, but yes, you can. There's no sign of concussion. I'll check her through the night and tomorrow. It wasn't your fault, Fred," she added as he squeezed past her.

A gusty expulsion of breath was his only response before he clomped up the stairs.

"And then there were two." She said it with a twinkle that amazed Logan almost as much as it confounded him. Was there anything a shrink couldn't or wouldn't rationalize?

Taking the beer back, he walked away, tipped the bottle for a long swallow. "Any point in me repeating that you could have been killed tonight?"

"What, because I'm not under the bed quaking with fear, you think I don't know that?"

"I have no idea what you do or don't know, Sera. I know I was thirty-five when I left here this morning, and I'm at least ten years older now. Beyond that—" He drank again. "—not a clue."

"Then let me clue you in. Being scared pisses me off. Being pissed off makes me cranky. It's a chain reaction that winds itself around to simply getting through or past whatever's necessary in order to come out whole at the other end."

Giving the door a shove, she came toward him. Her footsteps might be measured, but her expression verged on dangerous.

Now why the hell, he wondered in mild annoyance, should that excite him?

The storm outside had circled. The atmosphere in the kitchen felt electric. He hadn't turned on many lights, mostly because he preferred a stark atmosphere. The resulting shadows heightened the tension in the room and made his already heated blood pump with more force than was probably healthy.

Facing her across the table, he gave his beer a slow swirl. "Do you know who you're dealing with, Sera?"

Her brows went up. "Are we talking about you or the Blindfold Killer?"

"I want this guy, and I'm going to get him. He wants you, and that's not going to happen. You'd think somewhere in that tangle, we'd find some common ground."

A glimmer he didn't need to see swam up into her green eyes. "Are you trying to defuse my really workable irritation-born-of-fear mood by suggesting that we might be able to work together?"

He half smiled. "Believe me, Doc, it goes against the grain, but not knowing every last detail of the current case puts me at a disadvantage. I've got what Sig had in his files, but I don't have what was in his head. And I sure as hell don't have a window into the Blindfold Killer's mind."

"So enter Mata Hari?" She started around the table, with a seductive walk that was sixty percent female and forty percent nitro.

He didn't reach out and haul her in as she approached, but it was a close thing. Setting the bottle aside, he let her stroke a finger over his cheek to the corner of his mouth.

"And still he resists. You're a man of spectacular control, Logan."

He held her eyes even as his own began to glitter. "You think?" And giving in, let the last threads of his restraint snap.

He crushed his mouth to hers in a kiss that wanted to punish as much as pleasure. Not her but him. Sensation swept in on a swell of emotions so strong he wondered how he'd ever managed to bury them.

He used his tongue to explore, his lips to taste, his hands to discover. When she pressed herself into him, he was already rock hard.

Her hands fisted in the ends of his hair and tugged. She nipped at his mouth, tempting him to take her right there, in the middle of the kitchen, in the middle of the night.

He ran his lips over her cheek to her ear and along the side of her neck. Somewhere in the jumble of need and greed and hunger, he expected to feel the raw edge of pain. Or guilt. Something that would sweep in and blacken the moment or at least sucker punch the hell out of it.

He felt her smile against his mouth and heard the sound she made in her throat. She hooked her arms around his neck. "Just a little rough there, Logan." But when he drew back, she gave his lip a quick bite. "I like it," she said. And dived back in.

Without the threads, Logan knew he was alone on the

slippery edge. It started or ended here. He could ease away or take the plunge. His edge. His choice.

Smiling, she drew back far enough to tease, then with a velvet purr, jumped up to wrap her legs around his hips.

Every scrap of sanity flew out the window.

The crash he heard on the edge of his mind might have been thunder or something shattering inside. He'd have put it down to the last thing if the swinging door hadn't suddenly banged off the kitchen wall and jolted them apart.

Fred barreled in, shirtless and gesturing wildly. "I think a tree just fell on the barn."

Shoving his brain back in gear, Logan joined his deputy at the window. And swore. "That wasn't a tree."

Fred squinted. "Roof looks to be intact all right."

"It wasn't a tree," Logan repeated and handed Sera his cell. "Find Zack Walter's number. He's the volunteer fire chief. Then get your medical bag."

Already scrolling, she attempted to peer past him. "What is it? What happened?"

"Lightning hit the side," Fred declared. "I see flames."

"It wasn't lightning. It was a car." Logan headed for the door. "Bag, Sera."

Fred blinked. "Someone's car hit the barn?"

"Not someone's car." Logan grabbed the fire extinguisher from the mudroom shelf. "Flo's."

Chapter Twelve

Amazingly, Autumn wasn't injured, not in the crash or in the fire that broke out when sparks ignited the fuel leaking from Flo's rusty tank. But her breath smelled of whiskey, her pupils were dilated and she muttered "Dumb hick" the whole time Sera was examining her.

It took an hour to extinguish the flames, but less than half that to assess the damage. Fred moaned, Logan talked to the fire chief and Flo slept on unaware.

Sera took Autumn upstairs, undressed and covered her, then checked her vitals again. Being drunk and high, she figured the woman would sleep like the dead until she surfaced.

To punish himself for his daughter's misdeeds, Fred stationed himself at Sera's bedroom door for the remainder of the night. He refused to let her out of his sight the next day, even when cars and trucks began pulling up at the front gate. Apparently no clinic in town meant the patients she hadn't seen yesterday would come to her.

She palpated ribs, examined arthritic joints and treated a variety of peculiar rashes. Beth drove out mid-morning to help. She wore a bright smile and cowboy boots and toted two large platters of brownies.

The thunderstorm moved on and the sun returned. The temperature soared to ninety-four degrees. By six o'clock,

Sera was ready to follow Autumn's lead, steal Fred's truck and head for Alaska.

Her fingers sticky with frosting, Beth finally closed and locked the door.

"Clinic's done," she declared. "You tell Logan I'll send my son out here tomorrow to see about repairing his barn."

Fred shook the offer away. "I'll do it. Logan's being too nice not charging Autumn with anything."

Beth poked a chocolate-tipped finger into his chest. "And just what do you know about carpentry, Deputy Fife?"

"Enough to patch a barn." Fred snatched up his fifth brownie. "Back me up here, Doc."

"Taking the Fifth." She released her hair from its ponytail and headed for the swinging door. "I'm going to find a rock and watch the sun set. I'll take Ella," she added, grinning. "And I'll stay where you can see me."

"Do that," Fred warned. "Because I know for a fact that two of the Bulley boys were cut loose last night, and time's up on a third one tonight."

She patted his arm before she left. "Stop beating yourself up, Deputy. Moon Flower will be her usual sanguine self tomorrow. Poof." She spread her fingers in a starburst. "Worry bubble popped."

Rolling a cramp from her shoulder, she left Beth to badger him out of his funk. After washing up and snagging a Diet Coke from the fridge, she wandered into the backyard. Ella trotted dutifully behind her. The moment Sera settled on a rock, the dog flopped down to bask in the waning rays of sunlight.

The Big Horns rose clear and craggy in the distance, and for the first time all day, a breeze fluttered across Sera's cheeks.

Normal, she thought and smiled at the concept that somehow always eluded her.

The B movie of her childhood began to play in her head. Sparkles everywhere. Puff up the hair, strut, smile, own the stage, work the room. Don't smudge the makeup, flash the spray tan. Watch out for strap lines.

She paused there, her gaze on a fluffy white cloud. A man's arm appeared, but there was no khaki sleeve and no chrome watch. There was only a mark, a tan line where a watch should have been.

The image came and went in a heartbeat. Was it important, she wondered, or was she grasping at memory straws that meant nothing in the grand scheme?

Reclining on her elbows, she tried to empty her mind. Logan snuck in, but she was used to that and worked around him.

She brought back the smells, mildew and mothballs, and the sound—Bob Marley on Andi's computer—the arm, the sleeve, the watch, the grimace...

With the soda bottle poised at her mouth, she zeroed in on the last thing and saw it again. Gloved hands reaching, teeth clenched and bared.

They weren't particularly white teeth, and the lower front ones were crooked.

"Okay..." She drew the word out. "That's a good sign." A second later, her instincts kicked in, and a smile flitted across her lips. "Oh, yeah, really good."

At her side, Ella rolled over, blissfully unconcerned.

Sera counted down from five. As a shadow fell over her, she gripped the knife she'd taken from the kitchen and brought it around Bulley style so the tip touched the underside of a man's chin.

"Well, hey there, Chief," she greeted. Then using the tip to draw him forward, she set her mouth on his.

SERA KNEW LOGAN was up to something when he suggested they eat at Frank's Diner. He wasn't paying her back for the dinner he owed her, and, although he might be disarming her from across the table, she wasn't foolish enough to read this as a romantic whim on his part. Still, if he wanted to bide his time, she could play along.

While Tim McGraw spun on the jukebox, she indicated a man at the bar. "I recognize him from the other night."

"That's Travis. He's Abe's foreman."

"The guy he's talking to, the one with the curly brown hair and leathery skin, looks familiar, too. Probably from the clinic. And there's good old Wayne, the biker with the dirty laundry. No chance he's the Blindfold Killer, huh?"

"He's not Hugh Paxton if that's what you mean."

Something in Logan's tone brought her gaze to his shadowed face. "Isn't one the same as the other?"

"Maybe."

"Oh good, now you're going all mysterious on me. Please say you're not thinking that someone's copying the killer's MO."

"If someone is, he's copying details that weren't released to the media."

"For example?"

"The particular way the bandanna's folded. The fact that the Blindfold Killer always makes sure his victim's eyes are open and they're found lying face up."

"Why do I sense puzzlement?"

"Unlike the previous eleven, three of the four recent victims, Sig and his partner not included, had their wrists bound with red tape."

"That's very interesting." She drew a circle inside a square on the table. "I assume the one not bound was Andi. Because I interrupted him?"

"Possibly."

"You're being mysterious again, Chief. Any chance of an explanation?"

"Yeah. When I have one that works." He looked at the door. "Do you recognize those men who just came in?"

She had to squint through a sea of brawny bodies. "No, should I?"

"They're two of the new workers Abe took on right after Sig was killed."

"And?"

"They have alibis. One by his wife, the other by a maid and a motel clerk in Buffalo. People lie, though. It never hurts to double-check. Third guy on Abe's list ditched the site before I could talk to him."

"Does that say 'bad guy' to a cop?"

"It says question mark. The description I got was of an average-looking, forty-something male, several inches above average height."

Propping her elbows on the table, Sera pressed on her temples. "I think my head hurts." But she slid her eyes to the man standing next to Travis. "Maybe he's the one who's supposed to come back for a tetanus shot."

"Don't count on him keeping the appointment if he is."

Logan's expression made her laugh. "That's so cool. You went green at the thought. Tells me where your Achilles heel is—should I ever need to find it."

"You won't."

As Tim segued to Steve Earle, Sera's amusement faded. "You didn't bring me here so we could guess our way to the Blindfold Killer's identity, Logan. I sense an ulterior motive, and whatever it is, I sense much more strongly that I'm not going to like it."

"You're a perceptive woman." Sitting back, he rested a forearm on the table. "Okay, here's the deal. I know a guy.

His name's Hollis. I met him in L.A., somewhere between Vice and Homicide. He was quirky, but he got results, and that's all the department cared about."

"What kind of results and how quirky?"

Trapping her fingers, he rubbed a thumb over her knuckles. "Hollis lives in a trailer near a town called Starlight."

"Sounds pretty."

"Depends on your definition."

"Okay, not so pretty. Why?"

"Am I telling you about him?"

"Oh, no, I'm way past that. You want me to meet him. What I want to know is why, and—going out on a limb here, Chief—how it is you think he can help me smash through the wall in my head. Please say he's not a psychic."

"First six letters are right. He's a psychiatrist."

She stared in genuine surprise. "But you hate them—us."

"Having a problem with something or someone doesn't equal hate. Hollis is a friend first and foremost. I was on my way to see him two years ago when I stopped in Blue Ridge."

An intriguing statement. However… "Logan, if I thought a psychiatrist could help me, I know half a hundred reputable ones in California. What I really need is a mind reader. Or maybe another whack on the head."

He took a drink of the beer a harried Nadine plopped down at his elbow. "Hollis is a shrink, but his strong suit is hypnotism."

"Whoa." In a knee-jerk reaction, Sera jumped back in her chair. "Forget it. I mean, I have nothing against hypnotherapy. It has its place, and I've seen several cases where it's worked."

"But?"

"My mind, my memory, my call." Five tense seconds

ticked by before she offered a grudging, "What kind of results does he get, percentage-wise, I mean?"

Grinning slightly, Logan captured her chin. "What you really want to know is why he lives in a trailer in the back of beyond."

"Well, duh, Chief, wouldn't you? I'm picturing Brother Love here."

"You think I'd ask you to turn your mind over to a man who sells potions out of a fifth wheel?"

Although her blood was heating up, she didn't pull free. "We called them POHs in college. Professors of Hypnotology. Shysters who staged sideshow seminars to hoodwink gullible audience members into purchasing their expensive DVD collections. No, I don't think you'd take me to someone like that, but come on, Logan, a trailer in the woods? That's not quirky—that's weird."

"He graduated top of his class from Harvard."

"Even more weird."

"Rumor has it he's worked with politicians and royals."

"So having achieved such lofty goals, it makes perfect sense he'd go all mountain man and withdraw from the world."

"You're scared of being hypnotized, aren't you?"

"No—yes. Maybe." She tried not to hiss. "It's that control thing I told you about. I don't like relinquishing it, even to a Harvard grad." But her resistance wavered as her curiosity deepened. "Is it far to Starlight?"

"Four-hour drive. We can be there by midnight."

She flicked a disbelieving finger. "Midnight—as in you want to do this tonight?"

He drew her closer until all she could see were his unfathomable eyes. "I want this to end, Sera. Now. Before your luck and mine run out. In one form or another, the

Blindfold Killer's here in Blue Ridge, and he's losing what little patience he might have had."

Fear rose like bile in Sera's throat, but she held his gaze and refused to let it win. "Something's happened," she said. "Tell me, Logan, before the freak-out I'm having in my head spreads to the rest of my body."

He stared a moment longer, then reached into his shirt pocket and removed a folded paper. "I found this taped to the house after the excitement died down last night."

She didn't want to see it, really didn't want to know. But she made herself take the paper and read the killer's chilling words.

> Those who cannot see
> never will again.
> When fools rush in,
> sometimes the angel they meet
> is armed.
> I am the Angel of Vengeance,
> Sera Hudson.
> And you are DEAD!!

Chapter Thirteen

Logan didn't speak, just ran a contemplative finger under his lower lip and glanced at her from time to time as they drove north.

He knew when to leave someone alone. Before he'd resigned from the force, his captain and several other well-meaning superiors had pushed, prodded and finally ordered him to talk. Instead, he'd retreated into full stony silence. Two weeks later he'd packed up his truck and started driving.

Although he still wasn't sure how he'd wound up in Blue Ridge, living here for two plus years had worked for him. Then Sig had called, and the fabric of his new life had begun to shred.

He didn't want to care about Sera or any woman. Regardless of where you started, caring invariably led you to despair. But that was only the first stop on the road. Final destination? Hotel California every time.

They'd been off the interstate for thirty minutes before she shot him a vexed look. "You know, Logan, it's possible I didn't have a clear view of the murderer's face. It was dark, it was raining, Andi and I were alone in the office. We had our desk lights and computers on but not much else."

His lips curved. "You remember scratches on a chrome watch, Sera. You could see well enough."

She plucked a pine needle from the leg of her capris. Designer label, he reminded himself. Like the snug white halter top she wore and the green jacket she carried.

"I feel like there's something else, something connected to that watch." She fanned her fingers across the windshield. "I know it's out there in the vast universe that's my memory. I'm just not sure if this particular thing's blocked or simply eluding me."

"Is this thing more recent than your friend's death?"

"Feels like it."

He sent her a considering look. "It's possible you've seen the Blindfold Killer in Blue Ridge, and what your conscious mind didn't recognize, your subconscious one did."

She grinned for the first time since getting in his truck. "My how you've changed, Dr. Jung. Much hotter this time around. Definitely more persuasive."

"Sera, Hollis isn't going to make you cluck like a chicken every time you hear a bell."

She narrowed her eyes at him.

He knew better than to chuckle. "This is a good idea. Why are you fighting so hard?"

"Well, hmm, let me think. Maybe because it's me?"

His lips quirked. "Yeah, I've heard doctors make crappy patients."

"Given a choice, Logan, which would you prefer, a tetanus shot or turning your mind over to a stranger?"

"Stranger hands down."

"Uh-huh."

"I hate needles."

"Fine, you get hypnotized, I'll take the shot."

He continued to check his amusement. "Are you always so difficult in circumstances like this?"

"I wouldn't know, I've never been in circumstances like

this. You could at least let me test out my whack-on-the-head idea first."

"You already have." He turned off the rutted road onto a strip of dirt hardly wider than a cow path. "Barroom brawl, Sera. You wound up in the backseat of a truck stolen from Edgar Bulley's farm. Remember?"

She sighed. "At least *you* let me pack an overnight bag." She drew a vague air sketch. "Tell me, do you know why one of the side windows in Edgar Bulley's truck has Lamont Cranston as The Shadow painted on it?"

Frowning, Logan glanced over. "There's no Lamont Cranston in Edgar's truck, Sera."

"No? Huh. Well, whoever it was it looked like my childhood recollection of Lamont." She let her hand drop. "My uncle Geoffrey has a collection of old Shadow tapes."

"Sera, there's nothing painted anywhere on Edgar's truck. The body itself is more than half rust."

"Look, I know I saw…" She trailed off, reconsidered. "Maybe not a drawing." Her eyes came up. "Maybe a tattoo. On the Blindfold Killer's—" her fingers danced from side to side "—left shoulder. His shirt was torn, or coming apart at the seam."

"Are we talking about the night he murdered your friend, or the night he carried you out of the bar?"

She ran both scenarios. "I'm going to speculate that the truck memory is transference. When I think Shadow, I see a khaki coat." Clearly frustrated, she huffed out a breath. "Maybe this hypnotism thing's not a bad idea after all. Just please don't let him take me into my childhood."

A dark brow went up. "Afraid of what you might find, Doc?"

"More afraid of what I might say."

"So you'd rather die than risk an unconnected revelation."

Before she could respond, a lopsided trailer came into view. Around them the trees and towering boulders gave way to a tiny mountain clearing. But her gaze wasn't fixed on the trailer. Instead, she watched an enormous bearded man walk slowly toward them. He had an ax in one hand and a burlap bag in the other.

"There's a sight you don't see every day," she managed. "Grizzly Adams on steroids."

"That's not Grizzly Adams." Logan shoved the door of his truck open. "And it's not Hollis either."

"I SWEAR, MICHAEL Logan, you were born suspicious." A man with a long gray beard and features much finer than those of the hulk outside smiled benignly as he handed Sera a cup of tea. "Drink up, Doctor." He winked. "It's my own special blend."

"Black tea and bats' wings?" she countered with a twinkle.

He chuckled. "Chamomile and rose hips actually. For tranquility and trust. Although," he glanced at Logan, "I think you brought your own trust with you. If it sets your mind at ease, I'll tell you that man outside was gathering mushrooms for soup. He insists they taste best if they're collected at night. Never mind about the ax. Moving on, Logan informs me you're having a problem accessing a certain pivotal memory. I hope it won't shake your confidence if I tell you I've had that same problem on a near-daily basis since becoming an octogenarian."

Sera regarded him in amazement. "You're eighty years old? I would never have guessed that."

"Which could be a compliment or not, as I recently celebrated my eighty-seventh birthday. Thank you again for the satellite phone, Logan." His blue eyes sparkled. "The boy worries."

"I've noticed."

"To business, then." He removed a watch from his shirt pocket, noted Sera's reaction and chuckled again. "Simply checking the time, Doctor. I'm something of a night owl. I do my best work in the wee hours. Used to drive the police and my colleagues crazy."

He had a very soothing voice. Coupled with the serenity of his manner and the comforting sight of the half million books he had crammed in his trailer, Sera imagined he would have little trouble taking a person under.

Pushing aside a strand of gray hair, he tapped the multifaceted crystal earring that dangled from his left lobe.

"Focus on the center, Sera. A crystal is a maze of planes and angles, but the mind is far more complex. What can't be accessed from one direction must be approached from another.

Sera knew she could resist, and for a moment she almost did. But if she never remembered that horrible night, Andi and Sig's killer would remain at large, free to murder again.

Taking a deep breath, she focused on the crystal.

As if drawn by a magnet, her mind moved toward the glittering center. She saw faces reflected in the facets—Logan's, Fred's, Jenny-Lynn's, a cluster of Bulleys'.

She heard the roar of a motorcycle, the same sound as last night. Dirty Laundry Wayne rode an old Kawasaki. He had an attitude and the word "nasty" stamped on every feature. But Logan said he wasn't Hugh Paxton, and she believed him. She might even…

No, stop. Not going there.

Switching directions, she let her mind tiptoe through a welter of memories, some nice, some not. When the mist surrounding them cleared, she was in her office.

It was dark, after hours. She'd had a difficult day. The

police wanted an evaluation done on one of their own. She'd have to squeeze that in. And an Oakland social worker named Jody Frost wanted to talk to her.

She had called thirty minutes after the office closed. She'd just returned from a funeral. She said it was urgent. Sera mentally penciled her in for late the following day.

"I'm going down to the deli," Andi called from reception. "I've been sorting through our inactive files. That old guy of yours with the freako son died last Christmas, right? His name was Gould, Harvey or Henry."

Sera scrolled through a current patient file. "It was Harvey," she called back. "He died two days after Thanksgiving."

"What about Ballard? And Tristan Teas?"

"Those were your patients, Andi."

"Yes, but your memory's better than mine. Really, you should be going through this stuff. Come on, Ballard and Teas, dead or alive?"

"Both gone. Ballard died nine months ago in state prison. Teas committed suicide in February."

"We're not having much patient luck, are we?" Andi's voice began to fade. "Sometimes our job sucks."

A door closed. Rain streamed down the office window. In the distance, the Golden Gate Bridge was slowly being consumed by fog. Meant the rain was moving on. Beneath her fingers, the computer keyboard went dark.

Suddenly, she had a patient chart in her hand. The outer door closed again. "I'm back," Andi called. "Now before you tell me off, I'm sorry about the wet, but I didn't come prepared today."

Already immersed in the chart, Sera only half heard her. She started for the door, still scanning. "Andi, this patient's..."

A desk lamp burned in front of her. Did she look straight

at it? Is that why she couldn't see the man behind it? She could see Andi clearly enough, lying face up on the floor while raindrops plopped onto the carpet from the hem of her red trench.

Sera felt her lungs constrict. Fear—no, terror—rushed in.

"You're safe," a soothing male voice intervened. "He can't hurt you this time. Tell me where you are, Sera."

"I'm in Reception. No, I got away. I'm in my office. I'm calling Security. Len answers. I tell him to come, to hurry. Andi's dead. I can still see her face, her eyes. I can hear rain dripping onto the carpet. But in my mind it's not rain, it's blood."

"What about Andi's murderer? Can you see him?"

"I see a coat—maybe a coat. It's khaki, very light. He's wearing a watch, high up on his right forearm. I see his hands and his teeth. He looks wild. He's wearing black latex gloves. I drop the phone and run."

"He can't hurt you, Sera, even if he catches you. You're safe no matter what he does."

"He's strong." Her breath hitched. "Really strong. That's rage mixed with adrenaline. He has a knife. He's going to use it. His coat smells like it's been stored in wet mothballs. This time I miss when I kick him.

"The coat's open, his shirt is torn. I see a tattoo. It's The Shadow. Good masquerading as evil, except with this man it's the other way around.

"He shoves me away, but I can't run. I can't even move, and there's a pain in my head. Really sharp, like he got me with his knife. I keep seeing Andi's face, and I can still hear the blood—no, the drops of rain—hitting the carpet. Nothing's left after that." Both her voice and her mind hazed. "I'll burn the coat, Andi, promise. I'll never wear red again..."

SURFACING WAS MUCH like waking up from a nightmare, except for some reason she felt oddly peaceful. She still hadn't put a face to the Blindfold Killer, and God knew, all she wanted to do when Hollis eased her back into the now was sleep, but for the first time since it happened, the night made sense. There was a logical sequence of events.

"I left a tiny imprint in your mind." Hollis pushed a steaming mug of hot cocoa into her hands. "Nothing that will harm you or likely last for more than a few days, but perhaps the means to expand upon those things of which you're now aware."

He could have said he'd planted an alien transmitter in her head, and she wouldn't have cared. When her eyes closed, Hollis, his crowded trailer and even Logan simply dissolved.

She didn't dream about Andi as she'd expected. It was Logan who followed her into sleep. Sexy, mysterious Logan. One of the few men she trusted with her life. The only man she trusted with her heart.

It should have startled her to realize that, but it didn't. It didn't even make her want to run. So she'd rationalize it instead. He'd risked his life more than once to save hers. What woman wouldn't fall just a little bit in love?

Except it wasn't a little bit, and he wasn't open to love. Which might be the only reason she wasn't panicking in her sleep.

Without warning she heard the Blindfold Killer growl. The sound came from below, above and all around her.

Bob Marley played in Andi's office, but it was the steady plop, plop, plop of rain on the carpet that commanded her attention. She hadn't noticed it before.

The killer lurched toward her. His teeth were clenched, but she thought his lips moved. Was he shouting at her?

She picked up snatches of words, something about a graveyard ghoul.

His mouth stopped moving, and he grabbed her. She fought. Although she hadn't before, this time, she freed an arm.

While Bob Marley sang and the raindrops plopped next to Andi's lifeless body, she plowed her fist into his shadowed face.

Chapter Fourteen

Logan avoided the worst of the punch, but she still managed to clip his jaw and a portion of his right cheekbone.

In the darkness behind him, Hollis chuckled. "There's nothing passive about that one, Logan. Having met her, I'm hoping, though likely in vain, that you've set aside what happened back in Los Angeles and are willing to move into a more positive phase of your life."

Logan waited until Sera rolled onto her stomach on Hollis's bed before sliding his friend a dry look. "So the fact that she just tried to deck me says nothing to you, huh?"

"It says she's a fighter, but I deduced that much when she let me take her under against her will."

"She wants her friend's murderer caught. It also pisses her off that people are dying simply because they stand between the killer and her."

"Your uncle for one." Hollis handed him a large mug. "Special blend. Coffee with a kick. I'm sorry about Sig, Logan. He was a good man."

"I know." His eyes slid back to Sera. "He gave her his Sedona rock."

"I see."

Logan wished he did. He made a final check—she was sleeping peacefully now—gave his shoulders a tired roll and drank some of Hollis's coffee.

The concoction burned all the way to his stomach. It would have made his eyes water if he hadn't been prepared.

"Stronger than usual." He sucked air in through his teeth. "Some reason you think I need it?"

The old man shrugged, smiled, and turned away. "Emotions, floodgates, gut instinct. I went over the short list you sent of the Blindfold Killer's recent victims. My sense is, it's a new set of murders, a new vendetta if you will. You've got a social worker, age fifty-six, a waitress, forty-one, a retired insurance broker, seventy-four and a psychiatrist, twenty-nine. No apparent connection among any of them, and yet under hypnosis, Sera mentioned that a social worker wanted to talk to her."

"Jody Frost." Logan made a long sweep of the clearing through the window. "She's Oakland based. The woman who died worked with troubled kids in San Francisco."

"There still might be a connection."

"It's possible the department didn't go deep enough there. Under hypnosis, Sera said she agreed to meet the Frost woman, but there was nothing on her appointment calendar."

Hollis drained his mug. "Because it wasn't a patient meeting, maybe she left it at a mental note. I did that all the time."

"Yeah, but you're off the wall. Sera isn't."

"I gather you've never heard of her uncle. Dr. Jeffrey Hudson spends five days a week immersed in medical research and development. He's made not strides but leaps in treatment options for more life-threatening conditions than you can name. He runs a clinic and workshops on the side, all pro bono. The man's a complete workaholic. He's also a genius—and you know what they say about genius versus insanity."

"Yeah, I know. Fine line between." Logan's gaze strayed to the bedroom. "She likes cities, Hollis. It's where she belongs and I don't. You'd call us diametrically opposed."

"Would I?" Although the old man's eyes twinkled, he let it go. "Back to your serial killer then. I believe the red tape's key. It could be entirely literal—reference to a system that bogged him down to the point where whatever tether he'd managed to use on his homicidal urges snapped. Or there could be a complex reason. It could also be that each victim added to the strain on that tether. Once unleashed, the monster within went hunting."

"That's comforting."

"Theories only, Logan. I'm sure you have a few of them yourself." He squinted at his novelty owl wall clock. "It's closing on 3:00 a.m., and I'm betting small town living is slowly but surely turning you into a morning man."

Logan glanced at Hollis's bedroom again. "Three o'clock's morning in most people's books. You want to work on our chess game, I'm up for it."

Chuckling, Hollis went in search of the board. "With that lovely lady in there taking up a good three-quarters of your mind, our seven-month-old game will be concluded by dawn. As the potential victor, I have only two small requests." His clear blue eyes met Logan's. "Find the bastard who wants her dead. And if you don't want to marry her, give me the all clear, and I certainly will."

"I LIKE HIM." In the passenger seat of Logan's truck, Sera twirled her hair around one finger. "He's kind, he's clever and he's a better cook than I'll ever be. I still don't like turning my mind over to another person, but at least I don't feel violated. He's a good hypnotist."

"And a crafty chess player." Logan glanced in the rearview mirror. "He wants to marry you."

"Relocate the trailer and I'll think about it." Amused, she surveyed the barely visible strip of road ahead. Rain and murky darkness obliterated everything that wasn't directly in front of them. "You shouldn't have let me sleep for fourteen hours, Logan. Taking into account a two-hour dinner, plus another two hours of hellish driving time, it must be after 9:00 p.m."

He turned the wipers on high as the rain streaming over the windshield came down harder. "We're almost at the highway. Two more hours, and it'll be Flo who's forcing food on you."

Releasing her hair, Sera concentrated on capturing a memory that had been teasing the edges of her brain since she'd woken up.

She spread her fingers out in front of her. "It's like there's a thin layer of smoke between my eyes and his face. All it would take is one good... Whoa." She grabbed the dash when the truck gave two rough, sideways lurches. "Was that a rut?"

"Felt like a trench." Logan shook his head for silence. "I need to hear."

Unless the clatter coming from the rear of the vehicle was normal, Sera suspected a very big problem.

Pulling over, Logan reached into the back for a flashlight. He drew the gun from his waistband and gave it to her along with a quick kiss. "Stay here."

"Logan..." She sighed as the door slammed. Thankfully, Hollis had insisted she borrow his rain gear. Shoving the door open, she hopped into a puddle.

Even with extra socks, Hollis's boots were far too big. The mud made sucking sounds around her ankles every time she lifted a foot. She wore a hat and an oversized raincoat, but she thought it might be less work simply to get wet. Hindered by rubber and canvas, it took her twice as long as it should have to find Logan.

He was playing his light through the undercarriage when she did. "Pretty sure I told you to stay inside, Sera."

"The last time I did that, I was attacked by a Bulley. I'd rather stick with you." She waited until he drew the light out. "And the verdict is?"

"Cracked axle. We'll have to walk to Moosekill."

The name of the town sounded more daunting than the prospect of slogging through the rain and mud to reach it. She tried to shift a foot and almost left her boot behind. "Is it far?"

"Three or four miles, half of them on the highway."

Bending, she yanked on the stuck boot. "Please tell me there's no danger. You can't believe the Blindfold Killer followed us to Hollis's place, or you wouldn't have taken me there."

Logan scanned the area. "Hollis was a munitions specialist in two wars, and he can still beat the crap out of me in a target shoot. You wouldn't know it by looking, but his trailer's alarmed to the max. He has three dogs you didn't see because he figured they might scare you, and a webcam link with the ax man we saw when we first got there. Even so, the answer to your question is no, I don't think we were followed. At least not all the way." Handing her his flashlight, he opened the driver's door. "Feel better?"

"Tons." Careful to steer clear of the big puddles, she peered through the trees. "What makes you think we were followed at all?"

"Probably the gallon of coffee I drank yesterday."

"Caffeine-induced paranoia's not an answer."

"Cop instinct then. Target leaves town, murderer leaves town. But I'm guessing he's not up for a difficult trek. A few miles on a worse than bad road, chances are he turned back."

"Oh good." She slid her arms through the pack he passed over. "All or partway back?"

"Sixty-four-thousand dollar question, Doc. Can you handle a rifle?"

"Not as well as a gun. Logan." She caught his sleeve as he slung the strap of a badass Winchester over one shoulder. "Are you sure Hollis is safe?"

"I'm sure."

"But us, not so much."

Curling his fingers around her nape, he gave her a kiss that rocked her right down to the toes of Hollis's boots. "I promise he won't hurt you."

Which made her feel better. Until she realized he hadn't made the same promise for himself.

IF THEY'D GONE IN, then they would come out. He said that every time the hatred and fury simmering inside threatened to boil over.

He sat in his stolen vehicle on the edge of the highway. He ate stale donuts, drank cold coffee and listened to country music to stay awake.

He'd get her this time. Her luck couldn't hold forever.

But neither could his. The cop was looking in more than one direction. He was asking more questions, questioning different people. Eventually he'd ask the wrong person and wham, end of charade.

No, he ordered himself, don't think like that. Don't panic. Outmaneuver them. Listen. Learn. Stay one step ahead. It was all about details—and being invisible.

In a controlled movement, he unfolded the white bandanna he always carried and removed the length of red tape hidden inside. When his breath began to heave, he wrapped the tape around his hands and gave it a vicious snap.

He'd blind her and bind her, kiss the nightmare she'd become goodbye and move on to his next victim. Hudson? Problem solved.

Four down, three to go.

SERA NOTICED THAT Logan walked half a pace behind her during the difficult hike to the highway. His pack had to weigh twice as much as hers, and the rifle was no lightweight either. But even with the barrel propped on one shoulder and his eyes in constant motion, he looked like a man out for a nighttime stroll in the woods.

She checked the exasperation that rose when he reached down one-handed to extricate her boot from a mud hole. "How is it that you weigh more than me, and yet I'm the one who keeps getting stuck?"

"You're stepping in the wrong places. Keep to the edge of the path."

"News flash, pal—there hasn't been a path since we veered off that collection of ruts and potholes that no one except the Mantracker would call a road." She breathed out her tension. "You think the Blindfold Killer's waiting for us on the highway, don't you?"

"I think there's a good chance."

"Are you sure your phone can't get a signal?"

"I'll try again when we clear the trees." He steered her around another hole with a gentle nudge on her spine. "You're not going to start complaining, are you?"

"That would be bitchy and pointless." She swatted at a low branch. "I hate bitchiness, and I prefer point-blank to pointless." A moment later, a wet branch slapped her in the face. Shoving it up, she went with her preference. "Why did you leave Los Angeles? You can tell me it's none of my business, but please don't lie and tell me you wanted a change of pace."

"I did."

"Logan."

"There's more to it, but pace factored in."

She glanced at his profile in silhouette. "Is that a polite way of telling me to butt out?"

"No, it's a pragmatic way of saying that here and now might not be the best place for this conversation."

"That response could be construed as avoidance, Chief." But her teasing undertone took the sting out of her words. "Hollis told me he won a long-term chess match against you last night. He also said he thinks you're taking the recent Blindfold Killer murders in a different direction than the San Francisco police. Is that true?"

"All I'm doing is broadening my scope where the murderer's concerned."

"Translated into English that means…"

"I'm leaning toward a copycat."

"Despite the unreleased consistencies in his MO. Why?"

He squinted at a gap in the trees. "Gut feeling, nothing concrete."

"Did I say something under hypnosis?"

"You said quite a lot. I'm still processing most of it." He nodded through the rain. "Highway's up there. I want you to stay back while I check it out. There should be a small filling station and diner just south of here."

She wondered if his mental ruler measured in yards or miles and how, once on the highway, he expected to differentiate between a regular motorist and one with murderous intent.

At least walking would be easier. Except for the ditch

they had to wade through and the fact that, in the open, the wind was whipping the rain around in circles.

Lowering the rifle to his side, Logan shrugged off his pack and stepped up onto the pavement. Sera couldn't see any vehicles, but some of the larger boulders looked like they could easily hide one.

She forced herself not to follow him up. If the murderer was waiting, he wouldn't hesitate to take Logan out. He'd probably take anyone at this point.

Something rocketed out of the bushes behind her. Swinging around, she snapped her gun up, and for an instant, stopped breathing.

She'd seen him. As the rabbit she'd startled had darted out of the underbrush, the killer's face had blinked on and off in her head.

He'd been lunging at her, his mouth moving, the fingers of his gloved left hand outstretched, a bloody knife clutched in his right. Had he been calling her a ghoul as he ran?

"Come on," she urged her resistant brain. "Let me see him again. Just for another half second. That's all I need."

"Sera."

She cut off most of the gasp as a hand came down on her shoulder. She couldn't stop her other reaction, which was to jerk free and spin. And thankfully recognize before she fired.

Logan regarded the gun lodged against his rib cage. "I know the wind's loud, but I did call your name three times before I actually touched you."

She dropped her head onto his chest. "I saw his face. Just for a moment, but there was no smoke or shadows this time. Then, blink, it went dark."

"Nothing stood out?"

She looked up. "Sorry. I wasn't expecting a breakthrough.

A rabbit caught me off guard. Suddenly he was there. Then he wasn't. Next time, I won't let it go." She waved the tip of her gun toward the road. "Anything?"

"Nothing and no one." His lips twitched. "That I could see."

She gave him a kiss. "I love a positive man. Shall we go?"

For an answer, he held out a hand.

The highway consisted of two thin lanes with pitted shoulders and no lights. Which meant Sera could see about two feet in front of her at any given time. Still, walking was a piece of cake by comparison, and Logan's presence, coupled with the promise of a twenty-four-hour filling station, lifted her spirits to the point where her nerves only went zing every few seconds.

"It must be hell to be part of a witness protection program," she remarked above the whip and whirl of the wind. "Anyone you know ever done that?"

"One or two."

"Do you know where they are?"

"Yeah." His eyes combed the darkness. "They're dead."

"Ah." New topic, she decided. "How long were you…?"

He didn't need to silence her. Sera did it herself as a pair of headlights careened into view around a sharp bend. Something about the movement of the vehicle set her nerves on alert. She swore she heard tires squeal above the rush of rain and wind.

"Get down."

Not waiting, Logan tossed her across the ditch into a patch of prickly bushes.

What sounded like a truck minus its muffler roared closer. For a moment, Sera thought the driver might simply be a joyriding teenager. Then the back end fishtailed, and the entire vehicle swung out. Skidding sideways on the wet pavement, it screeched to a halt in front of them.

For a moment, there was nothing except the growl of the truck's engine. Steaming headlights cut through the gloom.

In the bushes, Sera choked back a scream when a hand gripped her ankle.

"Get behind a tree," Logan told her.

She struggled to separate Hollis's raincoat from the thorns poking through it. "Can you see him?"

"Not yet. Tree, Sera."

Finally, the prickles released her. She located the nearest pine and crawled toward it, skirting the base until the trunk stood between her and the truck.

A second later, two bullets winged the outer edge and sent strips of bark flying.

She spied the vague outline of the driver, but of course Logan was gone. Lamont Cranston had nothing on the Blue Ridge police chief.

More shots grazed the bark. Sera counted to bolster herself, then brought her arms up and fired at the killer's outline. She knew by the sound that she struck metal.

To her left, Logan used his rifle. He blew out one of the headlights and possibly the right front tire.

A spray of bullets peppered the air. She heard feet sloshing through the ditch and up the other side. She thought she glimpsed two guns in the man's hands, but she couldn't be sure. Squeezing off three more shots, she prepared to run.

Logan snared her by the waist before she could move. "Other direction," he said and motioned northward.

"But we can't get help that way."

"Shhh."

Although she wanted to protest, Sera clamped her mouth shut and did as he said—as quietly as she could.

The wind whistled around them. Rain pellets stung her cheeks. She had no idea where the Blindfold Killer was. Ahead, behind, in the ditch tracking them.

"Stay low," Logan cautioned.

Like she could stand with his hand pressed to her neck.

The bushes thickened. "Stop." He said it so softly she almost didn't hear him. "Don't move."

Ten seconds ticked by. Twenty. "Where is he?" she whispered.

"Not sure. Hiding, rethinking." Logan's eyes skimmed the overgrown bramble. "He's not a hunter."

Sera supposed that was a point in their favor, but lucky shots happened, especially when the aggressor carried two high-powered weapons.

A branch cracked close by. Shoving her behind him, Logan shouldered his rifle and fired. A howl like an enraged bull erupted but was swiftly silenced.

"Was that him?"

"Yes. Go." He gave her a push. "Make your way back to the road."

"What are you going to do?"

"Keep him busy. Take the gun. Use it if you see him."

"But…"

"Do it, Sera. Get as close to the road as you can, but keep out of sight."

Arguing would be a waste of time and an unneeded distraction so she swallowed her objections and started off.

The black strip of highway seemed miles away. She eased down into the ditch and up the other side. Logan must have a plan. Unless he was just Marshal Dillon squaring off against a particularly nasty villain.

She was crawling through soggy vegetation when a fresh round of bullets blasted through the air over her head. She thought about firing back, but the sound of rifle shot kept her moving forward.

Far ahead on the road, she spotted a glimmer of light. And another. Her heart jumped into her throat. Someone was coming.

Bullets continued to whiz above her. She couldn't stand and wasn't sure she should. If the unsuspecting driver slowed, the Blindfold Killer might switch targets and another innocent person could die.

Logan got off three more shots. Breath held, Sera waited for the murderer's reply. But there were no more bullets, and, as if a curtain had lifted in her mind, she realized why.

Not only were there headlights on the approaching vehicle, but also the familiar red and blue flashers of a police car.

The cavalry had arrived.

Chapter Fifteen

"Sorry I didn't pursue him, Logan, but you said you were near Willie's Bog, so I stopped when I saw you. You're lucky you got a message through to the station from there. Nine times out of ten, all you get's dead air."

The Moosekill police chief handed Sera a towel to wipe the mud from her hands and face.

"I'm gonna guess that at this particular moment, neither of you cares about what-ifs or apologies. Still, I'll spread the word and send someone out to tow your truck." He indicated a blurry log structure nestled among a heavy stand of trees. "Moosekill Lodge, dead ahead. It'll be full up, but the owner usually leaves one room free for emergencies. I figure this qualifies."

A naturally chatty man, he didn't seem to require any responses. He pulled up outside the lodge, had a word with the manager and, while Logan talked to Fred on his cell, returned dangling a key for Sera who was in the process of shedding her sodden gear.

"You're good to go in the executive suite. Car dealer from Billings is booked for the day after tomorrow, but until then, the manager says enjoy."

Replacing Hollis's boots and socks with a pair of wedge-heeled sandals, Sera thanked him. She made a detour to the washroom, then handed her dripping outerwear to a woman in a leather vest and hat who promised to have it dried out by morning.

Ten minutes later, the manager ushered them into the third floor corner suite. He turned two lamps on low and told them to make full use of the facilities, which included a hot tub and a mini bar. Winking broadly at Logan, he tipped his hat and left.

Logan tossed his backpack, hat and wet coat aside while Sera checked out the simple but pleasing decor. "You thought there'd be animal heads on the walls, didn't you?" he asked.

"Maybe." A large fruit basket sat on the bar. "I like the watercolors better. How come I got valet service, and you didn't?"

"You probably look like you expect it, and I don't."

"There's that snob thing again." A package of dates caught her eye. "Is there a restaurant here?"

"Two, and room service."

She hit a button on the remote and searched until she found the Eagles. Giving her damp hair a shake, she bit into a date. She turned to offer the other half to Logan, then spied a streak of blood on his left arm and choked.

"What?" He frowned when she strode over to tug at the front of his shirt. "Not that I mind, but why are you undressing me?"

Changing tactics, she yanked his sleeve up and made a sound of exasperated disbelief. "You might have mentioned that you'd been shot."

He looked down, still frowning. "That? That's a graze. Shot involves an ambulance, a hospital and occasionally a blood transfusion."

"If you don't know it, Logan, infections are frighteningly easy to come by."

"Are you always this dramatic?"

"Are you always this pigheaded?"

He trapped her wrist before she could probe further. "Trust me. I've had worse."

"Oh, I'm sure of it." She batted his hand away. "Now you can be a good cop and let me look, or I can sedate you and force compliance. Your choice."

"You weren't upset when you punched me last night."

"I punched... Really?" She thought back. "I don't remember that."

"I think I took one for the Blindfold Killer."

Momentarily sidetracked, she touched a finger to the faint mark on his jaw. "That was me?"

"You have a mean right hook, Doc."

Reluctant humor bubbled up. "Bear that in mind when I tell you that you could use a few stitches. However, seeing as you saved my life, I'll let you off with antiseptic, gauze and a single shot of whiskey from the mini-bar."

"Sounds like a deal." Locking his eyes on hers, Logan fingered the narrow strap of her silk top. "Tell me, do you ever not dress to seduce?"

A tremor shimmered through her. "Are you trying to distract me?"

"Not particularly. I already avoided the needle."

"Uh-huh." She hooked a finger in the front of his shirt. "So having shied away from your deepest fear, you're thinking mission accomplished, is that it?"

"Not exactly." Either they were moving, or the walls were closing in. "What I'm thinking is that a bandage can probably wait."

"Because life is short and I'm wearing a sexy top?"

"That works as a starting point."

So did the lamplight that pooled like silver on the dark wood floor. Around them, the Eagles sang about dreamers and signs and taking things to their limit.

At that moment, Sera felt there were no limits or barriers anywhere. Desire spiked through reason and created a jumble of sensations in her body and mind.

Logan kept his eyes fastened on hers. "You should run, Doc. Or at least slap a hand to my chest and tell me to back off."

Setting both hands on his chest, she let them slide upward until her fingers tangled in his hair. "Why is that, exactly?"

"Because having sex will complicate the hell out of both our lives."

Laughter sparkled in her eyes. "Nothing about my life has ever been anything less than complicated, Logan." Letting temptation win, she gave his lip a tantalizing bite and at the same time rolled her body against him. "I've dreamed about doing that too many times to count."

"Only that?"

She bumped him hip to hip. "What do you think?"

"That some of the things I've imagined during more than one sleepless night might actually happen."

When his mouth covered hers, every part of her responded. It was like she'd been zapped with a thousand volts of silken electricity.

Careful not to touch his wounded arm, she ran her hands from his shoulders to his wrists and held. She wanted the bed under her and Logan on top. She wanted to feel him fully aroused with the barrier of their clothing still between them. Then piece by piece, she wanted those layers gone, until they were skin to skin, heat pouring into heat. Until they both sizzled and burned.

Using her hold on him against her, he hauled her forward, then drew back so his mouth was a mere inch from hers. "Last chance for that slap, Sera."

She heard the words, but only in a distant, foggy part

of her brain. The second his mouth came back onto hers, every thought, every scrap of reason simply vanished.

His tongue plunged in, hot and hungry. She met it with a greed that intrigued her.

Pressed against him, she felt his muscles tense. Her fingers slid up under his shirt to explore the sleek, smooth skin of his back.

She didn't want to stop kissing him. His tongue was sparking incredible sensations in her body. Pinpoints of light glittered behind her eyelids, but in the end, it all came down to taste and touch and wanting him inside her.

With an impatient sound, she brought her hands around to the button of his jeans. The stubble on his jaw scraped her cheek as he kissed her face and throat. She nipped the corners of his mouth, then gasped out a laugh when they landed on the mattress.

Raising her arms above her head, she let him dispose of her slithery top. Her lace bra followed. A shiver raced across her skin. Recognizing it for what it was—pure desire—she shifted her hips.

Her crop pants vanished. So did her lace thong. She pushed his jeans away, then, kneeling to face him, ran her palms over his torso and lower, until she reached the hot, hard length of him.

With a cryptic half smile and a smoldering look in his eyes, Logan cupped her face and took possession of her mouth again. When he drew away, she let her head fall back. And hissed in a breath of shock and pleasure as his tongue circled her breast.

Desire surged from nipple to thigh, each spike driving deeper than the one before. When he raised his head, she took the lead, capturing his mouth and pushing him onto the mattress.

A smile stole across her lips as she got her first full look at his naked body. Straddling him, she moved her hips in a slow, sensuous motion.

A moment later she was flat on her back with no idea how she'd gotten there.

He went up on one elbow just far enough to stare into her eyes. "I knew you were a damn witch the first time I saw you."

She took him in her hands again. "Flattery won't get you out of this, Chief."

His features shadowed, he lowered his mouth to hers. "So who wants out?"

Those were the last words Sera heard. When his fingers plunged inside her, her head arched on the pillow. She bucked against him. Her nails dug into his hips and the world crumbled to dust.

She felt herself racing upward, desperate to discover that place only Logan could take her.

A shudder of release rocked her from the inside out. Heat flared. She knew she said his name, wondered hazily if she screamed it, as he took her up and up and up.

Heat streaked through her veins. When she wrapped her legs around him, his muscles, already straining, went rigid. Eyes open, she brought him inside.

Together they rolled until she was on top and he was holding her, pumping himself into her.

Her body bowed back, absorbing each long, hard thrust. Color and sound collided. Sensation swept through her. For an instant, the world went absolutely still, then burst apart in a shower of sparks that had her crying out as she spiraled into the fiery center.

He might have said something. She couldn't hear over the throb of blood in her head. She knew he caught her before her muscles gave out and she toppled from the bed.

"Stay with me, Sera," he murmured.

Still inside her, he brought her lower, until her hair fell on either side of his face. He kissed her cheeks, then her mouth and finally, easing her down beside him, pressed his forehead to hers.

She skimmed wondering fingers across his shoulder. "If I can feel you, I must still be alive." Sliding her leg over his, she nuzzled the bruise on his jaw. "Pretty sure you are, too."

"Don't count on it." He closed his eyes and breathed out. "We're slow to die in my family."

She had just enough strength to laugh. "You've got a family?"

"Yeah. Of vipers."

Touching a finger to his lower lip, she pressed down, kissed the imprint. "That was amazing, Logan."

"No, that was great."

"Excuse me?"

His eyes gleamed in the wash of watery light. "Night's young, Sera. I'm betting we can take it from great to way past amazing by morning."

With her humor and some portion of her strength restored, she pushed him onto his back. "You're on, cowboy." She kissed him hard and deep, felt him stir inside her and grinned. "I hope you're up for a very long ride."

THERE WAS NO room service available at 2:00 a.m., so they ate dates and black olives in the hot tub. Afterward, dripping and ravenous, they made love again.

The wind died. The clouds broke apart. The rain turned to mist and for a heartbeat of time, the horror that was the Blindfold Killer disappeared.

Later, on the floor, with Logan's hat on her head and wearing the cop shirt from his pack, Sera poured them both a glass of California red.

Their room overlooked a small lake surrounded by woods. Now that the clouds had dispersed, stars sparkled on the water, bouncing back diamond points of light. An almost dizzying number of them, she thought and turned her eyes, shielded by the brim of Logan's hat, to the man who was and had been for some time, the main source of her curiosity.

"Is your arm okay?" She glanced at the makeshift bandage she'd fashioned after their second blistering round of sex.

He sat with his back against the sofa, facing both her and the window. "It never wasn't, Sera." A smile touched his lips. "But as a physician you won't believe that, so yeah, it's fine, and thanks for killing what little pain there was."

She set the wine bottle aside. "Why am I sensing a mood? You were amiable enough a few minutes ago."

"Conversation's not necessary when you're making love. Heart rate slows, sanity returns, and I know what's coming."

She chose to be nice and moved from a sexy curl to a cross-legged position on the carpet. "You don't have to tell me anything you don't want to, Logan. I don't like being pushed either. I only asked you about L.A. earlier because I was feeling cranky."

Balancing his glass on a single raised knee, he regarded the contents half-lidded. "I was born in northern Montana, in a town called Sorley, population six hundred and twelve. My parents were churchgoing Baptists. Every Sunday, my father asked for forgiveness for beating the crap out of my brothers and me. Seven brothers," he added with more of a smile than Sera would have expected. "Six were older, one was younger. My mother raised chickens, canned garden vegetables and prayed for all our souls.

"One by one, we got out. Four of us wound up on the

West Coast. One joined the Marines, one became a cop, two went into business for themselves."

Sera knew by his tone that "business" was merely a euphemism for… "Drugs?" she assumed, watching what little she could see of his face.

"Pretty much. Might have been some other illegals thrown in from time to time, but mostly they stuck to what they knew."

She touched his ankle. "You don't have to do this, Logan."

"Hollis thinks I do." He raised his glass, drank. "And you're curious."

"Not at the cost of… Okay, yes," she admitted, "I'm curious."

"So I'll give you the short version and satisfy both of us. Ethan was the real bad ass. He hated me for being a cop. I met a woman, Sherry, also a cop. We got involved, worked out a routine, worked ourselves into a rut. Things got rocky, but that's how it is for cops. Relationship deteriorated. Then, one night, she got shot."

"Oh, damn. Logan, you really don't…"

"Sherry didn't die, but the guy who shot her did. Dead man's name was Spider. Spider shot Sherry, Ethan shot Spider. I discovered that Ethan and Sherry were lovers and had been for months. She knew what he was, but being what she was, she turned a blind eye. Until—wrong place, wrong time. One of Ethan's cronies tried to take her out. Now my brother's in prison for murder, and Sherry, who was dismissed from the department, is doing the books for a small chain of movie theaters in Nebraska. I stayed in L.A. for a while, then decided to hell with it. Sympathy sucked. Clean break worked better. I headed north to see Hollis, got sidetracked, got a new life."

"Got a life you like," she corrected. "Maybe the life you should have had from the start."

"That would depend on your view of fate. Fred thinks it was meant to be. I say detours happen. Sometimes they're good, sometimes not. The trick is to keep things simple, don't get attached."

"So you can take Blue Ridge or leave it?"

"Leave it in the lurch, no. But knowing the job's been competently filled, yeah, I could walk."

"Uh-huh." When he arched a brow at her tone, she set her glass aside and got to her knees. "Still a shrink, Chief." She batted his bent leg until he straightened it, then, kneeling over his lap, played with the dusting of dark hair on his chest. "As a shrink, I'll say that psychoanalysis has its place, and this isn't it. So I'll go with my feminine intuition and speculate that if you hadn't liked where you ended up, you'd have taken off two plus years ago. I'll also add that you're not the only person in this room who's chosen the wrong lover. I almost got engaged to a man three years ago who insisted I was the woman of his dreams."

"Which made him wrong because?"

"Oh, his claim might have been true, except in his fantasy, he married the woman he loved, then had sex with— well, pretty much any other woman who caught his eye. Like I said, Logan—my life, very complicated."

When he shifted her to a more telling part of his lap, she grinned. "Does this mean we're good?"

His eyes began to gleam as he gripped her hips. "Good's never been the problem, Sera. In fact, right now, I'm not sure what the problem is."

"In that case, let me fill you in." Pushing his hat back, Sera lowered her mouth until it was only a whisper away from his. "From my perspective, it's a problem of time, distance and should we try for the bed? Or say damn the consequences, and make love right here on the floor?"

OUCH, OUCH, DAMMIT, ouch!

He had to twist the red tape tightly around his thigh where the bastard police chief's bullet had gone in. Thankfully, it had also come out. But he'd lost both blood and a golden opportunity because of it.

He'd had to change a flat tire in the rain, fight through the dizziness that had threatened to swamp him and in the end spend another night in his stolen truck.

He toughed it out on a side road between where he'd been and where he needed to be.

Sweat beaded on his forehead and upper lip. His thigh was on fire, and he was having monstrous dreams.

He heard his mother scratching at the door. She wanted to come back. Papa said okay, but this time she had to stay.

She did—for a month. Then she left again, and Papa's heart, already half broken, crumbled to pieces.

"It's you and me now, son. Just us, no one else…"

Time rolled on. Years became decades.

"No one else," Papa insisted. "Just you and me…"

"Just us," the killer agreed in his sleep.

That's how it had been—until it hadn't.

That's when he'd gotten mad.

Eleven dead, murdered by the Blindfold Killer. Suspect arrested. Released. But the cops kept tabs on him. For a while.

Released suspect vanished. Did the dumb cops find him? Not so far. Maybe not ever.

The rain drumming on the roof of his truck slowed and finally stopped. The fire in his thigh made his leg go numb.

Maybe he'd die because of the Blue Ridge police chief. Maybe he'd never reach his goal of seven dead. But he'd get Sera Hudson. One way or another, he'd take her out.

Papa would give him a hero's welcome.

Chapter Sixteen

"This isn't exactly how I envisioned our morning going, Logan." Sera waved at the cloud of mosquitoes that swarmed out of the weeds around her. "I figured at 7:00 a.m. we'd be eating, not be eaten for, breakfast. Won't the rain have washed away any blood the Blindfold Killer lost? Assuming you shot him and that howl we heard last night wasn't him breaking an ankle in this rat hole of a ditch."

Crouching, Logan separated a wet patch of crab grass and thistles. "Answer to that long-winded question is possibly, but it's still worth a look."

Because he was right, and Fred wouldn't arrive to pick them up for an hour in any case, she squelched past him in Hollis's boots, shielded her eyes and endeavored to recreate the scene.

Last night's rain was nothing but a memory at this point. The sky was blue, the road was dry and the temperature had already climbed past eighty degrees.

Pivoting, she located the tree she'd used for cover, then slapped at a persistent deer fly. "I think we were twenty or thirty yards to the right of this spot."

"You were." He shifted a heavy tangle of vines. "I was moving toward him."

Something glinted ahead of her. Bending, Sera sloshed over to check it out.

Through the tall blades of grass, she spotted a gray metal cylinder. "I found a bullet casing," she called to Logan.

"Gun or rifle?"

She raised her voice. "Rifle, I think."

He waded over bare-chested, oblivious to the teeming insect life. "It's one of mine." Then he took another step and reached out to shift a thistle.

"What?"

With his free hand, he pulled her down next to him. "Blood," he said. She saw the gleam in his eyes. "And I'm betting it isn't mine."

BETH RUSHED OUT of the clinic the moment Logan and Sera braked at the police station in Fred's four by four.

"People have been asking for you since you left town. I thought you'd be back yesterday so I've been taking appointments. We're booked solid today." She popped her head around Sera to beam at Logan. "Morning, Chief. Toby's got Edgar Bulley waiting in your office. Trouble with your truck?"

"It's a long story," Logan told her. He glanced at the clinic and saw a lot of movement inside. "Looks like you'll have your hands full today, Doc. I'll send Toby over to keep an eye on things."

The look she slanted him had guilt twisting in his belly, but he was used to that. Shutting it down, he left her to deal with Beth and a raft of expectant patients alone.

Although he hadn't told her everything about his life last night, he'd said enough. Too much by his standards and with too little urging.

"Chief, hi. Thank God you're back." Stressed to the point where his hair stuck up, Toby vaulted to his feet. "Old Edgar's in your office. He wants the rest of his grandsons released, says stuff's going on at the farm and there's only three there to keep watch. He might be telling the truth because some of the site workers who are camped in that field Abe leased from him say they've heard buckshot in the ravine. Plus we've had a bunch of small thefts and burglaries lately."

"I know. I'll talk to him." Logan took a last look at Sera, then turned his attention to his young deputy. "I have to drive down to Casper this morning. I want you to stay at the clinic until Fred gets back from Moosekill with my truck. Make sure the back and side doors are double locked and Beth goes into the examining room with every patient. Send Annabelle out to my place to get Ella, and tell Walter to take a drive around the resort site, see if he can locate Wayne Postle."

"The biker guy you ticketed? Is he still here?"

"Sera and I saw him on our way in. He was heading north."

"Got it." Toby kept a pencil poised above his notepad. "Anything else?"

Logan glanced at the florist's shop on the corner but shook his head. "No, that's it."

Hostile voices emerging from the cells had his deputy edging toward the door. "I hope you got lots of rest in Moosekill, Logan. Lester's on a tear, and you know what Victor and Lloyd get like."

"Yeah, I know. Don't worry, Toby, they'll be free by sundown."

"Uh, are you sure that's—well, I guess you know what you're doing."

With the Bulleys, yes. With any other part of his life, not at all. Except for one thing, he thought, moving his grazed arm. He had a bullet casing and two samples of blood for the lab in Casper. If Hugh Paxton was behind the recent killings, he'd know about it by tomorrow. If not—well, one way or another he'd get the person who was.

And decide when he had him whether the guy was going in alive.

OKAY, SO NOW he was going to avoid her. Sera thought she could have scripted this part.

Night falls, make love. Stars and wine come out, talk, make love again. Sun rises, reality hits, dive back into the investigation. Stay there, focus, until what's familiar reappears. Then, big sigh, duck out.

If she hadn't been so busy, she would have been annoyed. She might even have confronted him. But patient after patient filed into the clinic, so many of them that the waiting room was never anything short of SRO.

Toby brought Ella over within half an hour of her arrival. The young deputy settled into a folding chair while Ella made herself at home between examining rooms. Beth created new files, kept track of names and made appointments for return visits.

Benny, the first Bulley she'd met, limped in after lunch with several nasty lacerations above his right ankle.

"What?" He fixed her with a bloodshot glare. "Stepped in a rabbit trap is all. Nothing illegal about trapping varmints."

Sera examined the bruised and bloody wounds. "Must have been some big rabbit you were looking to trap, Benny. When did this happen?"

He had trouble climbing onto the table, which was no wonder—he smelled like a distillery. "Only been out of jail for two days," he muttered, then caught sight of an anatomical diagram and shuddered. "Guess it was the first night."

"So you were just wandering aimlessly in the dark."

"I grew up on that farm. I could wander around blind-folded and not get lost."

"Is that why you stepped in a trap? Because you were wearing a blindfold?"

He flung an arm out. "I stepped in the frigging trap 'cause someone moved it. My brother set 'em one place, and suddenly they were some place else."

"Some place far away?"

"Far enough. Are you gonna make it so my foot doesn't turn green and have to be sawed off or not?"

"Would you feel anything if I did saw it off?"

He jerked back so fast, he almost pitched off the table. "You're as crazy as Prichard."

"Not crazy, Benny, observant. Swing yourself around and put your leg up so I can do a more thorough examination."

"No saws, right?"

"Do you see any saws?" she asked patiently.

Clearly mistrustful, he did as she instructed. "I don't want no vitamin shot either," he warned.

"Tetanus, yes. Vitamin, no."

"Right." He scowled. "What's tetanus?"

"Lockjaw," she said cheerfully. "Extremely unpleasant, sometimes even fatal. Don't worry, though. You're young and healthy, and I'm a whiz with needles. If you're squeamish, we can keep talking, take your mind off what I'm doing."

Noticeably less belligerent, he gave a hesitant nod. "Yeah, we can talk... About what?"

Smiling, she tore the leg of his filthy pants and watched him go from pale to pasty. "Why don't you start by telling me where the trap you stepped in was supposed to be and who you think might have moved it?"

DAMN THE WOMAN, Logan thought in irritation. She haunted him all the way to Casper and back. She was still in his head at four o'clock when Fred returned from Montana with his truck.

"You'll be riding on a used right rear axle stripped from a Dodge that's been sitting in some geezer's barn for the last two years." The big man swiped a layer of sweat from his forehead. "It was either that or order a new one, and I didn't figure you'd want to wait three days." He wrinkled his nose and sniffed. "Thought old Edgar wanted his grandsons released."

Perched on one of the front office desks, Logan perused a clipboard. "When old Edgar becomes chief of police, he can put revolving doors on the cells. Until then, it's my call."

Victor Bulley rattled his cell door. "You're not playing fair, Logan. You put Lester in here after Lloyd and me, but you let him out before. He's the one pulled a knife on the doc, not us."

Without raising his head, Logan called back. "We found a wad of cash under the floorboard of your truck, not Lester's."

"Lester trusts banks, I don't."

"Yeah? Thing is, Victor, I don't trust you."

He heard voices and knew the two remaining Bulleys were arguing. With a glance at Fred, he grinned. "Something you want to tell me, Lloyd?"

"No," Victor bellowed.

"Yes," his brother snapped.

Another squabble erupted, prompting Fred to shake his head. "How old are they now?"

Logan watched a man with curly brown hair and a cloth pressed to his cheek go into the clinic. He also saw a lot of bunting and banners that hadn't been there when he and Sera had left for Montana.

Blue Ridge Days had arrived. The bleachers would go up tonight, the booths and signs tomorrow. Tourist numbers, already increased, would double by Thursday for the three-day celebration. Add in a carnival, food tents, detours all around Main Street, and you had one big headache waiting to happen.

Back in the cells, Victor finally exploded. "Oh for crap's sake, Logan, you win. Guy paid us to start something in Tommy Gray Wolf's bar the other night. Said we should go for the pretty doc because you'd be on us like a buzzard on a carcass."

Logan returned his attention to the clipboard. "Give me a name."

"Didn't get one."

"A description then."

"Don't have one." When Logan didn't respond, the big Bulley heaved out a breath. "Look, he kept to the shadows, okay? Stood there, said his piece, paid up, took off."

"And stunk like Aunt Linda's hope chest," Lloyd shouted. "You met Aunt Linda, Logan. She lives in our…"

"I know where she lives." Standing, he motioned Fred to the front window and headed for the cells. Resting a shoulder on the corner, he said, "Keep talking."

Lloyd made a jerky motion. "Nothing else to tell. Money's money. We took it and—well, I s'pose I got kinda curious at that. Asked him did he know the doc from somewhere."

Logan nudged his hat forward. "And he replied…?"

"Didn't at first. But when he started to go, I heard him say she was a detail he'd screwed up. Said he shoulda known better than to judge a book by its cover."

SERA WAS MAKING notes and Beth was on the phone when a man came in holding a wad of cotton to his cheek.

"Got sprayed with a bunch of sparks and cinders while I was wiring the resort kitchen." He grimaced. "Some of the cinders stuck."

"That's gotta sting." Sera set the chart aside. "Come on, I'll take a look."

"Wait, Doctor." Beth covered the mouthpiece. "Sue, our midwife's got a breech baby trying to be born, a big one. She wants you to come because there's a lot of blood, and it's a long ambulance ride to Casper."

Blanching, the man with the cinders waved her away. "Don't worry about me. See to the baby."

Reaching for her medical bag, Sera gave the contents a quick check. "Have I met you?" she asked him.

He managed a grin. "Not yet, but I saw you out at Frank's Diner a few nights ago. Reckon I'll see you once or twice more as the work gets sparkier."

Beth wrote down an address and stabbed the paper at Toby. "You get the doc to Green Street lickety split, or my granddaughter's picnic basket will be off-limits to you at the auction this weekend."

What did she know about breech babies? Sera wondered. In the real world, what did she know about delivering babies at all?

Time for an emergency phone call.

She used her speed dial while they wound their way through the streets of town. "Be home, be home, be home," she pleaded under her breath.

For a minute, she thought she was going to get her uncle's voice mail, but he picked up at the last second.

"Hi, Uncle Jeffrey." Not wanting to shake an already-nervous Toby's faith, she twisted in her seat and lowered her voice. "No, I'm fine. I need a quick refresher on breech babies." She glanced out the windshield. "I can't remember if…"

A disbelieving double take stopped the question cold. "Toby, look out!" she shouted and barely had time to brace as a battered blue truck shot down the center of the sloped street.

The driver was speeding and weaving and, by the time he straightened the vehicle out, heading straight for them.

A DOMESTIC DISTURBANCE call that came in after five o'clock put Logan and his deputy Annabelle a mile from the station when the crash occurred. His two-way went off while he was muscling a hotheaded Bulley cousin into his truck.

"What was that sound?" he asked Fred on the other end.

"I hate to think. I'm on my way to Fourth and Spencer Hill."

"Is Toby still with Sera?"

"He is, but they left so the doc could help deliver a baby. I was giving a juvenile shoplifter a stern warning, or I'd've been on their tail."

Fear wrenched in Logan's stomach. "I'll be there in five." He shoved the sulking cousin in Annabelle's direction. "Take this one, too. Front seat, backseat. Any more trouble, JT, you're in for a week."

"She started it." The man glared at his wife who twitched a tattooed shoulder at him.

With one last shove, Logan left Annabelle to deal.

It took him less than four minutes to reach Spencer Hill. What he saw sent ice water spurting through his veins.

The back end of Toby's truck was impossibly wedged between two large trees. Across the street, resting on its crumpled roof, an ancient blue Ford rocked back and forth as its angry driver rattled the undercarriage.

Logan spared him a look—he didn't appear to be injured—dismissed the stream of questions being hurled at him by several excited bystanders and located Toby at the curb.

"What happened?" He spotted Fred and motioned him toward the driver of the battered Ford. "Where's Sera?"

"Guy's brakes failed. No one was hurt, so Sera went on to Green Street. I didn't know if I should go with her or not, but I figured not. It's only a short drive, and I made her take Ella. I tried to call it in, but my truck's a mess, my cell phone won't work and I lost my two-way."

Logan looked at Fred, who gave him a thumbs up. "What's the address, and who drove her?"

"One-seven-one Green. My minister took her, so I know she's okay."

She might be okay, Logan thought, but he'd be a mess until sometime next week.

His cell phone rang as he turned back toward the gathering crowd. Mildly annoyed, he unhooked it. "Logan."

"It's a girl," Jenny-Lynn sang. "Doc Sera and Sue were awesome. They got her turned, and she popped right out, pink and healthy."

"Glad to hear it. Who's with you?"

"Nadine and Jessie-Lynn. Proud papa's on the front porch with his head between his knees."

Logan relaxed. He told Jenny-Lynn he'd be there in half an hour and ended the call.

"What do you think?" Fred dogged Logan around the flipped Ford. "Could someone have rigged this to happen?"

"In a paranoid world, yes. In the real one..." He crouched for a better view. "Lot of vehicles breaking down lately."

He stood. "Toby, has Walter rounded up that out-of-town biker yet?"

The young deputy joined them, shaking his broken phone. "Last I heard, no, and the guy hasn't showed up at the work site lately, so Abe's not happy."

Fred poked his shoulder. "Don't forget, Logan, the guy was shooting beer cans off one of Edgar Bulley's fences last week."

"I haven't forgotten."

"He's also got a record."

"And a confirmed ID."

"I still don't trust him. He's up to something, and two'll get you ten it isn't good. Any ideas what it might be?"

"One or two." But nothing he intended to share. His cell phone beeped as a pair of calls came in simultaneously.

Regarding the screen, he smiled. "Get to Green Street, Fred. Toby, with me." Zinging nerves were replaced by a surge of adrenaline. "Your cousins are using their knives again."

ENERGIZED AFTER THE birth of a healthy baby girl, Sera returned to the clinic. She dispatched her last patient at 8:45, sent a frazzled Beth on her way and, leaving Fred in the waiting room with a fast-food order, straightened up the second examining room. She refused to think about Logan any more. She'd been doing it for most of the day and hadn't gotten anywhere.

So, naturally, when her cell phone rang, it was his name that appeared on-screen.

The best-laid plans, she reflected and pressed Talk. "I'm fine, Chief. Closing up shop and still pumped."

"Congratulations. Any memory breaks?"

"I wish." She locked the medicine cabinet, dimmed the lights and released her hair. "Whatever it was Hollis planted in my head, it hasn't kicked in yet. Except I keep humming Bob Marley, and I'm visualizing a forearm now with a tan line on it instead of a scratched chrome watch. Go figure."

"Would a late dinner help?"

Despite the lazy drawl, Sera sensed he was revved. "Are we talking payback here?"

"Not unless you'll settle for take-out pizza on the ridge."

Curiouser and curiouser. "Should I wear sneakers for this mysterious outing?"

"Might be an idea."

She sighed. "You're such a puzzle, Logan. You don't like anchovies, do you?"

"Hate 'em. We'll stop by the house so you can change. Ten minutes?"

"No problem." Hoisting the strap of her medical bag over one bare shoulder, Sera turned the radio off, dug her iPod out and popped her earbuds in.

From the waiting room, Fred mimed that he was going to the washroom.

Sera nodded. Head bent, she scanned for U2. Then froze when the dead bolt on the alley door snapped back and the knob began to turn.

Chapter Seventeen

"I swear, Logan, I thought I was looking at a Victorian undertaker—tall, hollow-cheeked and quietly furious with me for invading his medical space." Sera shivered off the unpleasant recollection. "By the way, your office and the mayor's are going to hear about this, so fair warning there. Doctor Rufus Prichard is supremely pissed off and looking to kick my butt out of town, right before he mounts his high horse and rides snottily into the sunset."

"Leaving us one physician and a jackass down." After parking his truck near the top of Blue Ridge, Logan pulled out a backpack and a large flat box. "Pizza's thermal wrapped—in case we get sidetracked."

Sera slid her arms into a black cotton shirt to combat the night insects. She'd gone with designer hiking boots and jeans, a ball cap and a ponytail. Who said urban and country couldn't meet in the middle?

"Are we planning to get sidetracked?" she asked as they undertook the remainder of the climb on foot.

He smiled a little. "It could happen."

"That's an intriguing answer. Will I enjoy this side venture?"

"You might—if I'm right and Flo and Fred are out of the frame by the time we get back."

"Or Doc Prichard isn't waiting in ambush on your back porch."

"He's not that energetic."

"Maybe he needs a vitamin shot." Planting her hands on her hips, she sized up the rock ledge in front of her. "Logan, why aren't we using flashlights? Please tell me we're not setting a trap for the Blindfold Killer."

"We're not, but he's one of the reasons we aren't using flashlights. I'm hoping that blood we found today means he'll be laid up for a while."

"Long enough for me to figure him out anyway." She gave her temples a double tap with her index fingers. "There are more than a dozen disconnected details flitting around in my brain, like puzzle pieces I can't capture long enough to fit together."

"It'll happen." Setting his hands on her waist, he helped her scale a craggy rock wall. "Twenty feet, and we're there."

It was an optimistic assessment, but she made it—and only scraped one palm in the process. She noticed that Logan wore a shoulder holster with his two-way radio attached to the upper strap. So much for any romantic notions she might have been harboring. Both his manner and his equipment said he was on duty tonight.

From the top of the ridge, she made out the shadowy sprawl of a farm below.

Logan shed his pack in a patch of soft scrub and grinned at her. "You're straying awfully close to the edge, Sera."

"Am I?" But she didn't back up until he hooked a finger through her belt loop. "That's the Bulley house, isn't it?"

"You have good eyes."

She indicated a collection of lights about a mile to the right of the dilapidated structure. "That must be the campsite for the project workers." She also spotted a rickety barn, a ramshackle collection of outbuildings, a large pond and several patches of black woods. When something fluttered in her peripheral vision, she found herself smiling. "You brought a blanket?"

"Can't have a picnic without one." He spread it on the scrub and tugged her down beside him. She sensed he was as surprised as she was when his fingers wrapped around her neck and his mouth came down on hers in a kiss that chased away any hint of cool in the night air.

Although she could have taken it a lot deeper, suspicion had her drawing back. "I know you, Logan. Much as I'd love to, I don't think you brought me up here to have wild sex under a nearly full moon."

"You don't have a very romantic vision of me, do you?"

"Oh, I have many naked visions of you. But sometimes, like now, you're not."

"You think naked's romantic?"

Catching his T, she gave him a hot kiss. "Look in a mirror, Chief. You'll figure it out. Meantime," she ran a finger around his radio, "I think I can answer my own question. I had a chat with Benny Bulley today. He was wasted. He'd also been bitten by a leghold trap."

Logan chuckled. "What did he tell you?"

"He insists someone moved the traps. Not far, just out of the way. Of what, he wouldn't say, but he mentioned trespassers and that his grandfather fired off several rounds of buckshot when he spotted a group of them sneaking through the woods toward the ravine. I believe he called the spot Dilly's Drop."

"Dilly was his grandmother. It's not a pretty story. Go on."

"Old Edgar claims the farm and a few of his relatives' homes in town have been burgled more in the last week than they have in the past ten years. You'll be pleased to know, he doesn't hold any of that against you, but he's starting to wish he hadn't rented his empty pastureland to Abe. On the flip side, Benny says he and his brothers can deal with the trespassers from now on, so you shouldn't worry your head about it."

"Man's a prince."

Spotting a light below that hadn't been there earlier, Sera followed Logan's lead and got down on her stomach. "What?" she asked when he removed a pair of binoculars from his pack. "Is it a Bulley?"

"No. Someone's leaving the workers' campsite and heading for the ravine." He shifted the glasses. "There's a light in the old Morgan house."

"Is that bad?"

"Probably kids smoking up."

"Or making out."

"You think that, you haven't seen the old Morgan house."

Reaching up, she altered the trajectory of his glasses. "The first light's closing in on the ravine."

"Apparently the guy behind it is unaware that the last of the Bulley boys was released this afternoon."

Sera rested her weight on her forearms. "They have another still down there, don't they?"

A smile touched Logan's lips. "They have two. One in the ravine—which accounts for old Edgar's buckshot—and a second in the outhouse. Danny and Lester pulled their knives this afternoon and went after a couple of guys from the work site who swear they were only trying to use the thing."

"Don't you just love a bad lie?" She borrowed his binoculars. "Question, Chief. Gross outhouse aspect aside, if the Bulleys are going to keep building stills regardless, why don't you let them have one? Control's in your camp then."

"Because they don't drink everything they brew. They sell more than half of it."

"Well, yes, but… Ah, right. They sell to anyone with cash, including minors." Her brow knit. "I can't believe Edgar would condone that."

"He doesn't. Unfortunately, Edgar and his grandsons don't subscribe to the same moral code."

"So what's the next move?"

Logan shrugged. "We wait. We eat pizza. We don't get sidetracked."

"Well, you're no fun."

Cupping her nape, he turned her head to kiss her long and deep. "Wanna say that again?"

She grinned. "You're no—" the amusement faded "—ghoul," she finished slowly and with a frown. "That's so weird."

"You're telling me."

"No, really." She went through it in her head. "As the Blindfold Killer was running toward me, I'm sure he said something about a grave and a ghoul."

Logan's two-way radio squawked. "Something?" he asked.

"I've got a pair of Bulleys heading for the ravine," Fred's voice crackled back. "Should we move in?"

"No, let them go. They'll threaten whoever wants to steal their hooch, but they won't hurt him. Jail cell'll still be fresh in their minds."

"If you say so." His disappointed deputy signed off.

Logan's gaze held steady on Sera's. "Anything else?"

"If I'm a ghoul for witnessing a murder, I'm a ghoul who loves pizza and a movie. Already got the pizza." She tapped the thermal box, then indicated the light now retreating quickly back to the campsite. "I can't wait for the feature presentation."

LOGAN'S PATIENCE AND timing amazed her. Two pieces of pizza and a brief surveillance later, he had the Bulley boys plus their grandfather lined up, fined and grumbling in resigned frustration.

"You'd think they'd learn." Fred followed Sera up the back porch stairs to the house. He waved a hand to activate the light sensor. "Flo and Babe play bingo twice a month," he explained. "That's why the place is dark."

So either their daughter was upstairs sulking, or she'd gone out for the evening. Fifty-fifty either way, Sera figured.

In the kitchen, Fred exhaled. "Guess I'll have a look-see for Autumn. Logan said he'd be home inside half an hour. Kinda wish he hadn't kept Ella, but she's good at sniffing out hidden whiskey barrels. Do you mind being housebound for a while, Doc?"

Sera plucked a twig from the tip of her ponytail. "All I want to do is take a bath, sing Bob Marley and think about ghouls and tan lines. Don't ask," she said at her companion's perplexed expression. "Just be happy you've never been hypnotized."

Fred trudged up to the third floor while she nabbed a bottle of cold water and started toward her room.

Except it wasn't her room, it was the guest room. Logan's guest room, in Logan's house. It hadn't taken her long to stake a claim. It had taken even less time to fall...

She halted with the bottle raised to her lips. "Whoa, okay, back up, Sera. You don't know what you're feeling right now. Think in maybes, not certainties."

But that was the shrink in her talking, and the further

she strayed from that particular branch of medicine, the cloudier she became about going back.

Did those clouds mean she loved Logan, or that she only thought she did because of circumstances and proximity?

Taking a drink, she continued walking. All in all, she'd be better off pondering ghouls and graves and speculating on why a killer had been uttering words like that as he'd run toward her.

She needed to go through the night again, frame by frame. She could thank Hollis for making that much possible.

A protracted creak of floorboards from above brought a smile to her lips. Glancing at her scraped palm, she released her ponytail, rearranged her cap and started to hum.

The moment she did, the killer burst through her office door, charging toward her, coat flapping. No—she held herself perfectly still—not a coat, not exactly. It was a three-quarter-length protective work jacket, the kind the maintenance people in her office building wore.

She stared at the corridor wall, careful not to rush the memory.

The mothball and mildew smell struck her strongly. The words he shouted echoed and overlapped. He wore a watch. Then, in a blink, he didn't. There was only a tan line. Same man, she realized, two looks. And the smell was gone, too.

"'He's dead, in his grave,'" the killer raged. "'No one puts a ghoul in his grave…'"

She frowned. That couldn't be right. But she sensed it was close.

When the image went irretrievably fuzzy, she opened the door to her room and went inside. An unexpected movement near the bathroom snapped her into the moment. Swearing, she spun and shouted automatically.

"Fred!"

Awkward hands grabbed her from behind. She tried to turn but couldn't, so she jabbed an elbow into her attacker's solar plexus and used her heel on his foot.

A stiletto would have been better, but the hiking boot worked because he yelped and thrust her into the wall.

Something hit the floor. He gave her another rough shove.

"Fred!" When he yanked on her hair, anger overrode fear. "Bastard," she hissed and groped for the table lamp.

As her fingers curled around it, she wrenched herself out of his grasp just enough to swing the base like a bat. She'd been going for his head, but the strike on his shoulder did the job. He tossed her into a small table and went for the partly open door.

Stairs creaked. She heard footsteps in the hall. Feet pounded. Then everything stopped.

"Fred?" Running across the room, she set a hand on the doorframe and swung out. Giddy relief swept through her. Not Fred, she realized, resting her head on the wood, but Logan.

It had to be mild hysteria that made her want to laugh. Logan had a knee planted in her attacker's back and a hand clamped around his neck.

Letting out a deep breath, she asked, "Who is it?"

"Old barmate of ours."

When he dragged the man's head up, her eyes widened and the laugh escaped. "Are you serious?"

There, lying on the floor, with one of her purses wrapped around his arm, was the biker Logan had ticketed several days earlier—Wayne Postle.

"So it was Wayne who jumped me in your room the night the power went out."

"The night it was cut." Logan handed her a mug containing the dregs of the day's coffee. "For the record."

With a doubtful glance at the contents, Sera braved a sip. "This is the second time he's assaulted me then. That pisses me off."

"You're not alone."

Smiling at his dark tone, she pushed the mug back into his hands. "Your coffee's terrible."

"Toby makes it."

"From the by-products of an outhouse still?" she countered sweetly and made him chuckle.

He was on station duty for the remainder of the night, thanks to Annabelle's in-laws who'd shown up unexpectedly for Blue Ridge Days. After bringing Wayne in, Logan had cut her loose and sent his night deputies out on patrol.

Sera poked a finger into the soil of a withered cactus. "Talk to me, Chief. Who did what the night Wayne blindsided me in your room?"

"Wayne is Autumn's boyfriend."

"What?" Astonishment halted her halfway to the sink. "Did Wayne tell you that?"

"He didn't have to. She had the keys to his Kawasaki in her pocket the night she crashed Flo's car into the barn. That's why she took off in the first place. To rendezvous with him. She met him where he'd been holed up—in a work shack on the Bulley farm. He used the shack both as a flop and as a storehouse for everything he's stolen since coming to Blue Ridge. It's a sizeable stash, and it explains the recent rash of thefts."

"About which I'm guessing you already had your suspicions."

"What can I say? He fit the profile. As for the night in

question, the Bulley boys were all in jail, and Wayne, being an opportunist with a nose for hooch, saw the still he'd been fortunate enough to stumble across in the ravine as a liquid gold mine. He and Autumn went there, swiped a couple quarts and got wasted. He passed out, and she drove back home."

"Via the barn. She kept saying 'Dumb hick' while I was putting her to bed. She must have been talking about Wayne."

"Yeah, well, first he kept her waiting, then, when he finally showed up at the shack, she discovered he was out of commission for the night thanks to you."

Sera filled a small watering can and cast a smile over her shoulder. "I'm jumped, I fight back. So you're saying they got drunk after Wayne broke into your house."

"Call it a medicinal bender." Logan dumped the cold coffee and rinsed the mug. "Far as I can tell, he wasn't sure if Autumn was there or not when he arrived at my place. She wanted to keep their relationship quiet, so he skulked around outside, saw you and Flo in the kitchen and decided to climb up the trellis to my room."

Sera gave the cactus enough water to soften the soil. "So we know Wayne's inside the house. Can we skip to the Blindfold Killer?"

"He probably used the side door. Flo's mind's been tied up with Autumn, and until recently, she hasn't been turning locks."

"Oh good, more guilt."

"Why? Because you witnessed a crime? Screw that, Sera. The guy got in and got lucky. The breaker box is right inside the door. He must have flipped off the house lights thinking it would be easier to dispose of you in the dark. Flo came in. He whacked her and went after you. But you had a weapon, and his balls, while expanding, aren't that big."

Boosting herself onto a cabinet, Sera let her eyes sparkle. "See what happens when you hang out with a shrink? You start analyzing every little thing."

"'Little' being the operative word here."

"You think the more people he murders, the more inflated the killer's ego is becoming, don't you?"

"Don't you?"

"I see an insignificant individual with grandiose dreams. Or maybe I should say a grandiose goal. He kills once—there's a weight off his chest. It can be done. Kill again, that's affirmation. With each successive death, his confidence builds. He goes in, bang, slash, stab, he gets out, fist pumped. Yes! He's got a signature, but he's a phantom, a fearsome one. Achieving his goal's gonna be a piece of cake. Then, uh-oh, sudden glitch. Not so easy this time around. But it's fixable. He has to back up, think the problem through, revise his plan, first with me, then, on the spur of the moment, with Flo."

"Revised plan fails," Logan continued. "One glitch leads to another. Maybe he's rushing. In any case, he's inside the house now. Power's out, Flo's a non-factor. He's back on track."

"Except—woo—I have a gun. I might fire, could get lucky. Then, dammit, Flo wakes up, finds me. But he's still got the dark and, for the most part, the upper hand. Flo and I go upstairs. No problem. He'll follow, kill us both. But, double damn, he spots headlights on the road leading to the house. Gotta be the police chief. Time to leave."

"He who fights and runs away, Sera."

"A sentiment the Blindfold Killer apparently shares with Wayne."

"You and Flo came into my room. Wayne panicked."

"He ran for the door, heard you, reversed and took a header out the window."

"Roared off on his bike, rendezvoused belatedly with Autumn, then drowned his pain and frustration in Bulley whiskey."

"Didn't learn any lessons in the process, but that's hardly surprising." Hopping down, Sera started toward him. "Do you think the killer and Wayne knew about each other?"

"I doubt if their paths crossed, although from what you've told me, Wayne might have heard the murderer taunting you. If he did, I'll get it out of him."

She didn't doubt it. However, at that moment, she didn't care. Or more accurately, she cared about something else and no longer wanted to think about thieves, murderers and or any person not standing directly in front of her.

Logan had a sofa in his office—not large, but adequate. Only a third of the station lights were burning, his night deputies were on patrol and the street outside was empty.

Drawing closer, she unbuttoned her black shirt, teased him with her movements. "Your prisoners are asleep. I can hear them snoring through two closed doors. You won't get anything out of Wayne tonight, and, although that pizza was good, all it really did was put an edge on." At his unreadable expression, she widened meaningful eyes. "My appetite." She walked her fingers up his chest. "Anything you can do to help me out there, Chief?"

He didn't say a word, just hauled her against him and crushed his mouth to hers. His eyes were glittering when he raised his head. "Answer your question, Doc?"

It might—if she could remember what it was. Every thought in her head had just been blasted apart. Only a shimmering haze remained—and somewhere in the nether regions of her mind, Bob Marley crooned softly.

Rather than fight it, Sera used the hypnotic rhythm to her

advantage. She swayed into Logan, slid her arms around his neck, reached for his mouth. And only smiled when he swept her up in his arms and started for the back room.

Forget dinner in a fancy restaurant. This topped food by a landslide.

Poker debt paid in full.

HE COULDN'T NURSE his gunshot wound properly. He'd been forced to suck up the pain, drive into town, park on a side street and take a stiff-legged walk out to Main.

Had it been good luck or bad that he'd come around the corner at that particular moment?

The town had been in an uproar—people hammering and drilling, others on ladders, hanging flags and baskets and colorful ribboned signs. It had been an easy enough matter to secrete himself behind a stack of crates, but what he'd seen caused him to break out in a cold sweat.

What were the odds that this would happen?

He'd breathed slowly to calm himself. Odds didn't matter. The worst had transpired, but he was still ahead of the game. Of equal importance, he was ahead of the Blue Ridge police chief. He hoped.

What should he do? What could he do?

Don't panic for a start. Think, calculate, rectify.

He'd stood there, sweating like pig. And then, not half a minute later, a possible reprieve.

He'd looked around the crowded street. Busy, preoccupied people rushed every which way. It could be done. It must be done.

Relaxing his muscles, he'd pulled his hat down over his face, stuffed his hands in his pockets and wandered through the crowd toward the clinic.

Chapter Eighteen

"You're looking mighty pleased with yourself, Logan." Fred clomped into the station at 7:00 a.m. "Night crew punched out yet?"

"Half an hour ago." Feet propped, Logan examined the barrel of a rusty Winchester. He read the crudely carved initials and grinned. "Looks like we recovered Edgar's daddy's rifle."

"Part of Wayne Postle's loot?" Fred inspected the collection of stolen merchandise Logan had spread out over three desks and the floor. "Aw, what's this? He stole ladies' purses? What's the matter with him?"

"He was after the contents, Fred. You saw him with two of Sera's bags last night."

"And my silver dollar collection, and Sig's autographed Mickey Mantle baseball, your laptop, Sera's pretty diamond earrings and two tins of Flo's chocolate chunk oatmeal cookies that she baked for the potluck picnic raffle."

Setting the rifle aside, Logan swung his feet down. "Guy's in jail and loot's been recovered. We'll have a list of stolen items posted around town by noon. We dismantled two more stills, and Annabelle's in-laws have decided to stay at the hotel instead of her place. All in all, I'd call it a good night's work."

Fred tapped the side of his nose. "You and Sera've got something going, haven't you? I know it's…"

"None of your business." Logan glanced at the clinic, considered for a moment, then returned his gaze to the desks. "I've got most of this stuff sorted. All you have to do is tag the items and post the list."

The big man deflated. "Logan, about my kid…"

"She's an accessory after the fact, Fred. Get her into rehab, and stop beating yourself up. Autumn's getting a second chance. What happens next is her choice." He reached for his ringing cell. "Logan."

"I've got the lab report for you, Chief," one of the deputies from Casper said. "We e-mailed the results, but I thought you'd want the gist firsthand."

"And that is?"

"We brought up the breakdown on Hugh Paxton's blood work, then ran the samples you gave us and eliminated yours straight off. Left us with two. And point for point they're about as dissimilar as blood types get. Read into that what you will, Logan, but one thing's sure. I don't envy you your job right now."

A DOZEN CREAM-COLORED roses laced with baby's breath were waiting for Sera when she arrived at the clinic. They were artfully arranged in a clear glass vase and stood front and center on the reception desk. The attached card read:

Sera,
    If I am where I'm meant to be,
    Then where are you?
    Logan.

The cryptic question, not to mention the gesture itself, would have occupied Sera's thoughts all day if she hadn't gone into the second examining room and discovered the contents of a dozen or more patient files strewn across the floor.

Her first thought was that Dr. Prichard had let himself in and flung them from the cabinet where they'd been stacked. Her second was that 8:00 a.m. had come and gone and Beth, who'd promised to open the doors promptly at 7:30, still wasn't at her desk.

When she hadn't appeared by 8:30, Sera called both her home and her cell—and got no answer on either phone.

Nudging a curious Ella aside, Toby crawled around on his hands and knees. "If you're right, Doc, Prichard must have had some kind of mad on to do a thing like this."

Wearing jeans and a pale-blue halter-top, Sera took advantage of the early morning lull and joined him. Still unsure about Beth, she sat on the floor next to the alley exit and began sorting.

Her hair remained damp from the fastest shower she'd ever taken. Logan's fault, of course. They'd made love twice on his lumpy office sofa. When the night patrol returned, they'd driven to his house to rush through one of Flo's hearty breakfasts, change clothes and somehow pretend they'd gotten at least an hour of sleep last night.

Reaching over, she felt for the door beside her. If it hadn't been ajar and stuck, she might not have noticed the tiny scratches around the lock. But she did notice them—and didn't like what they implied.

Kneeling, she studied the marks. "Uh, Toby? Does Dr. Prichard still have his keys?"

"Mayor says we can't take them away until he's officially dismissed or quits."

A chill feathered along her spine. "In that case, we need to get Logan over here. I have a feeling it wasn't Prichard who went through the files last night."

HE DIDN'T LIKE the way the nurse scrunched her mouth and wouldn't look at him. The whole left side of his body throbbed like a bad tooth, and no matter how dire the circumstances, she was supposed to be a caregiver.

Abandoning discretion, he showed her his wound. "It's infected, isn't it?" he demanded.

She glanced up, then back down. "Judging from the ooze and the swelling, I'd say yes. But then I haven't got my glasses, and I didn't sleep very well last night."

He ground his teeth. "You took an oath to help people."

Her voice was quietly spiteful. "Nurses make vows, doctors take oaths."

"Fine, then I'll just kill you now and be done with it."

His lash of temper closed her mouth quick enough and actually made her lips tremble. "If you wanted me dead, you'd have killed me at my place. Not stolen my car and brought me here."

"I don't want you dead at all." Snarling, he hobbled back and forth in front of her. "The only person I'm after is Dr. Hudson. This is about justice, not how many corpses I can rack up. People stay out of my way, I leave them be. I'm not a homicidal maniac."

"Then why do you want to kill Doc Sera?" At his vicious look, the nurse dropped her gaze to the floor. "If you need medical attention, she's the one who can give it to you."

He would have laughed if a shaft of white-hot pain hadn't shot along his leg from hip to ankle. A few pointy fingers actually kicked up into his chest and made him cough.

He set his face close to hers and drew strength from his fury. "Maybe I'll enlighten you before I'm done. Dr. Hudson might not remember what I look like, but she'll see me clear enough when I get her here." Whipping out a white bandanna, he gave it a snap. "I'm veering off the path with her. She's put me through hell, so I'm going to pay her back in kind. No easy death for her. I'm doing this for Papa. And trust me, Papa's really pissed off."

TOBY FELT CERTAIN it was one of his cousins who'd broken into the clinic, but despite the Bulleys' collectively vindictive natures, Sera wasn't convinced.

Whether Logan would have agreed or not became a moot point when a family of six rushed through the front door, shouting for her to help their grandfather.

The seventy-six-year-old man was having chest pains. His terror spawned a panic attack in his wife and caused his daughter to hyperventilate. Sera dealt with the most serious problem and was forced to leave the other two patients to Toby.

She thought he coped admirably, juggling mother and daughter and even thinking to contact the local paramedics for help. Unfortunately, they were out on a call. A five-car pileup ten miles south of town meant they'd be tied up for hours.

Sixty minutes flew by before she and Toby got things more or less under control. Then Logan's deputy, Walter, called to inform her that a pair of adolescents out four by fouring had rolled their truck. From the description, Sera suspected a broken leg and numerous fractured ribs.

She thought it was a good thing the old man's attack had turned out to be nothing more than indigestion. Still, considering it was barely 10:00 a.m., she foresaw a marathon day ahead.

Maybe it was the moon, Logan reflected, that was turning the town upside down. The pile-up on the Interstate had, as far as he could determine, been caused by an angry wasp trapped inside the lead driver's shirt.

On the heels of that unholy mess, two boys who shouldn't have been behind the wheel, let alone scaling ridges in their father's Land Rover, had flipped the thing and gotten stuck inside. Fortunately, by the time Sera showed up, he and Walter had the boys free.

Five minutes later, Fred radioed with the news that shots were being fired at the Bulley farm.

Logan wasn't sure what he expected to find when he pulled up, but it wasn't Benny Bulley running out of the house in his underwear, shaken and clutching two knives. "Aunt Linda's gone nuts," he shouted. "She's got Gramps up in the attic, and she won't let him near the door." He lowered his eyes. "It, uh, could be she got her hands on one of our bottles."

Although he had weightier matters on his mind, Logan also had a job to do, and he trusted Toby not to let Sera out of his sight. He had to believe she'd be safe until he figured out how to resolve the problem here.

He was rounding the front of his truck, running his gaze along the uneven line of old Edgar's roof, when the attic window shattered and a shower of bullets hit the rocky ground at his feet.

BLACK CLOUDS BEGAN massing over the Big Horn Mountains early in the afternoon. Sera noticed them, but because they didn't lighten the patient load or ease the nerves that had been fluttering in her stomach for most of the day, she put them out of her mind. They were clouds, she told herself, not portents of doom.

That she couldn't reach Beth bothered her. That Logan

hadn't returned to the station by 3:00 p.m. bothered her even more.

Walter agreed to check on Beth. Twenty minutes after leaving, he called to say she wasn't home and her car was missing from the driveway.

An unconcerned Toby informed her that Beth had a number of quirky friends in Casper. He figured she'd simply received a call from one of them during the night. Toby's girlfriend, Beth's granddaughter agreed, but said she'd try to locate her once her shift at the post office was done.

Outside, the black clouds continued to gather over the mountains.

"People are hustling their butts to get the bleachers up," Toby remarked. "Word has it old Joe's predicting a bad storm."

"The weather channel said sunny and hot..." Sera moved a humorous hand from side to side. "But you prefer to go with old Joe."

"Absolutely. Another month in these parts, and you will, too."

Sera opened her mouth, then closed it and picked up a chart. "I have a patient waiting. Let me know when Logan gets back."

Ella padded obligingly from room to room. Toby manned the phones and did his best not to squirm when a rancher began describing his hemorrhoids in detail.

The clouds crept closer. The sound of hammers and power saws moved farther down the street. Sera was snapping off a pair of latex gloves when a familiar head with curly brown hair poked around the examining room door.

"Looks like you've got a bit of a break going on, Doc.

D'you have a minute to look at my leg? It's burning like the devil."

She tossed her gloves in the trash. "You didn't step in a rabbit trap, did you?"

He rasped out a laugh. "Trap'd need to be two and half feet across to get me where I'm hurting."

Taking his arm, she helped him onto the examining table. "Is that blood on your pants?"

"Yeah."

Tight-lipped, he held fast to her wrist. His grip was so tight she had to pry his hand free. "Hold on to the table," she suggested.

Thunder rolled in a single, ominous peal across the sky.

"Radio said sun all day," he noted in a rasp.

She smiled. "Guess the weather people forgot to check with old Joe. He's the local…"

She broke off as the tan line halfway up the man's right forearm slapped her like an open palm. Bob Marley began to sing. She was transported instantly to San Francisco. A man's hand squeezed her arm. He wore a scratched chrome watch—and then he didn't.

Back in the present, her eyes snapped up. And she saw him. Same face, same man, both in her San Francisco office and here in Blue Ridge.

Her patient's pained expression transformed into a slow, evil smile.

"And there it is," he said softly. "Recognition. You see now the person you saw then. What you don't see is what brought this about. But you will." His left hand whipped up to clamp around her throat. His right pushed the tip of a gun into her ribs. "Before you die, Sera Hudson, you'll see what it is to be helpless. And you'll know what it is to beg."

LOGAN DIDN'T ANTICIPATE a three-hour melodrama at the Bulley farm. But as a jittery Benny informed him, Aunt Linda knew her way around a thirty-thirty.

Apparently, she wasn't drunk. Edgar simply hadn't been giving her her medication.

"He said it was making her loopy," Victor revealed with a shrug. "But I say better loopy than loony. Good luck coming up with a plan, Logan. The attic has windows on every side. She'll see you coming no matter what."

Because he didn't have the power to become invisible, Logan opted to wait her out. But only to a point. When she showed no sign of backing off, he decided to call her bluff and go in through the front door.

Black clouds slunk in to obscure the setting sun. He heard a trill of laughter as he stepped into the open. It didn't surprise him that she fired three bullets into the dirt in front of him. It didn't stop him either.

The laughter continued. The cloud cover thickened. Logan kept his eyes on the shattered window and his footsteps measured.

She fired again. And again. But she didn't hit him, and if her eyesight held, he didn't think she would.

Altogether, it took about five minutes to cross the yard and climb the stairs to the attic. The knob turned easily under his hand. With his gun lowered, he gave the door a shove—and held his position when she snapped the rifle toward him.

Motioning Edgar out, he forced her to focus on him. She tracked him as he circled the room. But there were no more bullets, and she offered no resistance when he wrapped his fingers around the rifle barrel and gently tugged it out of her hands.

For a moment, she simply stared. Then her face lit up, and she reached out to slap his shoulder.

"Well, hey there, Logan. 'Bout time you came calling." All smiles now, she pointed at a wooden tray. "Care for a cup of tea?"

"THIS IS WHY you're the chief of police and the rest of us are deputies." Fred clapped Logan on the back. "Damn but that was good."

It had also eaten up a lot of time, and Logan wanted to get back to town.

Leaving Walter and Annabelle to clean things up, he pushed Fred into his truck and answered his ringing cell.

"Yeah—Logan."

"Oh, hello," a woman replied. "My name is Jody Frost. I'm returning your call from last night. You wanted to know why I contacted Sera Hudson earlier this month. The answer is, because my sister's friend Kate was murdered... By the Blindfold Killer."

The hesitation in her voice wasn't something Logan could miss. Or ignore.

He started his truck and swung it around in a half circle. "You called Sera—Dr. Hudson on her personal line the night her colleague was killed, is that right?"

"Yes. I used a pay phone. Dr. Hudson answered and agreed to meet me. Of course that meeting never happened, but because it was her colleague who died, I realized I'd been wrong in any case."

"Wrong about what?"

"A possible connection between Kate and Dr. Hudson. Let me backtrack. I found Dr. Hudson's name and her work number written on a sticky note in Kate's address book. It had an arrow to another name—Harvey Gould. I don't know why I remember this, but a few years ago, Kate mentioned a man named Gould to me. Through a twisted sequence of events, Mr. Gould was removed from his home and put in a mental facility."

"Why?"

"Because that's where he needed to be. Kate didn't go into great detail about the case as such. She couldn't because it wasn't actually hers. Her part in it was more that of a bystander, a concerned citizen if you will."

"Concerned in what way?"

"It's a rather convoluted story. Suffice to say my hunch was wrong. You see, I thought what with Kate writing down Dr. Hudson's name, then drawing that arrow to Harvey Gould's name, then Kate getting killed, and, well, knowing how enraged Harvey Gould's son became after his father's commitment and subsequent death, that maybe he—Harvey Gould's son—might be the one who'd done the killing."

"You thought Harvey Gould's son murdered your sister's friend, Kate."

"Exactly. And if he had, then that would make him the Blindfold Killer. I know it sounds crazy, but it made sense to me at the time. So I called Dr. Hudson and arranged to meet her because if I was right, then she was in terrible danger. She was part of the Gould case, so in my mind it stood to reason. But as I said, when I heard about her colleague being killed, there went my idea.

"My sister told me to let it be. Don't dig into it on my own, don't contact the police, just go back to my day to day and leave the detecting to those best qualified to do it. I decided she was right. No one ever followed up, and I thought it was over. I was out of it. Until you called."

It took all of Logan's police training to keep his emotions in check. "What was the son's name, Ms. Frost? Do you remember?"

"Owen. Owen Gould." She gave a rueful laugh. "I don't know what made me think he might be a cold-blooded killer. I mean, after all, angry or not, he must have undergone some form of scrutiny before he was hired."

Logan's eyes narrowed. "Hired?"

"Yes, as a maintenance person. For the San Francisco Police Department."

Chapter Nineteen

The first thing Sera saw when the killer shoved her into the old farmhouse was Beth slumped against a crumbling plaster wall.

He'd tied her hands at the clinic and forced her out the back door into the alley. She had no idea what he'd done with Toby or Ella. She could only pray he hadn't killed them. Or Beth.

"Nurse isn't dead," he growled as if reading her mind. "Only sleeping."

He shoved her again, this time onto a rough wooden chair. "You don't remember me, do you?"

Sera swallowed as much of her terror as she could. "I do now."

"I don't mean from the clinic."

"Neither do I."

"Not from your office either. I'm talking about before that. Back when people started sticking their noses into things that didn't concern them." At her silent stare, he bared his teeth. "First his neighbor's niece got involved. Butted in even though her aunt had moved away by the time the shinola hit the fan. Then, there was that idiot insurance man. Any driver who can't see a twenty-pound cat in the middle of a quiet street has no business owning a car. And let's not forget the social worker, Kate Something, who was out of her jurisdiction but just had to interfere the day he suffered a little episode in the park. Did he ask for help? Did I? No. Just go away, lady. I can handle him."

"Him," Sera repeated carefully. "Who is he?"

The man's face reddened. "He is—he was—my father. The buttinsky niece insisted on talking to her aunt's soon-to-be-ex-landlord. Landlord hemmed and hawed, but didn't do much except warn me to keep him quiet. Fine, I would. But then the social worker from the park tracked us down, said she felt duty bound to help. She talked to the landlord, who called the niece, who talked up a storm even though auntie dearest was living in Minnesota by then. Enter idiot insurance man who steamrolled companion cat and sent my father over the edge. I stepped in, told everyone to calm down and back off. It was just another episode. I'd get him a new cat. Things would settle down, so please, go away.

"But Kate the social worker wouldn't leave it alone. She was gonna help that delusional old man. Oh dear, did I say delusional? Enter medical doctor. I haven't done him yet, or the weaselly landlord, but I will because medical doctor led to psychiatrist, and psychiatrist led to my father being carted off to a hospital. It was supposed to be him and me, always, just the two of us, but suddenly there were people everywhere. Busybodies and do-gooders. Except my father died a month after he went into that hospital."

"But if that's the case…"

"Shut up," the man spat. "He died. Did the judge who put him in that hospital care? No. None of you cared, but oh, how you congratulated yourselves. Look what we did. We got a noisy nuisance the care he needed. Applause, applause. Too bad the old guy died, but that's not our problem. We did what we could, what was best."

The man's breath heaved with the force of his emotions. The hatred in his eyes burned right into Sera's head… And prompted a memory that feathered along the edge of her brain.

Something in the killer's expression and the semi-lucid story he'd related rang a hazy bell. About an elderly man in the advanced stages of dementia, who'd been admitted to a San Francisco hospital. About a medical doctor who'd called in a psychiatrist, who'd conferred and examined and agreed with his diagnosis. About a hearing, and a decision, and an ending that wouldn't sit well with many children.

The killer limped around her chair, shooting poison bullets with his eyes. One more look at his face and the haze cleared. "Gould," she exclaimed softly. "Your father was Harvey Gould. That's why you were shouting at me. *That's* what you were shouting. Not 'ghoul' but 'Gould.'"

A sickly layer of sweat coated the killer's face. Leaning over from behind, he grasped the back of her chair. "I made a vow the night he died. I'd cut through the red tape you wrap yourself in and kill all of you. I'd copy another murderer's MO and add my own special twist—I knew it would work because I knew the real Blindfold Killer's story. And I knew the story because I know how to blend in. I've been doing it for years. Insignificant maintenance worker, Owen Gould. No one really sees him."

"But where...?"

"Shut up," he shouted again. "I've come all the way from San Francisco to kill you. So make your peace, and be grateful for the chance to do it. It's more than your predecessors got."

A length of red tape and a white bandanna landed in her lap. His breath rasped in her ear. "It's all about details and using what you have, what you've learned. It's about shadows and determination and thinking on your feet."

The barrel of his gun grazed her cheek. Her shudder of revulsion drew a low chuckle.

"Say hello to the real Blindfold Killer when you see him, Sera. He's been waiting to greet you for eighteen long months—in the deepest pit of hell."

"I DON'T KNOW what happened, Logan." On the clinic floor, in the corridor between the washroom and the waiting room, Toby rubbed the back of his head. "I was walking and thinking how finally there was no one but me and the doc in the building and that maybe we could close up soon. Then, bam, everything went black. Next thing I knew, you were calling my name and I heard Ella barking."

Locking down his fear, Logan focused on the facts. The killer had shut Ella in the utility closet. He'd whacked Toby and God knew what he'd done with Sera. Or to her.

His stomach tightened into slippery knots. She'd been his target from the start. Killing her colleague had been a mistake. That's why the police hadn't been able to connect Andrea to any of the other victims.

Sera was the link—to the social worker and undoubtedly to all the others. For whatever reason, the police hadn't considered the possibility of an accidental victim. Neither had he.

Slamming the door on the worst-case scenario, Logan worked with what he had—not much. There was no blood and no sign of a struggle. And no one on the street had noticed anything out of the ordinary.

He squashed the slimy tendril of panic that clawed through his restraint, and, although he knew it was dangerous, pushed his deputy for more.

"When did this happen, Toby? What time?"

"A little after five, I think." He clutched Logan's forearm. "Am I floating, or has the floor gone spongy?"

Setting his hands on Toby's shoulders, Logan checked

the young deputy's eyes, then called to Fred. "Are the paramedics en route?"

"Three minutes," Fred promised. "Back door's open in
Room Two."

"I know." He motioned to Annabelle who pressed a cold
cloth to Toby's neck.

"I'm sorry, Logan." The deputy's eyelids drooped. "I
thought Ella was with her, but now I think whoever took
Sera must have locked Ella up while I was on the phone,
then waited for me in the washroom."

A face formed in Logan's head. Portrait of the Blindfold
Killer. A dozen thoughts swirled in behind it, but the face
remained at the forefront.

He knew he could have reasoned it out, rammed it into
some kind of order, but Sera was gone and time, if any even
existed, was running out. All he had were those fragments
of thought, his gut instinct and about five seconds to make
a decision.

"Where do we start?"

Logan looked up at Fred, stricken and unmoving, wringing the clinic's handset. And went with his gut.

"Stay with Toby," he ordered. "I'm going after Sera."

"Where?" Fred waved the handset in a desperate circle.
"You're hunting for a ghost."

"A ghost with a name." Standing, Logan checked his
gun.

"But how do you…?"

Fred's voice died with the slam of the clinic door.

Thunder resonated overhead, a dark warning. But his
sights were set on the name stamped in his head. Owen
Gould. If the man had a driver's license, he'd have a face,
and Logan would know who to look for.

All he had to do was figure out where to look.

"I CAN HELP you."

The words rushed from Sera's lips, a knee-jerk response to the gun now pointed in her face.

"You're bleeding. I can see you're in pain. Unless you want to risk losing your leg, you should let me take a look."

He jammed his gun up hard under her jaw. "Let you kick me in the nuts, you mean. Or stick a needle in that'll knock me out cold."

Sera's voice wanted to tremble, but she ground her teeth and spoke around it. "I don't have my medical bag, so no needles. The best I can do is clean the wound for you."

His breath hissed like a steaming pipe in her ear. "Your nurse gave me the names of some antibiotics. That's why she's still alive. I'll get them from the next town I pass."

"You won't be alive to take those antibiotics if that infection gets much worse."

He jabbed her with the barrel to emphasize his point. "No tricks," he warned.

"No tricks," she agreed.

"I'm not untying your hands until I've immobilized the rest of you. Twitch wrong, and there'll be a big red splat on the wall. Then I'll put holes in all four of your nurse's limbs and watch her bleed to death."

Sera controlled her breathing with difficulty. Keep him talking, she told herself. The clouds had created a premature darkness. He'd switched on two battery-powered lamps, and the windows had no shades. Someone—Logan—would notice.

"You help me, and I'll make it fast for both of you." He grimaced. "Screw me around, and your brain'll be the last part of you to hit the wall. You got that?"

"Yes."

Wiping his upper lip, he gave Beth a rough shake and

ordered her to secure Sera to the chair with the roll of red tape he pulled from his duffel bag.

"Should I leave the knots loose?" the nurse whispered, but Sera shook her head. The killer was watching them closely, sweating heavily, trembling in spasms. It wouldn't take much for him to squeeze the trigger.

Buying time was the only chance they had. She had no instruments and no way of knowing what his pain threshold might be.

The bowl of water he made Beth set out looked murky and smelled like a swamp. The lamplight was bad, and her hands, although steady enough, had turned to ice.

"I don't kill for enjoyment," he bit out as he bound Beth's ankles. "I only took Florence Nightingale here because I saw a certain patient going into the clinic yesterday. A minute later, I saw you come out with the redheaded deputy. Did you know, I wondered, or was fortune on my side? It took balls, I'm telling you, to stroll over and eavesdrop outside the door. But to my amazement, Florence was too busy to twig and you were gone, so I figured—I hoped— crisis averted. Still, I knew she made up the charts and the truth might hit her during the night. Potential result? Puzzled call to you or the police chief."

Beth's chin went up. "Lucky for you, it was a madhouse all afternoon. With Doc Sera away on an emergency call, I was run off my feet. I didn't have time to think, let alone sort through the new files. I left them on the cabinet when I went home last night."

"At which time I stole the one that mattered." His eyes glittered. "Then I came and stole you."

Considering her terrified state of mind, Sera was surprised the answer came so quickly.

"You used someone else's identity," she said. "You hung around the project work site and found the closest physical match you could. Then you injured yourself and came to the clinic under his name."

"Smashed my hand into a wall after the bar fight," he admitted. "Logan screwed me up, or I'd have had you that night. So scrap Plan A—it was on to the clinic. I knew I'd have to be clever. And flexible. If you'd recognized me, I'd have been forced to kill you on the spot. Not the best solution, but I figure I'm an innocuous-looking man. I'd have left town and blended back into the city easily enough.

"As it turned out, however, you didn't recognize me. I was able to take what I'd overheard in Gray Wolf's bar and use it to buy myself some time, get you all looking in the wrong direction. I actually presented myself to Logan. I described Hugh Paxton just well enough that there'd be no doubt he was the man who'd tried to abduct you the night before. Then the helpful witness faded back into the shadows."

His mouth twisted downward. "You know what happened next. The worker whose name I'd used got injured and came to town for treatment. He's not a particularly sociable man. Still, I'd always known there was a risk my story wouldn't hold forever. Way I see it now, it held just long enough."

He gave the tape around Beth's ankles an angry jerk. "Chance after chance fell apart one way or another. It took me awhile, but I finally figured out why." He broke the tape with his hands.

Screwing his gun into the underside of her chin, he showed her his top and crooked bottom teeth, breathed his hatred through them. "I planned and I planned, and you messed me up. You, your shrink friend, your so similar dark hair, your red coat, the rain."

Sera regarded him calmly, despite the metal barrel

lodged against her windpipe and the fear scrambling around in her stomach. "You found him, didn't you?"

"Found who?" he demanded testily.

"The Blindfold Killer."

Beth sucked in a breath, but the man made a disgusted motion. "Of course I did. I worked at the police station, didn't I? And cops talk all the time. They jabber away, leave files open, go for coffee or to hit on the new blond dispatcher. What can an invisible person do?" The grin reappeared. Opening his shirt, he tapped the tattoo on his shoulder. "He can absorb and follow and if he's lucky, get where the cops are going first. He can use his luck and obliterate the very person he needs to fulfill his brand new mission in life. So long, original Blindfold Killer. Say hello to your successor, your shadow, Blindfold Killer Two. Better than the first because no one will ever suspect him. They'll keep right on looking for Hugh Paxton. They'll look, but they'll never find. Because Papa's watching over him, and I watch over Papa."

"Doctor..." Beth began, but Sera kept her eyes on the man in front of her.

"You are a clever man, Mr. Gould. Attention to details explains why you've been so—successful."

He wiped his lip, then his forehead. "Messed things up with you, though, didn't I? You wore a red coat to work that day. It was dark. I thought it was you getting that take-out food. I forgot to check the face. But there's always a way to fix things. Papa fixed old clocks. He said there was always a way. And he was right. So here we sit, you, me and an innocent victim. Your victim. Your fault. Just like the detectives were your fault. And, of course, your associate. Never lend, never borrow." Both his features and his smile hardened. "Most of all, though, never mess with a madman's head."

In a sudden, vicious move, he caught hold of her hair. His mouth took an ugly downward turn. "That's what you're doing, isn't it, Dr. Hudson? You're trying to distract me, thinking maybe the kook will bleed to death and that'll be the end of it. But it won't be me who dies today. Clock is ticking, Sera."

Releasing her, he yanked a battered chrome watch from his shirt pocket and clasped it around his right forearm. "This was my father's. I wear it at home like he did and again when I'm avenging his death. I gave it to him when I was ten years old. Do you see the time? It says 7:20. That's when my father died. It's only right that you who caused his death should die then, too. When I brought you here it was 6:30. You've got less than twenty minutes to live, Doc. If my leg feels better when you're finished working on it, you'll die fast. If not..." He moved his mouth and the gun next to her ear. "Splat, splat."

RAIN BEGAN TO fall as Logan cut the flashers outside Abe's trailer. The builder met him at the door with a wave and a grin, both of which faded at Logan's dark expression.

"What? Am I under arrest?"

"Listen to your damn messages more than once a day, Abe." Logan shook the rain from his hat. "Roy Parsons. Get him here."

"Sure. Uh, any reason?"

"Yeah."

"Gotcha." Abe scanned a list, punched a number, told his assistant to hustle the man over. As the silence stretched out and the minutes ticked away, he lowered himself onto the edge of his desk.

Finally, he craned his neck and nodded at the window. "I told him to step on it, and he did... Get in here, Travis, and close the damn door before the rain shorts out my electrics."

Abe's assistant booted the door closed and, pulling off his hat, slapped it against his thigh. "Hey, Logan. What's up?"

The man behind him nudged his cap back, fingered the bandage on his cheek and appeared impressed. "Doc said this plaster'd stick, and she was right." Stepping forward, he stuck out his hand. "Pleased to finally meet you, Chief. Travis said you wanted to see me. Name's Roy Parsons."

OWEN GOULD TORE his pant leg open at the hip and positioned his chair parallel to Sera's. He planted Beth on a crate and stuffed his gun under her left breast.

"Move it, Doc," he advised gruffly. "I'm feeling woozy. I might have to abandon my plan and off the nurse here in one quick shot, save the torture for you alone."

Sera ordered herself to breathe, go slowly, stall without being obvious.

"This is going to sting," she warned and tipped some non-Bulley whiskey onto one of the man's wadded-up shirts—a shirt that smelled of mothballs and mildew.

"What?" he demanded when she rearranged it.

"Nothing. Too bulky. Are you ready?"

"As I'll ever be." But he turned a sickly shade of green when the whiskey met infected flesh. "Son of a…" He whistled in and out, then shot her a baleful glare. "You don't like it, but you recognize it, don't you?"

She raised her eyes.

"The smell," he barked. "Mothballs. I heard you say it in the bar, before I knocked you out." Moving his gun, he tapped the barrel against Beth's temple. "Details, Doctor. My father loved the smell. My mother hated it. She was a clean freak. Wash, dry, iron, hang." He gave a contemptuous snort. "Hell with that, my dad and me said. Wear it, toss it on the floor, dig it out when you need it. Mothballs'll cover any smell that needs covering. Powerful little suckers. And you remembered them, even when you didn't remember my face." Gripping the neck of the whiskey bottle, he took a long swig, his fifth in as many minutes.

The battery lamps were dying, Sera realized, and with them her hopes. Still, where there was light there was hope.

Rain lashed the windowpane. Owen Gould took another drink, then startled her by thrusting the bottle into her hand and leaping to his feet. He put two bullets through the chattering pane and fired two more into the rain.

"I know someone's there!" Livid, he bent over Sera's chair and wrapped an arm around her throat. "Untie yourself," he snapped. "Do it." He cocked the trigger.

She fumbled with the knots on her waist and felt the gun dig into her nape as she worked on her ankles. The second she was free, he dragged her to her feet. His arm was a steel band across her windpipe.

"Is that you, Logan?" he demanded. "Come out where I can see you, or your girlfriend's dead in five...four... three..."

Someone moved on the porch. A face swam into view. Not Logan's but Benny Bulley's. Soaking wet and terrified, he gaped open-mouthed at the man with the gun.

"I was—looking for a new—a place," he stuttered. "I saw the lights and thought maybe one of my brothers beat me to it."

"Get in here." Gould jerked his head sideways. "Sit next to the nurse, and keep your mouth shut. I need to think."

He tossed Sera forward the moment Benny lowered himself onto a crate. "You know the drill, Doc. Tie him up tight, or someone in this room's going to take a bullet."

Sera knelt and picked up the tape Beth had used on her.

Benny's eyes went to the window but dropped to the floor when Gould darted a look at the shattered pane.

"Who else is out there?" he demanded.

"No one." Benny moved a foot. "My brothers and me don't travel in clumps."

Sera kept wrapping. Gould glanced at her repeatedly as he edged toward the window.

Benny moved his foot again, this time into her knee. "Not so tight, Doc."

Looking up, she watched his eyes and mouth. Rain gusted in, created puddles on the floor. Gould was sidling closer to the opening when his foot slipped on the broken glass.

As if someone had pushed a start button, the room came alive. Benny shot from his seat to tackle Sera. "Get down," he shouted and gave Beth's crate a kick that sent it flying.

A bullet from outside caught Gould in the shoulder. Reeling backward, he went for Sera, but she managed to roll away.

Roaring, he sent both lamps crashing to the floor. What light they'd been giving off immediately winked out.

Sera heard a moan. "Beth?" Unable to see, she stayed low. "Are you hurt?"

Hands shoved on her butt.

"Get behind the table," Benny whispered. "He wasn't supposed to kill the lights."

Gould knocked aside everything in his path. Bullets ricocheted off walls. Sera located Beth, but the nurse must have hit her head in the fall. She was groggy and only partially responsive.

"Untie her, Benny," she said, "and get her behind the table."

"But…"

"Where's your knife?"

"In my back pocket."

She reached around him and groped until she encountered the hilt.

"Everyone dies in pain," Gould ranted. He shot in all directions and from everywhere in the room it seemed.

Leaving Benny to splutter, Sera worked her way along the wall to what she hoped was Owen Gould's position. She estimated she was halfway there when another shadow moved and a hand closed around her wrist.

"Stop," Logan told her quietly.

Even as relief flooded through her, a bullet whizzed past her head.

"Logan, he's…"

"Shh." His fingers curled around her neck. "He's circling."

She gave his arm an urgent shake. "Beth and Benny."

"I know. Stay here. I'll draw his fire."

He was gone with the last word. Where, she had no idea. Until…

Above the approaching thunder, she heard bangs and grunts and shouts and finally a heavy thunk.

A body slammed into the wall directly in front of her. Gould's body, she realized. Her eyes had adjusted enough that she could see him shoving a new clip into his gun.

She didn't move, didn't twitch or even breathe. But somehow he knew. Before she could evade him, he reached down and tangled his hand in her hair.

"You die first, Sera Hudson," he growled. "At least I'll get that much satisfaction from this night. First you, then your bastard lawman lover."

As he started to yank her upright, Sera tightened her grip on Benny's knife. Double-handing it, she shoved the blade into his injured leg.

He howled in pain, dropping her instantly. She heard a single gunshot. For a moment, he didn't move. Then she saw his eyes widen and his jaw drop. To her shock, blood spurted from the center of his throat.

His gun arm swung around in a wild, drunken circle. He pointed it at her, but only for a second before his arm gave out and the weapon clattered to the floor.

"Should have stayed invisible," he burbled. And, head lolling, slithered down the wall into a motionless heap.

The physician in Sera had her crawling to where he sat, lopsided and staring. She pressed her fingers to the pulse point in his neck. When Logan came up behind her, she rocked back into him. "He's dead," she said quietly. "You're a good shot."

Setting his chin on top of her head, Logan asked, "Do you remember him now?"

She nodded. "Suddenly, I saw his face, my wet trench coat, Andi's body, all of it, as clearly as if the whole nightmare had happened yesterday."

He kissed her temple. "Yesterday's done, Sera."

While lightning flickered over the mountains, Sera let her tension slide away and savored the warmth of the man behind her. Through today and into tomorrow.

Epilogue

The story raced through town faster than one of Nadine's outlaw horses.

Benny Bulley lapped up praise for his participation in the showdown at the old Morgan farmhouse—even though his arrival mere minutes before Logan probably hadn't been as innocent as he claimed. Motive aside, however, he'd done what Logan asked. He'd clued Sera in by nudging her knee while she was tying him up and in doing so had earned himself and his brothers a free night at Tommy Gray Wolf's Bar.

The rain moved south, Blue Ridge Days opened with a bang—and, shortly after sunset, a minor brawl started between Victor Bulley and Abe's assistant Travis.

Abe apologized profusely to both Sera and Logan. The photo Logan had showed him of Owen Gould posing as Roy Parsons, although clear enough to most people, had been anything but to a man not wearing his much-needed glasses.

"It's all my fault," he moaned over and over again. Then he brightened as an idea struck. "Say, Doc, I'll bet your clinic could use some new equipment…"

Her clinic?

Sera might have corrected him if Jessie-Lynn hadn't tugged her aside to whisper that Doc Prichard had decided to pack up and move on. She claimed her alien friends had planted the thought in his head, and lucky for everyone in town, it had taken root.

As the night wore on, she watched men and women bid on their favorite picnic baskets at the annual Blue Ridge Days dinner auction. She watched Babe dance with Walter and a fully recovered Beth do a jig with Flo. She made a point of not watching a patched-up Toby sneak under the bleachers with Beth's granddaughter.

She'd like to have spent more time—well, any time really—with Logan, but a moment here and there was the best they could manage given the demand for their attention.

Sera supposed it was only natural. Still, she wasn't sorry when darkness descended and the first starburst exploded in the clear night sky. With Ella nosing her leg, she edged backward across the street—and straight into someone's chest.

She knew it was Logan before she looked. Lips curving, she let her head fall onto his shoulder. "Hey there, stranger. Shouldn't you be busting Bulleys or getting hit on by every single female in town?"

"As tempting as those options sound, I'd rather escape for a while with one particular female."

A bottle of wine appeared in front of her. "Sonoma Valley Cabernet." She ran a fingertip over the label. "Sig's favorite."

"He claimed the most worthwhile hangover he ever had came after a night spent with this stuff. I agreed with him—until I spent a night with some freshly distilled Bulley whiskey."

"Think I'll stick with the wine."

She heard the amusement in his voice when he lowered his mouth to her ear. "In that case, come with me, and I'll show you the best place in town to watch fireworks and get drunk."

Two minutes later, they were alone on the roof of the station house. Red, gold, silver, green and blue bombs burst overhead, filling the sky with jewel-toned sparkles.

Logan leaned against the rooftop door and Sera leaned against him. For a long time, neither of them spoke, just sipped Sig's favorite wine and watched the glitter rain down.

After awhile, she sighed. "Why does this feel so ridiculously perfect to me?"

"Probably because it is. Perfect moments happen, Sera. They're rare, but not unattainable."

"Even when people you care about are dead?"

"Even then."

His simple response had her pushing off to face him. Setting her glass aside, Sera raised her eyes to Logan's shadowed face and ran a finger along the brim of his hat. "Sig told me you were the best chance I had to stay alive. He was right."

"You're the one who remembered his face, Sera."

"Yeah, two seconds before he hauled me out to his hiding place in the old Morgan house—which you also figured out."

"Lights on where they shouldn't have been—it wasn't hard to figure. Locals have more sense than to use that place for anything, and we already had Wayne Postle in custody. FYI, Postle did hear Gould threatening you the night the power was cut at my place, but all he cared about at that point was getting out before he got caught."

"Killers and thieves." She ran her finger from hat to cheek. "Different mentalities."

"Snakes and weasels." A smile touched his lips. "Different species."

"Gould was insane for a very long time, Logan, if he was ever sane to start with. He murdered the real Blindfold Killer. But you suspected that already, didn't you?"

"Crossed my mind. Gould was also the leak Sig talked about within the department. As for Paxton's body—no, idea."

"Ah, well, I've been thinking about that. You might want to check out his father's grave. If I'm right, you could discover that Harvey Gould is no longer alone."

"Sounds like you neglected to mention a few significant points in your statement yesterday."

Her eyes danced in the shimmering light. "Yesterday's done, remember? Today's just beginning and tomorrow's a magical mystery tour." She moved her hips against him. "Beth thinks I should give up psychiatry and stay right here in Blue Ridge. Recruit other doctors, expand the clinic." She drew a circle on his chest, set her tongue on her teeth, angled her head. "Anything you want to say to that?"

"No."

Undeterred, she bumped against him. "You sure?"

"Yeah, I'm sure." She sensed his eyes on her face and felt his thumbs slide along the line of her jaw. "Words are cheap, Sera. Action works better for me."

As his mouth came down hungrily on hers, Sera slipped the Sedona rock he'd given to Sig as a child into the pocket of his jeans.

* * * * *

HIS CASE,
HER BABY

BY
CARLA CASSIDY

First published in Great Britain 2011
by Mills & Boon, an imprint of Harlequin (UK) Limited,
Eton House, 18-24 Paradise Road, Richmond, Surrey TW9 1SR

© Carla Bracale 2010

ISBN: 978 0 263 88549 1

46-0911

Harlequin (UK) policy is to use papers that are natural, renewable and
recyclable products and made from wood grown in sustainable forests. The
logging and manufacturing processes conform to the legal environmental
regulations of the country of origin.

Printed and bound in Spain
by Blackprint CPI, Barcelona

Carla Cassidy is an award-winning author who has written over fifty books. In 1995, she won Best Silhouette Romance from *Romantic Times BOOKreviews* for *Anything for Danny*. In 1998, she also won a Career Achievement Award for Best Innovative Series from *Romantic Times BOOKreviews*.

Carla believes the only thing better than curling up with a good book to read is sitting down at the computer with a good story to write. She's looking forward to writing many more books and bringing hours of pleasure to readers.

Curtis Cassidy is an award-winning author who has
written five ... books. In 1998, she won her ... award
for ... short, Roman ... Times, RONA ... the ...
Award for Romance ... In 1999, she also won a ... Cuga ...
... Romance Award for Best Innovative ... Romance ...
Romance Times ... Award.

Curtis ... says she only joins ... to ...
a good reason to write ... she is looking forward to ...
many more hours ... bringing ... of ... to ...

... ...

Chapter 1

Peyton Wilkerson finished mopping her kitchen floor, pleased by the shine on the tiles and the clean scent of bleach that hung in the air. She put the mop away and then went to the window of the cozy ranch house.

She stared outside, where the day before the concrete company had poured a beautiful new patio inside the six-foot privacy fence that surrounded the backyard.

Pride ballooned in her chest. It was all finally coming together for her. After years of working two and three jobs, of attending college nights and weekends, some of her dreams were beginning to come true.

She not only had her very own house, but she also had a brand-new patio where she could have a barbecue and invite neighbors who would hopefully soon be friends.

She turned from the window at the sound of a soft coo coming from the portable infant rocking seat in the center of the kitchen table. Her heart swelled as she smiled at her four-month-old little girl.

"Hey, Lilly girl," Peyton said as she scooped the baby up in her arms. Lilly flailed her arms and cooed again, her rosebud little lips turning upward in a happy smile.

It almost frightened Peyton, how happy she'd become, how many of her dreams were beginning to blossom into fruition. In a month she would begin teaching first grade at the Black Rock Elementary School. And even though Lilly hadn't been planned, she was the greatest gift Peyton had ever been given.

Although things hadn't worked out between Peyton and Lilly's father, Rick, Rick had promised to be there for his daughter, and Peyton knew he'd do just that. He was a good man, just not the man for Peyton.

"Are you hungry?" Peyton asked as she placed Lilly back in her seat.

Lilly bounced and wiggled and smiled, a faint trail of drool making its way from her mouth to her chin. Peyton laughed and grabbed a towel to wipe her mouth. "Or would you rather I just get your piggies?" She grabbed Lilly's foot and tickled her toes. Lilly squealed and kicked her feet as Peyton laughed again.

The ringing of the doorbell interrupted the game. Making certain that Lilly was secure in the seat, Peyton left her and hurried to the door.

She peeked through the spy hole on the door and

saw the tall redhead on the other side. She quickly unfastened the dead bolt and opened the door. "Kathy! I didn't expect you to stop by today," she said.

"I decided a little exercise would do me good, so I thought I'd walk over for a visit, but it's hot as blazes out there." She flipped her long red hair over her shoulder and smiled. "Hope you don't mind a hot and thirsty friend dropping by unexpectedly."

"Not at all. Come on into the kitchen. I was just about to make a bottle for Lilly, and I'll get you something cold to drink."

As they entered the kitchen, Kathy beelined to Lilly as Peyton got a bottle of soda out of the fridge and set it on the table.

Kathy baby-talked to Lilly for a moment, then sat at the table and watched as Peyton prepared Lilly's bottle.

The two women had met two months earlier, right after Peyton had moved to the small western Kansas town. Kathy was new to town as well and the two had hit it off immediately.

"I see you got the patio poured," Kathy said as Peyton sat in the chair next to her and began to feed Lilly.

"Yesterday. I can't wait to have a real barbecue outside. I want to get one of those umbrella tables and invite all my new friends for burgers and hot dogs."

"At least wait until it cools down. This heat is about to kill me," Kathy exclaimed. "I'd forgotten how hot it gets in Kansas in July. Besides, you have to meet some new friends in order to invite them."

"I know, and I will," Peyton replied. "Now that I'm finally settled in and Lilly is getting older, I plan on getting out more." Peyton had been reluctant to take Lilly outside and around strangers while she'd been so small, and she'd had the work of settling in to keep her from going out and socializing.

"Did Rick stop by last night? You mentioned that he was planning on driving out to visit with the baby."

"No, he didn't make it. He's working some big trial and scarcely has time to breathe right now." Rick Powell was an assistant D.A. Handsome and ambitious, he and Peyton had dated for six months, and ironically Lilly had been conceived on the night they mutually decided to break up.

"He could have married you," Kathy said with a touch of censure.

Peyton laughed. "I didn't want to marry him. We had a great time together, but I realized I wasn't in love with him. Besides, Rick is already married to his work."

Lilly finished her bottle and yawned around the nipple. Almost immediately she closed her eyes and fell asleep. Peyton put her back in the cushioned seat in the center of the table and brushed a strand of the pale blond hair away from her forehead.

"She's such a doll baby," Kathy said, then frowned and raised a hand to her temple. "You don't happen to have anything for a headache, do you?"

"Nothing stronger than an aspirin," Peyton replied.

"Could I have a couple? I have a killer headache."

"Sure, hang on and I'll be right back. I've got a bottle under the sink in the bathroom."

"Great, thanks."

As Peyton walked through her living room with its gleaming polished surfaces and simple furnishings, she thought of how far she'd come from her roots.

She'd done it. She'd climbed out of the filth and the fear of her childhood. She was in a place where she couldn't get evicted, where filth would never exist again.

The guest bathroom in the hall was decorated in cool shades of mint-green and white. She straightened the hand towel next to the sink before she bent down to look for the aspirin bottle.

She was on her knees when she looked up and saw Kathy standing in the doorway. "Here you are," she said as she grabbed the bottle and began to rise.

"And here you are," Kathy said, and she slammed something into the side of Peyton's head. Peyton reeled backward, unable to keep her balance. *What? Why?* These two words exploded in Peyton's brain just before her head hit the edge of the bathtub and everything went black.

Consciousness came in bits and pieces. The faint scent of pine cleaner filled her nose and she winced from the nauseating pound of a headache. She opened her eyes and saw the mint-green bathroom rug beneath her face. She frowned in confusion. *What?* How did she get on the floor?

Kathy. Kathy had come into the bathroom and

attacked her. Kathy had hit her. As she got to her feet it all came back to her. Why? Why had her friend attacked her? It didn't make sense.

Lilly! She had to get to Lilly. The baby wasn't crying. Maybe she was still napping. Peyton's heart crashed against her ribs, like an off-balance washing machine on the spin cycle. Please, God, let her still be napping.

Woozy and unsteady on her feet, she stumbled down the hallway. She needed to call for help. She'd been attacked. But before she could do anything she needed her baby in her arms.

As she stepped into the kitchen she froze. The infant seat was in the center of the table, the receiving blanket a swath of rose color against the empty seat.

"No." The word whispered out of her as her knees buckled. Horror pressed against her chest, making it difficult for her to draw breath. Where was Lilly?

She reeled out of the kitchen and ran down the hall to Lilly's bedroom. Kathy must have put her in her crib. Even though Peyton knew it made no sense, that nothing made sense, she clung to the hope that Kathy had tucked Lilly into her crib before she'd left the house.

She clung to that tenuous, fragile hope as she raced into the small bedroom she'd decorated with pink ruffles and teddy bears. She stopped in the doorway and stared at the empty crib.

And screamed.

Sheriff Tom Grayson pulled his car into the driveway of the neat little ranch house and got out before the engine had completely shut off. His youngest brother, Caleb, waited for him on the lawn, his khaki deputy uniform the same color as the sunburned dried grass beneath his feet.

"What's up?" Tom asked. The late July heat felt as if it seared his lungs with each breath he took.

Caleb's brown eyes were darker than usual, a sure sign that he was troubled. "A missing baby."

Tom's stomach flipped. In all his years as sheriff of Black Rock, Kansas, there had never been a child missing or murdered.

"Details," Tom demanded.

"The woman, Peyton Wilkerson, says she was entertaining a friend and she went to the bathroom. She says the woman attacked her and knocked her unconscious, then stole the baby. But, I got to tell you, Tom, it all seems pretty fishy. Her wounds look superficial, she just had a new patio poured yesterday, and the kitchen smells like bleach."

Bleach, the best thing to use to clean up traces of blood. Tom tried to keep his mind open as he nodded and went into the house.

He stepped into the living room, and his first impression was one of obsessive neatness and order. The furnishings were simple and the room smelled of lemon furniture polish and glass cleaner.

He heard the sound of his brother Benjamin coming from the kitchen. It didn't surprise him that Benjamin was the one in the kitchen with the potential victim while Caleb had been the one pacing the grass outside.

Benjamin had an affinity for anyone he thought might be a victim of a crime. Softhearted to a fault, he would be consoling Peyton Wilkerson. On the other hand, impulsive, impatient Caleb was always ready to believe the worst in a situation, always ready to investigate and arrest.

Before going to the kitchen, Tom turned down a hallway and stepped into the first bedroom he came to. It was obviously a nursery. Decorated in shades of pink, it was tidy and held the faintest scent of baby lotion.

He left that room and went farther down the hall, passing a bedroom and coming to the master bedroom. Decorated in yellow, white and green, it gave the aura of a peaceful garden with sunshine. As with all the other rooms, nothing appeared out of place. Even the nightstand held nothing more than an attractive reading lamp.

Tom frowned as he thought of his own nightstand, which often held the remainder of a bedtime snack, whatever book he was currently reading and little notes to himself of things he thought of just before drifting off to sleep.

He touched nothing; he was just trying to get a quick feel for the person who lived there. So far he learned that Peyton Wilkerson definitely took pride in her surroundings and probably had more than a touch of obsessive-compulsiveness.

The first thing Tom noticed as he stood in the doorway to the kitchen was the faint, underlying scent of bleach. The second thing he noticed was that Peyton

Wilkerson was a stunner. Even red-rimmed eyes from crying and an angry gash on the side of her forehead couldn't detract from her fragile beauty.

Both she and Benjamin sat at the kitchen table. In the center of the table was an empty infant seat covered in pink material and ruffles.

Tom knew most of the people in the small town of Black Rock, but he'd never seen Peyton Wilkerson before. If he had, he definitely would have remembered.

As he stepped into the room she jumped up from her chair. "Thank God," she said, tears shimmering in her already swollen eyes as she reached out and grabbed his hand. "Sheriff, you have to do something. You have to go get my Lilly."

Her hand was fevered and trembled in his. The sense of urgency that he'd felt when Caleb had told him a baby was missing welled up inside him.

"Who took her?" Tom asked.

"Her name is Kathy Simon, and she lives in the Black Rock Apartments. Please, we have to get my baby back. She's only four months old." A sob escaped her as Tom led her back to the chair where she'd been seated.

"You know what apartment she lives in?" he asked, aware that Caleb had come into the room.

Peyton frowned. "No, not specifically. Whenever I've dropped her off, it's always been at the front entrance."

"What does she look like?" Tom asked.

"She has shoulder-length red hair and blue eyes.

She's taller than me and very thin. She told me she was twenty-nine, the same age as me."

"Caleb, Benjamin, head over to the apartments and check it out," Tom said. "Get out an AMBER Alert and have Sam run a check on a Kathy Simon. Tell Clay and Eric to set up roadblocks on both ends of town and to check every car leaving town."

"I want to go to the apartments, too," Peyton exclaimed.

"You and I are going to stay here so I can ask you some questions," Tom said firmly. "My deputies will check things out." He nodded in dismissal to his brothers, who immediately left.

He returned his attention to Peyton, who looked as if she were hanging onto her very sanity by a thread. "Tell me what happened this morning."

For a moment he thought she was going to break down altogether. Her lips trembled and tears filled her eyes. "Please, Mrs. Wilkerson. I know this is difficult, but the more information I have the easier it will be to find your baby."

She drew a deep breath and visibly pulled herself together. "I had just finished cleaning the kitchen when Kathy showed up." She gripped a tissue in her hand so tightly her knuckles were white.

"I smell bleach. Is that what you were cleaning with?" he asked.

She nodded. "I always use a little bleach when I clean, especially when I mop the floor."

Tom watched her carefully, trying to discern any

deceit in the depths of her blue eyes. "You and this Kathy, you were friends?"

She nodded, a single curt nod. The sunshine streaming through the window sparkled in her pale blond hair. "We met about two months ago, right after I moved here. She was new to Black Rock, too, and we hit it off right away."

Tom pulled a small notepad and a pen from his pocket.

"You have a phone number for her?"

"No, she told me she didn't have a phone. She said she was short on money and had to cancel her cell phone and hadn't yet gotten a landline."

"What about a car? Do you know what kind she drove?"

She raised a trembling hand to her forehead and frowned. "I don't know. She mentioned something about it being in the shop."

"Do you know where she was from?"

Her frown deepened, the gesture doing nothing to detract from her attractiveness. "Chicago, I think."

"Where's your husband? Can I call him for you?"

She shook her head. "I'm not married. Lilly's father lives in Wichita."

"What's his name?" Tom asked. Maybe this was some sort of parental kidnapping, he thought. God, he hoped so. At least then he'd know the baby was safe.

"Rick, Rick Powell," she replied. Her eyes widened. "Surely you don't think he had anything to do with this.

He wouldn't. He's an assistant district attorney. He'd never be part of anything like this," she exclaimed.

She scooted back from the table and jumped up, her slender body vibrating with energy. "We don't have time to sit here and talk. I need to find Lilly." She reached up and grabbed the back of her head and grimaced.

Tom wouldn't have thought her face could get any paler, but it blanched of any lingering color. He jumped to his feet and grabbed her by the arm. "Are you all right? Do you need medical attention?"

She dropped her hand to her side, her body weaving slightly. "I sent the ambulance away. I'm all right. I just hit my head on the bathtub when she attacked me."

She allowed Tom to guide her back into the chair at the table. He could smell her, a scent of fresh flowers and despair, and he tried to maintain emotional distance, knowing that it was possible that all was not what it seemed.

As he asked her about the particulars of the attack and listened to her answers, he assessed the kitchen which was now a crime scene.

Did she like things so neat and clean, or had she sanitized the house before calling for help? Had a terrible accident taken place here and now she was trying to cover it up?

Certainly the news was full of stories of babies who had been shaken to death or suffocated by an overwrought parent. Or was it as she said, and a kidnapping had really occurred? It was too early to know the truth.

As quickly as possible, Tom got the pertinent information from her, and then he called in two of his deputies to fingerprint and collect evidence from the bathroom and the kitchen. He called another deputy to check with the garage to see if Kathy Simon had a car being worked on there.

With the arrival of the two deputies, Tom moved Peyton into the living room, where she paced the floor and looked as if she were about ready to jump out of her skin.

Tom had placed a call to Rick Powell and had gotten in touch with his secretary, as Rick was in trial. She'd promised to pass a message to him as soon as possible for him to call Tom.

Peyton had been seated on the sofa, hands wringing and her delicate features taut with tension as Tom directed his deputies attempting to lift fingerprints from the surfaces Kathy might have touched.

Although she appeared calm, but stressed, Tom sensed an explosion coming. He saw it in the white of her knuckles as she folded her hands together, in the deepening hue of her blue eyes as she watched him.

So far she'd been patient and cooperative, but he had a feeling that that was coming to an end quickly. As if to prove his intuition, she sprang up from the sofa when the phone rang.

The tight composure she'd kept cracked as she tearfully told Rick what had happened. Rick promised to come as soon as possible, but it was a two-and-a-half-hour drive from Wichita to Black Rock.

"You have to do something," she exclaimed after she'd hung up with Rick. For the first time there was an edge of frantic anger in her voice. "Why haven't we heard something? What's taking so long?"

Tom had been thinking the same thing. "We should hear something from them any minute. We have the AMBER Alert out and I have a deputy checking background on Kathy. At this point there's nothing else we can do but wait here until we have more information." He glanced toward her phone.

She followed his gaze, then looked back at him, her eyes widening slightly. "You think maybe she'll call?" A half-hysterical sob escaped her. "She won't call. This isn't about a ransom. Kathy knows I don't have any money."

"Then what do you think this is about?"

"I don't know," she cried. "I feel like this is all some horrible joke, or a terrible nightmare. I can't imagine why Kathy did this. I just can't wrap my mind around all of this."

She whirled around as the door opened and Caleb and Benjamin walked in. Caleb gave a small shake of his head.

"What does that mean?" Peyton asked. "Why are you shaking your head?"

"There's no Kathy Simon living at the Black Rock Apartments," he said.

"What do you mean? I know she lives there. I dropped her off there several times." Peyton looked from Caleb to Tom, then back to Caleb again.

"We checked with the manager. There's no Kathy Simon on a lease. We also knocked on every door and asked if anyone knew her. Nobody did," Benjamin added.

Peyton's eyes widened in horror as she looked at Tom. "Then where is she? And where has she taken my Lilly?"

Chapter 2

Peyton felt as if the ground beneath her feet was no longer solid. The world was no longer as it should be, and she'd never felt such fear. *Lilly!* Her heart cried in anguish. Where was her baby?

Who was Kathy Simon, and why had she done this? Had anything she'd told Peyton about herself been true? One thing was certain: Peyton had wasted enough time sitting around waiting for something to happen.

She needed to find Lilly, and she wasn't going to find her sitting around and answering questions. Without saying a word to the sheriff or his deputies, she headed down the hall to her bedroom.

Sheriff Grayson followed just behind her, as if afraid to let her out of his sight for a minute. "What are you doing?" he asked as she grabbed her purse from the top of her dresser.

"I'm going to find my baby." She turned to face him. "If I have to knock on every door of this town, I'll find Kathy and my Lilly."

"I don't think that's a good idea," he protested.

She raised her chin and embraced the anger that was so much easier to tolerate than her pain. "The only way you're going to stop me, Sheriff Grayson, is to arrest me and lock me up."

Despite the fact that he was easily six inches taller than her and had shoulders as broad as mountains, she shoved roughly past him and headed for the front door.

She'd gone only a couple of steps when he grabbed her by the arm. "I'll take you wherever you want to go." His dark eyes held her gaze intently. "We don't know if this woman is dangerous. She might not harm your baby, but she would definitely be a threat to you."

She considered his words and gave him a curt nod. "Then let's go. I can't sit here another minute."

She was vaguely surprised to see that the sun was still high in the sky. It had been less than two hours since Kathy and Lilly had disappeared, but it felt like an eternity.

Even the intensity of the late afternoon sun overhead couldn't warm the glacier that had become Peyton's heart. She slid into the passenger seat of the sheriff's car and was instantly engulfed by the scent of leather and, more faintly, the spicy cologne he wore.

As he got in behind the steering wheel he turned to look at her. "Do you have a plan?"

She'd shot out of the house lit with the fire of a frantic mother seeking her child, but she realized with the question that she didn't have a plan; she just knew she couldn't sit still another minute.

"The pizza place on Main Street," she said suddenly. "Kathy told me she was working there until she could get something more permanent."

He nodded, started the car and pulled away from the curb. Peyton stared out the window, irrationally hoping that Kathy would suddenly appear on the sidewalk.

The only thing that kept Peyton from losing her mind altogether was the belief that Kathy wouldn't hurt Lilly. "She was good with Lilly," she finally said aloud. "She seemed to love her."

"Did she mention wanting children of her own, maybe not being able to have them?" Sheriff Grayson asked.

"No, nothing like that. I just know she was always very sweet to Lilly. Surely the pizza place will have her address on file."

"What I need you to do is think of all the conversations you had with her, any tidbit of information that might be helpful as to where she might go and who she might be with," he replied.

For a moment Peyton was overwhelmed. "Sheriff Grayson, we talked almost every day, about everything and nothing." She frowned and tried to ignore the headache that pounded in the back of her head, the continuous frantic race of her heart.

"Call me Tom," he said. "There are four of us Graysons working law enforcement in Black Rock. First names make things easier."

"Caleb and Benjamin are your brothers?" she asked.

He nodded. "My sister is also a deputy, then I have one other brother who doesn't work for the town of Black Rock." He frowned. "Did Kathy mention dating somebody here in town? Perhaps somebody she was interested in?"

"No, in fact just the opposite. I got the impression she was a bit shy and was having trouble meeting people." She released a sigh of frustration. "God, what did I miss? What didn't I see or hear in all those conversations, in all the time we spent together?"

"You can't beat yourself up about that. How could you guess that something like this would happen?" He pulled into a parking space in front of the Canyon Pizzeria and cut the engine, then he turned and looked at her with his dark, intense eyes. "You let me ask the questions. I need to do my job."

She nodded and unbuckled her seatbelt, butterflies like little kamikaze pilots hitting the sides of her stomach. *Please, let us get some answers,* she thought as she got out of the car.

It was nearing dinnertime and the air outside the restaurant smelled of tangy tomato sauce and baking crust. The food smells only upset Peyton's stomach even more. The last thing she was interested in was food.

All she wanted was her sweet Lilly back in her arms.

She needed to smell her baby scent, feel Lilly's wiggly warmth against her chest.

She followed Sheriff Grayson through the front door. Inside, about a dozen people were seated at various tables and booths. Most of them raised a hand in greeting to the sheriff.

He went to the woman standing behind the cash register. "Hey, Linda, is Don in?" he asked.

"He's in the back. You here to arrest him for spicy sauce?" The blonde gave him a saucy, flirtatious smile.

"I need to talk to him. Can you get him out here?"

Her smile faded as she apparently heard the seriousness in his voice. "Sure, I'll go get him."

She disappeared into the kitchen and a moment later a big burly man clad in a tomato-splattered apron walked out.

"Hey, Tom. What's up?"

"You have a Kathy Simon working here for you?" Tom asked.

Peyton watched in horror as Don shook his head. "I've got a Stacy, a Katie and a Linda, but no Kathy," he replied.

"Are you sure? Maybe she was going by another name," Peyton said desperately. "She's tall with red hair?"

"Sorry, nobody like that works for me," Don replied.

Peyton staggered back outside where dusk was beginning to fall, vaguely aware of the sheriff right behind her. Nothing Kathy had told her had been true. She'd lied about where she worked, where she lived. Why?

She got back into the passenger seat and Tom slid in behind the wheel. "You okay?" he asked as he started the engine.

"Of course I'm not okay." She reached for anger, knowing that if she didn't hang on to something she'd lose it altogether. "Nothing she told me was the truth. Why would she lie to me about the most basic things? God, she was good. She had so many details. She told me about a man who had tipped her twenty dollars, about a little girl who wanted pizza crust and cheese but no sauce. She was so good with her lies."

A sickness welled up inside her as she realized night was falling too quickly and she was no closer to finding Lilly than she'd been when she'd regained consciousness on her bathroom floor.

"Any other ideas?" Tom asked as he backed out of the parking space in front of the pizza place. "Or are you ready to go back to your place?"

"No, we can't go back," she exclaimed. She didn't want to be there without her baby. "Just drive around. Maybe we'll see something."

For the next thirty minutes he drove up and down the streets of the small town. Peyton kept her gaze on the sidewalks, on the houses they passed, hoping for a glimpse of the woman she knew as Kathy Simon.

He received only one phone call during the drive.

When he hung up he told her that there was no driver's license matching what they knew about Kathy Simon.

"So that's probably not her real name," Peyton said flatly. She was numb; in a place where her fear was so great she couldn't process it any longer.

"Probably not," he agreed.

"How are we going to find her if we don't even know her name?" Peyton wanted to scream.

"We'll figure it all out," he replied. "Have you had any problems with anyone here in town?"

"No, nobody. Oh, there was a young man who cussed me in the parking lot of the grocery store. I was getting Lilly into her car seat and my shopping cart accidentally rolled into his truck."

"Did you exchange information?"

"No, nothing like that. It didn't scratch or dent the truck. He cursed me, then got in his truck and roared off."

"When did this happen?"

"About a week ago. Surely you don't think that has anything to do with Lilly's kidnapping," she said.

"I'm not taking anything for granted at this point," he replied. "What did this guy look like? What kind of a truck was he driving?"

"It was a black pickup, but I don't know the year or model. He was tall with brown hair." She sighed in frustration. "That doesn't help much, does it?"

"Sounds like half the men around this area," he replied.

As he once again drove down Main Street, Peyton

knew this probably wasn't standard operating procedure, that he was just indulging her need to be out looking. She also knew that there was no way she would see Kathy casually walking down the street with Lilly in her arms. She knew in her heart that Kathy had probably run out of town mere minutes after grabbing Lilly.

"I noticed you had a new patio in your backyard."

Peyton shifted her gaze from the window to him. "It was poured yesterday. What does that have to do with anything?"

"Just curious."

She stared at him, her heart beating an unsteady rhythm. She had a feeling this man didn't indulge in idle curiosity. There was a sharp intelligence in his sexy dark eyes that made her believe he was a man who didn't miss much.

As the realization of what he might be thinking struck her, she gasped. "You can't really believe that I had the patio poured to hide my baby's body?"

"It doesn't matter what I believe. I have to think of all possible scenarios," he said without apology.

"Pull over," she exclaimed. "I think I'm going to be sick."

He whirled the car to the curb and she unbuckled her seat belt, opened the door and stumbled outside. She bent over, feeling the need to throw up. He thought she'd killed her baby. He thought she'd killed her Lilly and buried her beneath the patio.

She dry heaved, her stomach rolling as tears blurred her vision. She was vaguely aware of a big, broad hand on her back, and she shook it off, the need to be sick swallowed by a rage she'd never felt before.

Her rage wasn't directed at Sheriff Tom Grayson, who was just doing his job, but rather at the woman who had pretended to be her friend and support over the past two months. The woman who had hit her in the head and stolen her baby.

She finally straightened up and stared at the sheriff. "If and when we find her, if she's hurt Lilly in any way, I'll kill her." She didn't wait for his reply but instead turned and walked back to the car and got into the passenger seat.

It was at that moment, with the fire of rage burning in her eyes, that Tom believed her. He hadn't been one hundred percent sure what to believe up until that point. There had been far too many cases of murdered children when the mothers concocted a story to cover the fact that they'd either accidentally or purposely hurt or killed their child.

He liked to believe he was good at assessing people, at recognizing liars and criminals. He didn't believe Peyton was either, and that meant they had a missing baby on their hands.

When they pulled up to her house, a luxury sports car was parked in the driveway. "That's Rick's car," she said, emotion thick in her voice.

As she and Tom got out of his car, the front door of the house opened and a tall, well-dressed blond man stepped out.

Peyton ran toward him, and Tom would have expected Rick to open up his arms, to hug the woman who was the mother of his missing child. But she stopped just short of him and Rick shoved his hands in his expensive slacks pockets. "What exactly happened?" he asked.

Peyton began to cry as she explained to him what had occurred. When she was finished, Rick looked at Tom. "Sheriff, Rick Powell." He held out his hand to Tom. "What's being done to find my daughter?"

Tom gave his hand a perfunctory shake, then motioned toward the front door. "Why don't we all go inside and talk."

As he followed them inside he found himself wishing that Rick had hugged her. If anyone needed the security of strong arms around her, it was Peyton. The thought hit him from left field and he pushed it aside.

"We have an AMBER Alert in place, and several of my deputies are out knocking on doors and seeing if anyone knows this woman who called herself Kathy Simon," Tom explained once they were all seated at the table. "It would be helpful if we could get a picture or a drawing of this woman to send out across the state."

"Do you have a picture of her?" Rick asked Peyton.

"No, I never took her picture," Peyton said miserably.

"My brother Benjamin is a pretty good artist. Why don't I get him in here to work up a sketch, and Rick and I can go into the living room and talk," Tom said.

Peyton nodded as he and Rick stood. Within minutes,

Benjamin was seated with her at the table, and Rick and Tom went into the living room, where Rick sat on the sofa and looked at Tom expectantly.

"Peyton told me you're an assistant D.A. in Wichita," Tom said.

"That's right." He leaned forward and ran a hand through his short hair. "I can't believe this has happened. Peyton's a terrific mother. She would never intentionally put Lilly at risk."

"You have no idea who this woman might be? You never met her?"

"No, but I have to confess that since Peyton moved here I've only been to visit a couple of times," Rick replied. "With my work schedule it's been difficult getting back and forth. In fact, I'm in the middle of a big trial now. I got the judge to call a continuance until day after tomorrow, but I've got to be back in Wichita first thing Thursday morning. Hopefully we'll have Lilly back long before then."

"Why did Peyton decide to move here?" Tom asked.

Rick leaned back in the chair and unfastened the buttons of his suit coat. "When our relationship fizzled out, she decided she wanted a new start someplace else. She started shooting out résumés, and when Black Rock Elementary School made an offer, she jumped at the opportunity."

"Your breakup was amicable?"

Rick released a small sigh of impatience. "Look, Sheriff, I know how these things go. I understand that you have to look at all angles, but let me save you a little time. Peyton and I dated for six months. We had a good time together but eventually realized we wanted different things from life. The split was amicable. In fact, it was the night we decided to call it quits that Lilly was conceived. Even though we weren't going to be together as a couple, we were both excited to be parents. We've had no problems, no issues since Lilly's birth. Peyton is one of the greatest women I've ever known. She would never do anything to hurt Lilly, and neither would I."

Tom fought back a sigh of frustration. He knew Rick was trying to be helpful, but there was nothing worse than investigating somebody who knew the system from the inside out. "You know I have to go through all this," Tom said.

Rick nodded. "I was just trying to cut to the chase by letting you know that there's nothing to investigate except the woman who stole my daughter. There's no point in wasting time speculating about Peyton or myself."

"I appreciate your help, but you know I'm going to do this investigation my way," Tom said. He kept his voice friendly but firm.

"Understood," Rick replied. "I just want my little girl back." For the first time since he'd arrived, emotion cracked his voice.

"Is it possible this has something to do with a case you're working on? An enemy you've made through your work?" Tom asked.

Rick frowned thoughtfully. "I don't think so. Very few people knew about Peyton and the baby. I wanted it that way for their own protection."

At that moment, Benjamin and Peyton came into the room. "We have a sketch," Benjamin said. He handed the paper to Tom, who looked at it closely.

Benjamin was a talented sketch artist, a talent he'd kept hidden for many years. The sketch showed a woman with a slender face and long hair. Her eyes were slightly deep set and her chin square.

Tom looked up at Peyton. "This looks like Kathy Simon?"

"It could be a photograph of her." For the first time her eyes shone with a hint of hope. Tom was struck again by her prettiness.

He handed the sketch to Rick. "Have you seen this woman?"

Rick studied the sketch with a frown, then shook his head. "No, I've never seen her before."

Tom looked back at Peyton. "You have a recent picture of Lilly?"

"I do. I just had her pictures taken at that little studio on Main Street a couple of weeks ago." She went to the desk in the corner of the room and opened a drawer. She withdrew a large envelope and from it pulled a 5x7 photograph.

She gazed at the picture for a long moment, her eyes filling with tears, then she handed it to Tom. Lilly was a doll, one of those exceptionally pretty babies with bright blue eyes and a tuft of curly blond hair.

Tom turned to his brother Caleb, who had returned to the house moments earlier after interviewing more of the people who lived in and around the apartment complex. "Take these to the office and get them over the wires," he said as he handed the photo and sketch to him. "Make up flyers and get them distributed around town."

When Caleb went out the front door, Tom turned back to Peyton. "Somebody will see them. Somebody will know where she is," he said in encouragement.

"I hope so," Peyton exclaimed.

The next couple of hours passed in agonizing slowness. Peyton sat on the sofa looking as if a loud noise might shatter her. Rick sat next to her, but at no time did the two touch in any way.

Tom found their relationship rather intriguing. Was their lack of physical touch an indication that their relationship hadn't had the mutual easy ending that both of them had implied? And what, if anything, might that have to do with the case?

Throughout the evening, Tom coordinated efforts to find the baby, speaking to his deputies by cell phone to keep updated. As night fell, Tom didn't expect anything to happen. People were in their homes, getting ready for bed, and wouldn't see the flyers until morning.

Rick must have recognized the same thing. At ten-thirty he stood. "I checked into the hotel downtown when I arrived. I think I'll head over there for the rest of the night. I'm in room 112. Somebody will let me know if anything happens?"

"Of course," Tom replied, vaguely surprised by his decision to leave.

Rick reached down and grabbed Peyton's hand. "Stay strong," he said. "I'm sure we'll have her back tomorrow." He dropped her hand and with a nod to Tom left the house.

Almost immediately, Peyton got up from the sofa and went to the front window. She stared out with her back to Tom, and he was struck by how alone, how achingly fragile, she looked.

"Do you have children, Tom?" She didn't turn to face him but remained staring out the window into the darkness of the night.

"No wife, no kids," he replied. He stepped closer to her, close enough that he could smell the pleasant scent of her perfume.

"So you can't know what this feels like." She turned to face him and raw pain radiated from her eyes.

"No, I can't know exactly what it feels like," he said softly.

"I feel like Kathy reached inside my chest and ripped my heart out." Tears slid down her cheeks. "Nothing matters except Lilly. I need her back, Tom. I need her back in my arms." A deep sob exploded out of her and she nearly crumpled to the floor.

Before she could, Tom reached out for her and pulled her tight against his chest. She sagged against him and buried her face in the front of his shirt while she cried.

He wrapped his arms around her and held tight,

knowing it was the only comfort he could offer her at the moment. As he held her he went over it all in his mind, satisfying himself that everything that could be done was being done.

Now it became a waiting game. Hopefully somebody knew this woman who had called herself Kathy Simon, somebody who would call with information that would lead them to her and the baby.

But the last time Tom had held a weeping woman in his arms, everything had ended badly. Tragedy had pulled her away from him, and he'd nearly been destroyed.

He hoped at the end of all this that Peyton would have her baby safely back in her arms. He hadn't been strong enough to help one woman deal with grief, and he prayed he wouldn't have to help Peyton.

Chapter 3

Peyton didn't realize how much she'd needed to be held until Tom's strong arms surrounded her. The fact that it was a relative stranger's arms that brought her some comfort wasn't lost on her. But his arms were solid and warm and the clean, slightly spicy scent of him was comforting, making her reluctant to leave his embrace.

She finally raised her face to look up at him. "Thank you. I needed somebody to hold me for just a minute or two." Reluctantly she dropped her hands from around his neck and stepped back from him. "As you probably noticed, Rick isn't very good in the hug department."

"Yeah, I noticed that. Why don't you make some coffee for us?" he asked as he took her by the elbow and led her back into the kitchen. "You should probably try to eat something, too," he said as he leaned against the counter.

She shook her head. "I can't even think about food right now, but if you're hungry I have some sandwich stuff."

"Sure, I'd take a sandwich," he replied.

As the coffee began to fill the air with its fragrance and Peyton got out the lunch meat and cheese to build a sandwich, she realized he was keeping her busy, trying to keep her mind off the reason he was here, the reason Lilly wasn't in her bouncy chair on the table.

When she finished making the sandwich she set it on the table in front of Tom. She poured them each a cup of coffee and joined him there.

She still wanted to weep and wail, to walk the streets and rip open each and every door she came to in order to find Lilly, but she knew in all likelihood that Kathy was long gone. She also knew Tom had set in place the means that would hopefully find her baby.

"It's going to be a long night," she said aloud as her gaze drifted toward the window where the darkness was profound. "I can't believe she's out there somewhere and not here with me."

"Tell me about your relationship with Rick," he said.

She looked back at him and knew he was once again trying to take her mind off Lilly—as if that were possible. Still, she wanted conversation. She wanted to talk about everything and anything so that she wouldn't hear the screaming voice inside her head that said her baby was gone.

She wrapped her cold fingers around the warmth of her coffee cup and frowned. "There isn't a whole lot to tell. I met Rick in a coffee shop where I was working near the courthouse in Wichita. He was handsome and charming, and when he asked me out I was thrilled. We got close really fast, but it didn't take me long to realize I would never be first in Rick's life. I'd always be a distant third behind his work and his colleagues. For a while I was okay with that. But toward the end I realized that for once in my life I wanted to be the first priority in somebody's life, and it wasn't going to happen with Rick."

She paused and took a sip of her coffee. "Anyway, we both agreed that we weren't right for each other and had one last fling that resulted in Lilly."

"A surprise?"

"Definitely," she replied. "But, the minute I saw the test result and knew that I was pregnant, I also knew I wanted the baby more than I'd ever wanted anything in my life."

"And what about Rick? How did he feel about it?"

She frowned thoughtfully. "Initially I think he was a little bit upset. Any man would be. Neither of us had planned to become parents so soon, but he quickly came around. He was one hundred percent supportive through the pregnancy and was right there with me when Lilly was born."

"What about support and visitation rights? Did you

work those out legally?" His chocolate-brown eyes seemed to see everything that was inside her soul.

"No. I know Rick will do the right thing where Lilly is concerned, and if he doesn't then I'll be fine on my own." For the first time since this horror had begun, she noticed that Sheriff Tom Grayson was a very handsome man. The warmth of his dark brown eyes tempered the stern, stark lines of his face.

She leaned back in her chair, slightly disconcerted by her spark of feminine interest. "Anyway, I figured if Rick wants to be a part of Lilly's life he'll make that happen. I didn't want some legal form to bind him to us if he didn't want that."

"You said for once in your life you wanted to be somebody's priority. What about your parents?" He took a bite of his sandwich and looked at her expectantly.

"I never knew my father, and I was always a distant third in my mother's life, right behind her drugs and her newest boyfriend." She couldn't hide the touch of bitterness that crept into her voice.

"Doesn't sound like the makings of a great childhood," he said softly.

"It wasn't." She stared back out the window, tossed back into painful memories she tried never to access. "It was nothing but fear and uncertainty and one cheap, filthy motel room after another." She looked back at him. "I promised myself then that if I survived eventually I'd have a place of my own that would never be dirty, a place where nobody could kick me out onto the streets."

He took another bite of his sandwich and looked around. "Looks like you've succeeded."

She nodded. "It's taken a long time to get here, but I'm happy where I'm at," she replied. "But now that somebody has taken my Lilly—"

Emotion clawed up the back of her throat, and she felt as if the darkness outside the window were seeping into her blood, taking over her heart. Just as she thought she'd be swallowed whole, Tom reached across the table and grabbed her hand tight in his.

"We're doing everything that can be done to find them," he said. "You have to stay strong. You said you didn't think Kathy would hurt Lilly. You have to believe that, hang on to that."

She squeezed his hand and nodded. "I do believe that. She was good with Lilly." She released a sigh. "Maybe she can't have children of her own. Maybe she only befriended me because she wanted Lilly."

He released her hand and leaned back in his chair. "If that's the case, then somebody in her life will realize she suddenly has a baby. She can't stay underground forever. Somewhere somebody is going to see her and Lilly and make a phone call."

"You sound so optimistic," she said.

He smiled then. It was the first real smile she'd seen on his face, and it was a nice one. It softened the sternness and deepened the warmth of his eyes. "I'm generally an optimist. I'd rather think on the positive side unless I have a reason to think otherwise."

"What's positive about all this?" she asked, needing something, anything to hang on to.

"It's encouraging to me that she didn't kill you. According to you, you blacked out and you aren't sure how long you were out. She would have had a perfect opportunity to kill you then, but she didn't. I'd rather be chasing a kidnapper than a killer."

He got up from the table and walked over to the coffeemaker. For a big man he moved with an innate grace, as if perfectly comfortable in his own skin. He picked up the coffee carafe and carried it to the table.

"No more for me," she said. He filled his cup, then returned the pot to the machine and once again sat down across from her.

"Your brother doesn't believe my story about Kathy, about anything I said," she said. "He thinks I did something to Lilly." The very idea threatened to squeeze the breath from her lungs.

Once again a small smile raced across his features. "Caleb is the cynic in the family. Half the time he doesn't believe anything I tell him."

"Tell me about the rest of your family." She needed something to take her mind off the ticking of the clock, off the deepening of the night and the fact that her baby girl wasn't in her crib where she belonged.

"I'm the eldest. I'm thirty-six. Jacob is next. He's thirty-four. He's the only one of us who didn't hang around Black Rock. Instead of joining the sheriff's department like all of us did, he became an FBI agent, working out of the Kansas City field office. A little over a month ago he quit his job and came back to Black Rock. He's been staying in a little cottage we have on the ranch property." A deep frown furrowed his forehead and he glanced out the window as if in deep thought.

"You're worried about him," Peyton said softly.

His gaze shot back to her. "Yeah, I guess I am. He hasn't told any of us what brought him home. He refuses to leave the cottage and has become a recluse." He shrugged. "I guess he'll tell us what's going on when the time is right."

"And what about the others? Benjamin seemed very kind."

"Benjamin is the softie of the family. Even when he was a kid he was trying to save the whales, adopt a pet, sponsor a starving child or whatever to help. Besides being a terrific deputy he also runs the family ranch on the northern edge of town."

"And you mentioned a sister?"

This time his smile was full of fond indulgence. "Brittany, she's twenty-four and the baby of the family. She's also a deputy."

"What about your parents? You haven't mentioned them."

"They died six years ago in a private plane crash. They were adventure junkies. The minute we were all old enough to take care of ourselves, they disappeared to one exotic location or another. The end result was that it made us kids closer than most big broods. What about your mother? Where is she now?"

"She died in prison when I was eighteen. I was

thirteen when she was arrested for manufacturing meth. She went to prison and I went into the foster care system. Unfortunately, I wasn't one of their success stories, and when I turned sixteen I ran away."

She couldn't believe she was telling him all this. Usually she was reticent to share the details of her ugly past with anyone. She hadn't even told Rick much about her childhood.

Maybe it was because it was dark and the middle of the night and she was feeling especially vulnerable. Or perhaps it was because his eyes were soft and without judgment and there was a solidness about him that made her think she could tell him anything.

"Sounds like things haven't been easy for you," he said.

She shrugged. "They say what doesn't kill you makes you strong." The darkness that she'd tried to push away all night suddenly slammed into her. An unexpected sob caught in the back of her throat.

"If anything happens to Lilly, it won't make me strong," she exclaimed. "It will kill me, Tom. It will honestly kill me."

As she began to cry once again he stood and pulled her back into his arms. This time his embrace not only felt welcomed, but familiar. She leaned into him, absorbing the strength she instinctively knew he possessed.

If she could just get through this night, then surely Lilly would come home. All she had to do was get through the agonizing long, dark night.

* * *

It was four in the morning when Peyton finally fell into an exhausted sleep in a chair in the living room. Tom considered moving her to her bedroom but was afraid in rousing her she would never go back to sleep, and she needed to sleep.

So did he.

When he was sure she was down for the count, he called Benjamin to come and sit with her so Tom could head home for a couple hours of sleep.

As he waited for Benjamin to arrive, he thought of everything that had been done so far in an effort to find Kathy Simon and the missing baby. Throughout the evening there had been a steady influx of deputies checking in to tell him what had been accomplished.

The sketch and picture of Lilly had gone over the wire services, the AMBER Alert was in effect and everything that could be done was being done. Now it was just a matter of time.

He met Benjamin at the front door and motioned him into the kitchen. "Hopefully she'll sleep for a couple of hours."

Benjamin nodded. "And hopefully in the next couple of hours we'll start getting some phone calls that will lead us to the baby."

"I'm going to catch an hour or two of sleep then head into the office and coordinate things. I'll try to be back here by noon."

"You okay?" Benjamin asked, his brow furrowed with concern. "I know this one must be tough for you."

"No tougher than any other," Tom replied curtly. There was no way he'd admit to his brother that for just a moment, as he'd looked at the photograph of Lilly, he'd remembered another little girl and an unexpected knife had pierced through his heart.

He shoved this thought away as he left Peyton's house and got into his patrol car. A deep weariness gripped him as he drove the short drive home.

He hoped Peyton was right and this Kathy character wouldn't harm the baby, and he hoped that when morning dawned phone calls would start flooding into the office, tips from people who either knew or had seen the woman calling herself Kathy Simon.

Tom's house was a white two-story with a wrap-around porch and hunter green shutters at the windows. It was the second house he'd owned. The first had been sold five years ago after his divorce, when he realized the memories that resided there were too painful to avoid.

He'd bought this particular house for a song because of all the work it needed. He'd thought it would be a terrific project in his spare time, a hobby to keep painful thoughts at bay.

As always when he entered the foyer a faint sense of satisfaction swept over him. The wooden floor gleamed beneath his feet and the throw rug in shades of copper and brown emphasized the beauty of the wood beneath.

He tossed his keys on the small table in the hallway and went directly up the stairs to the master bedroom.

He'd give himself a couple of hours of sleep and then head into the office to see if anything had popped.

It took him only minutes to place his gun and holster on the nightstand and undress and get into bed. Even though he was exhausted, his mind refused to turn off as it replayed the events of the day. He believed Peyton's story of what had happened, but he'd still instructed Sam to run background checks on both Peyton and Rick. The last thing he wanted was for something unexpected to jump up and bite him on the butt.

Every base needed to be covered, and he was certain as he closed his eyes that he'd covered them all. They were a small town, with a small force of law enforcement officers, but Tom was confident in his team. They were all smart and committed to their work.

As sleep began to edge in, his thoughts turned to Peyton. She'd touched him on levels nobody had reached in a very long time. She had to be strong in order to have survived her childhood, and yet there was that frailty about her that made him want to take care of her.

If he were completely honest with himself, he had to acknowledge that as he'd held her in his arms he'd been stunned to realize that although his intent had been to comfort, there had been a part of him, a strictly male part, that had enjoyed the feel of her in his arms.

In fact, he had more than enjoyed it. A quick fire of desire had swept through him as he'd felt the press of her soft breasts against his chest, as he'd smelled the fresh scent of her hair. It had stunned him, first because it was so unexpected and second because it was inappropriate, considering the circumstances.

He drifted asleep with thoughts of her in his head and awoke to his alarm clock ringing two hours later. He rolled over and punched it off, then bounded out of bed, eager to get to the office and find out how things had gone while he'd been sleeping. A sense of urgency chased him. Somewhere out there was a baby who needed to be brought home.

He was in the office by seven-thirty, and Sam greeted him as he walked through the door. Sam McCain was a big, burly black man who had come to Black Rock after working as a policeman in Chicago. He and his wife had moved there for the slower pace and a safer place to raise their kids.

Every day Tom was thankful that Sam had landed here working for him. "Hey, Sam. Please tell me the phone has been ringing off the wall with tips on Lilly Wilkerson's whereabouts."

Sam frowned and shook his head. "We've only had two calls so far this morning, and if you think real hard you'll be able to tell me who they were from."

"Sally Bernard called threatening to kill her husband, and Walt Toliver called to report that Lilly was probably taken into the spaceship that landed in his field last night," Tom replied.

"And the kewpie doll goes to the big fella with the gun on his hip," Sam exclaimed.

Tom grinned. "It wouldn't be a normal day without the two of them calling in." His grin flattened into a frown. "I was really hoping somebody would have seen this Kathy Simon."

"It's early yet, boss. It's possible she's holed up somewhere for the night, but eventually she'll have to get out and around, and somebody will see her."

"Where's Brittany?"

"She hasn't shown up yet," Sam replied.

Tom looked at his watch. She should have been in a half an hour ago. "Has she called in?" Sam shook his head. Tom sighed. "This is the third time in the last couple of weeks that she's been late. Guess I'm going to have to kick some sister butt."

Sam grinned. "Benjamin called earlier to tell you that everything is under control at the Wilkerson house and Caleb is waiting for you in your office."

"As soon as I check a few things here I'll be heading back over there," Tom said as he walked to his office.

Caleb sat in the chair in front of Tom's desk, his big feet propped up on the polished oak. Tom slapped Caleb's legs as he passed by and frowned in disapproval. His younger brother hurriedly straightened up.

"You heard from Brittany this morning?" he asked Caleb as he eased down into the chair at his desk.

"Why would I hear from her?" Caleb asked.

"She's late...again."

"She's probably hung over. She's spending way too much time down at Harley's bar. I think she has a crush on the new bartender there."

"I don't care what she does in her time off, but I can't have her ambling into work whenever she feels like it."

Tom definitely needed to have a stern conversation with his baby sister. "But in the meantime, I'm headed back over to the Wilkerson place to check on Peyton."

Caleb frowned. "Don't you find it odd that nobody saw this woman who supposedly stole her baby? She didn't know where this Kathy lived, doesn't have a picture of the woman and doesn't have any evidence to support that this woman even exists."

"Do you have pictures of your friends?" Tom countered. "Peyton only knew Kathy for two months, a span of time when Peyton wasn't taking her baby out much. Odd? Maybe. But impossible to believe? No."

"I think you should order that new patio ripped up," Caleb said. "I think if you want to find that baby then that's the first place you should look."

"I'll tell you what you're going to do today," Tom said. "According to Peyton, this Kathy Simon has been in town for at least two months. During that time she had to eat, so I want you to spend the day taking a sketch to every grocery store and every restaurant in town and find out who saw her when."

"Sounds like a waste of time," Caleb exclaimed.

"Your time is mine as long as you wear that deputy badge, little brother. Oh, and another thing, apparently Peyton had a run-in with somebody in the parking lot of the grocery store last week. She said the guy was driving a black pickup and had shaggy brown hair. See if you can figure out who that might have been."

"Now, that sounds like a bunch of busy work," Caleb exclaimed.

Tom smiled. "So get out of here and get busy."

As Caleb left, Tom called Sam into his office. "Coordinate with the others and start a door-to-door campaign to find somebody who knew Kathy Simon. I'm headed to the victim's house. Keep me updated on any calls that come in, anything that smells just a little bit like a break."

"Got it," Sam replied and followed Tom out of his office.

"Oh, one more thing. Call Brittany and tell her to get her butt in here, and call the men off the roadblocks. My guess is that Kathy Simon scooted out of town as fast as she could and is probably long gone."

Minutes later, as Tom drove toward Peyton's house, he wondered what condition she'd be in when he arrived. Although he didn't know personally what it was like to have a kidnapped child, he certainly knew personally how to grieve for a child.

His head filled with a vision of a baby face with merry brown eyes and chubby cheeks. Even though it had been five years since he'd lost her, his heart constricted with pain.

Nobody should have to suffer the loss of a child, and he certainly didn't want Peyton to know that kind of pain. She was hurting now, but if her baby wasn't returned to her and all hope was lost, she would be cast into a hollow darkness that Tom knew too well.

But he couldn't think about his own loss. He needed to focus on making sure that everything was being done to bring baby Lilly home. He also needed to decide if the FBI needed to be called in. At the moment, his plan was to give himself and his deputies twenty-four more hours to find Kathy Simon. If they didn't succeed, then they would have to proceed under the assumption that Kathy Simon had crossed state lines with the kidnapped infant.

Rick's car was back in Peyton's driveway as Tom parked at the curb. Benjamin's car was also still there. It was Benjamin who opened the door to his knock. He looked tired.

"Heard anything?" he asked Tom.

"Nothing. How are things here?"

"A bit tense. She didn't sleep much, hasn't eaten at all. Rick showed up about an hour ago and they're in the kitchen now."

Tom clapped his brother on the shoulder. "Go home. Get some sleep."

As Benjamin headed out the door Tom walked toward the kitchen where the murmurs of Peyton and Rick's voices drifted out.

"Tom!" Peyton jumped up from the table as he entered the room, looking relieved to see him.

"I hope you've brought us some news," Rick said. He started to rise as well, but Tom motioned him back into his chair.

"Unfortunately, I don't have news," Tom said, hating the way the hopeful expression on Peyton's face fell away. "The roadblocks on either end of town yielded nothing."

"She had plenty of time to get out of town before you

put those roadblocks into effect," Rick replied. "Peyton isn't even sure how long she was unconscious. She might have had as much as a half an hour head start before Peyton called for help."

"I'm aware of that," Tom replied. He leaned against the kitchen counter and tried not to notice how Peyton's jeans hugged the long length of her legs, how the blue T-shirt she wore perfectly matched her eyes and molded to the full breasts that had been against his chest the night before.

He focused his attention on Rick. "We're starting door-to-door canvassing this morning, hoping somebody knows something about Kathy Simon. She was in town for at least two months. She had to be living somewhere, and if we can find out where that was, then maybe we can get some clue as to where she might have gone."

Rick nodded. He looked tired, as if the night had been unkind to him and sleep had not come easy. "I just hope we get her back today. I hate to leave here without everything being resolved."

Tom focused again on Peyton. "How are you holding up?" His heart squeezed in his chest as he saw the dark smudges beneath her eyes, the lines of strain on either side of her mouth.

"I'm okay." She lifted her chin, but the defiant gesture only added to her fragile appearance.

"I'd like to hand out some flyers," Rick said. "I'll go stir crazy if I have to sit around here all day."

"If you go to the sheriff's office on Main, my deputy

Sam McCain can give you some flyers to pass out," Tom said.

Rick cast Peyton a worried look. "You'll be okay if I leave?"

"Of course." She sat back down at the table and curled her slender fingers around a mug of coffee.

"Have you eaten anything?" Tom asked Peyton the minute Rick had left the house.

She waved a hand in dismissal. "I'm not hungry."

"You have to eat," Tom said firmly. "You're running on nothing but nerves and energy, and that will make you sick." He went to the refrigerator and pulled out a package of bacon and a carton of eggs. "Now point to where you keep your skillet." She pointed to a lower cabinet and Tom got to work.

"I've racked my brain trying to think of something Kathy might have said to me about her past, but I can't think of anything concrete. I just feel like with every minute that passes Lilly gets farther away from me."

Tom searched for a response that would give her hope but wouldn't sound like a meaningless platitude. He continued to search for positive things to say to her as the day wore on and little news came in.

What bothered Tom most was that Kathy Simon had seemingly managed to drift around town for the last two months like a ghost, with nobody seeing her and nobody interacting with her.

Except Peyton.

And as the day wore on Peyton's emotions grew more raw, more difficult for Tom to witness.

As evening approached, Rick returned to the house to check in before he headed back to Wichita.

"We have flyers up all over town," Rick said as he raked a hand through his hair. "Surely somebody who sees them will know something and come forward."

"God, I hope so," Peyton exclaimed.

"As much as I hate to leave, I've got to get back to Wichita," Rick said, his gaze going first to Peyton and then to Tom. "I'm sorry. I don't know what else to do."

"Go, Rick. There's nothing more you can do for now," Peyton replied.

"You'll call me with any news?" he asked Tom.

"Absolutely."

With a nod to Tom, Rick left the house.

When he left, Peyton turned to Tom, her eyes filled with an agony he felt in his own chest.

"I can't believe it's going to be night again and we're no closer to finding her than we were last night." She stuffed the back of her hand against her mouth as if to keep a sob from escaping.

Tom wanted to take her into his arms but didn't, perhaps because he wanted too badly to hold her once again. Instead, at that moment his cell phone rang.

"Sheriff Grayson," he answered.

"Tom, it's Jack Warner. The missus and me just got back from spending a couple of days with our boy in Kansas City. I just saw one of those flyers you're circulating around town. You know that garage apartment I rent behind my house? Well, I believe the woman you're looking for is renting it, except she rented it by the name of Sarah Johnson. She's been here about two months. Her car is there now if you want to get over here."

Tom's heartbeat kicked up a thousand notches. "You sure it's the same woman?"

"If it's not, then it's her twin."

"Thanks, Jack. Do me a favor, stay away from the apartment and I'll be right there." He hung up and looked at Peyton, who was staring at him with a glimmer of hope shining from her eyes.

"I think we might have an address for Kathy Simon," he said.

She was out of the chair and at the door to the kitchen before the words had completely left his mouth. "Let's go."

He hesitated. He wasn't sure why, but he had a bad feeling. "I think it would be best if you stay here."

"Yeah, right." Without waiting for his reply, she headed for the front door.

As Tom followed behind her he hoped that his bad feeling was nothing more than heartburn.

Chapter 4

The thrum of excitement that filled Peyton was almost as sickening as the helpless, hopeless feeling that had been with her all day long.

"Four years ago, Jack Warner and his wife renovated their detached garage and made it into a small studio apartment," Tom said. "Their son rented it from them until he got married and moved into his own house, and since then they've rented it out to whoever needed it. Jack told me a woman by the name of Sarah Johnson rented it and has been living there for the past two months. He said Sarah Johnson looks exactly like the woman on our flyers."

"So, she used a fake name to rent the place. Surely we'll find something there that will give us a clue to her real identity," Peyton said. "A fingerprint or maybe something she left behind." Excitement roared through her. "We're a step closer, Tom. We're a step closer to having Lilly back where she belongs."

He frowned, and with that gesture some of Peyton's excitement waned. "What's wrong?" she asked. "What is it you aren't telling me?"

"Jack said her car is parked out front. I'm trying to figure out why a woman who snatched a baby didn't take her car when she left town."

A faint disquiet swept through Peyton. "Maybe she was afraid we'd find out about the car and could broadcast the license plate information with the AMBER Alert?"

"Maybe, but then the question becomes how did she leave town? There's no bus service in Black Rock, no airport or train station."

"Maybe she didn't leave town. Maybe she's crazy enough to think that she could steal my baby and stay in that garage apartment and nobody would know." Even as Peyton said the words, she didn't believe them.

It didn't make sense. But then nothing had made sense since the moment Kathy had attacked her in the bathroom.

"She'd be stupid to hang around here," Tom replied. "And a woman who was able to so thoroughly manipulate you and plan Lilly's kidnapping wouldn't be stupid enough to hang around town."

"So, she'd have to have an accomplice, somebody working with her." The idea that there might be two people who had wanted her baby was almost as frightening as anything else that had happened so far.

"Maybe a husband or a boyfriend," Tom said.

"How could a man allow himself to be a party to such a crime?" she asked.

Tom shot her a quick glance as he turned off Main Street and onto a tree-studded residential road. "My brothers and I call that crazy love."

"Crazy love?"

He nodded. "You see it in the headlines all the time. A woman who helps her husband kidnap women for his sexual pleasure. She does it because she loves him. Or a man who might help his wife run a credit card scam because he loves her too much to tell her no."

"That's not crazy love. That's two crazy people thinking what they feel is love," she replied.

"You wouldn't break the law for a man you loved?" he asked.

A nervous laugh escaped her. "I'd never be with a man who would ask me to break the law," she replied.

"That's good to know," he replied.

Every muscle in her body tensed as Tom pulled the car to the curb in front of a neat ranch house. An older man sat on a wicker chair on the front porch and rose to his feet at the sight of them.

Tom unfastened his seat belt and then turned and looked at her. "Peyton, I need you to stay in the car until I assess the scene. I don't want to put you in danger, and I certainly don't want to put your baby in danger if she's somewhere on the property."

Although she desperately wanted to be beside him when he went into the apartment, she reluctantly nodded her head. The last thing she would want to do was put Lilly at any greater risk.

"I don't want to make things more difficult for you." She placed a hand on his forearm. "But, if Lilly's in there and you get to her, you'll bring her right to me, yes?" Her heart beat loudly in her ears and she felt half-breathless with anxiety.

"Of course, but you know, Peyton, the likelihood of them being here is pretty low."

She squeezed his arm. "Just go find something, Tom. Find something that will get my baby back in my arms." She released her hold on him and watched as he got out of the car and met the man she assumed was Jack Warner in the middle of the front yard. She quickly rolled down her window so she could hear the conversation taking place between the two.

"She was no trouble at all," Jack said to Tom. "Paid the rent in cash on time and kept to herself. I never saw anyone here visiting her."

"Did you have her fill out a background form before renting to her?"

Jack laughed and shook his head. "Now, Tom, you know that's not how we do things here in Black Rock. She seemed like a nice young woman and she had the cash in hand. She told us she wanted a fresh start and had fallen in love with Black Rock. That was good enough for me and Martha."

"Did she mention where she was from?"

Jack frowned. "I don't believe it came up." As the two men began to walk around the side of the house, their voices were lost to Peyton.

She unfastened her seat belt and tried to still the frantic pounding of her heart. Even though she knew it was completely irrational, she hoped and prayed that Tom would open up that apartment door and Kathy would be sitting on her sofa with Lilly on her lap.

Closing her eyes, she imagined Lilly in her mind. Her head filled with the sweet baby scent of her daughter, and a vision of Lilly's toothless smile nearly made her cry out loud.

She felt as if she'd been so strong, had tried so hard to keep it all together, but at the moment she felt as if the smallest thing could shatter her completely apart.

All she could do was pray that wherever Lilly was, she was safe and with somebody who was loving her and taking care of her until the time she was back in Peyton's arms.

One thing was certain. She was grateful for Tom. His calm, steady presence through all of this was part of what had kept her sane. All she had to do was look in his dark brown eyes and she felt the calm soothing her rising hysteria.

The hours spent with Rick had only reconfirmed the fact that they hadn't been right for each other. Although he'd tried to be supportive in his own way and she knew he was hurting, too, she'd almost been grateful when he'd gone back to Wichita.

It wasn't lost on Peyton that she'd found comfort

in Tom's arms and not in Lilly's father's arms. On some level it surprised her to realize that she felt more comfortable with the handsome sheriff than she had in all the months of her relationship with Rick.

Rick was self-contained, rarely showing any deep emotion. He was a bundle of suppressed energy. All qualities that she knew made him a wonderful assistant district attorney but didn't bode well for personal relationships.

Tom was different. She sensed a tremendous capacity for love in him. It shone from his eyes when he spoke of his family, and it had radiated from his very being when he'd held her in his arms.

She sighed with impatience. She knew what she was doing—thinking of anything and everything except what might be taking place in the apartment where Kathy Simon had lived.

What was taking so long? Why hadn't Tom come out to tell her what he'd found? With each agonizing minute that ticked by, it became more apparent to her that Lilly wasn't inside the apartment.

Something was wrong. She felt it in the sudden weight of her heart in her chest. Something was wrong and she needed to know what it was, what was happening. She needed to know right now.

Even though she'd told Tom she'd remain in the car and stay out of his way, the need to get out of the car and go to the garage apartment was stronger than her half-hearted commitment to Tom to stay in the car.

She opened the car door and got out, a terrible

foreboding washing over her. It was taking too long. Something just wasn't right.

As she began to walk toward the side of the house where Tom and Jack had disappeared, she felt as if her feet were weighed down by the inexplicable dread that coursed through her.

When she reached the side of the house, the detached garage came into view. Two things caused a screaming alarm to go off in her head. The first was Jack Warner seated on the grass next to the building with his hands over his face. The second was Tom standing off to one side talking frantically into his cell phone.

Tom's features were taut with tension, and that tension electrified Peyton. A screaming protest came from her. Then she whispered, "No." Suddenly she was running, deep sobs welling up inside her as she raced for the open front door.

"Peyton, wait! Don't go in there," Tom exclaimed.

She ignored him. She ran into the front door and stopped short as a deep moan escaped her. On the floor just inside the door was Kathy Simon. Dead.

The young woman was sprawled on her back like a broken doll. Her blue eyes were wide open and staring up as if in surprise. Her hair was no longer long and red but instead was cut short and dyed black. Still, there was no question it was Kathy.

A large knife protruded from her chest.

"Oh, God. Oh, God," Peyton gasped. "Lilly!" The name ripped from the depths of her being as she nearly fell to her knees.

"Peyton." Tom gripped her firmly by one arm. "She's not here. Listen to me, Peyton. I promise you Lilly isn't here. You need to come outside now. This is an active crime scene."

She stared up at him with incomprehension but allowed him to lead her back outside, where she drew several deep, steadying breaths. "I don't understand. Who would do this? What's going on? And where is my baby, Tom?"

"I don't know, Peyton," he replied.

For the first time since Lilly had disappeared, Peyton faced the possibility that she might never see her daughter again.

Tom stepped outside the garage apartment and drew a deep, weary sigh. It was just after midnight and the scene had been processed. Kathy's body had been taken away to be looked at more thoroughly by the local medical examiner.

Peyton had left the scene hours earlier. Benjamin had taken her home and was staying with her so Tom could sort things out there.

The medical examiner had tentatively determined that death had probably occurred sometime the evening before. Cause of death had been the single deep stab wound to the chest.

Tom now not only had the job of finding Lilly but also of solving a murder. The only sign that Lilly had been in the studio apartment at all was a tiny pink bootie he'd found next to the sofa.

He drew in a deep breath of the hot night air as his brain worked overtime to try to make sense of everything. Why would somebody murder a kidnapper? And where had Lilly been taken?

Caleb stepped outside and joined Tom. "We found her purse in the closet. She's got a driver's license in the name of Kathy Simon and another in the name of Sarah Johnson. To my eyes they both look like very good fakes."

Tom frowned. "We'll run her fingerprints through the AFIS system and see if anything pops." He knew it could take anywhere from twenty-four to forty-eight hours for the Automated Fingerprint Identification System to make a match and that was only if she'd been arrested or had her fingerprints taken in the past.

"Maybe with a real identification it will be easier to make sense of all this," Caleb said. "I'm glad you didn't rip up Peyton's patio looking for a body. Guess I was off base where she's concerned."

Tom clapped a hand on his brother's shoulder. "You were right to be suspicious of Peyton's story." He dropped his arm back to his side. "What a mess."

"I hate to add to the mess, but nobody's heard from Brittany all day," Caleb said. "I drove by her place on my way here, and her car is gone."

"God, I hope she hasn't gone and done something stupid." Tom released another deep sigh. "I suppose she'll eventually call one of us." He would be more concerned if Brittany hadn't done this before.

Brittany was only eighteen when their parents had

died, and despite the support of her brothers, she'd taken the deaths hard.

Tom had been thrilled when she'd decided to follow her brothers' footsteps and make her career law enforcement. She was not only beautiful, but she was also exceptionally bright and had become a valuable team player in the Black Rock Sheriff's Department. Unfortunately, far too often her personal life interfered with her professional one.

"I'm going to have to talk to her. I can't let her just disappear every time she gets a new boyfriend or feels like she needs some time alone. If she's going to work for me, then I have to know I can depend on her," Tom said.

"Don't be too hard on her. She's just having trouble growing up," Caleb replied.

"In the meantime, I've got a murder to solve and a baby to find," Tom replied. His thoughts turned to Peyton. She had to be hysterical over this latest turn of events.

He wished he had the time to go over to her house, to somehow find the right words to assuage her fears, but he didn't. He didn't have the right words and he didn't have the time.

He and his deputies needed to go over the crime scene again and canvass the neighborhood to see if anyone had seen anything related to the murder.

Besides, it bothered him that he wanted to be there for her, that all he could think about was how badly she needed to be held right now.

It had been a very long time since he'd had any interest in a woman. Five years earlier, his heart had been ripped out of his chest and he'd thought the wound was fatal, that he'd never feel anything for another woman again.

Peyton was the first woman since the tragedy to make him feel again, and he didn't like it. The last thing he wanted was to get close to a woman, to fall in love again.

He raked a hand down his face, inwardly cursing his own foolishness. The only interest Peyton had in him was as a lawman who could bring her baby home. But he couldn't do that until they got an ID on the dead woman in Jack Warner's apartment.

They worked through the night. The fingerprints lifted were sent to a lab in Topeka, along with any other forensic evidence they'd collected. Black Rock was far too small to have anything resembling a crime lab, so they used the lab in Topeka.

Sam was dispatched to physically drive the evidence to Topeka, although the fingerprints were already being run through the AFIS. Neighbors were contacted and statements were taken, but nobody had seen anything that might give a clue to the killer.

The evidence pointed to Kathy Simon opening her door to her killer. There was no sign of forced entry at any of the doors or windows.

Tom could only speculate on why Kathy had stayed in town, and his theory was that somebody—a partner— had met her there and she had planned to leave with that person. Not only had her hair been cut and dyed, but a suitcase containing all of her clothes had been packed and was waiting in the closet.

She'd been ready to run, but why had she waited so long? Waiting for her accomplice to show up? There was no way to know if that accomplice was male or female. Was it somebody from Kathy's life before she moved here or somebody here in town?

He hated to think that it was somebody in his town, a friend or neighbor who smiled at him or raised a hand in greeting but secretly had the capacity for kidnapping and murder.

It was after six in the morning when Tom finally headed to Peyton's place. He wished he had something to give her, but he had nothing. His men were out canvassing the streets, the evidence was on its way to the lab and so far there had been nothing from the AFIS.

He'd sent photos of the victim to all the news sources hoping that somebody would see the photo on the news and be able to make an official identification.

It was a waiting game…waiting for the physical evidence to turn up something, waiting to see if her fingerprints would identify her. Until they knew her real name, he had no idea in what direction to take the investigation.

As he parked in Peyton's driveway, the sun appeared in the eastern sky, promising another hot, clear day. He was exhausted but felt he owed it to Peyton to stop by and check in with her.

Wearily he pulled himself out of his car, wishing he

had something to tell Peyton that would bring a smile to her face, irritated with himself by how badly he wanted to see a smile from her.

When he reached the front door he knocked softly and Benjamin answered. "How's she doing?" Tom asked as he stepped into the small foyer.

"She napped on and off during the night. She's been real quiet, very self-contained." Benjamin frowned. "And I'm assuming there's nothing new."

"Nothing," Tom replied. "Hopefully by the end of the day we'll have a good identification and can go from there. Where is Peyton now?"

"She's in the nursery."

"Go home, get some sleep, I might need you later today," Tom said.

Benjamin nodded and Tom clapped him on the shoulder. "I'll talk to you later," Tom said.

He stood at the door and watched as Benjamin got into his car and drove off, wishing he could go in and tell Peyton something positive, but he had nothing to offer her. As he went down the hallway toward the nursery, the silence of the house pressed in around him. He summoned what strength he had left to face Peyton.

He stepped into the doorway of the nursery and found her sitting in a rocking chair facing the window. She wasn't aware of his presence, and for a moment he merely stood, his breath stuck in his chest as he looked at her.

The morning sun caught in her hair and sparkled with a thousand pinpoints of light. There was no question that something about this woman resonated deep inside him. It wasn't just her physical beauty that fired through him, that was a given.

It was more than that. It was a need to right her world, a desire to be a hero for her. It was like nothing he'd felt before, and it scared him more than just a little bit.

"Peyton." He spoke her name softly, not wanting to startle her.

She swiveled the rocker around to face him, and his heart nearly broke. She clutched to her chest a pink teddy bear and her tired eyes held all the sorrow of the universe.

"Nothing?" she said, her voice a mere whisper as she motioned him into an overstuffed chair in the corner.

"We're working on getting an identification from her fingerprints. Once we know who she is and where she's from we'll be much closer to finding Lilly." He sat in the chair, wishing he had more for her.

She rocked for a moment, the chair squeaking slightly with each back-and-forth motion. "Despite what she did, she didn't deserve to die that way," she finally said. She stopped rocking and her eyes were midnight-blue as she looked at him. "It was awful. I can't get the imagine of her on the floor out of my head."

"I know. I'm sorry you saw it," he replied.

"You look exhausted. You shouldn't be here. You should be home getting some sleep," she said.

"I didn't want to go home before stopping by here to talk to you," he replied.

She turned and looked back out the window, the

rocking chair once again creaking with her movement. His eyes felt gritty with lack of sleep, and the longer he sat in the chair the heavier his body became.

This felt familiar, this intense desire to fix things, to somehow make sense of tragedy, the need to comfort a woman's pain.

"I had a child once." The words fell out of his mouth before he'd realized they were even in his thoughts. She turned once again to look at him, a quizzical and cautious look in her eyes.

"You said *had*," she said softly.

He nodded. "Her name was Kelly. My wife used to like to call her Kelly belly." Emotion pressed tight against his chest. He hadn't intended to talk about this, had spent the last five years of his life trying not to think about it. "She was two when we lost her."

He stared past her and out the window, but in his mind's eye he saw a chubby little girl with laughing brown eyes and tousled dark curls. The pain he'd once felt when thinking about Kelly wasn't as sharp as it had been, although he would always ache for the child he'd lost.

"What happened?" Peyton's voice pulled him back to the present.

"I was at work when it happened. My wife, Julie, had taken Kelly out in the front yard to play. Kelly was already a handful. She never talked if she could sing, never walked if she could run." He felt the smile that curved his lips for just a moment and then felt it fall away.

"It happened in the split second of a heartbeat," he continued. "Julie looked away, Kelly took off running and the driver in the car coming down the street never saw her."

He heard Peyton's gasp and he smiled and shook his head. "She died instantly. Six months later, Julie left me. She couldn't forgive herself even though I told her there was nothing to forgive, that it had been a tragic accident. But she told me she couldn't look at me, that it was just too painful for her to be with me, and so we divorced."

"Oh, Tom, I'm so sorry." She got up from the rocking chair and placed the teddy bear in the crib.

He knew he should stand and go home, but the weariness that suddenly swept over him made any movement near impossible. "I didn't tell you this to make you feel sorry for me," he said as she walked closer to where he sat. "I just wanted you to know that I know what it's like to miss a child."

To his surprise she sat on his lap, curled her arms around his neck and laid her head on his chest. He wrapped his arms around her and held tight.

There was nothing sexual in the embrace—they were simply two parents grieving for what might be and what would never be.

With the sweet scent of her hair in his head and the warmth of her arms around his neck, Tom closed his eyes and prayed that she would never know the finality of loss that he experienced every day of his life.

Chapter 5

"**I**ndia Richards," Tom said to Peyton that evening. He'd left her place that morning and had gone home to get some much-needed sleep and arrived back at her house a few minutes after five. "Does that name ring a bell?"

Peyton shook her head. "That's who she was?" She motioned him onto the sofa, glad to see he looked rested.

Even with the drama and uncertainty in her life at the moment, she wasn't oblivious to the fact that there was something crazy between them, a connection on some level she'd never felt before with another person.

"Not only that, but she had a rap sheet as long as my arm," he said as he eased down on the sofa cushion.

"Seriously?" Peyton sat in the chair facing him and

remembered how his arms had felt around her that morning, how somehow their pain had mingled together and become more tolerable.

"Nothing violent. Three years ago she was charged with shoplifting and petty theft in Kansas City, also a prostitution charge there. She got off on probation each time, then apparently moved to Wichita and two years ago was charged with shoplifting once again."

"Wichita. So she might have seen me and Lilly there, possibly followed us here to Black Rock." The thought of being singled out and stalked sent a chill up Peyton's spine. "Do you know where she lived in Wichita?"

"Last known address was on Grand Road."

Peyton frowned. "That's clear on the other side of town, miles from where I lived."

"Maybe she saw you in a grocery store. Maybe you shared the same hairdresser or dental office. You could have run into her in a million places and not known it. Now that we know her name, we're working with the authorities in Wichita to find out everything we can about her. Hopefully they can tell us who she associated with and from there we can figure out who might have had reason to kill her. In the meantime, news agencies are requesting anyone with information regarding India to contact my office or the authorities in Wichita. I've also sent Caleb to Wichita to do some investigating."

"So hopefully somebody will come forward with information that will lead us to Lilly," she said.

"That's what we want, Peyton. That's what everyone wants. Have you heard from Rick?"

She nodded. "He's been calling about every two hours to see if there's any progress. He's worried sick."

"He should be here with you," Tom replied.

She heard the faint edge of scorn in his voice and smiled. "To be perfectly honest, he wanted to drive out, but I discouraged him. There's nothing he can do here but pace my living room floor and make me even more on edge than I already am. I don't need him here."

It was a bit unsettling for her to realize she'd known Tom for less than a week and yet he was the one she wanted to be with her, to support her.

She knew better than to trust her feelings where Tom was concerned. She was certain that it was the situation that had her feeling so close to him. After all, he was the man she was depending on to bring her baby home. The fact that he'd told her about his wife and baby girl had made her feel even closer to him.

"Do you want some coffee or something?" she asked. She got up from the chair, needing to do something to take her mind off her growing feelings for a man she barely knew and the ticking of the clock racing down to another night without Lilly in her arms.

"Coffee would be good," he agreed.

He followed her into the kitchen, where she busied herself making the coffee while he sat at the table. She'd been so strong through the day, but as the sun dipped in the western skies anxiety and grief began to build inside her. Like a scream waiting to be released.

She poured the coffee and joined him at the table.

"Now our goal is to try to retrace India's footsteps

before this all occurred. There's obviously somebody else involved in the kidnapping," Tom said. He took a sip of his coffee and eyed her over the rim of the cup. "Are you sure there's nobody else from your past that might want to hurt you? Did you date anyone before Rick? Somebody who might not have been happy that you hooked up with Rick and had a baby?"

"I only dated one other man before Rick. He was a waiter at one of the restaurants I worked at. We dated off and on for two years, then I met Rick."

"What's his name?"

"Cliff Gunther, but I can't imagine him having anything to do with this," she protested, then frowned. "But, I also couldn't imagine Kathy doing anything like this."

"When was the last time you saw him?" he asked.

"Just before I moved here. I went to visit him at the restaurant where he worked and told him I was moving."

"What restaurant?" Tom asked.

"Henry's Italian Cuisine in Wichita."

At that moment Tom's phone rang.

Peyton immediately felt the tension that wafted off him. He shot her a glance, then rose from the table and carried the phone into the living room. She stared after him, fear piercing through her. Who was he talking to, and why had he felt the need to leave the room? *Don't let it be something terrible about Lilly,* she prayed.

Her heart thundered in her chest painfully fast, and for a moment she couldn't breathe. *Had somebody found*

Lilly? Had something bad happened? Was Lilly dead?
The thoughts crashed through her brain, the kind of
thoughts that no mother should ever have in her head.
She only breathed again when Tom stepped back into
the kitchen. "What is it? Has something happened?"
she asked.

"I've got to leave," he replied, his features without
expression.

Peyton jumped up from her chair. "Tom, what's
happened?" The scream she'd been fighting against
for the past two days rose up in the back of her throat.
"Is Lilly dead?" The dreadful words yanked out of the
very depths of her.

"No. No!" He grabbed her by the shoulders. "That's
not what the phone call was about."

"Then what?" She stepped away from him. "I know
it was about the case. You have to tell me."

He hesitated, the frown once again digging into his
forehead. "We got a tip from a woman who says her
neighbors have a new infant. They told the neighbor
it's an adopted baby, but the neighbor is suspicious. The
couple lives in Laville, a little town about thirty minutes
north of here."

"And you're going there to check it out?" she asked.
"Then I'm coming with you," she said as he nodded.

"Peyton, this could very well be a wild-goose chase,"
he protested. "It could be nothing more than a waste of
time."

"I have plenty of time to waste," she replied. There
was no way she wasn't going to be in that car with him

when he went to check it out. "Please don't fight with me, Tom. I can either ride with you in your car or I'll be following behind you in mine, but one way or another, I'm going along."

"I don't want you getting your hopes up," he said moments later as he backed out of her driveway. She'd brought along Lilly's car seat, which was now buckled into the back of the patrol car. "It's possible we're going to get a lot of tips that are going to be without merit."

"And I'll be hopeful with each tip that comes in," she replied. "I don't know how to be anything else."

They drove for a few minutes in silence. Even though Peyton knew he was right, that she was a fool to get her hopes up, she couldn't help the wild hope that filled her at the possibility that they could be driving to a sweet reunion with her baby.

She had to continue to believe that Lilly was going to be returned to her safe and sound. Any other thought was too horrible to consider.

"You're the strongest woman I've ever met," he said, breaking the silence. "No matter what happens, I want you to know that I admire the way you've handled yourself through all this."

"Blame it on my childhood. Surviving that took a healthy dose of strength." She stared out the side window, infused with painful memories of her past. "It's ironic. My mother did everything wrong to assure that I would survive my youth. I've tried to do everything right, and look where we are."

"You can't blame yourself for what's happened with Lilly."

"I don't." It was true. Peyton didn't blame herself. "I trusted a woman I thought was a friend. I had no way of knowing she wasn't who she presented herself to be. If I blame myself for that then I'll never trust anyone in my life again."

"And that would be the real tragedy in all this," he replied.

"Why haven't you remarried, Tom?" she asked. She couldn't imagine that it had been for lack of female interest.

He was hot, and more than that he seemed to be kind and sensitive. He was the total package, and she couldn't believe that all the single women in Black Rock hadn't noticed.

"Just not interested," he replied. "Until the accident it was pretty good. Sure, Julie and I had some issues, no marriage is perfect, but for the most part it was all pretty good. I just don't want to do it again. It's as simple as that."

"So, you don't believe in second chances at happiness?"

He shot her a quick glance. "I can be happy and single. Besides, I've got a big family, it's not like I'll ever be lonely." He turned off the main highway and onto a county road.

"I want to be married," she replied. "I feel like I've been alone all my life and I can't wait to find that special man to share the rest of my life with me."

They fell silent once again, and the rise of anxiety pressed tight against Peyton's chest. She needed Lilly. She couldn't imagine having to spend the rest of her life with the kind of grief that Tom lived with, with the ache of a child lost forever.

As they got closer to the address Tom had been given, he felt Peyton's hope fill the car, and he was sorry she was with him, afraid that if the infant wasn't Lilly then the composure that Peyton had maintained for so long would finally crack.

He'd been a fool to let her come along. He shouldn't have told her what the phone call had been about. This wasn't just about finding out if Lilly was there; it was possible they were going to the home of India's murderer. Having Peyton along with him was not only unprofessional, but it could also be dangerous.

He glanced over where she stared out the window. There was no question that he found her more attractive than he'd found any woman in years. Her blond hair fell to her shoulders in a soft wave, and even the worry that furrowed her brow couldn't diminish her beauty.

He was compromising his professional ethics by allowing her to be with him and wondered why he was having such a problem keeping his personal feelings out of this case.

He'd always found it easy to maintain a professional distance, an emotional detachment on the cases he worked as sheriff. In the years he'd been in charge he'd had to occasionally arrest people he thought of as friends, he'd had to investigate neighbors and never had he allowed his personal feelings about the matter get in the way of his duty.

Maybe it was because this case was about Lilly. Maybe it was impossible to separate himself from Peyton's emotions because in many ways they were so close to his own.

He tightened his grip on the steering wheel as he turned down a dirt road that would take him to the farmhouse they sought.

He was familiar with the area, as it was part of his jurisdiction, although he didn't know the people who lived in the particular house where they were going.

"Peyton, you have to wait in the car while I check it out," he said. "That's not a suggestion, it's a command. You can't forget that somebody murdered India and we don't know if one of the people in this farmhouse is responsible for her death. I need you to stay in the car to assure your own personal safety, but more importantly it might assure Lilly's personal safety if she's in there."

She looked at him with her amazing blue eyes and offered him a nervous half smile. "I won't do anything to jeopardize Lilly's safety. As difficult as it will be for me, I'll wait in the car until you tell me to get out."

He nodded. "I appreciate your cooperation."

She released a small sigh. "I want it to be her so badly I feel sick."

He fought the impulse to reach over and cover her hand with his. Somehow he had to stop wanting to touch her all the time. Eventually this case would end, hopefully with a happy ending, and she could move on with her life and find a man who wanted to marry and spend forever with her.

He definitely wasn't that man.

He pulled to the side of the road and shut off the engine. "What are you doing?" Peyton asked.

"Benjamin is meeting me here. I didn't want to go in without backup," he replied. He could tell that this information frightened her.

She needed to be frightened. There was no assurance that there wasn't danger in coming here.

By the time Benjamin pulled up behind them, Tom wasn't sure whether it was her tension that filled the car or his own.

He got out of the car and met his brother, who had gotten out of his own vehicle. "This might be nothing but a wild-goose chase," he said to Benjamin. "Maybe a neighbor with a beef blowing a whistle on an innocent set of new adoptive parents."

Benjamin flashed Tom a tight smile. "Won't be the first wild-goose chase we've shared."

"Be ready for anything. I don't know what we're walking into. Somebody put a six-inch blade into India Richards's heart and it's possible that somebody is in that house."

Benjamin nodded. "You watch my back, I'll watch yours."

"Then let's do it," Tom said and got back into his car. He turned and looked at Peyton, whose eyes radiated electric blue with anxiety.

"Promise me you won't move from the car until I come out to you."

"I promise," she said, her eyes shining earnestly. "Just hurry and tell me if she's in there or not."

With her promise ringing in his ear, Tom started the car and turned into the long driveway that led to the house.

It was a small home, and the deepening shadows of twilight couldn't hide the look of neglect that clung to the place. Still, lights spilled from the front window and a beat-up pickup was parked in the front.

Tom parked and cut the engine and without another word to Peyton got out of the car. As he approached the front door he hoped like hell he'd find inside the one thing that would erase the pain from Peyton's eyes.

Chapter 6

Peyton's heart was in her throat as she sat and stared at the house Tom and Benjamin had just disappeared inside of.

A young woman who had looked at Tom and Benjamin in surprise had opened the door. A thin young man had appeared at her side, then the two lawmen had gone into the house and Peyton hadn't been able to see anything else.

This whole thing felt wrong. What would that young couple have to do with a kidnapping, with a murder? They looked like teenagers. Why would they want to steal her baby?

She rubbed a hand across her forehead where a headache squeezed like a tight band. She leaned her head toward the open car window and drew in a deep breath of the warm night air.

She could hear nothing from the house. What was going on inside? Surely if Lilly were in there Tom would have already come out to get her.

Tom had said this was just the first of the tips to come in. Peyton had seen enough missing-children newscasts to realize that often in these cases thousands of tips came in from all over the country. The child was spotted in California or in Texas or in Florida, often all at the same time.

It could take weeks or even months to chase down all the leads this case might generate. Weeks and months that she wouldn't have sweet Lilly.

Hot tears burned her eyes as a well of grief threatened to consume her. The inner scream begged to be released, but she swallowed hard against it.

Lilly was at that stage of development where she changed almost every day. Peyton would be missing some of the most precious moments in her daughter's life.

She squeezed her eyelids closed and for the first time wondered if she would ever have Lilly back in her arms. How would she get through the rest of her life if they never found her baby?

How did Tom get up mornings without his little girl? How did any parent who had lost a child survive the grief?

She had to stay strong. She refused to break now. Right now all she knew was that Lilly was out there somewhere and hopefully would be found alive and well.

The minutes ticked by and twilight was replaced by the darkness of encroaching night. A glance at the clock let her know that Tom had only been in the house fifteen minutes, but if felt like hours had passed since he'd disappeared inside.

She felt as if in the space of seconds passing she'd transformed into a very old woman, with nothing but grief to keep her company.

The opening of the front door snapped her eyes back open and she looked toward the house to see Tom's silhouette as he approached the car.

He was halfway across the yard when she realized he was carrying something in his arms. Peyton froze and for a moment it felt as if her heart had stopped beating.

She heard the distinctive sound of a fussing baby, her baby. "Lilly?" The name whispered from her. She threw open the car door and sprang out, nearly tripping in the grass as she ran toward Tom.

"Lilly!" Tears half blurred her vision as she met him and he held out the infant.

Her baby! Oh, God, it was Lilly.

The deep sobs that Peyton had held in for so long ripped from her as she took Lilly from him and clutched the baby to her chest. She was laughing and crying at the same time as Tom grabbed her by the elbow and took her back to the car.

"I've got things to finish up inside. I'll be back in a

few minutes and we'll get the two of you home where you belong," Tom said. "I'll have a doctor come to check her out, but she seems okay."

She nodded absently, barely hearing him as she focused all her attention on her baby. Happy tears escaped her as Lilly smiled up at her.

The baby was wrapped in a pink blanket and Peyton quickly unwrapped her, needing to check her from head to toe to assure herself that Lilly was really okay.

She was clad in a pink T-shirt and a diaper and she smelled sweet and clean. It was obvious she'd been well taken care of, and for that Peyton was grateful.

At the moment Peyton didn't care how Lilly had come to be here and what the people inside the house had to do with India Richards. All she cared about was the baby in her arms, her beloved Lilly.

"Mommy missed you," she whispered as she held Lilly tight. She kissed her cheeks, her eyelids and forehead. She kissed Lilly's little toes as her heart sang. "Mommy missed you so very much." Lilly cuddled against her and within minutes had fallen asleep.

Peyton felt as if the world was suddenly right. Nothing mattered other than the fact that Lilly was safe and sound and back in her arms where she belonged.

Silent tears of joy fell as Peyton waited for Tom to come back to the car. What she wanted now was to get Lilly home.

It was nearly thirty minutes before Tom came back outside. He took Lilly from her arms and placed her in the car seat in the back, then got in behind the wheel and started the engine.

"Benjamin is going to stay here while I take you home. We're still in the process of taking statements from them. Their names are Benny and Molly Morris. They're nothing but a couple of kids playing house. Got married last year when they were eighteen years old."

"How did they get Lilly?" she asked.

"Apparently Molly is India's second cousin. India showed up here out of the blue on Tuesday afternoon with the baby. She told them that the baby belonged to a friend of hers who couldn't take care of her anymore and wanted to put her up for adoption. Molly has been trying to get pregnant for the last year without success, so India thought they might be interested in adopting. They took one look at Lilly and said they fell in love with her."

"They didn't question the legality of just being handed a baby?" Peyton asked incredulously.

He flashed her a quick glance. "Did I mention that they're really young? According to them, India was working with a lawyer and told them she'd be back with legal papers for them to sign."

"You think she just wanted to give them a baby? That's what this is all about?"

"I don't know yet," Tom replied. "According to the couple, they weren't close to India."

"Is there something physically wrong with them that they can't have a baby of their own?" she asked, trying to make sense of it.

"I asked them that and they both assured me that there was nothing wrong with them. But Molly had gotten impatient because it wasn't happening fast enough. She said the last time she'd talked to India she'd mentioned how frustrated she was about not getting pregnant."

"So she apparently went directly to their house right after she took Lilly," Peyton said thoughtfully. "And then went back to Black Rock and to that motel room? Why wouldn't she have run as far away and as fast as possible?"

"That's what I need to find out," he replied. He flashed her a quick smile. "At least this has a happy ending where you and Lilly are concerned."

Peyton's heart crunched a bit as she returned his smile. This must be a bittersweet moment for him, that he'd been able to return her child to her but had not been able to save his own little girl.

"Thank you, Tom. Thank you for everything you've done for me and for Lilly."

"Just doing my job," he replied lightly.

She felt his emotional distance and suddenly realized he was moving on. He'd achieved what he'd wanted in returning Lilly, and now it was time for him to get back to solving a murder and resuming his own life.

Even though she'd only known him a couple of days, she was surprised to realize she was going to miss him, that the intensity of emotions they had shared had forged a bond in her, but one that he obviously didn't feel.

He'd just been doing his job. When he'd held her as

she'd cried, it had been his duty as an officer of the law and nothing more.

Lilly slept the entire way home, and Tom and Peyton didn't speak for the remainder of the ride. It wasn't an uncomfortable silence but rather one of two people who were occupied with their own separate thoughts.

"What's going to happen to Benny and Molly?" she finally asked when he turned down the street where she lived.

"I don't know yet. It's too early to know if they'll be charged with anything." He pulled into her driveway and cut the engine. They both got out of the car and he opened the back door to get the sleeping Lilly from her seat.

As they walked up to the front porch he looked right carrying a baby in his arms, and Peyton's heart hurt for him as she thought of the child he had lost.

"I'll be in touch if I need anything from you, but Peyton, this isn't over yet. We still have a killer out there, and we don't know what his relationship might have been to you. You need to be careful, okay?" He transferred Lilly from his arms to hers. "I'll have a squad car stop in to check on you periodically."

"I don't know how to thank you enough," she said as tears once again burned at her eyes.

"You don't have to thank me. We got lucky, that's all," he replied.

She couldn't tell him that not only did she want to thank him for the return of her daughter but also for the fact that he'd instinctively known when she'd needed his strong arms around her. He'd known when to cover her cold, trembling hand with his own.

On impulse she reached up on her tiptoes with the intent of pressing her lips against his cheek. At the very last minute he dipped his head down and instead of his cheek her lips met his.

His mouth was softer, warmer than she'd anticipated, and what she'd meant as a simple thank-you kiss became so much more. Although his arms remained at his sides, a flicker of heat licked at her insides just before he stepped back from her.

His eyes were dark, impossible to read. "Good night, Peyton. I'll be in touch." Without another word he turned and left her porch.

She watched him go and felt a ridiculous stab in her heart as she realized he was for all intents and purposes out of her life.

She had her baby back and Tom had a killer to catch. There was no reason for their lives to intersect again in any real, meaningful way, and she wasn't sure why that thought made her incredibly sad.

The kiss was everything Tom had imagined it would be. Sweet, yet hot enough to flood his veins with heat. It had made him wonder what her skin would taste like beneath his lips, if she'd moan while he made love to her.

As he got into his car and left her house, he tried not to think about how soft and yielding her mouth had been against his, how much he'd wanted to deepen the kiss with his tongue.

Thank God they'd found the baby alive and well. Thank God there had been a happy ending for Peyton where the baby was concerned. In a million years he would never forget the look on Peyton's face when he'd returned Lilly to her. It had been such exquisite joy. He would love for her to experience that kind of joy every day for the rest of her life.

Unfortunately, the case wasn't wrapped up neat and tidy. One loose end was the fact that somebody had killed the kidnapper and Tom not only wanted to know who, but he also wanted to know why.

Cliff Gunther. The new name whirled around in his head. He needed to get Sam on finding out what he could about the waiter who had dated Peyton before her relationship with Tom. It was another loose end Tom didn't want to leave untended.

The next morning he was no closer to having answers than he'd been the night before. Not only did he have the weight of the India Richards case on his shoulders, but he was also wondering if Peyton was truly out of danger.

As he went into his office Sam greeted him with a frown. "Don't have much information for you on Cliff Gunther," he said.

Tom sat in the chair next to his desk. "What have you got?"

Sam pulled some papers in front of him. "Cliff Gunther, thirty-two years old. Born and raised in

Wichita and has a clean record except for a couple of speeding tickets. He quit his job two weeks ago and hasn't resurfaced anywhere else."

"Did you get an address?"

Sam nodded. "But one of his coworkers at the restaurant said he hasn't been at his apartment since he quit his job."

Tom frowned. "It could mean nothing, it could mean something. We need to dig a little deeper to find out where he is and what he's up to. If nothing else I need to exclude him in this case and move on to somebody else."

"Have you heard anything from Caleb?" Sam asked.

"Not yet. I'm hoping to hear something from him today about India Richards's life in Wichita. Meanwhile, I intend to spend the day trying to trace her movements while she was here in Black Rock."

"At least the baby is back where she belongs," Sam replied. "Peyton is probably having the best morning of her life this morning."

Tom nodded. He wished Sam hadn't said her name, hadn't put her back in his head. "I'll be in my office. Let me know when you have something more for me on Cliff Gunther."

"Will do," Sam agreed.

Tom went into his office and closed the door and tried to put Peyton Wilkerson out of his mind, with little success.

It felt strange not going directly to her house this

morning. In the span of just a couple of days, being with her had become a habit. But it was a habit he had to break.

Even though Peyton had been the first woman in a very long time to interest him on a male/female level, he could never be the man in her life.

He knew enough about her past, enough about her hopes and dreams to know that what she was looking for was a fantasy storybook ending. Tom was grounded in harsh reality too much to believe in those kinds of happily-ever-afters.

When he'd buried his precious Kelly he'd buried half his heart with her, and when Julie had walked away from him she'd taken the other half. There was nothing left for anyone else, and in any case he never wanted to be that vulnerable to the capricious nature of fate again. It was much safer, much easier to keep himself from ever caring too deeply about the people in his life.

He had to forget that kiss they'd shared, he had to stop thinking about Peyton as a sexy, loving woman and think of her only as a victim of a crime.

Besides, he had more important things on his mind, like the murder of India Richards. He also wanted to figure out who Peyton had had her run-in with at the grocery store. It might have nothing to do with what happened, but he wouldn't be satisfied until he checked out all leads.

Tom spent the morning chasing down information about India Richards. He knew there was no way she could have been in town for two months and not have met anyone but Peyton. Although the apartment where she'd been living had yielded few clues as to the life of the occupant, there had been some.

A discarded foam cup had held the name of a convenience store on the edge of town, and that was the first stop Tom made. Armed with a photo of India Richards, he entered the shop.

He recognized the older woman behind the counter and offered her a smile. "Hi, Margie."

"Morning, Tom. What brings you to this neck of the woods? I know it's not that sludge we call coffee."

Margie Meadows was a widow who lived in the house next to the Grayson ranch. At sixty-five years old she was as feisty as a woman half her age and had made it known that she was actively looking for a husband to replace the one she'd lost to a heart attack a year before.

"Or maybe you've finally come to your senses and decided what you need most in your life is a hot, sexy cougar like me," she added.

Tom laughed. "Ah, Margie, I have a feeling I could never keep up with you." He pulled the picture of India from his pocket. "I was wondering if you could tell me anything about this woman." He slid the picture across the counter to her.

"This is that woman who kidnapped that baby," she said. "Yeah, I've seen her in here a couple of times."

"Was she ever with anybody?"

Margie frowned. "Only once. I saw her get out of

Buck Harmon's truck and she came in and bought some beer then got back in his truck and they took off."

Buck Harmon. A burst of adrenaline shot through Tom. Buck was a twenty-four-year-old tough guy who lived fifteen miles outside of Black Rock and only ventured into town to frequent Harley's bar.

He was tall with sandy-colored hair and drove a black pickup. The only reason Tom hadn't thought of him before now was because he rarely saw Buck.

Was it merely a coincidence that Buck fit the description of the man who had cursed Peyton in the parking lot of the grocery store and had a connection to the woman who had kidnapped Lilly? Tom didn't believe in those kinds of coincidences.

He left the convenience store and headed out to Buck's place. Even with the little bit of information he now had, he couldn't make sense of the whole mess. He had the pieces of a puzzle but no puzzle box to look at to see how the pieces were supposed to fit together.

Buck lived in a small house that had belonged to his parents before they retired to Florida. He worked as a mechanic in the neighboring town of Little Creek and from what Tom knew had few friends. A phone call to the garage let Tom know that Buck didn't work on Saturdays, so Tom hoped to catch him at home.

Buck's pickup was in the driveway when Tom pulled up in front of the house, which looked as if it had been neglected for years. The paint was faded and peeling and a collection of old beer cans sat on top of the porch railing. The front yard was a graveyard of old tires and car parts.

As Tom approached the door he unfastened the snap of his holster, allowing for immediate access to his gun if it became necessary. He had no idea what role, if any, Buck might have played in either the kidnapping or the murder.

Buck answered Tom's knock. Clad in a T-shirt and a pair of boxers and with his hair disheveled as if he'd just climbed out of bed, he didn't looked pleased at the intrusion.

He narrowed his blue eyes and glared at Tom. "What's up? What are you doing here?"

"I need to ask you some questions, Buck. Can I come in?"

Buck raked a hand through his messy hair, then opened the screen door to allow Tom entry. "Excuse the mess," he said as he swept a pizza box and a newspaper off the shabby couch. "I don't usually get much company."

He threw his lanky body into the chair opposite the sofa. "So, what's going on?"

"I want to ask you about India Richards," Tom said.

"Who?" Buck frowned in incomprehension.

"You might have known her as Kathy Simon," Tom replied.

Buck's eyes narrowed once again. "Crazy chick. I met her one night at Harley's, and we kicked it together for a couple of hours. I didn't have anything to do with whatever trouble she got herself into, and I sure as hell didn't kill her."

"What can you tell me about her?" Tom asked. He wasn't sure if he could believe a word that came out of Buck's mouth, but for the moment he was willing to listen to whatever he had to say.

"Not much. She liked to dance, liked to drink and I thought she was going to like other things, too, if you get my drift. But she told me she had a boyfriend and wasn't going to cheat on him."

"Did she say anything else about this boyfriend of hers?"

"Not really. I got the feeling he might be married."

"Did she tell you that?" Tom asked.

Buck shook his head. "Nah, it was just the impression I got, that she was just hanging out here in Black Rock until he could be with her."

"Did she say if he was from Black Rock?"

"Not specifically, but I assumed he was."

Back and forth it went as Tom continued to question him. By the time Tom left just before noon, he didn't have any definitive answers, but he had more directions to explore in his investigation.

Buck had told him that on the night of India's murder he was in Harley's back room playing pool. Tom knew it was going to be difficult to check the alibi. The crowd that hung at Harley's could be a tough one, and few of them would be willing to answer questions.

Tom was in his car and headed back to his office when his cell phone rang. It was Caleb telling Tom that he was back from Wichita. The two agreed to meet for lunch at the local café.

It was just before noon when Tom parked in front of the Black Rock Café. He'd skipped breakfast and his stomach rumbled with hunger. The food at the café was the best in town.

Harry Thompson, the owner, greeted Tom as he walked through the door. Harry was a walking advertisement for the quality of the food he offered. Heavyset and with a broad cheerful smile, he looked like a man who knew how to enjoy a good meal.

"Your brother is waiting for you in a booth in the back," Harry said. "And the chicken fried steak is exceptional today."

"Thanks, Harry. Sounds good." Tom made his way through the tables to the booth where Caleb waited for him. As he sat, the waitress appeared and they placed their orders.

Tom relayed to Caleb what he'd found out from Buck, and by that time their lunches had arrived. "So, what did you find out in Wichita?" he asked.

"First of all, Rick Powell has a great reputation in town. Tough on crime, a stand-up guy. Nobody I spoke to had a bad word to say about him. He's definitely ambitious. According to his coworkers, he has an eye on the D.A. position and eventually wants to get into the national politic scene. On the other hand, India Richards didn't have that kind of a reputation."

Caleb paused to cut into his chicken fried steak. He took a bite then washed it down with his soda and continued. "I contacted a friend of hers. Her name is Brandy Wine—no joke, that's her real name. Anyway, she told me India ran with a rough crowd, that she always figured she'd wind up either dead or in prison."

"Did she say what brought India to Black Rock?" Tom asked.

"A man, although Brandy didn't have a name."

Tom frowned. "Buck said basically the same thing. He also thought the man might be married."

"Maybe India mistook an affair for something more important. Maybe she was pressing Mr. Married to come clean to his wife and he wasn't prepared to do that," Caleb said.

"Then it's possible her murder had nothing to do with Lilly's kidnapping." Tom leaned back in his seat and released a deep sigh. "It seems like the more information we learn, the more complicated things become."

He looked up and froze at the sight of Peyton coming in the door. He'd spent the morning trying his damnedest not to think about her, and there she was, bigger than life, beelining toward him with Lilly in her arms and a wide, joyful smile on her face.

The sight of her reminded him of the kiss they had shared and a small flame ignited in the pit of his stomach.

As she reached their booth she nodded to Caleb, then turned to Tom. "Hi. We were just on our way to your office when I saw your car parked outside."

She looked gorgeous in a pale pink sundress that

bared her creamy, slender shoulders and emphasized her cool blond coloring.

"What's up?" he asked, trying to maintain his professional composure.

"Lilly and I would like to invite you to dinner tomorrow night as a thank-you," she said.

"That's not necessary," he protested.

"Don't be silly, brother," Caleb said. "When a pretty lady invites you to dinner you should always accept."

"Tom, please. I'd really like to do this for you," she said.

Thanks to Caleb, Tom felt as if there was no way to decline the offer without looking like a jerk. "What time?" he asked, deciding it was easier to give in that to make a big deal out of it. After all, it was just a meal.

Her eyes lit with pleasure. "Shall we say around six-thirty?"

"All right," he agreed.

"Wonderful. And, Tom, be sure to come hungry." With the smile still on her face, she murmured a goodbye and walked away.

Tom watched the sway of her hips as she left. *Come hungry.* What she didn't realize was that she stirred a hunger inside him, a hunger that shouldn't be sated.

"I think you might need this," Caleb said as he pulled out his wallet and withdrew a condom package. He laid it on the table between them.

"Jeez, Caleb, put that away," Tom exclaimed.

Caleb grinned. "If you want it put away you'd better put it in your wallet."

Tom snatched it up and shoved it into his pocket. "I don't know why you think I'll need it. She invited me for dinner, that's all."

Caleb leaned back in the booth with a grin. "I might not know everything there is to know about investigating crimes, but one thing I know is women, and brother, that woman has the hots for you."

"That's ridiculous," Tom scoffed. "You heard what she said. She just wants to thank me."

Caleb leaned forward, the smile on his face fading away. "Why don't you allow yourself to enjoy whatever it is she's offering? Haven't you punished yourself enough for the past?"

Tom stiffened. "I'm not punishing myself for anything—this subject is now officially closed." He picked up his fork to finish his lunch. At this moment he wasn't sure what was going to be more difficult, solving India Richards's murder or getting through tomorrow night's dinner with Peyton without doing something stupid.

Chapter 7

The house was spotless and the scent of chicken and freshly baked rolls filled the air. Peyton felt ridiculously nervous as she poured herself a glass of wine and sat at the table adorned with her good dishes and silverware. Lilly was in her infant swing nearby, cooing with happiness as she swung to and fro.

This was supposed to be a simple thank-you meal, but for Peyton it was much more. With the trauma of Lilly's kidnapping behind her, over the past day she'd been able to think of nothing but Tom.

Without the fear for Lilly that had gripped her heart, it was now open to all the feelings she'd suppressed where the handsome lawman was concerned.

She liked him. She liked him a lot. Her feelings for him had little to do with the fact that he'd successfully gotten her baby back into her arms. It was so much more than that.

His quiet confidence was so different than Rick's bravado, and yet she felt so much more comfortable in Tom's company. His quiet, steady ways soothed her, but at the same time his sexy brown eyes sparked a flame of excitement in her that she wanted to explore.

She'd thought she'd seen a flicker of desire in his eyes, especially in those moments just after they'd kissed. The truth was she wanted Tom Grayson. She wasn't a fool enough to believe herself in love with him, not after knowing him only a couple of days, but she wanted to get to know him better, and that's what tonight was all about.

Even though she was excited to spend time with him, the nerves that fluttered through her as she waited his arrival surprised her.

A glance at the clock let her know he was due to arrive within minutes. She had a feeling Tom was a man who would rarely be late.

Rick had rarely been on time for anything. There had always been one last phone call he needed to make, one more e-mail to send before he could give her his attention.

At precisely six-thirty her doorbell rang. She downed the last of her wine, ran quick fingers through her hair and then hurried to the door to greet him.

As she opened the door, her heart swelled at the sight of him. It was the first time she'd seen him out of uniform. He looked amazingly masculine and hot in a pair of jeans and a blue striped short-sleeved dress shirt.

"Tom, I'm so glad you came," she said as she opened the door to allow him inside.

"Thanks for inviting me," he replied. He looked ill at ease as he stepped into the living room. He held out a bottle of wine. "I didn't know if I should bring white or red, so I guessed at white."

"It's chicken, so that's perfect," she replied and took the bottle from him. "In fact, I have to confess, I've already had a glass of wine. Come on in and I'll pour you a glass so you can catch up."

She was acutely conscious of him just behind her as she led him into the kitchen. She could smell the familiar scent of him, that spicy cologne that somehow smelled like a combination of sweet comfort and heady desire.

As Tom walked into the kitchen his lips curved into a smile as he saw Lilly. "It's nice to know she's where she belongs," he said as Peyton gestured him into a chair at the table.

"You have no idea," Peyton replied as she poured him a glass of wine and handed it to him. "The night I got her home I could barely let her go so she could sleep in her crib." A new burst of emotion welled up in Peyton's chest as she thought of how close she'd come to losing Lilly forever.

She shoved those terrible thoughts aside. Tonight was the time to be happy, to celebrate that Lilly was home and Tom was here.

"Dinner should be ready in about fifteen minutes," she said as she poured herself another glass of wine. "I hope you like chicken cordon bleu."

One of his dark brows lifted. "I do, but that's a lot of work."

"Cooking has become a hobby of mine," she said as she leaned against the counter. "When I was seventeen I got a job in an upscale restaurant and the chef became a mentor of sorts. In our slow time he would teach me cooking techniques."

"So why teaching? Why didn't you become a chef?" he asked.

She could tell by his posture that he was beginning to relax. She wanted him relaxed. She wanted him to enjoy dinner with her.

"I love kids. I always wanted to be a teacher. The other jobs I had were just the means to get me money to pay for my college education. What about you? Did you always want to be a sheriff?"

He leaned back in the chair and his eyes held the warmth of memories. "When I was eighteen years old I was flirting with the other side of the law," he admitted. "I thought I was a tough guy and was always ready for a brawl. The sheriff at the time was a close friend of my father's, and my dad arranged for me to work with him part-time on the weekends. It was the best thing my dad ever did for me. When I was twenty-one I became a full-time deputy, and when I was twenty-eight I became sheriff."

"And what a wonderful role model you've become for your siblings," she said.

"Yeah, law enforcement in Black Rock has definitely become a family affair." He finished his wine, and Peyton began to put the meal on the table.

"Is there anything I can do to help?" he asked.

"Absolutely not," she replied. "You just sit there and relax."

It took her only minutes to get everything on the table and join him there. As they ate, Lilly smiled and babbled, perfectly satisfied in her swing and with her mother in sight.

The conversation continued to flow throughout the meal. She was delighted by the stories Tom told of growing up with his brothers and sister. His obvious commitment to and love of his family only made him more appealing.

She shared with him the loneliness she'd felt as a child, growing up virtually alone in a world of adults behaving badly. "I remember one particular night when we were homeless and my mother left me alone in the car. It was in a scary part of town where the only people on the streets were thugs and prostitutes. I hid in the backseat beneath on old blanket and prayed that I'd still be alive in the morning."

Tom gazed at her, his eyes dark and filled with concern. "How old were you?"

"Nine. That night I swore to myself I'd have something better when I grew up, that I wouldn't make the same choices my mother made and that my husband and any children I had would be the most important things in my life." She grinned. "I managed to get it all a little bit backward and got the child before I got the man."

By that time they had finished eating and Tom insisted he help her clear the table. Instantly the kitchen seemed to shrink as he filled it with his presence. By the time they'd finished clearing things from the table, Lilly had fallen asleep in the swing.

"How about some coffee?" she suggested as she put the last plate in the dishwasher.

"Sounds good," he agreed.

"Why don't you make yourself comfortable in the living room and I'll put the coffee on and put Lilly to bed."

"Why don't you take care of Lilly and I'll make the coffee?" he suggested.

She nodded. "Sounds like a plan." She scooped the sleeping baby up and left the kitchen.

As she walked down the hallway holding Lilly she thought of the man in her kitchen. Throughout the meal she'd been intensely aware of him, the memory of the kiss they'd shared replaying over and over in her head.

The hunger she felt for him was like nothing she'd felt for Rick. This was stronger, more intense, and she wondered if it was because of the kidnapping, because of India's murder.

She was struck with a feeling of how important it was to grasp every moment of life, to reach for what you wanted because life was too short. She wasn't in love with Tom, but she was in serious lust, and right now that felt like enough.

Gently she placed Lilly in her crib, kissed her on her sweet cheek and left the room. She had no idea what to expect for the rest of the evening, but she was eager to see how the night would unfold.

The minute Peyton carried Lilly out of the kitchen, Tom set about making the coffee and mentally cursed his younger brother. The condom Caleb had given him burned in his back pocket, but it didn't burn as hot as the desire he'd fought all through the meal.

The burn had begun the moment she'd opened the door. Dressed in a blue sundress that perfectly matched her eyes, and with her hair pulled back at her nape exposing dainty ears and the lovely length of her slender neck, she'd taken his breath away.

There was something about her that broke his heart just a little bit. Maybe it was because he could so easily imagine her as that small, frightened girl struggling to survive in a world where she didn't belong.

But it wasn't sympathy for what she'd gone through that boiled the blood in his veins, that made him think about running his mouth down the length of her neck.

It was the evocative scent of her, the press of her breasts against the blue material and the slender, curvy bare legs beneath her dress that had him half dizzy with desire.

It would be absolutely wrong to make a move on her. He knew what she wanted most in her life, and Tom wasn't and could never be that man. She wanted a man who would love her, and Tom had no love to give. But that didn't mean he had no desire to give.

He was pouring the coffee when she returned to the kitchen. "She's a good baby," he said as they carried their cups into the living room and sat side-by-side on the sofa.

"She's a great baby," Peyton replied. "She rarely fusses and has been sleeping through the night for a while now."

"Has Rick been back to see her since she got home?"

Peyton nodded. "He drove in yesterday morning and spent a couple of hours playing with her."

"Any chance you two will get back together?" He half hoped she'd say yes. Rick seemed like a stand-up guy, and that would put an end to what Tom felt, where she was concerned.

She laughed. "No way. Neither of us have any desire to get back together. Rick will probably always be in my life, but only as the man who is Lilly's father."

"I found the man who had that altercation in the parking lot with you," he said. Maybe he wouldn't notice the heat radiating from her and the heady scent of her perfume if he talked about work.

"It wasn't a real altercation," she countered. "But who is he?"

"His name is Buck Harmon. He lives in a neighboring small town, and he knew India."

Her eyes widened. "Did he have something to do with the kidnapping? With India's murder?"

"I don't know yet. According to what he told me, he met India at Harley's bar and they hung out together for a night. He says he had no idea that she was going to kidnap a baby, and he sure doesn't know who murdered her, but I'm checking him out."

"It's a mess, isn't it?"

"Yeah, it is. To make matters more complicated, Buck had the impression that India had a lover here in town, a married lover. Caleb got the same information from a friend of India's in Wichita."

Peyton frowned thoughtfully. "So maybe the lover couldn't have children and wanted them, so he and India cooked up the scheme to take Lilly, then run away and live together like a family."

"Maybe, although there's also the possibility that the married man didn't expect his lover to show up here in Black Rock. Maybe he murdered India to save his marriage."

"That's a lot of maybes," she said.

"And that's all we've got right now," he replied with a touch of frustration.

She smiled at him and placed her hand on his forearm. "You'll figure it out, Tom. I have all the confidence in the world that you'll solve this mess."

He would have been so much better if she hadn't touched him, but the feel of her warm hand on his skin reminded him of how soft her lips had been beneath his, how warm and sexy she'd felt in his arms.

It had been so long since he'd been with a woman, so long since he'd even allowed himself the pleasure of feminine company. But there was something about Peyton Wilkerson that moved him both on an emotional and a physical level.

"I should probably go," he finally said. This woman felt dangerous to him, to his sense of peace.

"So early? I still have a cherry chocolate cake for dessert. Surely you'll at least stay for dessert." She looked at him wistfully.

"Since you went to all that trouble, I suppose I could stay for a piece of cake," he replied.

"Great! I'll just go get it."

As she left the sofa and went into the kitchen, Tom released a deep sigh. This was all Caleb's fault. If he hadn't given Tom that condom then Tom wouldn't have sex on his mind. And if Peyton didn't look so sexy and hot, he wouldn't have sex with her on his mind.

She came back into the living room carrying a tray with two dessert plates with cake, forks and napkins. She set the tray in the center of the coffee table and then handed him one of the pieces of cake.

"This looks sinful," he said, eyeing the dark chocolate with bits of cherries, but he was thinking about the curve of her breasts that were visible just above the deep neckline of her dress.

"My philosophy is that if it looks good, feels good or tastes good it can't be all wrong." She picked up her plate and fork.

Her words did nothing to dispel Tom's wayward

thoughts. He felt like an awkward teenager pumped with hormones and on a date with the school beauty queen.

"When do you start work at the school?" he asked.

"Two weeks." She frowned and looked down at the cake. "I have to confess I'm not sure what I'm going to do. I'm just not ready to leave Lilly with anyone, and I can't exactly take her to school with me."

"Where do you plan to take her?"

"Portia's Playpen."

"She'll be fine there," Tom assured her. "Portia Perez is devoted to the kids in her day care."

"She just seemed young," Peyton replied.

Tom smiled. "She's twenty-seven and has a degree in early childhood development."

"How do you know so much about her?" She slid a forkful of the cake into her mouth and then licked the side of her upper lip.

Tom stared down at his own piece of dessert as a new fire of desire crashed through him. "Portia and Caleb dated when they were in high school. They broke up when Portia went to college. Portia has a great reputation, and lots of mothers here in town trust her with their children."

"That makes me feel better. One of my goals over the next two weeks is to get out and meet some of the people here." She set her plate back on the coffee table and leaned back against the sofa cushion.

"One of the things I realized during the ordeal with Lilly is that I haven't made any friends here. I was isolated with just India hanging around. I don't even know my neighbors," she said with a frown.

"To the left are Jane and Harvey Carter. You probably haven't met them yet. They're retired and spend most of the summers at their son's place in Maine. On the right are the Burkes, Carrie and Mike."

He began to relax again as he told her about some of the people in her neighborhood, and it wasn't long before he was describing some of the more colorful characters in town.

He loved the sound of her laughter and found himself exaggerating quirks of the people in order to hear her deep-throated laugh.

His laughter halted abruptly when she reached out and ran her finger across the side of his upper lip. "You had a little frosting there," she said.

He reached for his napkin, his breath caught painfully in his chest. But before he could wipe his mouth, she leaned toward him, and he knew by the look on her face that she wanted—needed—to be kissed. And God help him, he complied.

He leaned forward and captured her mouth with his. In an instant she was in his arms, her mouth open to him. She tasted of sweet, dark chocolate and hot desire, and as her tongue met his he was momentarily lost in the simple pleasure of kissing her.

One minute they were kissing still seated side by side and the next moment she was on her back beneath him on the sofa.

Their tongues battled in a hunger that sprang up

instantly. Her arms wound around his back, and her fingers played in the hair at the nape of his neck, creating a sizzling electricity that stung through him.

He wanted her with a raging need and tasted her desire for him on her lips. It had been so long, so aching long since he'd lost himself in a woman, and as they continued to kiss he realized how easy it would be for him to lose himself in Peyton.

Still, someplace in the back of his mind he knew this was wrong, that he was absolutely the wrong man to be kissing her, to be feeling the warmth of her body beneath him.

Reluctantly he broke the kiss and sat up. "Peyton, we can't do this," he said even as he felt his arousal tight against his jeans.

"Why not?" Her voice was low and sexy as she sat up and gazed at him.

He couldn't look at her, not with her mouth moist and red from his kisses, not with her eyes so deep blue with desire. He got up from the sofa, needing to distance himself from her.

"Peyton, I'm not the man you're looking for in your life."

She got up from the sofa and smiled at him. "I'm just looking for tonight, Tom, not tomorrow or the day after. I want you, and I can tell that you want me, too."

His breath caught in his throat as she moved to stand in front of him, so close he could feel her warm breath on his neck, so close her breasts touched his chest. "We're not foolish kids, Tom. We're both adults, and I can't think of a single reason why we can't make love tonight."

Tom tried to think of all the reasons it would be a bad idea, but he couldn't think as she wound her arms around his neck and pressed herself intimately against him.

"I'm not the man you want," he finally managed to say.

"You're the man I want right now," she replied. "And that's enough for me."

Brain dead. He was completely and totally brain dead. She'd effectively removed every concern he had, and his desire to take her was suddenly far stronger than anything else.

She must have seen his answer in his eyes, for she took him by the hand and led him down the hallway to her bedroom.

His last rational thought was a mental thank-you to Caleb, who had made sure he was prepared for a simple dinner of thanks with Peyton.

Chapter 8

Peyton's heart beat wildly as they entered her bedroom. She'd told Tom the truth: at that moment, she wasn't thinking of the future. She only knew her need for him now.

It was crazy after knowing him such a short period of time, but she already felt intimately involved with him. What she wanted was to be naked in his arms, to feel his heart beating against her own as they made love.

The minute they were in the bedroom he claimed her mouth again, kissing her with such searing intent that her bones seemed to melt in her body.

As his mouth left hers and trailed down her neck, she began to unfasten the buttons on his shirt. With several of the buttons undone, she slid her arms around his warm, bare chest, and at the same time he unzipped the zipper that ran up the back of her dress.

He shoved it off her shoulders and it fell to the floor, leaving her clad only in a lacy bra and matching panties. "Just let me look at you," he whispered as she stepped back from him.

In the illumination from the bedside lamp, his eyes glowed like a wild animal's as he visually devoured her. She felt his gaze like pinpricks of heat lingering on the fullness of her breasts, lowering to her hips and legs.

"God, you're beautiful," he said as he pulled off his shirt.

"So are you," she replied as she gazed at his sharply cut, muscular chest. Before her legs could turn completely weak, she pulled down the bedspread and slid beneath the sheets.

"Peyton, are you sure this is what you want to do?" He shifted from one foot to the other. "I don't want this to be about gratitude."

She laughed. "Tom, I'm grateful for the guy who throws my newspaper on my porch in the mornings, but you don't see him in my bed. This isn't about giving you something, it's about giving myself something. I want you, and nothing is going to change my mind."

Her words snapped his inertia and her heart beat even faster as he placed his wallet on the nightstand and took off his pants.

"I'm glad it's not the newspaper man in your bed," he said as he slid beneath the sheets next to her and gathered her into his arms.

She smiled at him. "Me, too."

He captured her smile with his mouth, and there was no more time for levity. As he kissed her he reached around behind her and unfastened her bra and then covered her breasts with his warm palms.

She closed her eyes against the sensations that coursed through her, and as he moved down her body she wrapped her fingers in his thick, dark hair. A moan escaped her as he captured one of her nipples in his mouth.

His skin was hot against hers, and she loved the feel of it. She could feel the length of his hardness pressed against her thigh, and knowing she had caused his arousal only increased the sexual excitement that winged through her.

He kissed and nibbled and licked first one turgid nipple and then the other and she reached down and stroked the length of him through his cotton boxers.

He gasped and slid his hands beneath her buttocks to pull down her panties. She aided him, raising her hips to allow him to take the wisp of silk from her. When she was completely naked he took off his boxers and then pulled her back to him.

Her skin sizzled against his, and as he cupped her face with his hands and kissed her again she felt the absolute rightness of being with him.

Even though her entire body sang with sexual want, she'd never felt so safe in a man's arms. Although Tom caressed her with hunger and passion, beneath it was a tenderness that was as exciting and wonderful as anything.

As his hands slid down the length of her, over the rise of her breasts and down the flat of her stomach, her breath caught in the back of her throat as he touched her inner thigh with his hot fingers.

"Peyton," he whispered, his voice deeper than usual. "It's been a long time since I've been with anyone."

"And you make me feel as if this is the very first time for me," she replied.

He gazed down at her. "Then that's all the more reason it should be slow and sweet, but I don't think I have slow in me right now."

She smiled and placed her hand on the side of his face. "Just love me, Tom. Short and sweet or fast and frantic, I just want you to make love to me."

His mouth crashed down to hers, and at the same time his hand moved from her thigh to the very center of her. A deep moan built up inside her as his intimate touch shot sweet sensations through her.

He knew exactly where to touch, precisely how much pressure to use to bring her to the brink of climax. As he took her over the edge, she stiffened and cried out his name as wave after wave of pleasure crashed over her.

Before she could catch her breath he rolled over and grabbed his pants and pulled out a condom package. He ripped it open and put it on, then with his breath hitching in his throat he moved on top of her.

She welcomed him, opening her legs and grabbing

his shoulders. He moved into her and froze, his eyes narrowing as he gazed down at her. "Peyton, you feel so good." He lowered his head and kissed her with a tenderness that nearly brought tears to her eyes.

As the kiss ended he began to move against her, into her. Slowly at first, he stroked deep and easy, and she arched up to meet his every thrust. But it didn't take long for their movements to become faster and more frantic.

Peyton was lost in him, in the heat of his body and the arms that held her. She was lost to the fiery pleasure that he gave her as he thrust again and again.

A building tension welled up inside her and she knew he was reaching the end. His body shook with faint tremors and his grunts of pleasure brought her closer to her own climax.

As it rushed over her and she cried out his name, he stiffened against her and collapsed with his chest just to her side.

For several long moments neither of them spoke as they waited for breathing to return to normal and speech to become possible once again.

"Wow," he finally said.

Peyton giggled. "My sentiments exactly."

He stroked a finger down the side of her face. "You are amazing."

She smiled. "I never believe the praise of a naked man in my bed after lovemaking."

He laughed. "It's more dangerous to believe the words of a naked man in your bed *before* lovemaking."

She laughed again. "I never thought of that." Reluctantly she disengaged from him. "I need to go check on Lilly," she said. She leaned over and kissed him on the cheek. "I'll be right back."

She slid out of bed and grabbed the robe that hung on a hook just inside her closet. Wrapping herself up in the cool cotton, she left the room.

Her entire body tingled with residual heat from Tom. He'd been everything she'd wanted him to be—sexy yet tender, commanding but gentle.

It hadn't just been the physical aspect of what they'd shared that warmed her. Emotionally it felt right to be with Tom. He fit into her world like no man had before.

As she walked into the nursery, a smile curved her lips at the sight of Lilly sleeping soundly in the crib. There was a peace in her heart she hadn't felt for a long time.

She covered Lilly with a sheet and stifled the impulse to lean down and kiss her little cheek. She didn't want to awaken her.

When Peyton returned to the bedroom she was disappointed to see Tom up and with his pants on. "Oh, you're leaving? I was hoping that maybe you'd spend the night."

He reached for his shirt and shook his head. He didn't look at her as he pulled on his shirt and buttoned it up. "I've got to go. I've still got things to do tonight."

She could taste the regret in the air, coming off him in waves. He grabbed his wallet from the nightstand

and shoved it into his back pocket, then finally met her gaze.

"Peyton, I loved making love with you, but it's not going to happen again." He shoved his hands in his pockets, a gesture she recognized as defensiveness. "You deserve to find the man of your dreams, and I can't be that man."

"And I think maybe you're selling yourself short," she replied, but there was no way she was going to argue with him, to try to make him see that they had something special and should explore where it took them.

Instead she walked silently behind him as he left her room and headed for the front door. When he reached the door, he turned back to face her. "Thank you, Peyton, for being an amazingly strong, loving woman. You're going to make a wonderful wife for some lucky man."

He drew in a deep, visible breath. "And all that talk about you getting out and meeting people. I need to remind you that we don't know if the danger to you has passed. Until we know who was working with India and what connection they might have to you—to Lilly—the threat isn't gone. I don't want you leaving this house unless I or one of my deputies are with you. Make sure your door is locked at all times. I don't want to scare you, but until we have India's murderer behind bars, there's still danger."

He didn't wait for her response but turned and walked out the front door. She stood and watched as he got into his car.

She felt as if something had ended before it had really

begun, and what surprised her more than anything was the sadness that filled her heart. And as she thought of his final words, she quickly closed and locked her door as a new burst of fear rushed through her.

Tom didn't go home. He was too restless, too filled with alien emotions to try to sleep. Instead he drove north, toward the family ranch. He needed some time to process what had just happened, time so that the scent of Peyton would wear off his skin. A visit to Jacob was just what he needed. It had been too long since he'd spoken with him.

In another lifetime, under different circumstances, he might have found himself falling in love with Peyton. She was bright and brave, sexy and funny—she possessed all the qualities he liked in a woman.

But she was too late.

And he wasn't the man she thought he was.

As always when he turned down the lane that led to the Grayson ranch, a sense of homecoming filled him. The house where he'd grown up was once a three-bedroom ranch, but as the kids had come, additions had been added so that now it boasted four bedrooms, three baths and a huge family room addition on the back.

It was a working cattle ranch with acres of pasture and a large barn to house the horses they all owned. As he drove past the house and the barn he thought of his childhood.

It had been a happy one. Sure, there had been chaos and noise much of the time, but there had also been plenty of love and security, two necessities that Peyton hadn't known in her childhood.

A narrow dirt road took him past a large pond and to a grove of trees where a small cottage was visible amid the large, lush trees.

This house and the surrounding land had once belonged to a neighbor, but big Jim Grayson had bought him out. Through the years this little cottage had served many uses—a guesthouse for visiting relatives, a romantic getaway for the harried parents of five kids, and as home for one or the other of those kids as they became adults.

Even though it felt late as Tom pulled up in front of the cottage, a glance at the clock let him know it was just after ten. A single light burned in the front window, letting him know that Jacob was still awake.

Of all his brothers, Tom had always been closest to Jacob. It had just worked out that the two eldest were close, and Caleb and Benjamin were close, and they had all spoiled Brittany rotten.

A surge of irritation filled him as he thought of his wayward sister. This wasn't the first time she'd just up and disappeared. Six months earlier she'd gone to Las Vegas to marry a man she'd only known for three months. Thankfully, she'd come to her senses before the wedding could take place, but she'd hidden out for two weeks rather than face her brothers.

But what weighed on his heart more than anything at the moment was the fact that he'd made love to Peyton when he'd known deep in his soul that it was the wrong thing to do. Worse than that, he wanted to do it again.

He knocked once and heard his brother yell for him to come in. He walked in to see Jacob in the recliner in the small living room. As always, the sight of Jacob sent a small shock through Tom.

His black hair had become long and shaggy, emphasizing the lean angles of his face. His jaw held the growth of several days of whiskers, giving him the aura of a man who didn't care.

"Grab a beer if you want," Jacob said as he lifted a bottle of his own to his lips.

Tom went into the kitchen and grabbed a beer from the fridge, then returned to the living room and sank down on the sofa.

"Heard you've had a tough week," Jacob said.

"Yeah, it's been rough," Tom agreed. "Did Benjamin fill you in?"

"Yeah. Missing baby, pretty single mother, a murdered woman and our missing sister. I think Benjamin has told me everything except what he had to eat for lunch on Tuesday," Jacob said dryly.

"If you'd get out of that chair and out of this cabin, Benjamin wouldn't have to keep updating you with what's going on in town and with the family," Tom replied.

Jacob said nothing but instead tipped his bottle to his lips and took a deep drink. He'd been doing that a lot lately. He'd come home thin, his eyes shadowed with secrets he refused to share with anyone. But Tom knew that Jacob wouldn't talk about what had put the darkness in his eyes until he was good and ready.

For the next few minutes the two talked about the kidnapping and murder. "Likely suspects?" Jacob asked.

"That's the problem. There aren't many. Buck Harmon spent some time with India but insists he was playing pool in the back room at Harley's when she was murdered. Johnny Boyd confirmed it, but those two are thick as thieves, so who knows if it's the truth or not. Caleb is checking out some of the people from India's past, and Peyton came up with the name of an old boyfriend, but it looks like this murder isn't going to be an easy solve."

"Some of them never get solved," Jacob said darkly. He finished his beer and set the bottle on the table next to his chair. "So tell me about the woman."

"What woman?" Tom asked.

"Benjamin told me he thought there was something going on between you and the mother of the baby."

Tom frowned. Although this was what he'd come to talk about, he found himself reluctant now to discuss his crazy feelings for Peyton.

"She's an amazing woman, strong and bright and sexy. But, I have no interest in pursuing anything with her."

"You haven't had any interest in pursuing anyone since Julie left you," Jacob observed.

"I tried it once, and I have no intention of trying it again," Tom replied.

"You're in a box of your own making, Tom. You've convinced yourself that you failed, and that's not reality. If anyone should try it again, it should be you."

"That's funny coming from a guy who's locked himself inside this house and refuses to leave, doesn't even want anyone to know he's here."

"I have my reasons."

"You sure you don't want to talk about them?" Tom asked.

"Positive." There was a definite edge to Jacob's voice that warned Tom from pushing. "You know, someday you might want to let yourself talk about Julie and Kelly. You never really gave yourself any time to grieve."

"That's ridiculous, of course I grieved. Besides, there's nothing to talk about. Kelly died, Julie left and that's the end of the story," Tom replied.

For the next hour the two talked about safe subjects—the hot weather, the ranch and the new veterinarian who had set up practice in town.

"He was out here the other day to look at one of the horses who got into some brambles," Jacob said. "Benjamin seemed impressed with him."

"I haven't met him yet," Tom said.

"I'm surprised. From what Benjamin said, he and his wife and family have been in town a couple of months now."

"A couple of months? I didn't realize it had been that long. Maybe it's time I had a visit with the new vet in town. Did Benjamin mention where they're from?"

"No. Why? You've got that sheriff look in your eyes," Jacob said.

Tom shrugged. "Just a thought. One of our theories is that India came here to be close to a married lover. She moved here two months ago, and from what you've just told me, it might have been around the same time that the new vet showed up here in town."

"Sounds like you're grasping at straws," Jacob observed.

"I am," Tom admitted, "but at the moment straws are all I have left." He released a weary sigh. "Not only do I have a murder to solve, but I don't know if Peyton is out of danger yet. Until I find out who killed India, I won't know what the connection is with Peyton, and that worries me."

Jacob raked a hand through his thick, unruly hair and gave Tom a half grin. "Then I guess it's your job to make sure she stays safe."

"I guess so," Tom agreed.

Minutes later, when he was back in his car and headed home, he wondered how in the hell he was going to keep Peyton safe *and* keep his distance.

Chapter 9

It had been three days since Tom had come to dinner, three days since they had made love, and Peyton realized he had no intention of sharing any relationship with her other than a professional one.

He'd called several times each day asking if she needed anything, reminding her that he didn't think it was a good idea for her to go out and about, but he'd been cool and distant each time.

She couldn't help but be disappointed. Despite everything, she'd hoped for more.

Still, she tried not to sit around and mope, even though her heart had been bruised a little. Monday she cleaned the house from top to bottom and played with Lilly.

Although she tried not to think about Tom, thoughts

of him refused to leave her head. She'd thought he cared about her, beyond their roles of sheriff and victim. It had been in his touch when he held her hand, it had been in his eyes when he'd looked at her. There had been something there, something strictly male and female that had nothing to do with their roles in the drama.

Still, she couldn't make him acknowledge it or embrace it. He'd wished her well and sent her on her way—alone, as she'd been for most of her life.

Tuesday was a longer day. With little to do, she wandered the house and finally sat at the kitchen table and made lessons plans for the fall.

Today, Wednesday, had been the longest day of all. Cabin fever hit hard. How long could she stay cooped up in the house worried about some threat that might or might not exist? How long was she willing to keep her life on hold?

By evening she'd decided she wasn't willing to put off her life any longer. She wanted to get out of the house. She wanted to go to the park and breathe in some fresh air, sit and maybe visit with whoever might also be there.

With India's death, some of the fear for Lilly's safety had vanished. She believed Tom's theory, that India had moved to Black Rock to be near a lover. Peyton thought it was possible that India had stolen Lilly in the deluded belief that she'd present her lover with a ready-made family. Once she'd actually taken Lilly she must have panicked and instead of keeping her had taken her to her cousin's house.

Crazy love, that's what India had apparently felt for her lover. And Peyton believed it was that crazy love that had gotten her killed.

But Peyton couldn't remain locked up in her house until her killer was caught. What if the killer was never caught? At some point she had to start living again.

It was just after seven when Peyton called Tom. "I'm sorry to bother you," she said when he answered. "But I just wanted to let you know that I'm taking Lilly to the park for a little while. It's a beautiful evening, and if I have to stay in this house another minute I think I'll scream."

There was a moment of silence. "I'll meet you there," he finally said.

"Oh, Tom, I don't want you to have to babysit me," she protested.

"It's not a problem."

"But what would the taxpayers say if they knew you were spending time sitting in a park instead of doing your job."

"Keeping you safe is my job. I'll see you there in ten minutes." He hung up.

Peyton loaded up a stroller, several bottles of water for herself and a bottle of formula for Lilly and fought a deep-seated guilt that she was taking him away from his work because she had a touch of cabin fever.

The evening was still warm, but not as stifling hot as it had been earlier in the day. Many times as she'd driven by the park she'd seen mothers and children enjoying the shaded benches and playground equipment. She just wanted to hold Lilly and enjoy the beautiful evening.

The park was located two blocks from the sheriff's office, and as she turned into the parking lot she saw Tom's car already there.

He got out of his car and approached hers and she tried not to notice how handsome he looked in the evening sun.

He looked toward the park, where two women sat on the benches and several children were enjoying the playground equipment.

"See those women?" he asked as she got out of her car.

"That's Dawn Washington and Rachel Cook, two of Black Rock's most upstanding citizens. I've known them both for most of my life. If you want to meet good people, I'll introduce you to them. Then I'll go hang out in the car."

"Tom, I'll be fine here with them. I'll introduce myself. There's no point in you staying here with me. I'll visit with the women and when they leave I'll leave. Nobody is going to try to do anything to me or to Lilly as long as there are other people around. Please, I'd feel better about this whole thing if you'd just go back to the office."

He jammed his hands in his pockets and gazed at the park, then looked at her once again. "You'll leave as they do and go directly home?"

"I promise," she agreed.

"And you'll call me as soon as you get home?"

She nodded and he stepped back from her. "Then I guess you'll be okay." He raised a hand and waved at one of the two women, who waved back. "You'll make friends with them easily," he said to Peyton. "And don't forget to call me when you get home."

She watched as he got into his car. In the best case scenario she would have been sharing the evening in the park with him. They would be sharing dreams, making plans for their future and laughing with Lilly.

"Foolish thoughts," she muttered as she unloaded the stroller, then got Lilly settled in and pushed her toward the two women seated on one of the benches.

"Look at that sweet baby girl," one of them said with a friendly smile.

"Her name is Lilly, and I'm Peyton."

"Hi, Peyton. I'm Dawn, and this is Rachel. Nice to meet you."

Rachel, an attractive blonde looked at Peyton curiously. "Aren't you the woman whose baby was kidnapped?"

Peyton nodded.

"Oh, honey, sit right down here," Dawn exclaimed and made a place between the two for Peyton to sit. "You must have been terrified."

"It was the worst experience I've ever been through," Peyton replied. "Thank goodness Sheriff Grayson managed to find Lilly and return her to me safe and sound."

For the next few minutes they spoke about mothers' fears and shared personal information about themselves.

Dawn was married and had two little boys who were at the moment climbing on the jungle gym. Rachel was also married and the mother of a five-year-old girl who was on the swings.

With Tom's ringing endorsement of the women in her ears it was easier for Peyton to let down her guard just a little bit.

Dawn worked as a secretary in the mayor's office, and Rachel was a stay-at-home mom with a passion for making beaded jewelry.

For Peyton it was delightful to sit and chat with the two women, who were friendly and open and wonderfully ordinary. Rachel was planning a jewelry party in her home and took Peyton's phone number, promising an invite and the opportunity to meet more of the women of Black Rock.

"There's Caleb, making the evening rounds," Dawn said as the deputy's car rolled slowly by the park.

"Those Grayson men definitely got the luck of the hunk genes," Rachel exclaimed. "If I were single I'm not sure which one of their bones I'd jump."

Tom's name jumped right into Peyton's head. "They were all nice while investigating Lilly's kidnapping," she said.

"They're hot, they're nice and they all seem to have an aversion to marriage," Dawn said.

"Sheriff Grayson was married, remember?" Rachel said. "Poor man lost his little girl then his wife left him. I think it broke him completely."

These words pierced through Peyton's heart. Was it

possible that a tragedy like that could break a person so completely he could never love again? Would never seek that kind of happiness again?

If she'd never gotten Lilly back, would that trauma have made her never think about having another child? Would she have never loved anyone that much again?

She liked to think that wasn't the case, that her capacity to love was bigger than anything life could throw her way.

"Well, guess it's time to pack it in," Dawn said. Twilight had fallen, painting the park in violet shadows portending the imminent arrival of night.

She stood from the bench. "Shawn, David, let's go. It's going to take an hour to get the dirt off you before bedtime."

The little boys hollered protests but got off the equipment and headed to their mom as Rachel called for her daughter, Melissa.

"We're here most evenings," Rachel said. "Feel free to join us anytime. Maybe we can do lunch sometime before school starts."

"That would be great," Peyton agreed. As the others began the walk toward their cars, Peyton also got ready to go.

It didn't take long for the other two women to load up their cars while Peyton tried to unfasten the strap holding Lilly in place in the stroller.

It was stuck. She waved goodbye as the others pulled out of the lot and then knelt down to tug on the strap fastener.

"Did you have a good time at the park, Lilly?" She smiled at the baby and leaned down and kissed her cheek, then sighed in relief as she finally managed to get the strap unfastened.

"I think with all this fresh air we should both sleep like babies tonight." She unlocked the back door and placed Lilly in her car seat.

As she fastened her in, Lilly reached out and grabbed her nose and cooed. Peyton laughed and kissed the little hand. "We'll go home and you can have a nice bottle and I'll have a glass of wine. How does that sound?"

Lilly laughed, as if delighted by the plan. As Peyton closed the car door and folded up the stroller to put it in the trunk, she smiled at thoughts of the two women she'd met. They'd been nice, and wonderfully normal.

She thought of Kathy—or India—who had fooled her so completely. Part of the problem, Peyton now recognized, was that she'd isolated herself in the two months after making the move to Black Rock.

She should have been out making lots of friends, she should have had those friends and neighbors to support her when Lilly had been taken. Maybe that's why Tom had become so important, because he'd been the only thing she'd had to hang on to.

She opened the trunk and leaned over to place the stroller inside. As she raised up, something crashed down hard on her back. Her purse fell to the ground, and for a moment she thought that somehow the trunk lid had fallen on her, but she heard the scuffle of footsteps and felt somebody's hot breath on her neck. At the same time a vicious punch in her side sucked her breath away.

She crumbled to the ground, gasping for air. *Get up,* an inner voice screamed inside her head. *You have to get up and protect Lilly.*

Even as the thought exploded in her brain, a foot connected with her ribs and a crashing pain sent stars flying in her head.

She grabbed the fender and attempted to pull herself up and got her first look at her assailant. She couldn't tell anything about him other than he was tall and wore a ski mask that obscured not only his hair color but also any other identifying feature.

"Bitch," he hissed, his voice nothing more than a guttural snarl as he kicked her again…and again.

She tried to scream, but she had no air and she realized he was going to kill her if she didn't move, if she didn't somehow get up.

She tried to crawl away from him. She was light-headed and felt as if she were going to throw up. Still he kicked at her, as if she were a soccer ball he was trying to get through a goal.

"Please," she managed to gasp as her vision blurred and the dark edges of unconsciousness crept closer. *Somebody help me,* she mentally cried, just before the world turned black.

Tom rose from his chair in his office and stretched with his arms overhead. He checked his watch and

wondered how long it would be before Peyton called to
tell him she was home.

There were moments when he wondered if he were
over-reacting to an imagined threat against Peyton. The
only person who had hurt her was India, and she was
dead. But the fact that there was still a killer out there, a
killer who might be connected to Peyton, kept Tom from
letting his guard down where she was concerned.

The last three days had yielded no more information
on Cliff Gunther, and Tom wondered if maybe the man
had been upset that Peyton had begun to date Rick, if
perhaps he'd seen Lilly as the final straw?

Since Sunday night with Peyton he'd thrown himself
into work. First thing Monday morning he'd gone to the
farm where Dr. Larry Norwood, the new vet in town,
was now living.

Larry was an affable man, and his wife, Tracy, was
just as friendly. They had two beautiful little girls, and
it was impossible to imagine Larry risking it all for a
woman like India.

They were from Kansas City, and Larry explained
that they had been looking for some time to move to a
small town where he could focus his practice on farm
animals.

He and Dr. Johnson, the man who had been the town
vet for the last forty years, had begun to correspond
through a Web site. And after months of corresponding,
Hank, who was getting ready to retire, encouraged Larry
to move to Black Rock and take over his practice.

Although Tom hadn't seriously entertained the

thought that somehow the vet might have something to do with India's death and Lilly's kidnapping, he left the farm feeling that the vet and his family were a nice addition to the town.

He had spent much of the last two days on the phone, working with the Wichita Police Department to investigate some of the people India had associated with while living there.

Along with the growing list of names of lowlifes who had been in India's life before she'd moved to Black Rock, he also was trying to figure out if there was somebody here in town who might have been ripe for an affair, somebody who was capable of murder.

As he shut off the light in his office, his cell phone rang. "Sheriff Grayson," he answered.

"In the park, they're in the park! You need to come right away."

Even though the voice was excited and higher pitched than usual, Tom recognized Walt Toliver. Just what he needed to round out the day—a call from the local eccentric.

"Walt, calm down," Tom said. "What's in the park?"

"It was an alien, and he hurt a woman. You got to get out here, Sheriff, she's hurt bad, and the baby won't stop crying."

A burst of adrenaline shot through Tom. Walt called on a regular basis to talk about the alien invasion he thought was taking place in and around the Black Rock area, but Peyton had been in the park with Lilly.

"Is the alien still there?" he asked as he left his office.

"No, I chased him off, but the woman is on the ground and somebody needs to do something about that poor baby. Just listen to that crying." Walt must have held out the phone, for in the background Tom could hear the faint cries of an infant.

"Walt, I'm on my way." Tom clicked off and looked at Sam and Benjamin, who were sitting at their desks. "Benjamin, come with me. That was Walt, and he said somebody needs help in the park. Peyton was there earlier. I think she's in trouble." His heart crashed with rapid beats as he raced out of the office.

Within minutes they were in Tom's car and headed to the park. As he drove, Tom quickly filled Benjamin in on what Walt had said.

As the park came into sight and Tom saw the familiar car parked in the lot, his heart felt as if it had exploded in his chest.

Peyton!

He pulled the car to a halt several yards away from hers and jumped out of it with his heart pumping frantically.

Walt was pacing at the back of the vehicle, where Tom could see Peyton crumpled on the ground. The sound of Lilly's wails filled the air.

"I was afraid to move her," Walt said as Tom raced to her side.

"Benjamin, get Lilly and call for an ambulance," he said as he knelt down beside Peyton. "Peyton, can you hear me?" Oh, God, she looked so small, so utterly broken.

Her eyelids fluttered and opened. She stared up at him for a moment with bewilderment, then her eyes filled with horror. "Lilly!" she cried and tried to rise, but she groaned with the movement and collapsed back on the ground.

"Don't try to move," Tom said quickly. "Lilly is fine. Benjamin is getting her out of her car seat. We'll take care of her." She closed her eyes and for a moment he thought she'd lost consciousness again.

"He was kicking her, the alien was," Walt exclaimed. "I thought they might be landing in the park tonight so I came out here to check it out, and that's when I saw him attacking her."

Benjamin had Lilly in his arms and was walking with her. She'd stopped crying so the only sounds were those of Peyton's labored breathing and Walt's footsteps as he paced in the dry grass.

"I was putting the stroller in the trunk," Peyton said, her voice achingly weak. "He came up behind me and hit me in the back."

"Did you recognize him?" Tom asked.

"He had no face," Walt said, obviously overexcited. "He was one of those outer-space creatures without any features."

"He had on a ski mask," Peyton said. "I don't know who it was. I don't know what he wanted." A sob escaped her and she reached for Tom's hand. "I think he meant to kill me. He just kept kicking and kicking."

"Shh, don't try to talk," Tom said, his heart breaking as he saw the pain she was in. There would be questions for her later, after she'd been treated.

He released her hand and stood as the ambulance arrived. Thankfully they hadn't used the siren, which probably would have traumatized Lilly.

As the paramedics loaded Peyton, Tom assured her that he'd be at the hospital with Lilly as soon as possible. As the ambulance drove away he picked up her purse, which she'd dropped in the attack, detached the baby seat from the back and installed it in his car, then locked her vehicle.

"Benjamin, take a statement from Walt and call Sam and Caleb to start canvassing the area. I'll take the baby and head over to the hospital."

As he took Lilly from Benjamin, he tried to ignore the sweet memory of another baby in his arms. He quickly fastened her into the car seat, then got in behind the steering wheel.

What in the hell was going on in his town? He clenched the steering wheel hard as he headed to the small local hospital. Who had attacked Peyton, and why? Was there something about her past that she hadn't told him? Beneath the questions lingered a killing guilt. Why had he allowed her to go to the park? Why hadn't he stayed with her?

A million questions flew through his head as he parked the car and got Lilly out of the backseat. The baby had fallen asleep, and for that Tom was grateful.

The loudest question that pounded in his head was

about Peyton's condition. She hadn't been able to move without groaning. What kind of internal damage had been done?

The idea of any man laying his hands or his feet on her filled him with rage. She was so small, so fragile. And why would anyone want to hurt her?

He walked through the emergency room door, but before he could get much farther, he was stopped by Loretta McCain, Sam's wife.

"Whoa," she said as she stepped between him and the door leading to the exam rooms. "Where do you think you're going, and where did you get that precious bundle of love?"

"I need to check in on Peyton Wilkerson. She was just brought in, and this is Lilly, her daughter."

"You know you can't go back there right now. The doctor is with her. I'm sure he'll come out to speak to you after he's had a chance to check her out." She smiled at the sleeping baby, her chocolate eyes twinkling with a maternal light. "You want me to take that little bundle from you? I can put her in one of our bassinettes until we figure out what's going on."

"That's a great idea," he said, eager to relinquish the baby, who smelled of baby powder and innocence and a million old memories.

As Loretta disappeared with Lilly, Tom sank down on one of the molded plastic chairs to wait for an update from the doctor. He knew Benjamin and Caleb would be taking care of the investigation, which was good, because all Tom could think about at the moment was Peyton's well-being.

Every time he thought of her on the ground at the back of her car he felt sick to his stomach. He wanted to hurt somebody. He wanted to find the man responsible and smash in his face. It was definitely not the thoughts of a sheriff, but rather those of a man whose woman had been hurt.

It felt as if hours passed before Dr. Ryan Attenburg came into the waiting room. Tom leapt out of his chair. "How is she?"

"Two cracked ribs and a multitude of bruises, but other than that she's okay."

Tom inwardly cringed as he imagined the power of the kicks that had cracked her ribs. "You're releasing her?"

"I've got her bound up and with a prescription for some pain meds. There isn't much more I can do for her. She's going to feel like hell for a while, but it's just going to take time to heal."

"Can I go back and see her?"

"While you do that, I'll just get her discharge papers ready."

There were only three examining rooms in the emergency area, and she was in the first. He pushed the curtain back to see her seated on the table, her arms wrapped around her midsection and her face as pale as the bleached cotton gown she wore.

She looked up at him and her eyes widened. "Lilly? Where's Lilly?"

"It's okay. She's with one of the nurses."

"Oh, God, was she hurt?" Tears instantly jumped into her eyes.

"No, no. She's fine," Tom hurriedly assured her. "She fell asleep, so one of the nurses put her in one of the cribs in the nursery."

She released a small sigh. "What's going on, Tom? Why would somebody do this to me? It wasn't a robbery attempt. I dropped my purse the minute he struck me from behind."

"I don't know, but I swear I'm going to find who did this to you." He would move heaven and earth to put the guilty behind bars. It was all connected, the kidnapping of Lilly and this assault on Peyton. Somebody was after Peyton, and that somebody had killed India.

A young nurse's aide appeared in the doorway. "I'm here to help you get dressed, Ms. Wilkerson."

"I'll just wait outside. I'll take you home when you're ready." Tom left and returned to the waiting room, where he called Benjamin for an update.

Unfortunately, he had nothing to report. He could get nothing out of Walt except that it had been a tall alien with no face. The assailant had run down the street when Walt had hollered at him, but there was no sign of anyone in or around the area. They had knocked on the doors of the houses in the vicinity, but nobody had seen or heard anything.

So Tom was left with nothing but an eyewitness who watched the heavens for alien spaceships and believed an invasion from outer space was imminent.

Loretta appeared with a still-sleeping Lilly in her arms. "You best be carrying this one out. Her mama isn't going to feel like lifting anything for a couple of days."

As Tom took the infant into his arms, Peyton walked through the double doors with the doctor. She walked with tiny steps, as if every bone in her body hurt.

Once again a slow, seething rage built up inside Tom. He wanted to envelop her in bubble wrap, lock her in a padded room, do whatever it took to make sure nobody and nothing could hurt her again.

"I've given her some samples of pain meds since the drugstore is closed for the night. She has enough to last until tomorrow," Dr. Attenburg said. He turned and offered a sympathetic smile to Peyton. "I have a feeling you're going to feel like you've been run over by a truck when you wake up in the morning."

"What I'd like more than anything right now is my bed and a handful of those pain pills," she said.

"Let's get you home," Tom said.

It took several minutes to get Lilly back into the infant car seat and Peyton loaded into the passenger side. She leaned her head back and closed her eyes as Tom got into the car and started the engine.

"Can you talk about it?" he asked as they left the hospital parking lot. She opened her eyes and nodded.

"I had trouble unfastening the clasp on the stroller. By the time I got it unhooked and got Lilly into the car, the other women had left. I had just put the stroller in the trunk when I was hit from behind. Then it all happened so fast. I was on the ground and he was kicking me over and over again."

"Did he say anything to you?"

"No…oh wait, yes. He called me a bitch, but it was a deep snarl. I didn't recognize the voice. All I could think about was that he was going to kill me and take Lilly."

Guilt ripped through him. "Is that what you think it was about? He wanted to get Lilly?"

"I can't imagine what it was about. All I know is that if Walt hadn't been in that park, I'd be dead." She wrapped her arms around her middle as if seeking warmth.

Tom pulled into her driveway and cut the engine. As she got out of the car he pulled Lilly from her car seat. She was awake and her big blue eyes met his and a smile curved her little lips.

Tom steeled his heart against that baby smile as he and Peyton walked to the front door. Peyton carried the purse Tom had retrieved from the scene and she dug into it to find her keys.

"You need to go directly to bed," Tom said once they were inside the house.

"I need to give Lilly a bottle before I do anything," she replied. She moved slowly toward the kitchen, and Tom followed just behind her with Lilly still in his arms.

"She can sleep with me tonight," Peyton said as she fixed a bottle. "That way if she wakes up for any reason I don't have to get out of bed."

"She can sleep in her own bed," Tom said. "If she wakes up or needs anything, I'll be here. What you need most is uninterrupted rest, and if I know you, you won't take those pain pills because you're afraid Lilly might need you in the night."

"You shouldn't have to stay and babysit me through the night," she protested, but he thought he saw a hint of relief in her eyes.

"I'm not just staying through the night," Tom said. "I'm staying here until we figure out exactly what's going on." He hesitated a moment, then decided to give it to her straight. She'd proven herself to be a strong individual, and he needed her to be aware of just what was at stake here.

"If what you said was true, and you really believe that man's intention tonight was to kill you, then he was unsuccessful," he said.

She looked at him for a long moment, and the relief that had momentarily lit her eyes was replaced with a tinge of fear. "You think he'll be back."

It was a statement, not a question, and Tom simply nodded his head as Lilly began to cry in his arms.

Chapter 10

When Peyton awakened the next morning she didn't feel as if she'd been hit by a truck. She felt as if a hundred trucks had smashed into her.

A glance at her clock let her know it was just after six. The sun was just beginning to peek over the horizon, and she knew Lilly would probably sleep for another hour or so.

She closed her eyes again, not wanting to move, not wanting to breathe as each and every inch of her body ached.

He had wanted her dead. She'd felt it in the fierceness of the attack, in the hatred that had oozed from him. *Why?* That was the single question that kept replaying in her mind.

Why would somebody want her dead? Who hated

her so much to do something like this to her? A week ago she would have said she had no enemies, but if that were the case, then what had the attack been about? It had felt personal. The way he had growled "bitch" had definitely felt personal.

She shut her eyes and tried to think of somebody, anybody close to her who might harbor that kind of hatred. Rick? Impossible. They had moved on with their lives without any real entanglements, without any bitterness.

She'd worked a lot of jobs, met a lot of people before moving to Black Rock. Had there been somebody she'd angered?

Buck Harmon. The name jumped into her mind. Had he been more angry than she thought when she'd bumped his truck with her shopping cart? It seemed crazy to think that an incident like that could result in the vicious attack on her.

And then there was Cliff. She'd been dating him, although not seriously, when she'd met Rick. Had Cliff been more serious about her than she'd thought? Serious enough that he'd gone off the deep end and now wanted to hurt her?

With her thoughts making her head pound, she decided it was counterproductive to stay in bed and worry about questions with no answers.

Gingerly, she sat up, stifling a moan. A hot shower. Maybe that would help ease the bumps and bruises that covered her body.

She eased her feet over the edge of the bed and stood,

slowly making her way into the adjoining bathroom. She unwrapped the loose binding that the doctor had wrapped around her and gasped as she saw the black-and-blue marks that mottled her torso.

A few minutes later as she stood beneath a hot spray of water she thought about the fact that apparently Tom was going to be her houseguest for a while. She'd wanted to spend more time with him, but certainly not under these circumstances.

She'd hoped he'd want to spend more time with her, but it was duty and responsibility and not desire and attraction that had him back in her life.

Once she stepped out of the shower she dried carefully, then pulled on a pair of shorts and a short-sleeved blouse. A regular bra was impossible with the soreness of her ribs, but she managed to get on an old, stretched-out sports bra.

As she walked down the hall she smelled the scent of coffee and knew that Tom was awake. To her surprise, when she walked into the kitchen she saw Lilly, looking fresh and happy in her bouncy chair on the table.

Tom scowled at her as she walked into the kitchen and eased down into a chair. "You were supposed to stay in bed." He pulled a cup out of the cabinet and poured her coffee.

"I tried, but I woke up, and my thoughts started giving me a headache. Thanks," she added as she wrapped her fingers around the cup.

"You want a pain pill?"

"No, I'm okay as long as I don't move too fast or try

to breathe too deeply." She took a sip of her coffee then reached out a hand and grabbed Lilly's fingers. "How's my girl this morning?"

"I gave her a bottle and changed her," Tom said as he joined her at the table.

"I think that goes above and beyond your duties as a sheriff."

He frowned. "Yeah, well, I don't seem to be doing so well with my sheriff duties. No matter how I twist it all around, I can't make sense of anything that's happened."

"Trying to make sense of it is what gave me a headache before I got out of bed this morning," she replied.

Even though her body ached and her head pounded, a tiny flutter of pleasure swept through her as she smelled the familiar scent of him, felt the warmth of his eyes lingering on her.

She was not a foolish woman, but she felt foolish now, like a teenager with a crush on a boy when she had no hopes of winning his heart.

But there was something about Tom that made her believe his heart needed to be claimed again, that he was a man who not only needed, but deserved to be loved.

"I had Benjamin bring your car home last night," he said.

The ring of the phone swallowed her murmur of thanks. Tom jumped up and grabbed the cordless and handed it to her.

"Peyton, are you all right?" Rick's voice burst over

the line. "They told me somebody beat the hell out of you."

"I'm okay," she replied. "Who told you about it?"

"Benjamin Grayson called this morning to ask me where I was last night. I told him I was here in my apartment writing arguments for the trial I'm working, and he told me about the attack on you. Jesus, Peyton, what's going on there?"

"I wish I knew," she replied and watched as Tom left the room.

"Are you sure you're okay?" Rick asked.

"I'm fine, Rick. A little frightened, a little banged up, but I'm okay."

"Maybe you should come back here, stay with me for a while. I have plenty of room for you and Lilly, and I'd feel better if I knew you were here safe and sound."

A burst of warmth swept through her at his offer. Life would have been so much less complicated if they had truly loved each other. But she didn't love him and he didn't love her, at least not in a romantic way.

"I appreciate the offer, Rick, but I'm not going anywhere. I'm confident Sheriff Grayson will figure this all out soon and I can get back to a normal life."

"Do you need anything? Is there anything I can do for you? For Lilly?" he asked.

"We're fine, and we have everything we need," she replied.

"Call me if there's anything I can do. I mean it, Peyton. All you have to do is let me know."

"Thanks, Rick. I appreciate it."

They hung up and Peyton got up from the table to go in search of Tom. He was in the living room, standing by the front window and staring outside.

For a moment she simply stood and looked at him, noting the width of his broad shoulders, the way his khaki slacks fit across his tight butt.

He must have sensed her presence, for he turned around to face her. His features held stress, and she wanted to stroke her fingers across the lines in his forehead until they smoothed out.

"You had Benjamin check out Rick's alibi for last night?" she said.

Tom nodded. "If you knew the pope personally, I'd be having Benjamin check his alibi."

"I think it's safe to mark the pope off our list of suspects," she said in an attempt to bring a smile to his face. It didn't work.

"I was just thinking that it would be a good idea for you to get an alarm system installed," he said. "I could have somebody out here by this afternoon if you agree."

"At this point I think it would be a good idea," she replied. It would also allow him to leave her and get back to his work.

As much as she'd love to have him as a personal bodyguard, he was the sheriff and couldn't spend the rest of his life living here with her. There was a tiny part inside her that wished he could spend the rest of his life with her, not as a bodyguard but as a man who loved her.

"I'll make a phone call and get somebody out here as soon as possible," he said. "In the meantime, I've got Caleb coming over to sit with you while I take care of some business. I'll pick up your pain meds while I'm out. I don't want you leaving this house for anything right now."

As she looked into his somber dark eyes, it struck her just how serious this was, that somebody wanted her dead and might try to kill her again.

"Tom, what's happened to my life?" she asked softly. "Why is this happening to me?"

For a brief moment she thought he was going to take her in his arms, but instead he shoved his hands into his pockets and rocked back on his heels. "I don't know, Peyton. Is there anything you haven't told me, about yourself, about your relationship with Rick? Anything about past coworkers or friends that might explain this? Any old boyfriends before Rick besides Cliff?"

"No. Just Cliff, and that's it. That's what I was thinking about before I got out of bed this morning. I've racked my brain trying to figure out who might want to hurt me, and I can't think of anyone."

As Lilly wailed from the kitchen, Peyton left the living room and went back to where the little girl was in her infant seat.

Tom followed behind her and watched as she took Lilly from the seat and sat with the baby in one of the kitchen chairs. She fought the wince of pain that stabbed through her as Lilly snuggled against her ribs.

"Have you checked out Buck Harmon's alibi for last night?" she asked.

He nodded. "Apparently Buck was home alone last night, not exactly an airtight alibi. I've got Sam McCain going over the area in the park with a fine-tooth comb, looking for any evidence the attacker might have left behind, but I'm not very confident that he'll find anything. Right now the only thing we can do is to suspect everyone and trust nobody."

She sighed and stroked her fingers through Lilly's downy hair. "This is not exactly the way I want to live my life."

"This isn't going to last the rest of your life," he replied. "Whoever attacked you last night wants you dead, and I have a gut feeling that he's going to try again. Hopefully, sooner or later, he'll show his hand, make a mistake that will let us know who he is, but in the meantime the only thing we can do is stay on the defensive."

Peyton hugged Lilly tighter to her, fighting against the chill of fear that snaked up her spine.

By four o'clock that afternoon a security system had been installed in Peyton's house. Nobody would be able to get in through a window or door without an alarm sounding.

Dawn Washington and Rachel Cook, her new friends from the park, had stopped by just after noon, having heard the news about the attack on Peyton. Tom took the opportunity to question them both, but unfortunately they hadn't seen anyone suspicious lurking around the area, nor had they seen a vehicle approaching as they left.

Tom's frustration over the case was complicated by his frustration over his feelings where Peyton was concerned. He cared about her deeply, but taking care of Lilly that morning had only confirmed his desire to remain alone.

As he'd changed Lilly and heard her soft coos and baby laughter, memories of Kelly had played in his head, and the old familiar pain had filled his heart.

But the toughest thing he did all day was keep his hands off Peyton. There were moments in the day when he'd wanted to wrap his arms around her bruised and battered body, when he'd wanted to kiss the fear out of her eyes, but he hadn't.

He'd left the house for a couple of hours after Caleb had arrived and had picked up Peyton's pain meds, then he had gone to the office to check in.

The fact that still nobody had heard from Brittany added an additional fragment of worry in the back of his head. She'd disappeared before for as long as a week, but this was the longest time she'd been gone with no contact.

He could only hope that she was safe and sound. He had no reason to think otherwise, and besides, he already had plenty to deal with, like finding whoever wanted Peyton dead.

He'd returned to Peyton's place and sent Caleb back to the office, and now he sat in the kitchen while she fixed a salad and broiled a couple of steaks. Lilly was in her swing, smiling at Tom whenever she caught his eye, filling him with the memories of another family, another life.

Peyton was different than Julie. Julie had been needy, a woman who had required lots of attention and energy. Tom hadn't minded giving it to her because he'd loved her. But if he was perfectly honest with himself, when she'd walked out on him there had been a little bit of relief. It had taken every ounce of his energy to try to assuage her guilt and to shoulder her grief over Kelly's death.

He'd made up his mind to spend another night with Peyton. Even with the security system, he wasn't comfortable leaving her and Lilly alone.

"Rare, medium or well done?" she asked as she bent over to check the steaks. She winced as she straightened back up.

"Rare. Have you taken any of those pills I picked up for you?"

She shook her head. "I don't like to take pain medicine. I don't have any tolerance for it. It makes me groggy and out of it."

"I don't like to see you in pain," he said gruffly.

"It's okay, it's manageable at the moment. I might take a pill at bedtime, but in the past they've always hit me so hard."

"You know, if you take a pain pill when you need it, it doesn't make you a drug addict like your mother," he said.

She looked at him sharply as if he'd suddenly dived into her innermost fears. She set the bowl of salad on the table and sat in the chair opposite him. "Maybe I am a little afraid of that," she admitted.

"You aren't your mother, Peyton, and there's no reason for you not to treat the pain. It's one thing to try to be strong, but it's another to martyr yourself for no good reason."

"Okay, you win. After dinner I'll take a pill," she replied. "It's already seven, and by the time we finish eating I'll put Lilly down and feel more comfortable taking one."

As they ate the meal Tom tried to keep the conversation off the crime. He couldn't help but notice that with every hour that passed her features tightened with the pain from her ribs.

After dinner he cleared the dishes while she gave Lilly a bottle. Once Lilly had been fed he brought her a glass of water and two of the pain pills.

"Take these, and I want no arguments," he said firmly. "I can tell that you're hurting badly."

To his surprise she took the pills and swallowed them without protest. That, as much as the strained look on her face, let him know she was hurting more than she was letting on.

By eight-thirty Lilly was down for the night and Peyton was loopy from the pills. Tom had never seen anything like it before. He'd never seen anyone with less tolerance.

"I feel good enough to go dancing," she said. She

was half slumped on the sofa and her eyes were half closed.

Tom couldn't help but smile at her. "I think it's time you danced right into your bed."

She released a deep sigh. "Maybe you're right," she agreed. As she stood from the sofa she swayed, and Tom quickly jumped up and grabbed her before she could fall.

"Whoa," he exclaimed. "You weren't kidding when you said you have no tolerance."

She leaned heavily against him. "I told you I shouldn't take those silly pills." A giggle escaped her lips. "Those silly little pills make me just a little bit silly."

For just a moment all the tension that the day had brought fell aside as he looked into Peyton's laughing eyes. He was surprised by the chuckle that escaped him. "At the moment, you look smashed."

She nodded. "I feel smashed. Help me to bed?"

Every muscle in Tom's body tensed. He'd love to help her to bed. He'd love to stretch out next to her and take her in his arms and make love to her through the long, lonely night.

But of course he wouldn't do that. "Sure," he said. "Let's get you tucked in safe and sound."

He helped her to the bedroom, where she sat on the edge of the bed like a helpless child. He watched her as she fumbled unsuccessfully to unbutton her blouse.

"Let me help." He leaned down and quickly unfastened the buttons and tried not to breathe in the scent of her, a fresh, feminine fragrance that always stirred him.

Still, his blood heated in his veins and he mentally chastised himself for wanting a woman who was dopey on pain meds and hurting.

He pushed the blouse off her shoulders, and it fell to the bed behind her. He saw the dark bruises that covered her skin beginning beneath the band of her bra and disappearing into the waist of her shorts; a deep moan escaped him.

The sight of the ugly bruises threatened to bring tears to his eyes as emotion swelled up inside him. Although he'd known she was hurt, knowing and seeing were two different things.

"Peyton, I'm sorry. I'm so sorry." His voice was thick as he fought to control his emotion.

She placed her hands on either side of his face and forced him to look at her. "Don't be sad, Tom. It's okay. I'm okay. The bruises will heal, and at least I'm alive, but I don't want you to be sad."

She awed him, this woman who had been beaten up and might have been killed but didn't want him to be sad. "Let's get you into bed," he said.

Her nightgown was laid out on the nearby chair, and as she stood to remove her shorts he retrieved the gown. As she finished undressing to put on her nightgown, Tom averted his gaze from her and turned down the bed covers.

As she slid in beneath the sheets, she looked at him with a soft gaze. "Sleep with me, Tom?"

He wanted to tell her no, that there was no way he wanted to be next to her in the bed, smelling the scent of her, feeling her body heat. And yet he couldn't tell her no with those sleepy blue eyes gazing at him.

She was traumatized and she was drugged, and he knew if he just slipped into the bed next to her she'd probably be asleep within two minutes.

He kicked off his shoes, took off his shirt and pulled off his slacks and slid beneath the sheet next to her.

She sighed, as if at peace, and placed her small, warm hand over his chest and almost immediately fell asleep.

He realized he could love her if he allowed himself to. But as he thought of Lilly and family, his chest tightened as if squeezed by a steel vise.

He could love her, but he wouldn't. He'd catch the person responsible for the attack, the person he believed still posed a threat, then he'd walk out of her life and never look back.

Chapter 11

Peyton awoke the next morning feeling worse than she had the day before. Dawn hadn't yet lightened the eastern sky, and a quick look at her clock told her it was just after five.

She closed her eyes and tried to go back to sleep, but her body ached too badly and she was completely awake. She pulled on a robe and left the bedroom.

As quietly as possible, she went down the hallway, stopping first in Lilly's doorway to see her sleeping peacefully. She went on down the hall and stopped at the doorway of the living room, where Tom was asleep on the sofa.

She had a vague memory of him in the bed next to her the night before. He must have gotten up and moved here at some point after she'd fallen asleep.

The room was lit by the light over the sink in the kitchen drifting in, and she took a moment just to watch him sleep.

He couldn't be comfortable, with his feet hanging over the foot of the sofa and his head crammed into the corner. He had her spare pillow beneath his head and a sheet pulled halfway up his bare chest.

Even in sleep he touched her on a physical and mental level. She had a vague memory of his tenderness the night before when he'd helped her get ready for bed.

She was certain he had a great capacity to love, but he seemed intent on denying that in his life. Had the death of his child and the abandonment by his wife left him so damaged he could never reach out for love again? If that were so, then that would be the real tragedy in his life.

"Couldn't sleep?"

The deep voice startled her and she jumped in surprise. "How did you know I was here?"

"Just sensed you." He sat up and raked a hand through his tousled hair. "How do you feel?"

She frowned. "Worse today than I did yesterday," she admitted.

"They say the second day after an accident is always the worst."

She'd never seen him look as sexy as he did now, with his hair bed-tousled and his bare chest staring her in the face. The aches and pains that shot through her didn't stop the flicker of desire that roared to life.

In that moment she recognized that as crazy as it was,

she'd fallen in love with Sheriff Tom Grayson. It didn't matter that they'd known each other only a short period of time; it didn't matter than they hadn't even dated. She knew what was in her heart, in her soul, and it was love for this man.

"I'm going to go put on the coffee," she said, suddenly needing to be away from him. She escaped into the kitchen and started the coffee, then sat at the kitchen table and thought about Tom Grayson.

Loving him was probably a study in futility, and yet she couldn't help the tiny flicker of hope that burned in her heart.

Despite his firm words to her that he had no intention of getting involved with anyone again, she knew he cared about her, knew he cared about her more than he might be willing to admit.

But did he care enough that he'd want to pursue a relationship with her after all this madness had ended? She hoped so. She was sipping a cup of the fresh brew when he came into the kitchen.

He'd showered and was dressed in a clean uniform. His hair was neatly combed, and as he walked over to pour himself a cup of coffee she couldn't help but admire his attractiveness. But it was his inner qualities that drew her, his gentleness and intelligence, his ability to comfort and offer support under the worst of circumstances.

He got his coffee then joined her at the table, and she saw that despite the shower he looked tired. "You can't have slept well on the sofa," she said.

"I'm okay," he replied.

She drew a deep breath. "You could have stayed in bed with me."

"I didn't think that was a good idea. I might have accidentally jostled you in the night." He gazed at her a moment, then focused outside the nearby window—but not before she saw the flare of heat in his eyes. His mouth might say one thing to her, but his eyes told her something else altogether.

She wanted to tell him that she was in love with him, but she knew the timing wasn't right. He had India's murder and the attack on her on his mind. There wasn't space for her to speak her mind to him. She had a feeling it would only add to his burden. Eventually there would be a time when she could speak to him from her heart; she just knew that time wasn't now.

Peyton had just finished her cup of coffee when she heard the sound of Lilly awaken. She left the kitchen and went into the nursery to take care of her daughter.

Lilly greeted her with a happy smile, and as she changed her diaper, love filled Peyton's heart. From the moment she'd realized she was pregnant with her daughter, Peyton had prepared herself for being a single parent.

She knew how to be alone. She'd been alone most of her life, but there was a difference in knowing you would be okay alone and wanting something different.

She wanted Tom in her life, not just as a sheriff protecting her but as a man loving her. For the first time in her life she felt a need inside her where another human being was concerned, and that scared her more than just a little bit.

Once she had Lilly changed, she carried her back into the kitchen, where Tom was already on his cell phone. She placed the baby in the infant seat then made a bottle as he walked into the living room to complete his call.

When he returned to the kitchen, she was sitting and feeding Lilly her bottle. As much as she felt safe with him here, as much as she wanted him here with her day and night, night and day, she was struck by the fact that as sheriff he shouldn't be holed up in her house; he should be in his office taking care of business.

"Tom, if I had my way I'd have you living here forever." She felt the heat of a blush warm her cheeks as she realized perhaps her words gave too much away of what was in her heart.

"But you have a job and I know you can't do it effectively playing bodyguard here to me," she continued. "I have the alarm system and I feel relatively safe here. You need to get back to work, in your office. Find the man who killed India. Find the man who attacked me. That's your job, not babysitting me."

He walked over to the coffeepot and poured himself a cup, then turned to face her. "You'd have to agree not to leave the house for anything. If you or Lilly need something, anything, then you have to promise to call me and I'll take care of it."

"I can do that," she agreed. "Trust me, after what happened to me at the park, I'm not eager to leave this house for anything."

He took a sip of his coffee, his gaze remaining on her. "I've got my men working on various angles of both crimes. I'll hang out here until noon and see where we are with everything."

She nodded, pleased that she would have him with her for another half a day.

The morning passed all too quickly. As Lilly went down for her morning nap, Peyton made breakfast for her and Tom.

As they ate they talked about everything but the crimes. They talked about favorite foods and old movies, they spoke of the predictions of a harsh winter to come and the hot summer still here.

Each and every fact she learned about him only solidified her feelings for him. They were alike in the ways that mattered and not alike in ways that would be stimulating and exciting.

There was a part of her that believed that fate had somehow brought them together, that he was a man who needed to love and she and Lilly had all the love in the world to give to him.

But at noon as he prepared to leave, she realized it was equally possible that fate was toying with her, bringing into her life a man she loved but who would never allow himself to become a part of her life.

"I'm not entirely comfortable leaving you here alone," he said at the front door. "I'll make sure a squad car comes by periodically to make sure everything is all right."

"The security system will do the job, and besides,

how long can you be my bodyguard and let all the other business of Black Rock fall by the wayside?"

"You promise you'll call me if you need anything," he asked.

"I promise," she replied.

"And you'll take a pain pill if you need it?" He raised a hand, as if to touch her face, but then quickly dropped it back to his side. "You look like you need one."

She forced a smile to her face. "I'm fine. If I need one later I'll take one. You'll keep me posted on what's happening with the investigation?"

"Of course," he replied as he opened the front door.

She wanted to tell him she had fallen in love with him, but she was afraid to bare her soul to a man who she suspected was at this very moment telling her goodbye.

"Lock the door and set the alarm when I leave," he said.

She nodded. "I will."

His eyes were dark, fathomless, as he gazed at her. "We'll get him, Peyton, and hopefully very soon you'll be able to get back to your real life."

He didn't wait for her to reply, and she watched as he walked down the sidewalk and got into his car. As he pulled out of the driveway, an emptiness filled her.

Maybe she'd have the chance to tell him that she loved him after this was all over. When India's killer was in jail and Peyton's attacker had been caught, then maybe Tom's heart would be open to her.

* * *

Tom drove away from Peyton's and drew a deep, long breath of relief. He'd been on edge all night after helping her into bed, and that same tension had filled his chest all morning.

It was as if his body and his brain had disconnected where Peyton was concerned. He always figured he'd spend the rest of his life alone, and yet every time he looked at Peyton, each time she was close to him, a sweeping desire soared inside him.

It was more than the desire to make love to her, although that particular want roared through him with an intensity that stunned him.

The problem was he liked waking up to her presence, to that beautiful smile that warmed him from the top of his head to the tip of his toes. He liked sharing his first cup of coffee of the day with her, talking to her about everything and nothing.

If he looked deep in his heart, he'd even admit that he was charmed by Lilly, who rarely had a cranky moment and seemed to spend most of her days bestowing smiles on whoever came near.

"Crazy love," he muttered as he pulled into the parking space in front of his office. Surely that's all it was, a false sense of closeness induced by what they'd been through together.

He could never give her what she was looking for in a man, and in any case he wasn't willing to try. She needed a man whose heart was unfettered by loss, a man who could make her and Lilly number one in his life.

He got out of his car and tried to push thoughts of her out of his mind. He had work to do, and there was no question he'd do it better from his office than from Peyton's house.

What he needed more than anything was physical distance from her, and escaping into his office and work was what he did best.

Sam greeted him as he came in the door. "Hey, boss. I didn't know you were coming in today."

"I can't bodyguard for Peyton Wilkerson for the rest of my life. The best thing to do is figure out who's responsible and get them behind bars. But tell Caleb and Benjamin I want them to rotate hourly drive-bys on her house."

Sam nodded. "Done. On that note, I've got two things to tell you. I managed to track down Cliff Gunther. He's at his parents' home in Arizona, has been there since walking out on his job."

"So, he couldn't be responsible for the attack on Peyton."

Sam nodded. "Also, Benjamin is out interviewing one of Buck's neighbors. The neighbor says he saw India Richards's car parked at Buck's on more than one occasion."

"So Buck lied about hanging with India just one night. Gee, why am I not surprised?" Tom frowned thoughtfully. "Get Caleb to meet Benjamin at Buck's place. I want him brought in for questioning. Maybe sitting in our little interrogation room he'll feel more like telling the truth. And, Sam, I want you to do your magic on the computer and get me everything you can find on Rick Powell." From the moment Tom had met Rick, something hadn't felt right. Now he had a hunch that might or might not play out.

"Done," Sam replied. He was on the phone before Tom entered his own office.

Tom closed the door and at his desk pulled out the files on both crimes that were uppermost in his mind. He opened the file for India's murder. He'd read through it over a dozen times but hoped that this time he'd see something he'd missed.

He didn't know how long he'd been sitting studying the files, when their guest of honor arrived. Buck Harmon filled the air with a string of expletives as he was led to the interrogation room next to Tom's office.

A moment late Caleb poked his head in Tom's door and offered him a grin. "He's here, and he's not happy."

"He'll be even less happy after I'm finished with him," Tom replied as he got up from his desk.

There had been a rage in Tom since the moment he'd arrived at the park and had seen Peyton on the ground, and even though he'd managed to stuff that rage down for the last couple of days, he felt it now rising up inside him.

He couldn't help but think that the kidnapping, the murder and the attack on Peyton were all related; he just hadn't been able to figure out the missing link. Was Buck that link?

Time to find out what Buck was hiding and why.

As Tom entered the interrogation room with Benjamin, Buck glared at him with belligerent defiance.

"What the hell, Sheriff? What's going on?"

"We need to have a little chat, Buck," Tom said, his voice deceptively friendly. "You want something to drink? Maybe a coffee or something?"

"All I want is to get out of here," Buck replied. "Ask me whatever you need to so I can get out of here."

Tom eased down in the chair next to Buck at the table while Benjamin stood guard at the door. "India Richards," Tom said.

"We already had that talk," Buck exclaimed as he averted his gaze from Tom's.

"I think maybe you left some things out," Tom replied. "You told me that you'd only seen India one night, but we have witnesses that place her car at your place more than one night."

Buck shot up straighter in his chair. "Then they're lying."

"And why would your neighbors lie about you?" Tom asked.

Buck snorted, as if the answer were obvious to any idiot. "They think my truck is too loud and my place is an eyesore."

"And so they would lie to get you into trouble," Tom said, his voice filled with his disbelief. He stood with an abruptness that made Buck jump in surprise. "He doesn't want to play nice, so I guess I won't, either," he said to Benjamin. "Book him on murder charges."

"Whoa, wait a minute." Buck shot out of his chair

and Benjamin stepped forward, his gun drawn. Buck instantly raised his hands above his head to show he meant no menace. "Okay, okay. I'll tell you the truth." He eased back down in the chair and looked up at Tom.

Tom sat back at the table. "I'm listening."

"It's true that I met her down at Harley's and after we left there we stopped and bought some more beer and hung out at my place. After that she'd sometimes just drop in to talk and have a beer. We weren't having sex. It was nothing like that. She told me she had a boyfriend and wasn't going to cheat on him. I just got the feeling she was lonely."

"Why didn't you tell me all this when I first asked you about her?" Tom asked.

"I don't exactly have the best reputation around these parts," he said dryly. "I'd heard she'd kidnapped a kid, then had been murdered and I didn't want to be involved in any of it."

"You are involved, Buck, whether you want to be or not." Tom leaned back in his chair and eyed the young man across from him.

His mind filled with a vision of Peyton's ribs, black and blue from somebody kicking her with a bone-crushing force. He looked down to the boots Buck wore, and the rage he'd been fighting rose to the surface.

"Maybe you were worried that Peyton Wilkerson knew you were friends with India." He stood once again and leaned over Buck, invading his personal space. "Maybe you saw her the other night in the park and figured you could keep her from telling that you and India were friendly with each other."

A red haze fell before Tom's eyes. "Is that what happened, Buck?" Tom grabbed the front of his shirt and half pulled him from the chair. "Were you afraid that Peyton might know too much, and so you shoved her to the ground and kicked her over and over again?"

"Tom, that's enough." Benjamin's voice cut through the red haze, and Tom realized he was shaking Buck like a rag doll. He released his hold on him and stepped back, appalled by his own lack of control.

"Get him out of here," Tom said. "Lock him up until I decide what to do with him."

As Benjamin lead the protesting Buck away, Tom sank back into the chair. He could hold Buck twenty-one hours without charging him.

That gave him twenty-one hours to try to find out if Buck was a cold-blooded killer who had not only murdered India but had also attacked Peyton, or if he was just a dumb putz who just happened to run into the wrong woman at a bar.

The day seemed endless to Peyton. She played with Lilly, cleaned the kitchen and then paced the floor, wondering if her life would ever be normal again.

What if Tom never found the person who had attacked her? What if he never found out why India had kidnapped Lilly and who had killed India?

How could Peyton hope to live a normal life if there was no resolution to the crimes? She would forever be looking over her shoulder, wondering if her attacker might strike again, this time with deadly results.

If she wasn't thinking about the crimes, then her thoughts were filled with Tom. She wanted to believe that there was some sort of future with him, but she knew she was probably fooling herself.

At three o'clock when her doorbell rang and she peeked out and saw Rachel, she was thrilled by the distraction of a visit from this new friend.

"I just thought I'd stop by and check in on you," Rachel said as Peyton led her into the kitchen.

"I can't tell you how happy I am to see you. Sheriff Grayson doesn't want me leaving the house, and even though I don't need to go out for anything, I'm suddenly feeling like a prisoner in my own home." Peyton gestured her to a seat at the table. "Can I get you something cold to drink? Iced tea or a soda?"

"Tea would be great. How are you feeling?"

"A little rough today," Peyton admitted. "It's not too bad if I don't breathe too deeply or move too fast. And God forbid I sneeze or cough."

"And there's still no clue as to who did this to you?" Rachel asked.

"No. None." Peyton placed the tea on the table, then took the seat across from Rachel. "Where's your daughter?"

"Ah, twice a week I take her to Portia's Playpen for play time. She has a wonderful time and mommy gets a little downtime to visit friends or just sit and read a book without interruption."

"I've arranged for Portia to take care of Lilly when I start teaching. I have to confess, since the kidnapping the idea of leaving her with anyone is a little frightening."

"Portia is amazing, and she'll love your Lilly just like you do," Rachel replied. "Trust me, you're putting her in good hands."

"That's good to know. Tom only had good things to say about Portia. He said she and Caleb dated while they were in high school."

"Everyone just assumed they'd get married and live happily ever after, but I guess not all high school romances can go the distance."

"I didn't have time to have a high school romance," Peyton said. "I was working two jobs in high school and living on my own."

For the next hour the two women visited, sharing pieces of their past, talking about their present and their hope for the future for their daughters.

It was just after four when Rachel stood to go home. "I need to get dinner started. David likes to eat at five-thirty on the dot, and I'm trying a new chicken recipe tonight."

Peyton walked with her friend to the door. "I really appreciate you stopping by," she said as she unarmed the security system. "I'm eager to make lots of friends here in Black Rock."

Rachel offered her a friendly smile. "Consider Dawn and me two of your first."

Peyton was still smiling after Rachel left. Once Tom solved the issue of who had attacked her and life returned to normal, she knew she was going to like it here in Black Rock.

It was going to be a wonderful place for Lilly to grow up. There was nothing nicer than a real small town, with a café where everyone gathered and people who looked out for each other.

By eight that evening she'd put Lilly down for the night and had broken down and taken one of her pain pills. Feeling a bit woozy, she settled on the sofa and turned on the television, comforted by the sound of a sitcom.

Tom had called just after five to check in on her, and she'd assured him she was fine and didn't need anything. He'd told her there was nothing new on the cases, and the call had been brief.

As she stretched out on the sofa she felt as if her mind had fuzzy edges, thanks to the pill she'd taken. "You should just go to bed," she said aloud. Maybe she'd feel better in the morning.

Deciding to call it a night before she got too groggy, she got up from the sofa and turned off the television. She was headed down the hallway when the doorbell rang.

Instantly her heart leapt in her chest. Maybe it was Tom. She hurried to the front door and peeked out, surprised to see Rick.

"Rick, what a surprise," she said as she opened the door to allow him in.

"Sorry it's so late, but court has been cancelled for tomorrow so I thought I'd drive out to see you and Lilly."

He smiled apologetically. "I know I should have called, but it was a spur-of-the-moment decision, and I was afraid you'd tell me to wait until tomorrow. And to be honest, I was worried about you."

How she wished she could love him. Everything would be so less complicated if she and Rick were in love. But she wasn't in love with him. She was in love with Tom.

"Lilly's already down for the night," she said. "And as you can see, I'm fine, although a little dopey because I took a pain pill."

He stepped into the foyer and closed the door behind him. "I couldn't believe it when I heard what happened to you." The warmth of his eyes faded. "I couldn't believe I didn't break all your ribs when I kicked you."

Peyton stared at him, for a moment wondering if the medication was tampering with her ability to understand. "What?"

"Ah, Peyton, you've been a real pain in my ass. If India had done what she was supposed to, I wouldn't have to be here now to finish the job."

Peyton took a step back from him and tried to make sense of what he was saying. "You knew India?" The question whispered out of her on a labored breath.

"I met India at a bar one night after work. She was hanging around looking for a date, and by the end of the night she was crazy about me. She loved me enough to do anything for me. She moved here to get close to you and gain your trust."

He frowned with irritation. "But when it came right

down to it, she couldn't do it. She couldn't kill Lilly and she couldn't kill you. But you know what I always say, if you want a job done right, you should do it yourself."

He pulled a length of rope from his pocket, and horror washed over Peyton as she tried to make sense of what was happening.

Chapter 12

It was nearly seven when Sam brought Tom a pile of papers he'd copied off the Internet. "That's everything I could find about Rick Powell. He must like being in the news. I don't think he misses a photo or interview opportunity."

"Thanks, Sam. And now you'd better get out of here. Loretta is going to have my head for keeping you so late."

Sam grinned. "You know Loretta's bark is worse than her bite. Good night, boss," he said as he walked out.

Tom shuffled the papers together and stuck them into a manila envelope. He'd go over them at home. He left his office to see Caleb and Don Walker, another young deputy, ready to work the night shift.

"Heading out?" Caleb asked.

Tom nodded. "Going home."

"I see you're taking work home with you," Caleb said and pointed to the manila folder.

"Yeah, I'm checking into Rick Powell. Aside from Buck and Cliff, he's the only person in Peyton's life. And speaking of Buck, go ahead and cut him loose. We've got no evidence to hold him, and I'm doubtful that anything will suddenly show up. He might as well sleep in his own bed tonight."

Don stood and grabbed the jail keys from the top drawer of the desk. "For a tough guy, he's been doing a lot of whining since he got locked up."

Tom smiled. "You know the old saying—the bigger they are, the harder they fall. I'm out of here."

As he walked out into the hot night air he thought of Peyton. What was she doing right now? Was she curled up in bed reading a book? Was she parked in front of the sofa watching television? Was she missing him?

The last thought made him slam his car door harder than necessary. It didn't matter whether she missed his presence in her house or not. He didn't belong there.

By the time he got home, a weariness had invaded his soul. There was no question that he hadn't slept well on Peyton's sofa. He'd been haunted by memories of making love to her, angered by the vision of the angry bruises that darkened her skin and frustrated by the fact that he hadn't already made an arrest.

His house seemed big and empty as he walked through the door. The silence was deafening. He realized he'd grown accustomed to Peyton's voice filling the quiet, to Lilly's sweet coos adding music.

Once again irritated by his own thoughts, he walked into the kitchen, put on a pot of coffee to brew and sat at the table and spread out the items Sam had printed off the Internet.

Before he started looking at anything he poured himself a cup of coffee and called Brittany's cell phone. As usual, it went directly to voice mail.

He sipped his coffee and for a moment allowed himself to think about his missing sister. Even though he didn't want to believe anything sinister had happened, his frame of mind was dark, and he couldn't help but admit that he was worried about her; the worry was growing bigger and bigger with each hour that passed without contact from her.

He told himself not to worry, that there was absolutely no evidence to show that his sister might be in any trouble. Besides, he had real crimes in front of him to solve, and until he knew something different about Brittany, that's where he needed to focus.

He began to sort through the information Sam had pulled up on Rick Powell. Sam wasn't kidding: it seemed that Rick enjoyed having his mug in front of the cameras.

There were social events, charity appearances and work-related stories. The first thing Tom did was separate it all into three piles. Once he had the items separated he started on the work-related items.

It didn't take long for Tom to realize Peyton was

right—the man was definitely ambitious. Tough on crime, and with a winning smile, he was a perfect candidate for a future in politics, and there were several interviews where he told the reporter that's where he intended to eventually land.

In one interview given just after the date of Lilly's birth, he was asked about his single status, and Rick hadn't mentioned a word about Peyton or the baby.

In fact, the interesting thing for Tom, as he perused through the social and charity piles, was that although many of the photos had been taken during the time when Peyton and Rick were a couple, she was in none of them. He was either photographed alone or with whoever was in charge of the function he was attending.

Why wouldn't he take Peyton with him? Why hadn't he mentioned Peyton to his friends or family? The birth of a baby was something to celebrate. Perhaps Rick had never accepted Lilly's presence.

Tom frowned and shoved the paperwork aside, then poured himself a fresh cup of coffee and leaned back in his chair.

His mind whirled with the information he had about India, about Tom and Buck. He felt as if he was missing an important link.

Why had India taken Lilly? It didn't ring true that she'd simply taken the baby to give to a second cousin in the next town, a woman who was capable of having her own children. Tom had decided not to arrest the young couple. He believed their story, that they thought what they were participating in was a legal adoption of an unwanted baby. They had fully cooperated with him, and he believed their only crime was being young and uneducated.

He sipped his coffee and stared out the window, working the pieces of the puzzle around and around in his head in an attempt to make sense of everything that had happened.

Rick Powell was an assistant district attorney. India Richards had a record of petty crimes. Was it possible their paths had crossed at one time or another in Wichita?

It was definitely possible.

So why would Rick want to get rid of Lilly? Because he didn't want to be a dad? Peyton had said he was upset when he'd found out she was pregnant but that he'd eventually come around.

She had insisted that she'd told Rick he didn't have to be a part of Lilly's life, that he didn't have to pay child support or do anything that he didn't want to do.

It still didn't make sense, but he didn't trust Rick Powell. He wasn't convinced that the man was innocent in all of this. Maybe he had these feelings because there was no viable suspect left. Cliff Gunther had been cleared, and Tom's instinct told him Buck was nothing but a loser whose only crime had been trying to hook up with a new young woman in town.

It suddenly seemed important that he tell Peyton his concerns about Rick. Although Rick hadn't been around much since the kidnapping and Tom knew that Peyton refused to consider that he might have anything to do with what had happened, Tom would feel better erring on the side of caution.

As he grabbed his cell phone from his pocket he wondered if he was just manufacturing a reason to call her, to hear her voice before he went to bed.

He opened his phone and got ready to dial, then clicked it shut once again. He'd talk to her in the morning, when his head was clear and exhaustion didn't weigh so heavy on his shoulders.

He got up from the table and shut off the coffeemaker then headed for his bedroom. Maybe everything would be clearer in the morning after a good night's sleep.

"What are you doing?" Peyton asked as Rick grabbed her by the arm and lead her into the kitchen. He forced her into a chair and began to tie her there.

"I'm sorry to say that you and Lilly are going to be the victims of a terrible home invasion." He tied her tightly into the chair. "But before I take care of you and Lilly, I need to set the stage—a broken window, some items taken out." He flashed her a confident smile. "Believe me, I've prosecuted enough of these cases to know how to set a scene."

"I don't understand," Peyton said, her heart beating so fast she feared she might pass out. "Why, Rick? Why are you doing this?" She couldn't believe this was the man she'd dated, the man who had stood next to her as she'd delivered their daughter.

His smile faded, and for the first time since she'd known him anger blazed in his eyes. "I have dreams,

Peyton. Big dreams, and you and that kid are in my way. I never signed on to be a father. You were just a girl I was dating for a while. Did you really think it could be anything more than that? You come from nothing. Your mother died in prison. Your mere existence in my life is a detriment to where I want to go, to who I want to be."

She stared at him, wondering how she'd missed the selfishness, the utter depravity he possessed. "You don't have to be part of our lives," she said frantically. "I told you I'd never expect anything from you where Lilly was concerned."

"That's what you say now, but you would have changed your mind. You would have sucked the life out of me for the rest of Lilly's life."

"That's not true, Rick. Please, you have to believe that I want nothing from you. You can live whatever life you want, go after your dreams and we won't bother you." Tears blurred her vision as the reality of the situation penetrated through her foggy head.

Danger hadn't intruded into her home; instead she'd invited it in. She should have been wary when she saw him on the porch at this time of night, but she hadn't been thinking clearly.

"Rick, if you leave now I promise I won't say anything about this. You'll never hear from me again." She was begging not for her own life, but for Lilly's life. "At least leave Lilly alone." She struggled against the rope that held her hands to the chair rungs behind her, but there was no give.

"You don't get it." Wild rage rode in his eyes as he looked at her. "I'm going places, and in the world of politics an illegitimate child and the daughter of a convict are trouble. But a man who lost his daughter and his girlfriend to a violent crime is a figure of compassion. You're worth far more to me dead than alive."

He backed away from her. "Now I've got to take care of some things. If you scream, I'll kill Lilly right in front of you."

As he went into the living room, tears raced from Peyton's eyes. She pulled on the ropes, trying to free herself from the chair, but it was no use.

She heard the sound of the front door open and then close, and when there was no resulting alarm sounding she realized she hadn't reset the alarm after she'd let him inside.

A moment later she heard the tinkle of a window breaking in one of the rooms. Setting the scene. The police would assume that the killer had come in through the broken window. She guessed that he'd take her television and stereo, he'd steal what little jewelry she had and whatever else that would make it look as if she'd been the victim of a robbery gone bad.

A clawing panic rose up in the back of her throat. Once he was finished setting the scene he would kill her, then he'd kill Lilly.

She had to do something. She had to save her daughter, but how?

She heard him re-enter the house, and every muscle in her body tensed. She wished she'd moved a million miles from Rick. She wished she had the strength to break the rope and get free to fight for Lilly's life. Finally she wished she would have followed her heart and told Tom that she loved him.

The ring of the phone cut through the air as Rick came back into the kitchen. He picked up the cordless and looked at the caller ID screen with a frown. "It's Tom."

"If I don't answer he'll think something is wrong," she said.

"Get rid of him, and if you do anything stupid, Lilly will be dead before he can get here, and I promise you I'll make her suffer." He clicked the phone on and held it to her ear.

"Tom," she said. The scent of Rick's cologne, the feel of his body heat so close to her, made her want to vomit.

"Hi, Peyton. I just thought I'd give you a quick call to see how you're doing."

"I was just on my way to bed. I'm exhausted and my ribs are sore. I took three of the pain pills the doctor gave me about a half an hour ago, so I really don't feel like talking."

"Oh, then I guess I won't keep you. I'll come by in the morning—there are some things I want to discuss with you."

Peyton willed herself not to sob, not to scream. "Okay, I'll see you in the morning," she replied. As Rick disconnected, the sob she'd been fighting against erupted out of her.

She swallowed hard and looked up at Rick. "You murdered India, didn't you?"

He leaned with his slim hip against the counter. "She was a loose end. Talk about a stupid woman. She actually thought I was going to marry her, that we were going to live happily ever after."

"She was waiting for you at the motel. That's why she didn't run away after she took Lilly." She wanted to keep him talking. As long as he was talking, Lilly remained safe.

"I told her I'd come and get her, take her back to Wichita with me. She was in love with me. All I had to do was tell her that you and Lilly were ruining my life. Unfortunately, when it came to killing you and Lilly, she didn't have the guts to follow through."

Crazy love, Peyton thought. That's what India had felt for Rick. It had been the sick kind of obsession that really had nothing at all to do with real love.

"This all would have been over if that old man hadn't come running to your rescue in the park," Rick continued. "You'd be dead, Lilly would be gone and that would have been the end of things."

"You're going to be caught," Peyton said. "You're never going to get away with this. You're going to be the first person Tom looks at when I'm gone."

"Ah, Peyton, do you really think I'd come out here to take care of you without having a solid alibi lined up for myself? India wasn't the only woman in my life who would do anything for me. Right now there's a woman in Wichita who will swear under oath that I was at her house this evening having dinner. I'm five steps ahead of Sheriff Tom Grayson. Now, it's time for me to finish up my work here."

As he once again left the kitchen, an overwhelming sense of despair swept through Peyton. She had hoped that Tom would get the message and sense something in her voice, realize that she wouldn't take that many pain pills while home alone and with Lilly in her care.

Lilly! Her heart cried in anguish. Her sweet baby. Was he in there with her now? Placing a pillow over her face? Wrapping his fingers around her neck?

As the minutes ticked by and death crept closer, for the first time in her life Peyton felt all hope seep away.

Chapter 13

He'd had no intention of calling her, but as Tom had undressed for bed, he couldn't resist hearing the sound of her voice before going to sleep.

As he got into bed, the brief phone call played in his head. She'd sounded fine, so why did an electric current of worry zing through him?

She'd told him she'd taken three pain pills, but he'd had to fight with her to take two. She'd said she'd taken them a half an hour before he'd called, but when he'd given her the two pills, within a half an hour she'd been nearly comatose.

Something wasn't right. Had she been trying to tell him that something was wrong, that she was in trouble? He leapt out of bed as if the sheets were on fire.

It took him only seconds to get dressed again. As he left the bedroom he used his cell phone to call Caleb.

"Caleb, it's me. Meet me at Peyton's place."

"What's up?" Caleb asked.

"I think she's in trouble. Don't pull up in the driveway. Park down the street and we'll go in quietly. Wait for me. I should be there in five minutes."

Tom clicked off as he raced to the kitchen and grabbed his car keys. His heart thrummed an anxious rhythm as he left the house and got into his car.

He hoped he was wrong. He prayed the sick feeling in his gut was all a mistake. He'd get to Peyton's and she would be fine.

Maybe he'd misunderstood what she'd said about the pills. Maybe he was making a big deal out of nothing. He hoped so.

Still, with each minute that passed the anxiety inside him grew more intense. His heart beat so rapidly he heard it banging in his ears.

Buck Harmon had been released from the jail. Had he gone to Peyton's house? Or was it possible somebody else was there, somebody who had so far flown under the radar?

It took only minutes to reach Peyton's street. He parked his car next to the curb half a block away and a moment later Caleb pulled up behind him.

"What do you think is going on?" Caleb asked as the two men met at the front of Tom's car. "There's no vehicle in her driveway. Everything looks peaceful."

"I called her a few minutes ago and she said

something that didn't sound right. I don't know, maybe I'm overreacting, but I have a bad feeling and thought I should come over here and check things out."

"How do you want to handle this?" Caleb asked.

Tom frowned as he looked up the street at her house. "Let's head to the back and see if we can look through the windows and see if anything looks off. I don't want to go to the front door, because if somebody is in there with her, we don't know what the response might be. With Peyton and Lilly inside, I don't want to take that kind of a chance."

Caleb nodded. "Then let's do it."

Together the two moved through the dark of the night like silent shadows. They cut through the neighboring yards to reach Peyton's place. Tom mentally cursed as he saw the six-foot privacy fence. He'd forgotten all about it.

Caleb cupped his hands and gestured that he'd boost Tom over the fence. Tom nodded and with his brother's help dropped to the grass on the other side.

The back of the house was before him. Lights burned in both the kitchen and the living room. Tom drew his gun and approached the kitchen window, which was the easiest one to see inside.

He raised up to peek in and his heart crashed into his ribs, momentarily stealing his breath away. Peyton was tied to a chair. Her chin was on her chest and her eyes were closed.

Was he too late? Grief crashed through him—grief coupled with an anger he'd never known. He had to get to her. He left the window and moved to the back door. It was locked, but he used the butt of his gun and broke the glass so he could reach through and unlock it.

As he entered the kitchen, Peyton's head snapped up and her eyes widened, but instead of relief, they held fear. "It's Rick," she whispered. "Save Lilly. If it's not too late, please save my baby."

Tom felt gutted as he left her in the kitchen and slid into the living room, his gun leading the way. He had no idea if Rick had heard his entry into the kitchen, had no idea if the man was waiting for him now with a weapon of his own.

Every muscle in his body was tensed as he saw that the television and stereo were by the front door, obviously ready to be carried outside and taken away.

So he was going to make it look like a robbery gone bad. Tom's blood boiled, but beneath the rage was a fear so intense it cramped his stomach. If Rick had done anything to that precious little girl, then Tom wouldn't try to arrest him, he'd kill him.

He crept silently down the hallway, trying to get a handle on which room Rick was in, but he heard nothing that would give him any indication.

He whirled into the first doorway he came to, the bathroom, but it was empty. The next room was the spare bedroom, and once again there was nobody inside.

Lilly's room was next, and as Tom stepped inside he saw Rick leaning over the crib. "Freeze!" Tom said, fighting his impulse to pull the trigger.

Instantly Rick straightened. He whirled around and

threw something at Tom. For a moment Tom thought he'd thrown Lilly, and he dropped the gun in an effort to catch the baby, only to discover it was a stuffed bear.

Before he had time to process it, Rick was on him. They fell to the floor, where both of them grappled for the gun that had slid beneath the rocking chair.

The gun slid farther away, and Tom managed to drag Rick toward the doorway. Rick swung a fist and connected with Tom's jaw. His head snapped back and he tasted blood, but it fed the rage and he landed a hard right on Rick's nose.

More fists flew and they both gasped for air as the fight continued. The gun was forgotten as they exchanged blows.

Finally it was another fist to Rick's nose that brought the fight to an end. Rick fell to the floor on his back, his breathing labored and his eyes closed as Tom got to his feet.

He reached beneath the rocking chair to retrieve his gun, then looked into the crib and gasped a sigh of relief as Lilly's bright blue eyes met his and she smiled.

He looked up to see his brother standing in the doorway. "How long you been there?" he asked.

"Long enough," Caleb replied.

"Thanks for the help," he said dryly. Gently he picked Lilly up from the crib and suddenly remembered the bruises on Peyton's body. When he passed Rick's prone body, he kicked him hard in the ribs. Rick moaned and curled up in a fetal ball.

"Get this piece of crap locked up," he said. "I need to take care of Peyton."

As he left the room, Caleb was handcuffing Rick. Tom hurried down the hall toward the kitchen where he could hear Peyton sobbing.

As he entered the room and she saw Lilly in his arms she began to laugh and cry at the same time. Tom placed Lilly in the bouncy chair on the table, strapped her in, then moved to Peyton.

He began to work the ropes in order to free her. "Thank God you came," she exclaimed. "He was going to kill us. He killed India and he attacked me that night in the park."

"You were smart, Peyton. Telling me that you took three pain pills sent all kinds of alarms through my head," he replied.

"I wasn't smart," she scoffed, obviously stifling new sobs. "I let him in. I just opened the door and invited him inside."

Tom managed to get the last rope off her and she stood and turned to face him. Before he knew it she was against his chest, burrowed into him as her body trembled with residual emotion.

Tom tried to keep himself rigid, uninvolved, but as she wrapped her arms around his neck he gave into his need to hold her, to assure himself that she was really all right.

She cried against his chest as he held her. "It's over, Peyton," he said softly. "It's finally over, and he can't hurt you again."

When he finally released her, she went to Lilly and pulled the baby into her arms. "I need to get a full statement from you," he said. "And I'm going to have to get a couple of the boys in to process this scene." He pulled his cell phone from his pocket. "Why don't you go sit on the sofa and we'll get this all done as soon as possible."

He mentally shifted from man to sheriff. There were things that needed to be done to assure a successful prosecution of Rick Powell.

It was after ten by the time his team began to photograph and collect evidence. Tom had taken a detailed statement from Peyton as she held a sleeping Lilly.

"This is going to take a while," he said to her. "You want to go to a motel for the night?"

She shook her head. "I'm fine here. I don't think I could sleep anyway. I keep replaying it all in my head. I can't believe Rick would go to the lengths he did for some grand future he had planned for himself. And India, she was under his spell."

"At least she wasn't so crazy to follow through and kill you and Lilly," Tom replied. The relief he felt that it was all over was intense. She was safe, and hopefully nobody would ever try to hurt her again.

It took most of the night to completely process the house and Rick's car, which they had found parked down the street. It was five o'clock in the morning when the team packed up and Tom and Peyton were once again alone in the house. Lilly had been put back in her crib when Tom eased down next to Peyton on the sofa.

"You finally have your life back," he said to her.

"Rick is smart and he knows the system," she said with a touch of apprehension.

He took her hand in his, wanted to whisk away the last of her fear. "He's gone for good, Peyton. It doesn't matter how smart he is or how well he knows the system. He's going to spend the rest of his life behind bars. Now, what you need more than anything is to get some sleep."

He started to pull his hand back, but she squeezed and refused to let it go. "When I was tied to that chair all I could think about was Lilly and you." Her gaze held his, and in the depths of her beautiful blue eyes he saw a wealth of emotion.

"All I could think about was that I'd never get a chance to see Lilly walk, and she'd never get a chance to play with little friends or go to school." Tears sparkled in her eyes. "And the other thing I kept thinking about was the fact that I hadn't told you that I was falling in love with you."

Her words hit him from out of left field, and for just a moment an incredible joy filled him, but it was followed quickly by some of the deepest regret he'd ever felt.

He pulled his hand from hers and got up from the sofa. "Peyton, don't."

"Don't what?" She got up and stepped toward him. "Don't fall in love with you? It's too late, Tom. I can't stop what I feel in my heart, and I'm sure if you look deep in your heart you'll have to admit that you care for me more than a little bit."

"Of course I care for you," he replied uneasily. He didn't want to have this conversation. The light shining from her eyes as she looked at him shot into his heart. He knew he was going to hurt her and he hated it, hated himself for doing it.

"Peyton, you told me you want to be a priority in somebody's life, that you were tired of being a distant third. In my life that's all you'd ever be. I've already had my priorities with my ex-wife and my daughter."

"But, Tom, they're gone. They've been gone for a long time. Isn't it time for you to open your heart to love again? Won't you give yourself a chance at happiness?"

Tom felt himself closing in, closing off. There was a part of him that wanted to embrace what she offered, but there was a bigger part of him that wanted to run as fast and as far away as possible.

"Find a nice man, Peyton. Our town is full of them. Find a man who will love you and Lilly to distraction, a man who has an open heart and a loving soul."

"I've already found him." Tears escaped her eyes to shine on her cheeks. "What happened to India Richards was a tragedy. What almost happened to me and Lilly would have been a tragedy, but the real tragedy in all of this would be if you don't allow yourself to find happiness again." Her voice trembled. "I want you to be happy, Tom. I want you to love again, and if you can't find that with me, then I hope you'll find that with another woman." She stepped back from him. "I just wanted you to know how I feel about you. It suddenly seemed important that I tell you."

"Peyton, this has been a crazy time. I'm sure once things settle down and get back to normal you'll realize your feelings for me aren't as strong as you think they are," he replied. His chest felt tight, filled with an emotion he couldn't identify and didn't want to look at too closely.

She looked at him sadly. "Tom, I know the difference between crazy love and the real thing, and I know what's in my heart." She released a weary sigh. "Go on, you need some sleep and so do I. I guess I'll just see you around."

"I'll be in touch as the case goes forward," he said. There were a million things he wished he could say to her, but the words were trapped someplace deep inside him, in a place he refused to access.

There was nothing more to say, nothing left to do but leave. He turned and walked toward the front door without a backward glance.

As he stepped outside, dawn was just beginning to light the eastern sky, but even the promise of a new day couldn't lighten the weight of his heart.

He'd never meant to hurt her. He'd been clear with her from the very beginning that he didn't want a wife, any children in his life. He shouldn't feel responsible for her feelings, and yet he did.

Sleep, that's what he needed more than anything. He needed to put Peyton's words of love out of his head.

Eventually she'd meet somebody who would be the perfect man for her and a wonderful father for Lilly.

You're in a box of your own making. Jacob's words jumped into his head. *You never gave yourself time to grieve.*

Tom had intended to go right home, but he found himself at the entrance of the cemetery where Kelly was buried. He parked the car and stood just outside the iron gate, emotion like a steel band pressing hard into his chest. He hadn't been here since the funeral.

His head filled with echoes of a little girl's laughter, her sweet voice shouting "Daddy" whenever he came home from work.

Before he realized what he was doing, his feet carried him through the quiet dawn across the lush grass to her final resting place.

The headstone was tiny and held simply the name of Kelly Marie Grayson. Tom stared at the headstone and realized his brother had been right.

Jacob had been right. He hadn't taken the time to grieve for his daughter. He'd had a wife who had been overwhelmed with her grief, her guilt, and he'd had to keep it together for her.

But now there was nothing between him and his grief, and as it ripped through him he sank down to his knees in the dewy grass next to her grave. For the first time in five years, Tom wept for the child he had lost.

It took two full days for Peyton to really embrace the fact that the danger was over and her life was truly her own. The bruises on her ribs were beginning to heal, and she suffered no nightmares from her trauma—nothing except for the heartache that held the name of Tom.

She'd hoped that after he'd had a good night's sleep he would have a magical epiphany and realize he loved her, but as the first day passed and then the second, she accepted the fact that he hadn't felt the same way that she'd felt about him.

What surprised her more than anything was that once the story broke of what had happened to her, the town of Black Rock seemed to gather to offer her support and friendship.

Women stopped by with casseroles and little toys for Lilly. Even Walt Tolliver came by with a charm made of aluminum foil that he insisted would keep the aliens at bay.

It was the evening of the third day after Rick's attack on her that Peyton loaded the stroller into the trunk of her car. Lilly was already in her car seat in the back of the car, and the early evening air was warm, but not uncomfortably so.

As Peyton slid in behind the steering wheel she fought a little flutter of anxiety. She was meeting Rachel and Dawn and their children at the park.

When they'd called earlier in the day to invite her along, her first impulse had been to turn them down. She wasn't sure she was ready to face the place where she'd been nearly kicked to death.

But then she realized she didn't want to be afraid to

go back there. She hoped that the park would be a place of many happy memories for her as Lilly grew up.

As she pulled up to the park the two women were waiting for her. As she shut off her engine she wished it were Tom meeting her here for a walk in the park after dinner.

"Foolish woman," she muttered to herself as she got out of the car. She had to put Tom out of her head, somehow get him out of her heart.

She gave Dawn and Rachel a bright smile as she pulled Lilly from her car seat, then went to the back of the car to retrieve the stroller.

"Here, I'll get it," Dawn offered and took her car keys from her.

Within minutes the three women were on a park bench with Lilly in the stroller and Dawn and Rachel's kids on the playground with a handful of other children.

"Another week and a half and school will start. Are you all ready?" Dawn asked.

Peyton nodded. "I've been working on lesson plans and can't wait to get started." Part of her eagerness to get to work was that she hoped with the hours of the day filled she would finally be able to stop thinking about how safe she'd felt in Tom's arms, how safe and right it had been when they'd made love.

A pleasant, light breeze accompanied their conversation, and Peyton felt a sense of satisfaction as she realized these women were new friends...good friends.

Aside from the fact that seeing Tom on the streets of the small town, running into him in the café or at town functions would hurt, she knew she was on her way to building a wonderful life here for herself and her daughter.

She didn't know how long they'd been sitting and visiting when Tom's sheriff's car drove slowly by.

"Evening patrol," Rachel said.

"I've always felt safe here in Black Rock," Dawn said. "I think that's why what happened to you was so shocking to everyone."

"It must be a consolation for everyone in town that Rick wasn't from here and had no real ties to the community except for the fact that I happened to move here," Peyton said.

Dawn nodded. "You never want to believe that a friend or neighbor could be responsible for that kind of violence." She gave Peyton a bright smile. "At least it's over."

"Thank goodness," Peyton exclaimed.

Tom's car appeared again, and this time he turned into the park entrance. Instantly Peyton's muscles all tightened. She wasn't ready to see him. Her emotions were still too raw.

She narrowed her eyes and watched as he parked the car and got out. He looked achingly handsome in his khaki uniform, and her heart squeezed in her chest as he approached.

"Evening, ladies," he said.

They all returned his greeting.

Tom looked at Peyton. "Could I speak with you for a moment?"

"Of course," she said. He probably needed to talk to her about the case against Rick. As a victim of a crime and with him being sheriff, she knew there would have to be a certain amount of interaction between them. She got up from the bench.

"You can leave Lilly here," Rachel offered. "We'll keep an eye on her while you two talk."

Peyton hesitated a minute, then reminded herself that these women were truly her friends and she could trust them. Tom led her away from the benches to stand beneath a nearby tree. Peyton steeled her heart against the onslaught of emotion he evoked in her.

"How are you feeling?" he asked.

"Better every day," she replied.

"Rick was transported to Wichita right after his arrest. He's been officially charged with murder and attempted murder. It's a solid case, so you don't have anything more to worry about."

She forced a smile to her lips. "I wasn't worried. I know you did your job well, and there's no way he's walking on a technicality. But thanks for the information." She turned to go back to the women, but he grabbed her arm with his hand.

"Peyton, wait."

She turned back to look at him. She just wanted this conversation over. The smell of his cologne made her remember being held in his arms.

"When I left your house the other morning, I remembered something my brother Jacob had said to me. I had spoken to him about you after the night we'd made love. I told him what an amazing woman you were, that I found myself having strong feelings for you, but that I had no intention of following through on anything. He told me that I was in a box of my own making, that I'd never really grieved for all that I'd lost, and I told him he was crazy. But that morning after leaving you, I found myself at Kelly's grave and I realized he was right—I hadn't given myself a chance to grieve."

"Oh, Tom, I'm so sorry." She couldn't help the fact that her heart ached for him.

"No, don't be. That morning at Kelly's grave I realized that I couldn't move forward until I'd let go of the past. My grief for her filled my heart so completely I didn't have room for you or for Lilly."

He leaned with his back against the tree, his eyes distant as he stared across the expanse of the park. "I didn't know I had that many tears in me, but that morning they all came out." A faint pink tinged his cheeks, as if he was embarrassed by this admission. "I cried like a baby, and for the past two days I've been numb."

She couldn't stand it anymore. She had to touch him. She wanted to console him, to somehow help him heal. She took one of his hands in hers. "There's no shame in crying for somebody you love."

"I know," he agreed. "The thing is, I woke up this morning and the grief was gone, the numbness had passed and all I was left with were my feelings for you."

Peyton felt as if her heart stopped beating, as if

everything around her faded away and there was only Tom. "What feelings?" she asked softly.

"I'm falling in love with you, Peyton. I don't know if I can be the man you and Lilly want, the man you need in your life. All I know is that I want to try."

Her heart exploded with happiness as he took her into his arms and his lips met hers. The kiss was like nothing they'd shared so far. Yes, it had the wild passion, the gentleness of the other kisses they had shared, but this one simmered with sweet promise.

As the kiss finally ended, he smiled down at her. "You know by morning we'll be the talk of the town."

She laughed. "I'm already the talk of the town for all the wrong reasons. I don't mind being the talk of the town if it means I'm with you."

He dropped his arms from around her. "We've been through a life-and-death situation, we've shared our pasts and we've made love. Maybe it's time we go out on an actual date."

"Just name the place and the time," she replied.

"How about right now. We'll have some dessert and coffee at the café."

With a wicked little grin, she placed her palm against his cheek. "How about we have coffee at the café and dessert at my place."

His eyes flared with a heat that warmed her from her head to her toe. "We'll make it a quick cup of coffee," he replied, his voice thick and smoky deep.

As Peyton and Tom walked back to Lilly's stroller, Dawn and Rachel smiled at them with a knowing gaze.

"Looks like you're settling in here just fine, Peyton," Dawn said.

Peyton smiled as Tom took control of Lilly's stroller. "I think I'm at the beginning of a wonderful life," she said. "I'll see you guys later, Tom and I are headed to the café."

"You go, girl," Rachel said.

As Peyton walked with Tom and Lilly toward the cars, she remembered the dreams that had sustained her through her terrible childhood.

Despite the odds, she'd managed to get her education, land a wonderful teaching job and move to a quaint little town filled with good people. Best of all, she'd found a man to love, a man who found his capacity to love again after suffering a tremendous loss.

It was a new beginning for both of them, and as Tom gently lifted Lilly from her stroller and kissed her sweet little cheek, Peyton felt her future calling. She knew that future was going to be filled with warmth and laughter and the love of an amazing man.

Epilogue

He stood in the building that had become his playroom. Hidden by a grove of trees and brush in the center of a pasture, and after some major renovations, the old barn was perfect.

The wooden horse stall enclosures had been torn out and replaced by steel bars, creating individual jail-like enclosures, each with its own plumbing.

It was a perfect place for him to keep his collection, a place where nobody would bother him and, most important of all, isolated and insulated to assure that nobody could hear the screams. Ah, the screams. There was nothing more exciting than the sound of a woman screaming in fear, in pain.

He walked to the first "cell" and gripped the cool iron bars in his hands. She lay inside on a cot, her hair a spill of dark silk against the white pillowcase.

Brittany Grayson. She was beautiful and bright and all his. At the moment she was still drugged, as she had been for the past two weeks. Today he'd stop giving her the drug that had kept her out of it since the moment he'd taken her.

Eventually she'd regain consciousness and realize she was a prisoner, his prisoner. He wanted to be here when that moment happened. He wanted to see the fear etched deep into her pretty eyes, see it stretch her mouth into a scream.

He pulled up a nearby chair and sat, prepared to wait for that moment to occur. As he waited his gaze shifted to the other cells. There were five of them, and eventually they would all be filled. Then the games would truly begin. He fought a shiver of excitement at the thought.

Maybe a blonde next time, he thought. Or perhaps a redhead. After all, variety was the spice of life. He had to admit he was vaguely surprised that Brittany had been missing two weeks and nobody had raised an alarm.

Soon the alarms would sound. Soon the entire town of Black Rock would be in an uproar as they realized pretty young women were disappearing.

In the meantime, he was savoring the first of his collection. He couldn't wait for Brittany Grayson to wake up.

* * * * *

& *A sneaky peek at next month...*

INTRIGUE...

BREATHTAKING ROMANTIC SUSPENSE

My wish list for next month's titles...

In stores from 16th September 2011:

☐ Indestructible — Cassie Miles

& Enigma — Carla Cassidy

☐ Christmas Countdown — Jan Hambright

& Night Moves — HelenKay Dimon

☐ No Ordinary Hero — Rachel Lee

& Operation: Forbidden — Lindsay McKenna

☐ Boots and Bullets — BJ Daniels

Available at WHSmith, Tesco, Asda, Eason, Amazon and Apple

Just can't wait?

Visit us Online

You can buy our books online a month before they hit the shops! **www.millsandboon.co.uk**

New Voices is back!

New Voices
returns on
13th September 2011!

For sneak previews and exclusives:

 Like us on facebook.com/romancehq

 Follow us on twitter.com/MillsandBoonUK

Last year your votes helped Leah Ashton win
New Voices 2010 with her fabulous story
Secrets & Speed Dating!

Who will you be voting for this year?

Visit us Online

Find out more at
www.romanceisnotdead.com

Have Your Say

You've just finished your book.
So what did you think?

We'd love to hear your thoughts on our
'Have your say' online panel
www.millsandboon.co.uk/haveyoursay

- 🌹 Easy to use
- 🌹 Short questionnaire
- 🌹 Chance to win Mills & Boon®
  goodies

Visit us Online

Tell us what you thought of this book now at
www.millsandboon.co.uk/haveyoursay

YOUR_SAY